NOTHING
FEAR

SCARLETT FINN

Also by Scarlett Finn

GO NOVELS
GO WITH IT
GO IT ALONE
GO ALL OUT
GO ALL IN
GO FULL CIRCLE

EXILE
HIDE & SEEK
KISS CHASE

WRECK & RUIN
RUIN ME
RUIN HIM

**THE BRANDED
SERIES**
BRANDED
SCARRED
MARKED

**FORBIDDEN
PREQUEL DUET**
ALL. ONLY.
ONLY YOURS

THE FORBIDDEN NOVELS
FORBIDDEN DESIRE
FORBIDDEN WANT
FORBIDDEN WISH
FORBIDDEN NEED
FORBIDDEN BOND

**BOMBSHELLS & BILLIONAIRES
(ROXIVERSE)**
NOTHING TO HIDE
NOTHING TO LOSE
NOTHING IN BETWEEN: ONE
NOTHING TO DECLARE
NOTHING TO US
NOTHING IN BETWEEN: TWO
NOTHING TO SAY
NOTHING TO GAIN
NOTHING IN BETWEEN: THREE
NOTHING TO YOU
NOTHING TO THIS PREQUEL: ONE WILD NIGHT
NOTHING TO THIS
NOTHING IN BETWEEN: FOUR
NOTHING TO DO
NOTHING TO NO ONE
NOTHING TO FEAR
NOTHING TO DENY
NOTHING TO BEAT
NOTHING TO THE WEDDING
NOTHING TO TELL
NOTHING TO IT
NOTHING TO SEE
NOTHING TO WIN
NOTHING TO OFFER
NOTHING TO PROVE

**LOVE AGAINST THE ODDS
STANDALONE COLLECTION**
SWEET SEAS
HEIR'S AFFAIR
RESCUED
MAESTRO'S MUSE
GETTING TRICKY
THIRTEEN
REMEMBER WHEN...
RELUCTANT SUSPICION
XY FACTOR

KINDRED SERIES
RAVEN
SWALLOW
CUCKOO
SWIFT
FALCON
FINCH

MISTAKE DUET
MISTAKE ME NOT
SLEIGHT MISTAKE

LOST & FOUND
LOST
FOUND

**THE EXPLICIT
SERIES**
EXPLICIT INSTRUCTION
EXPLICIT DETAIL
EXPLICIT MEMORY

TO DIE FOR...
TO DIE FOR TRUTH
TO DIE FOR HONOR
TO DIE FOR VIRTUE
TO DIE FOR DUTY
TO DIE FOR LOVE

**RISQUÉ & HARROW
INTERTWINED**
TAKE A RISK
FIGHTING FATE
RISK IT ALL
FIGHTING BACK
GAME OF RISK

ONE

"HELLO?"

"You're connected to operator 1908," an automated voice echoed down the line.

No matter how good technology got, most humans recognized a non-human voice. Not the most comforting start.

"Hello?"

"Hi, you're speaking to Jacob." His deep voice rumbled right through her. Though there was something not quite right about it. Human? Automated? This couldn't be AI, could it? Maybe she should take her previous thought back. "Do you want to give me your name?"

Did she? Probably not, but what the hell was the point in calling if she wasn't going to engage?

"Anna."

Not completely true, but not a lie either, perfect.

"Hi, Anna." Reassurance came with the bass of his words. A vague picture of him formed in her mind's eye. Bet this Jacob wouldn't lie down and take abuse.

"Thank you for reaching out to Trauma Support at Lighting Darkness. Why did you call tonight?"

Why did she call? "My boss suggested it might be… a good idea."

Like a million years ago, but she'd been busy. That was her excuse anyway.

"Okay. Are you friendly with your boss?"

"Not overly," she said, sinking into the couch, twirling her finger in the cord of her rotary phone. "There was an incident at work, or work related and…" She exhaled. "This is stupid."

"Why is it stupid?"

"Because I'm not afraid and my trauma was… it's nothing to what some people go through."

"Do you always measure your experience against others?"

"Don't we all?"

"No," he said, plain and simple, just like that.

Well, okay then, way to call her weird. Shouldn't that be against some phone counsellor rules?

Inhaling, she held the breath until her lungs burned. "I have trust issues. Opening up isn't easy."

"That's okay. This is a free line; it costs nothing to talk to me. I've got nowhere to be. You've got me all night, if you want me."

The warmth in that statement did ease a little of her tension. But there were others, people waiting on hold, people who may really need help.

The "*Lighting Darkness*" charity helpline covered many needs neglected on a state and federal level, and by the healthcare system in general. Upon dialing, a user was given options, press one for this, two for that, and so on. Trauma, suicidal thoughts, grief counselling, loneliness, befriending, self-harm, etc. the list was comprehensive.

"How long have you worked for Lighting Darkness?"

"Lighting Darkness is staffed primarily by volunteers. Everyone is vetted and has experience in the area they answer."

"Experience?"

"Could be they're trained in the field or that they have dealt with similar issues themselves."

"Do you?" she asked.

"Yes."

"Which? Experience or training?"

"Both," he said. "Everything you say is held in confidence. It won't be discussed with anyone else. Your own judgment is valid. If you feel uncomfortable at any point, you have no obligation and can hang up without explanation or pursuit. The exception to this is if we believe you are a danger to yourself or others. In that case, we pass your number to the appropriate authority to ensure your safety."

A rehearsed spiel she'd bet. "I don't mistrust you; I don't know you."

"It's cliché to say, but this isn't about me. It's about you. I'm a sounding board, a sympathetic ear. Nothing about me matters. You are in control."

"What about continuity of care? You must have people who call up more than once. Do we have to start at page one with a new person every time?"

"At the end of the call, you'll be asked if you'd like to connect to the same agent in future. If you press one, your number will automatically be routed to my line whenever you call."

"You're on twenty-four, seven?"

"No, we have voicemail. If I'm unavailable, you can leave a message and I'll call you back. Alternatively, if you prefer something more concrete, we can schedule an appointment to talk."

"That's a lot of responsibility for a volunteer. Doesn't it take over your life?"

"Volunteers set their own parameters. Some people do dedicate their time to this twenty-four, seven. Some don't accept appointments. Each restricts the number of clients they take on at a time."

All very smart. The charity should be proud of itself. She'd been on the line for less than five minutes and was already impressed.

"How many do you take?"

"I don't discuss clients with clients." And it sounded like there was a smile in his voice though the wary edge added to her picture of him. He'd be tall, able, probably a guy who looked after his physique. Was he a meathead? Not so far. "Tell me something about you. What do you do?"

"I'm a sales associate."

"Sales. Do you enjoy it?"

"It pays my bills. My employer has always been fair. Though my direct supervisor can be… curt. Sometimes the power goes to her head." Folding her legs in front of her, they twisted into lotus of their own accord. "That wasn't nice, she's easily swayed by stress. Things get on top of her sometimes."

"Isn't that true of all of us?"

"You don't sound like the kind of man who understands stress."

"No?"

"No. How old are you?"

"Old enough to know age is just a number. I've met eighteen-year-olds who've seen more grief and trauma than any of us should. And eighty-year-olds who still believe in Santa Claus."

"That means you're young."

"It does?"

"Yes, you're defensive about it," she said, stretching the phone cord out to the side. "Society often dismisses young people as inexperienced and ignorant. It tends to place more value on older members of society when it comes to experience and wisdom. To a point anyway. After a certain age, the elderly are infantilized, treated as doddery or irrelevant." Silence. "There's a not-so-sweet spot, usually somewhere between seventy and eighty, depending on health, when many people subconsciously dismiss their older relatives as being on a downward slope. Like overnight everything they've seen and achieved is erased and replaced with senility. We love our older relatives and follow their example until we assume we know more than them." More silence. "Are you still there?"

"Yes, I—that's an interesting perspective."

Which, by the sounds of it, he didn't share.

"Sorry, that's... it doesn't matter."

"It matters if you want to talk about it."

"I don't want to talk about it, I just... The wider view is easier," she said, coiling the length of cord around her arm on and off over and over. "Talking in generalizations..."

"Gives the illusion of talking about something without actually talking about it," he said. "Do you keep everyone at a distance?"

"Most people, it's not like—why would they care?"

"Why would who care?"

"Anyone. People say they're friends. Colleagues, co-workers, neighbors, people are close until it doesn't suit them anymore. At work, you see the same people every day, share discussions of weekend plans, family events, bitch about your partner or your kids, but if you change job, how many of those friendships carry through?"

"Not many."

"Exactly. We might converse with our neighbors, even take on a common cause if it's relevant to the building or street or whatever. But when you move, you don't take those people with you, do you?"

"You take the experience with you."

"True," she said. "But you can't trust those people to be with you, to be at your side when it really matters."

"What about your family?"

"What about them?"

"Aren't they there for you when it matters?"

"My mother, my sisters, they're all about the drama. They live to spy on the neighbors and whisper in their circles. I wouldn't trust them with any secret." She sighed and her arm dropped, coiled in the phone wire. "That's not fair, I… It's not malicious, they just don't— they're not like me. Hence why I'm talking to you."

"You selected the trauma line. Do you want to tell me about what you went through?"

Did she? "It seems stupid to call and then not talk about it."

"This happens at your pace. Nothing is obligatory. If you want to just talk, we'll just talk."

"Are you close to your family?"

"Some more than others."

"Do you trust them?"

"Some more than others," he said. The whisper of his laugh prompted hers. "Who are you close to? A friend? Husband?"

"Oh, men, that's a whole other kind of trauma."

"You're not married?"

"No. You?"

"You always do that? Bounce questions back."

"Isn't it the polite thing to do? Reciprocity."

"Or it's a defense mechanism, to prevent anyone from asking a follow up question."

"There's no reason you should care about my answers."

"I care."

"Why?"

"Because I want to help."

"Why?"

"Because I can," he said.

Again, just like that. Either he was super genuine or the answer was rehearsed. That edge to his voice intrigued her again.

"How do you know? How do you know you can help me?"

"What makes you think I can't?"

"Now who's bouncing questions back?"

"Why did you pick up the phone tonight? It's late. You couldn't sleep?"

"Sleep's been a problem all my life. For as long as I can remember anyway. When I was a kid, our house was burglarized," she said. "I didn't see the guy, but just knowing he'd been there, taking our things, touching them…"

"You felt violated."

"I was a kid."

"Children understand more than society gives them credit for, just like you said."

"We moved and—we didn't have a lot of money. No insurance, so no replacement anything. Took us a long time to build everything back up again."

"How did that feel?"

"Great, until the fire." Licking her lips, she extended her arm again. "I'd say bad luck doesn't follow a person, or a family, but with us, it was always one thing after another. My mom is a professional victim and is always looking for someone to bail her out. She has the routine down to a tee. Taught it to my sisters too."

"Skipped you?"

"I'm the youngest."

"So that means…?"

"There wasn't enough to go around?" she hazarded in humor. "I'm not a great victim, but calamity follows me everywhere."

"More bad luck?"

"Do you believe in fate?"

"Do I…? I don't know, do you?"

Her shoulders rose and she swayed sideways, lying on the couch, legs still folded, but now propped on the arm. "We weren't raised religious… unless it suited the cause. A lot of charities are religion affiliated. Is there a higher power? A god? Maybe. Maybe not. It can't all mean nothing, can it?"

"It?"

"Experience. Life. Everything we go through."

"It makes us who we are."

"Right," she said, sitting upright quick. "Exactly. Everything we've ever done, said, seen, it's brought both of us to this moment right now, to this call, to this conversation, to each other."

"Why did it do that?"

She winced. "And that's the problem." Slumping again, she took her cord coiled arm to her forehead and closed her eyes. "I have no idea. Everything happens for a reason. What that reason is… isn't always clear."

"If I'm confused about where I am or why, I retrace my steps." Logical. "Narrow that wide focus. Why did you call tonight?"

"Because I was tired of staring at the ceiling wondering why."

"Why?"

"I follow the path, the signs, I give fate the reins and I trust that." Did she? "I try to trust that."

"What happened to make you doubt something you've believed in your whole life?"

"I still believe, what I doubt is the end goal. Maybe the goal isn't happiness. I believed the signs would steer me to contentment, as a reward, I guess. I still believe in fate, but maybe not the balance of the universe. Good doesn't necessarily follow bad. Not everyone dies happy."

"You're a pessimist?"

"Not until tonight."

"What happened tonight?"

"My ex called," she said.

"To upset you?"

"To hook up." Her eyes closed. "He was drinking, sometimes he calls when…"

"He wants to get laid."

"Right," she said on a grateful snicker.

"You can say anything here, believe me, I've heard it all. Sex, violence, even chick flicks with Kevin Costner." Huh, that was oddly specific. "Nothing is out of bounds. What do you usually do when your ex calls?"

"Tell him where to stick it."

"You didn't tonight?" Concern crept into his astute tone. "Did he hurt you? Force himself on—"

"No, God, it wasn't him, it was me."

"You?"

"For a minute, a few seconds maybe… I was tempted."

"If things haven't been going great for you, it's natural to want what feels good."

"Sex with Jeremy doesn't leave women feeling good." A harsh truth. "Not me anyway. And being with me didn't leave him feeling good either. All that baggage, all that history… I swore I'd never go back. How far have I sunk that for a minute I was willing to forget our past? I'd have let him have sex with me just so I didn't have to fall asleep alone. God, I'm a mess."

"Are you afraid at night?"

"Bad things happen at night, don't they? In the dark, when we're vulnerable."

"And Jeremy would've made you feel safe?"

"I never felt safe with Jeremy, he's… charismatic, personable, he can get along with literally anyone. Women are accessories to his brilliance."

"And you had a relationship with him? For how long?"

"Too long."

"But you didn't invite him over," he said. "You said no."

"I said no."

"And then you called me."

"A couple of hours later, yeah. I can't figure me out—God, I'm sorry. Isn't very traumatic, is it? Maybe I should've pressed the number for Whiners Anonymous."

He laughed and a ball of satisfaction built in her chest. Like there was less space for the air she sucked down, oxygen caught in her throat. What a sound. Something about him was genuine, his reasons for doing what he did were entirely his, but she couldn't deny her curiosity.

"Was that your trauma? Jeremy's call?"

"No, I… something happened to me, kind of recently, it's brought back old memories, I guess."

"Do you want to talk about it?"

"It's pathetic, I'm pathetic. I shouldn't feel like this over one stupid incident. Why can't I just get over it? Forget about it?"

"Trauma impacts individuals in different ways. Some people become jaded. Some shut themselves off. Some seek solace in the familiar… or the bottle. Your experience is valid. You are allowed to feel what you feel."

Was that what she needed? Permission?

"It's not on you to fix me though, is it?"

"I can't fix you, but I can listen. I can advise. I

can offer my opinion and guidance."

"That's what my boss said, that Lighting Darkness offers exercises for users to follow. That's what I need. I need you to tell me what to do, what steps to take, one by one, because if I look at the big picture, I'll hyperventilate."

He laughed again though it wasn't actually a joke. "What are you doing this weekend?"

"My supervisor is on a personal mission, competing with her nemesis. Has been for a while. The rest of us try to keep her on the tracks. We're taking part in a bake-off event in the park."

"Like the TV show?"

"Not exactly. It's for charity. Volunteers bake, whatever they can. Then we sell what we bake. There are stalls and booths, proceeds go to charity."

"That's a worthy cause."

"We put a team together at work. People can wander through the tent and watch, there are donation bins all around."

"Will that distract you from what you're feeling?"

Would it? Could anything?

TWO

SHE'D PRESSED ONE.

After being up most of the night with Lighting Darkness, she'd drifted off. The jarring automated voice had woken her with its insistence. *"If you would like to connect with Agent 1908 in future, please press one."* Yes, the voice had broken her slumber, but the sun was over the horizon by then.

Agent 1908.

He'd been in her head all through her gym workout. Since then and all the way to the bake-off. Had he stayed on the phone even after she was asleep? He couldn't have, surely. How embarrassing. What gave her the right? Other clients would've needed his attention. He must've disconnected at some point to return her to the automated voice.

"Ow, fuck!"

Tossing down the baking sheet, she stretched her stinging finger, already streaked with red from earlier burns.

"What is with you today?" Yvette came over to

rescue the sheet from its spot teetering on the edge of the counter. "Remember, Savanna, sweetie, this is supposed to be fun."

"Yeah, well, this is my version of fun. Wait a while, I'll end up in the ER. What a hoot that'll be."

"Let me see."

"It's fine," she said, but let Yvette pull her over to the sink to run cold water on it.

Celeste, her poised supervisor, was already popping cookies from the sheet onto the cooling rack.

"You're doing better than Nessa," Yvette said, increasing the pressure until the water spat up and out in tiny jets dampening her apron. "She's her own kind of special. At least you're producing something."

"Blood and burns, clever me, neither would get me past the health department. Thank God this is for charity."

"You're the only one who can do the cupcake frosting right."

Each of the thirty stations in the tent was manned by teams from various businesses around the city. Unofficially, a little healthy competition ran between the two Breckenridge teams. Not only in this event, but others they participated in too.

It was kind of a thing. A long running thing. Was it *completely* healthy on all their parts…? No, not exactly.

Many years ago, Celeste and her archnemesis, Maureen, from the luxury leather department, started at Breckenridge Retail together. At one point, according to legend, they'd been friends. Whatever went wrong happened way in the distant past, way, way, distant. There were so many versions that she couldn't make head nor tail of the truth. Not that she ever really asked or investigated with laser-precise focus… or any focus at all really. Still, nothing like a little palace intrigue to keep the peasants happy.

"Oh my God," Nessa gasped from further down the opposite side of their counter.

Celeste whipped around, following the younger woman's line of sight. She couldn't help but do the same when her boss's jaw fell.

"Shit." Yvette's sentiment matched the rippling intrigue of whispers and stares engulfing the tent. See, peasants happy. "That's Alice Breckenridge."

"With the bodyguards?"

"Those are not bodyguards, they're her boys… two of them anyway."

Big and broad, they dwarfed their mother who glided like she was on castors past flanking baking stations. Beautiful, with blonde hair in a French roll lined by pearls, real she'd bet, the lady reeked of class. The regal woman acknowledged all without stopping or touching anyone.

The Breckenridge family. American royalty.

Her boys were less refined, but no less entrancing.

"Go frost those cupcakes," Yvette hissed in her ear.

Yes, cupcakes. Look busy. Not like they were agog at the spectacle of the richest people any of them ever breathed near.

What was the point of charity when people like them existed?

Placing cherries on top of the already frosted cupcakes, they had to get those ones out of the way to make space for more. Concentrate. Nothing to see here, rich folks. Just common people, living out their meaningless existences. Ants in the farm, organized chaos. Underlings. Minions. Inferiors.

"Hello."

"Mrs. Breckenridge!" Celeste rushed past her. She didn't turn to see why, not with that Breckenridge voice so close. Cupcakes. Cherries. "Wow, this is unexpected."

"We're showing our support. Wonderful to see Breckenridge people working hard for a good cause."

"We take part in as many charity events as we can," Celeste said. Yeah, especially when Luxe Leather signed up. "Several a month." Keeping them busy. "We have a stall just outside, selling the produce."

"Yes, we saw that, it's very busy," Alice Breckenridge said. "We didn't want to interrupt."

"We have fresh baked goods here. Would you like a taste?"

"My boys would."

"Mom—"

"These women have worked hard. Appreciate their labor."

Two cupcakes were swiped from her station, including one she hadn't dressed.

"Thank you," a deep voice purred. "What's your name?"

"Celeste and this is—oh—" She got an elbow in the ribs. "Cherry. Cherry."

Right, cherry.

Spinning around, cherry aloft, her stomach bottomed out as a rush of heat flooded her head. Damn, dark, masculine eyes locked on her and suddenly she couldn't breathe let alone see to put the cherry in place.

"Thank you, Cherry."

Was that like—oh no. Whirling away from him, she meant to grab the counter to kill her momentum. But, of course, she overcorrected. Her hand sailed right past, sweeping cupcakes and cookies every which way.

"Damnit," Celeste yapped. "That's two hours work."

She winced. "I'm sorry."

"No, my son should apologize." Alice's

amusement did nothing to quell her embarrassment. Dropping to a crouch, she gathered the mess into her apron. "Darroch, apologize."

Oh, God, this was awful. Awful. Why did these things happen—she shouldn't be allowed near people, definitely not near super-rich people. Why did she have to learn that today? And in front of the family who owned the company that employed her?

"He has nothing to apologize for," Celeste said. "Savanna's a walking calamity. This always happens. She's a klutz."

Yes, story of her life.

Reaching around, she scraped the crumbs into a pile, noting the line of overlapping cookies shooting out toward the feet behind her. Her weight shifted and her butt slipped from her heels, landing her knee square on one of the dark boots flanking the cookies.

Great job!

"Shit," she hissed, cringing as she glanced upward to those same inscrutable eyes that wouldn't cut her a break. "Sorry."

"Don't swear at him," Celeste grumbled in a rush.

His large hand moved from his side toward her. What was she supposed to do? Not touch him probably, that would be the safest bet… Except, wouldn't it be rude not to accept—her fingers slid over his and his hold closed around them. Sure, strong, oh her heart couldn't take the pulse rate.

He yanked her to her feet, stealing her breath with his strength.

Better not to even try inhaling. Just stand there, Sav. Don't move. Don't breathe, just wait for him to let go.

"You're wet," he stated.

What the—her mouth dropped open and

immediately closed again as—did he really just say—how did he know that? Was she? Oh, God, yes. Mmm, he was hot. All dark hair, definition, and casual gravity sucking women under. Bet every female near him was wet, that's how he knew. Must happen every day, all the time. Women would be sliding off their seats left and right around him.

"I—" His chin rose in a gesture that took her gaze down to— "My apron." Shit, that's what he meant. "Yes! My apron is wet."

Which he knew because he'd just said it. God, please, ground, open up and swallow her down.

"Can I have it?"

Could he—what the hell was—oh, fuck. He could have anything he damn well liked and knew it, that glint in his eye was way too astute.

"My… You want my apron?"

A smirk quirked his lips for the briefest second and he licked his lips to hide it. God, given half a chance she'd have done that for him. Mmm, Mr. Breckenridge, that wide, dark pink enticement. Thank God he was so much taller than her or she'd be sucking on that like ice-cream from a spoon.

"The cherry."

Fuck, where was her head? Right. Because he hadn't—that would mean letting him go. Why was she still holding his hand? Let go, Savanna. Dropping one somehow released the other and the mess in her apron scattered on the floor again.

"Damnit." Crouching, she grabbed a cherry and straightened up, headbutting his hand in the process, sending the cupcake flying in a new direction.

"This is an interesting group," Alice said.

She couldn't break the lock his eyes held on hers. Swaying from the lack of oxygen in her brain, she raised the fruit between them.

"You want my cherry?"

Fuck. Did she really just say that? There was that smirk again, and someone laughed. A male, but not the one distracting her.

Someone, the other guy, smacked his brother's shoulder. "Best offer he's had all day."

"I did—I didn't—that wasn't what I meant." Her laugh was feeble. "I wouldn't—what a ridiculous thing to say. I'm no virgin, who is these days? You're sure as hell not. Have you seen you? Not that you would or anyone should—and I just said that in front of your mom. Why am I talking about sex in front of your mother? Why am I talking about sex at all? It's because you're attractive. I'm a jabbering idiot in front of hot men and you're like a twelve on the hotness scale—damn, twelve feels like an insult. I need to—I'm not doing myself any favors here, I should just…"

Squeezing her eyes closed, she was so grateful when Yvette put an arm around her.

"Forgive my friend," Yvette said, "she has a condition. We don't let her out much."

After that spectacle, no one should let her out at all.

"I'm Nessa." Their younger cohort slid between them. Small mercies were welcome. "And I'll share my cookies."

Okay, so that joke was deliberate, but the woman got away with it. That's what she should do, aim for flirt and maybe she'd hit tease… No, actually, that wouldn't happen at all, she'd probably end up in cuffs.

"Breckenridge Intimates are very welcoming," Alice said, her tone indecipherable. "I see our Luxe Leathers have a team as well. Did you consider joining forces?"

"We have a good-natured rivalry, an in-house contest, to see who can raise the most for the charity."

"Ah, good fun." Thank God the woman thought that way. "I sense my sons' piqued interest already. They can rarely resist a wager; it's a curse they got from their father. What is the prize?"

"Uh…"

"Glory," Yvette interjected.

The other brother spoke up. "We've got to do better than that."

"Caber?" Alice asked. "You and your brother—"

"What do you say, Roch? Want to make this interesting?"

"Forgive my boys for being competitive."

"Winner gets lucky."

"You're on," Darroch said. "Leather or lace?"

"I'm taking leather, you have a thing over here."

A disadvantage: her. The guy's eyes only flicked to her for a second, but she got it. With this Darroch guy around, she'd be a liability.

"You're attractive too," her voice said to the one Alice called Caber.

Her voice? Just all on its own. It wasn't her. Not "on purpose" her anyway. What was going on with her senses acting without direction… without permission?

"Two things Breckenridge boys don't share," he said. "The second is…"

"Women," the pair said in unison as their mother rolled her eyes.

As the men were about to part, Alice raised a hand, halting them both. "Rules?"

"Ah, Mom—"

"You work back here. I don't want either of you on the stalls drawing crowds. You are not in charge, follow orders."

"No money changes hands and no sabotage," Caber said. "We know the drill."

"Then let the games begin. I'll inform your father."

Caber dashed across the aisle to the opposite Breckenridge team, his mother not far behind him.

"Okay, team, what's the plan?"

The plan. Shit. It sure hadn't been for Mr. GQ model in designer jeans and a perfectly pressed tee-shirt to join their ranks.

"Cookies and cupcakes," Celeste said. "Do you have baking experience?"

"College."

"Excellent," Celeste beamed.

He kinda cringed. "I don't think that variety of brownie fit the theme."

Nessa laughed. Loud. So loud it startled the rest of them. "I can show you."

"No," Celeste said, ushering Darroch the long way round to the other end of the counter. "Yvette can show you, she's married."

Nessa came closer, until they were arm to arm. "Wouldn't stop me," she muttered. "Check out that ass."

Oh, God help her, but it was impossible to ignore. "We should stay away from him. Both of us."

"They said the winner got lucky. Shouldn't that count for us too?"

Lucky would be getting through the rest of the day without embarrassing herself any further.

From nowhere, Celeste materialized to crowd her. "You…" Grabbing her arm, she was forced to turn her back to the Breckenridge. "Stay at this end. Frosting is your world. I don't care if you have to paint faces on the cookies to keep busy, do not look at that man or waste anymore of our stock."

"No problem," she said, drawing out the sentiment. "Go, team."

Yeah, her gusto was gone. She'd keep her head

down and frost her heart out. The cause mattered; it deserved their best. Just so happened that day her best was less than stellar.

THREE

THE SUN HAD SUNK and the crowds thinned. Clean up was the only thing left to do. Well, cleaning and counting, but only one was on her agenda.

Outside stalls were being broken down and packed up. The day had been long, but whatever the total, it had been worth it, someone, some people, would benefit.

"Sorry we didn't get to work closer."

Hmm, with her hands deep in the suds, running away from that rough brogue wasn't an option. Head down. Maybe if she said nothing at all, he'd go away. Shoo, shoo, big Breckenridge. Read the room.

"You're not going to talk to me?" No, but if she held her breath much longer, she'd pass out right there. Wouldn't that be a great story to share at the country club? "You can talk about sex again."

No, that wasn't funny. She wouldn't laugh or relax or… Mmmm, his cologne smacked like a one-two punch and her chin rose, tractoring her gaze to his.

"That wouldn't be a good idea."

Stupid voice was acting on its own again.

"I'm great at talking about sex," he said. "Should we start with foreplay or just flirt a little? This happens at your pace, baby. How do you like it?"

He'd probably had it every which way. Was variety the spice of life or just the best way to tour pussy?

"You don't know what's good for you, Breckenridge," she said, laying a spoon on the drying rack. The last thing she expected was for him to pick it up with a towel to dry it off. How did a billionaire know how to do that? "Your mom make you do chores at home?"

"A man should know what to do around the house."

"Most of us don't grow up with a staff," she said, loosening as she washed and he dried.

This was normal. Two people. Could be any two people just shooting the breeze. Focus on the water and those dirty, dirty—wet, dirty, slick, slippery soap and— nope, switch route. No sex thinking, embrace logic. If she didn't think it, surely her mouth couldn't speak it.

"Don't know much about my family, do you?"

"I've worked in the Breckenridge flagship store for three years," she said. Work was safe. Boring. Normal. "I've heard a thing or two."

"Such as?"

"There are a lot of you, I know that. The Breckenridge brand is known across the world in retail, fashion, sport, want me to keep going?"

"Get to the part where we talk about sex."

She groaned and surrendered to her shame. "Okay, yes," she said, slapping a whisk onto his palm. "I made an idiot of myself, want to take out an ad?"

"I wouldn't say an idiot, but you made an impression."

One her boss wouldn't forget in a hurry.

Probably one Alice Breckenridge would share with her husband. Were her Breckenridge days numbered already? A compliment maybe wouldn't go amiss.

"Your mother is beautiful, refined." She'd made an impression too. "Breathtaking."

"Any Breckenridge you're not attracted to?"

Shit, his tease wasn't appreciated. No, breathe out, it was. She'd rather he took her with good humor than offense.

"Must be good genes."

He laughed. "You really don't know anything about my family at all."

And did he have to mock her for that? "Do you know about mine?"

His laughter died. "Why would I know about—"

"Why would I know about yours? Because you're rich?"

Nothing dented his confidence. "You'd know about them if we talked over dinner."

The curveballs just kept coming. "Dinner? Why would we—" Her hands sank into the water when her arms relaxed. "You're asking me to dinner? You're asking me out? On a date?"

He shrugged. "You did offer me your cherry."

Class didn't come with a price, and in that she found her confidence. "Oh, so you didn't mean dinner, you meant sex?"

"If we have one, the other might follow."

Working again, her smile stayed low. Nothing wrong with his ego. Why should there be?

"I'm not Breckenridge material and like my job. I do not want to be a Breckenridge booty call."

"Wouldn't worry about that, I'd put money on you not being the first employee tapped by a Breckenridge. I can ask for a show of hands at the next family meeting, if that'll help you decide."

This guy was a jokester, she'd never have pegged that. Or he was playing with her, but it seemed in good fun. Maybe this was his attempt to put her at ease.

"Nice."

"We employ thousands of people."

"Because that's what you meant."

"No, I meant we're all studs, always on the lookout for primo pussy."

"Smooth, buddy. Real smooth. Do you kiss your mother with that mouth?"

"Darroch," Alice's abrupt voice put the woman right there. Nearby. Close. Too close. How long had she been listening? "Are you being rude?"

"Expressing a healthy interest," he said, unperturbed by his mother's proximity. "Did I offend you, Cherry?"

Okay, that wasn't her name but... "No more than I offended you earlier."

"We have the results," Alice Breckenridge said, "if you'd both like to join your team."

The others were gathering a dozen yards away.

"Results?" she asked, taking the proffered hand towel from Darroch.

Two distinct sides formed. In the middle of one was Caber.

"We've got it locked here," Caber crowed to his brother. "Go back to your dirty dishes, Roch."

"Everyone in their place," Alice said.

Darroch laid a hand on the middle of her back to guide her into their cohort. The heat of it tickled up and down, but the span gave reassuring weight broad enough to support the width of her narrow waist.

"Hush, hush," Celeste said.

Eager, electrified silence descended.

"The numbers have been tallied and verified,"

Alice addressed her audience. "Though it was close, we do have a winning team…" Yes, yes, who? She'd never had a competitive bone in her body. Until right then. "Congratulations to… Breckenridge Intimates."

As a wail of joy exploded from her group, the other mirrored it with outrage.

Yvette hugged her and Nessa smacked a kiss on her cheek at the same time she was pulled the opposite way, up against a solid column. The cologne betrayed that column had a name, one she hadn't known that morning: Darroch Breckenridge.

"Now, please," Alice said, barely audible over the furor until Darroch vibrated, his loud, sharp whistle quieted all. "Thank you, sweetheart. We would like to invite the winning team to have dinner at our family table tomorrow night." More cheers and groans. "And in light of this incredible inspiration, my family and I would like to invite all of you to sign up to next year's Breckenridge Walkathon in aid of Lighting Darkness."

That got everyone chattering. The excitement was contagious.

"Are you going to sign up?"

Huh, oh, was he—he was. Darroch was talking to her. Only her.

"Oh, uh, I sign up for every charity event I can. We have another couple this month. Celeste and Maureen regularly go head-to-head."

"And the charity wins either way. Great hobby."

For her, it was more than that, but he didn't need to know the truth. He didn't need to know anything about her. If fate had any kind of mercy, they'd never cross paths again. And maybe a bout of viral amnesia could strike the group thus erasing this day of shame from everyone's memory. Perfect. Worked for her. Should she send a memo?

"Savanna!"

Celeste's cry startled her into jumping away from him and his still cradling arm. Though the momentary strengthening of his embrace suggested Darroch maybe didn't want to let go.

She went to her boss, encircled by colleagues, phone aloft.

"What is—"

"Sign here, we're putting your name in." The others were all there, why shouldn't she partake? "Don't forget the bowling tournament next weekend."

They'd see each other at work and at dinner too, apparently. It would be pretty difficult to forget their commitment.

"Are we doing the dinner thing?"

Because she'd get out of it if she could. Maybe the refined Breckenridge matriarch was only extending the invitation to be polite. Could be attendance wasn't compulsory.

"Yes, we're doing the dinner thing, and you better dress up. No one says no to Alice Breckenridge."

Few people would say no to any Breckenridge, she imagined.

"Might not be a good idea," she said, "for me. For obvious reasons."

Her boss took her elbow to lead her away from the others.

"Mrs. Breckenridge is already talking about joining and supporting other events. This could be a breakthrough, imagine how much we could raise and the higher the stakes…"

The more the charity would gain. That was the presumed answer, the socially acceptable one. Though she couldn't help but assume Celeste's motivation was snatching higher glory from Luxe Leathers.

Maybe that wasn't fair.

Cynicism was difficult to shrug off.

"I don't want to embarrass myself again."

"You were getting along just fine at the sink."

"The unexpected throws me off; I'm terrible with surprises. It helps when my energy stores are low and I'm focused on something else… and when I don't have to look directly at him."

"Then skip sleep tonight. There's no way any of our team are missing this meal."

It was a lock. Oh, goody. Sigh.

FOUR

"I THOUGHT ABOUT you today."

He answered.

Agent 1908 answered when she called. While dialing she told herself it was just to leave a message. Other people needed help. The agent must have a family and commitments of his own.

"Good thoughts?" he asked.

"No, of how I embarrassed myself last night. I want to apologize. I have to apologize. Truly. I can't believe that I—I don't remember saying goodnight. I think I just fell asleep."

"That's okay."

"No, it's not. I am not a child. You have other responsibilities. It's no excuse, but I haven't slept well this week. This month actually. It's harder to get up, to be motivated—"

"You have nothing to apologize for. I'm here for whatever you need."

Exhaling, her breath quivered. "I'm such a mess. I made an idiot of myself at the bake-off and upset my boss. Sometimes it's like I'm not even in my own head."

"After going through a trauma, some people report disassociation. Is it like that?"

"It's not a conscious separation. What happened, it was… I was alone. And after, people were shocked, they were kind, but then…"

"It all got quiet," he said. "Like it never happened at all."

"People don't know, do they?"

"Often unless they've been through a trauma of their own, they can't identify. There are also those who bury their own trauma."

"And hearing of another's can ignite their own neuroses. I get that."

"Was that what you wanted? To talk about it?"

"I wasn't raped or beaten to within an inch of my life." She took a calming breath. "Do you ever get lonely?"

"Doesn't everyone?"

"Not like a one off, like… it's not sadness, it's… a disconnect. All my life, I've never belonged anywhere. And when things happen, like this, it puts more distance between me and the rest of the world. Sometimes it's like I'm drifting in zero gravity, unable to get hold of anything to steady myself or gain control."

"If you want to work with a professional in person, we can refer you. Lighting Darkness also has funds that can be released—"

"Thank you, no," she said. "I shouldn't have called again, others deserve your attention. I only wanted to apologize for last night and—"

"Anna," he said. "I want to talk to you." He did? "I want you to call." Maybe that was his training again. "You have a bad habit of putting others ahead of yourself. Recognize your value."

"I value myself, I'm all I have. I just… These

things land on a spectrum. I haven't seen war or murder, I was held hostage, that's it."

"Held hostage? You say that like it's nothing."

"It was at work. I was alone, doing overnight inventory. I don't know how he got in or where he came from. The cops talked about it after, I didn't take any of it in. Already it's like it didn't happen."

"You're disassociating."

"What I went through, that night, it brought a lot back. From childhood when we'd have nowhere, sometimes we were in shelters, barely able to feed ourselves. At school, we didn't have time to forge relationships because we'd only up and move again when my mom got dumped by boyfriend number three hundred and fifty-eight. Only as an adult can I appreciate that other people's lives are not so transient. Standing in that room, with him, following his instructions like I would my mother's, it hit me…"

"What hit you?"

"No one would notice. If it hadn't happened in a place with cameras, somewhere people worked and so had to enter, no one would've noticed me missing at all. No one would notice if I died or disappeared." When no words followed, she dropped onto her back on the couch. "See, I told you, I should've called Whiner's Anonymous."

"I don't think you're whining, I think it's incredibly sad."

"Pathetic, yes, I know."

"No, not that kind of sad. I mean it's such a waste. You have an energy, in your voice, I can hear it. Don't sell yourself short. Today, you accomplished something with the bake-off."

"Yeah, accomplished embarrassing myself and my team in front of the family who own our workplace. Something happens, something just clicks, and I'm a walking disaster. There was this guy that I… God, I made a complete idiot of myself. At one point, I really thought I might kiss him. Just completely randomly I wanted to… What kind of a person does that? Fantasizes about being bent over and fucked by a stranger." Silence. "Sorry, too far."

Okay the thought at the time was kissing. Daydreaming later fleshed out all those carnal details.

"He had an effect on you."

"He was hot. I told him it was because he was hot. It's abandon, you know? So much that could be and so much that never will."

"Never say never."

"I doubt I'll ever see him again. If he has any sense, he'll stay far, far away. Men like that are propositioned every day, I'd never be secure. I learned my lesson on that. With Jeremy, I was oblivious, and his family aren't worth a fraction of what this guy's is. Some say with money comes security. Yes, that's true. But arrogance and entitlement come with it too."

"You can't tar everyone with the same brush. People are individuals."

"I know. You're right. That wasn't fair. It doesn't matter, I guess. I could never satisfy a man like that. If I wasn't enough for Jeremy, there's no reason to think any man would be happy with me."

"What about your happiness? What would that look like?"

"I love my job… it's naughty and nice. The detail, the fabric, talking to people. You'd be amazed what people tell their lingerie retailers. And Breckenridge Intimates isn't like a seedy sex shop. It's high-class. We do weddings, anniversaries, events in people's lives, their most intimate moments. And we do parties and—" she exhaled a laugh. "Sorry, you'll think I'm trying to upsell you."

"I have no problem talking about lingerie."

She laughed. "Your wife might object to that."

"What I do is important," he said, "Lighting Darkness leads us down various roads."

"Do you talk to her about it? Your discussions? She must ease your burden."

"I'm not married," he said. "Do you have someone to ease your burden?"

"You. That's as close as I get."

"Then it's important to maintain this link." Could she do that? "I want you to call. Anytime you need to talk to someone, call me."

"You don't owe me anything. It's not your job to—"

"What I do with Lighting Darkness is important to me. I choose who to work with carefully. I want to make a difference and I'm not always great at maintaining a professional distance."

"But if you're a trauma—"

"My clients have various entry avenues; I answer more than one line. You were taken hostage, that's what you said. That is a trauma and I hope one day you'll want to tell me more about that experience."

"There's something safe about you. Maybe it's the detachment from real life. It feels safe to talk to you."

"You are safe."

"I thought I was safe at work."

"And you weren't," he said. "What follow up was done? What did they charge him with? Did you go to court and—"

"Oh no, they didn't catch him," she said, astonished he would suggest otherwise. "He's still out there… somewhere." More silence. For a guy who volunteered his time to talk, he could say surprisingly little. "Probably far, far away."

"They didn't catch him."

That was a statement, not a question.

"Happens all the time. Crime is rife. So I've heard anyway, it's not like I go sleuthing around the city at night. Though with the insomnia, I probably could. My boss told me to skip sleep tonight, so at least I have an excuse."

"Why did she tell you that?"

"It's a long story. The short version is she doesn't want me to make an idiot of myself tomorrow the way I did today. If I'm sleep deprived, less chance I'll trip over my own tongue if I do see this guy again."

"Does he know you're following him?"

A joke. Just what she needed.

She exhaled a laugh. "It's boss driven, believe me. I tried to get out of it."

"Why? Do you resent the people you work for?"

"Why would I resent them?"

"Your trauma happened at work. Do you blame them for what happened?"

"It wasn't anyone's fault. I was in the wrong place at the wrong time."

"And the perp?"

"Sick, I think. Tough to tell without a professional diagnosis." She smiled. "I should've slipped him your number."

His humor faded to intrigue. "You shy away from it, avoid, don't confront."

"Confrontation rarely leads to anything good."

"Sometimes you have to get emotion out."

"I find it's better to bury it and just keep on smiling."

Maybe he was right. Confronting her experience might give her a better perspective, when she was ready. She wasn't ready yet. Not that she'd necessarily recognize readiness if it jumped up and bit her on the ass. Joy.

FIVE

DINNER WITH THE Breckenridge family started with a forty-five-minute limo drive. Talk of what the night might hold and future events occupied them. Having their Intimates team in close quarters, without work as a distraction, they searched online and signed up for events to raise money for various charities. At least they'd accomplished something, even if the rest of the night was a bust.

Such a long drive there would equal a long one home. Hmm. They had work bright and early. It wouldn't be a late night… Would it be a late night? Sharing a car there implied they'd need to share one back. How much would a cab ride to the city cost? Would slipping out early be rude?

When they slowed to take an offshoot with its own flanking columns, intrigue lit. They drove for a while, then a broad gate opened to grant them entry to yet more road.

Both inside and outside the gate were huts, security no doubt. Amazing. The rich could afford to take excellent care of themselves. They wouldn't be burglarized any time soon. Why was that in her head? It happened a million years ago. The Lighting Darkness call, that's why. Jacob.

The house came into view and none of them could find the words. Three floors high, the broad curved staircase at the front led to more columns.

"Wow," Nessa said. "This is like a palace."

Nothing "*like*" a palace. It was exactly that.

The car came to a halt and ushers rushed over to open both back doors. Shit. Celeste's order to dress up was opportune. Good save, boss. When choosing her outfit, she'd restrained herself and gone with a cocktail dress and heels. Maybe a ballgown would've been a better choice. Not that she owned a ballgown. Who owned a ballgown? Alice Breckenridge, that's who. The matriarch would have a bunch of them, probably got bored switching between them every weekend for glitzy occasions… If she wore one more than once. Maybe she got a new one for every new event. What a life.

They ascended and the doors seemed to open without assistance. That thought disappeared in the wonder of the glowing chandelier brightening a vast space with a gleaming white floor and breathtaking double staircase.

"Wow," came from more than one mouth, probably hers too.

Like Christmas in some movie, the walls, the corners, every inch glistened, pure gleaming luxe cleanliness. Who had the time to keep all this space spotless? How did someone even dust a chandelier? When the family were sleeping? Did they do it by candlelight? Wouldn't get a Swiffer duster up there with all the will in the world, not from floor level, and she didn't see a ladder.

"Good evening!"

Alice Breckenridge appeared on the overlooking

floor between the staircases. Like a balcony, it presented the woman aloft for all to behold. Fairytale stuff.

"Wow," Nessa murmured under her breath again.

Alice twisted as three kids came to join her and put her hand on the tallest one's head. "Allow me to introduce Astor, he's thirteen." And already as tall as his mother. "Dougie." The middle one got a touch. "Eleven." She took the smallest by the hand. "And this is Buoy. He's five. These are my three youngest."

Wow, she had a five-year-old? Caber and Darroch were definitely full grown. Very full grown, all adult developed in all the right ways full grown, and Alice was still raising infants? The woman must love risky sex... or the couple had a breeding fetish. Guess they could afford it.

"It's nice to meet you all," Celeste said, stepping up as the foursome descended. "I'm Celeste. This is Yvette, Nessa, and Savanna."

"Do you go by Savanna?" Alice asked.

"She's Savvy, mostly," Celeste answered.

"Anna's the name she gives to no-hope guys in clubs," Nessa offered.

What the hell value did that add to the conversation?

Celeste, luckily, re-routed the discussion. "Will your husband be joining us?"

"Yes. If you follow me..."

They went through a grand living room decked out in gold décor to a sort of reception space with a bar and beyond into a dining room that stopped her in her tracks.

The long table wasn't fully set. Only a few places at the top were prepared for diners. What a length though, how many people did the Breckenridges feed on a daily basis? There had to be at least ten spots down each side, maybe twelve.

Forcing herself to approach with the others, a guy in a suit, like a butler, showed them to their assigned seats. Before they could sit, a door at the head of the room opened to produce three men. Caber, Darroch, and an older man, Benedict Breckenridge, no question about his identity.

"Good evening," patriarch Benedict Breckenridge proclaimed. "Well, boys, it looks like we're in luck, dining with such accomplished winners tonight. Welcome, all."

He went to kiss his wife and help her into her seat before picking up Buoy to settle him too.

Someone behind her cleared his throat. Oh, Darroch. With one hand on the back of her chair, he gestured with the other.

Sit.

Right.

"You got the short straw," he said, sinking down at the next place.

"Sitting next to you?"

"No, sitting next to Boo Boo, the little guy on your other side. He's kinda attached to his mom."

"And you're not?"

"Not tied up in her apron strings." He slanted closer. "I'm no virgin, Cherry, remember?"

"That's not actually my name," she said, straightening a fork that was already straight. "And I think Buoy is adorable."

"Competition, huh? I forgot you love everything Breckenridge. Would you turn brother against brother?"

"Being I'm not attached to any one brother, how can I turn you against each other?"

"I've staked my claim."

"Oh, really?"

Turning her head was the mistake because when

their eyes met, she forgot how to verbalize.

"I like your getup tonight, beautiful."

And, uh… why was she suddenly singing scales in her head? Stop. No tunes. No melody. Language, vocabulary, respond. Why was she wearing—what was she wearing? Clothes. Ha. The dress. Would help if she could remember which one. Geez, she didn't even have that many—did it matter? Breathe. He was being polite. Just breathe. She could do this.

"Celeste…" she started on a half throat clear, eager not to choke on the words. "Celeste, my boss, she asked us to make the effort… for your mom."

"Mom doesn't care about things like that."

"And you do?"

"You don't need to dress for me either. Though if you want to undress for me…"

What a flirt. Could he be like this with every woman? Maybe. Except he hadn't taken his focus away. Celeste, Yvette, they weren't targets of his teasing. Nessa was the youngest, and the prettiest, yet she couldn't be sure he'd even noticed her.

Still, a little restraint never hurt anyone. "Your little brother is sitting right next to me."

Alice was whispering to the boy, something she couldn't hear.

"Playing it cool, I've got you," Darroch said. "Let start at the beginning, how long have you worked for Breckenridge?"

Arrogance wasn't scarce in this house. "My life didn't start at Breckenridge, but three years ago. I started as a model."

"I bet you did. In intimates?"

"Maybe." Before Jeremy and what came with that relationship. More life reflection. She really had to stop that. "A long time ago."

"Sorry I missed that."

"We all have to grow up sometime," she said, touching her spoon. "I thought fancy houses like this did a million course meals with a thousand different utensils. I think I can guess what these ones are for."

"We only do that with people we don't like."

Others chatted among themselves while the food was being served.

"So I should be honored?" she asked.

"I don't know what we're having. Maybe. You allergic to anything?"

"No."

"Vegetarian? Vegan? A lifestyle diet?"

"No."

"I'll keep you right."

You know, it was curious.

She tried to look deeper. "There's something about you."

"That you can't resist? Don't fight it, Cherry."

"No, it's… I don't know, I can't figure it out."

"Then you should stick close, wait 'til it comes to you."

And some part of her wanted to reach out. To touch, like contact might solve the riddle.

"How many women are you seeing right now?" she asked.

"Only you."

"We're not seeing each other."

"Yet."

Just the idea that he'd be so eager, so interested… What was she missing? Something… She couldn't figure it out.

"You and your brothers can have anything you want."

"I'd appreciate it if you kept that offer exclusive," he said. "Some of my brothers are young and others aren't that nice."

"And your sisters?"

"Don't have any of those."

Only boys. Interesting.

"How many of you are there?" she asked, leaning back to allow a server to put soup in front of her.

Darroch poured wine for them both. "Only one of me."

"Breckenridge boys," she said. "How many brothers are there?"

"Sixteen."

Her hand stopped midway to the spoon.

After a beat, restraint bolted, and her surprise flew to him. "Sixteen?"

A laugh from further up the table betrayed her lack of subtlety.

"Introducing our guest to the family, Darroch?" asked Benedict Breckenridge.

"Sixteen and counting," Alice said, stroking Buoy's cheek as she smiled down at him.

"I swear she'll never stop," Caber said. "We already have four family Christmas trees in the den because all the gifts won't fit under one."

"Sixteen beautiful boys," Alice said, glancing from Caber to Darroch. "And not one of them has brought me a grandchild."

"I'm working on it down here," Darroch said.

She bit her lip. Another outburst or disaster wouldn't ingratiate her with anyone.

In his arrogance there was a tease, it wasn't ego. He didn't take himself too seriously. Rare for a man as hot and rich as him. Were all the Breckenridge boys the same? Raised with confidence and, somehow, humility too?

"Is that when you'll stop?" Caber asked. "When we bring you babies? You know there's a chance those babies might have mothers who'd want a little input."

Benedict had an answer for that. "None of you would marry a woman your mother didn't like."

"To do that, we'd have to find one first. Mom sees the best in everyone."

"Not anyone who'd hurt my boys," Alice said. "Do you have children, Savanna?"

"No. Kids? Me?" Ha. Funny. "It would be an unlucky child who'd have a mother like me foisted on them. That alone would constitute child abuse."

Buoy blinked up at her with pure innocence glistening in his brilliant blue eyes. Was she allowed to reference abuse in front of a little one? Probably not. Best just eat the soup and be silent.

"I have two boys myself," Celeste said. "They're grown and out in the world now."

"Mine may be grown, but they all have a home under this roof."

She glanced at Darroch. "You live with your momma? How old are you?"

"Age is just a number. And I have an open account with the Grand Hotel in the city, if we need privacy."

She didn't need a hotel for that. "I have my own apartment."

"Great. We can go there."

There were those eyes again. Wasn't she supposed to be eating soup?

"Twenty bedrooms?" Nessa gasped.

Good to know she wasn't the only one overwhelmed by the Breckenridge clan.

"This is the original house. Each of the retreating wings were added as we increased our brood."

"Construction is underway on a postern block to enclose the courtyard within."

"With a dozen more bedrooms," Caber said. "You need more kids to fill them… or we could open a hotel. How do you think Bastian would like that?"

"I would be delighted to model the block for my grandchildren."

"None of us are married yet, Mom."

"My darling boy, there is no need to remind me of that."

"Imagine a wedding here," Nessa said, eyes wide as she took it all in. "This would be an incredible venue."

"Are you involved, Nessa?"

"She's only twenty," Celeste said. "Still finding her way in the world."

"If you want a lot of kids, you have to start early, right, Mom?" Caber asked. "How old were you when Rankin came along?"

"Nessa has time," Alice said, amused by her boy. "Each woman has to make her own choice about children and the number she wants."

"And it's the guy's job to go with it?"

"Would you consider it a hardship to satisfy your wife's wishes? I raised you better than that."

"A happy wife means a happy husband," Benedict said, taking his wife's hand to his lips. "Whatever you desire is yours."

Not so bad when it came with what had to be a few decades of solid sex.

"Sound good?"

Startled by Darroch's voice and the heat of his breath in her hair, her attention snapped to him again.

Shit, had he heard that thought? Please don't say she'd spoken out loud.

"Excuse me?" she asked him.

"Happy wife, happy husband. I can keep you happy."

"Oh you think so?"

The smirking confidence in his expression poked more fun at himself than her.

"Marriage takes work," Celeste said. "Young people these days don't understand that."

Says the woman who just got divorced. That wasn't fair. She shouldn't be snarky, even in her head.

"Family is the most important thing," Alice said. "The needs of the family have to be met. Work or not, a family comes together in times of happiness and endures through life's challenges."

"It's how we were raised," Caber said.

"Only thing we ever asked of our boys," Benedict said. "To be there for each other. To value family above everything else."

"It wasn't always an easy process," Alice said. "We don't love each other because it's easy. We love each other because we recognize the value of family and the individuals in it. Each unique part is just as valuable as the whole machine."

"Okay, Mom, sounds like you're recruiting them to our cult," Caber said, swigging his wine. "Let's get through a couple of barrels first."

"A subject change," Benedict said. "Bring me up to speed on our Intimates department. I'd be fascinated to learn each of your histories."

Celeste immediately seized on the opportunity to please their hosts. Good. Celeste could talk all night. Please, be her guest. Hold the floor until the last second, save her from opening her mouth.

Yvette caught her eye, grave in her silence. Yes, okay, she wasn't the best ad for Breckenridge Retail. Her history was not good dinner conversation, any conversation. In Yvette, she had an ally. Maybe her only one. Her friend had gotten her through, been a rock when she needed it most. If the night called for it, Yvette would cover and redirect, wouldn't be the first time.

If questions started flowing her way, she'd toss some pebbles in the stream and wait for the rain to cover them. Yvette was that rain. And if that didn't work? Well, the palace was big enough, there had to be a back door out of there somewhere.

SIX

"YOU WERE QUIET at dinner."

"You're welcome," she said to the man seated next to her.

"I don't think that was what I meant."

"If it wasn't, it should've been. Better I keep my mouth shut as much as possible."

"Trust issues?"

Yeah, trust in herself. "You could say that."

"I just did."

Okay, Mr. Sarcasm.

The rest of the table finished up and Alice said something about coffee somewhere else that put everyone on their feet. She was slower to rise. If this was the part of the night where things got cozy and intimate, and personal, it was definitely time for her to slip out a side door.

"I'll settle Buoy and join you in a few minutes," Alice said, accepting another kiss from Benedict before he crouched to speak to his littlest boy. "Caber, will you show our guests to the west terrace?"

West terrace? Very nice. Very not her. What was she doing in that building with these—

When fingers slipped between hers, the thick weight of them interrupted her thoughts. Except what replaced them?

"Let's go this way," Darroch said, pulling her toward the end of the table as others went back the way they'd come in.

"Shouldn't we stick with the group?"

"I've been getting lost in this house for three decades, I never missed a meal."

Bursting through another exit from the dining room, the dim lighting in the wide hallway required adjustment.

This didn't seem to be going a favorable way. Staying quiet was much more difficult with only two people in the conversation. How could she get out of this?

"Mr. Breckenridge—"

"Darroch or Roch is fine, Cherry. You start with that Breckenridge shit around here, you won't hit the mark 'til June. There's a lot of us around."

"People will notice we're gone."

"I'm okay with that, Cherry."

They veered left. "Those are my colleagues; your dad is my boss."

"Guarantee he doesn't make personnel decisions in the Intimates department. He's a happily married man."

Screeching to a halt, he dropped her hand and turned to, dramatically, throw open glass double doors.

Then their hands were joined again, and he led her into a stone tunnel.

"Where are we going?"

A cool breeze suggested they were no longer inside. Up ahead stone stairs awaited, but they didn't get that far. He diverted into a nook, flicked a switch, and dull light flickered behind a gauze curtain.

He drew the fabric aside. "What do you like?"

The bench around three sides reclined to a padded backrest strewn with scatter pillows. He swung around to sit right there, lights twinkling in the recesses above them.

"Is this your favorite spot for seduction?"

"You want me to seduce you, Cherry? Damn. If I'd known that, I would've worn different pants." He played it well, but his smile eventually broke. He patted the bench beside him. "I'd rather we just talk. Come sit."

"Okay," she said and sat with him, about a foot away. "I appreciate your hospitality tonight. You have a wonderful family."

"Don't take them for granted?" he asked like he was finishing for her. "A lot of people assume we take our privilege for granted. We don't. Our mom wouldn't allow it."

"Buoy is adorable, do you spend much time with him? A five-year-old must be a damper on your social life."

"You know what strikes me about you, baby?"

"About me?" She was almost afraid to find out. "I'm not refined or expensive or—"

"You jump to conclusions." When her gaze met his, her body relaxed into a sort of trance. "You're beautiful." His curled fingers met her jaw. "I get the feeling you don't know that."

"Doesn't sound like talking's on your mind."

"I'm whatever you need, baby. What do you like?"

He'd asked that before. "What do I like?"

The heat of his hand trailed to her chin. "Roses? Diamonds? Kittens?"

"Kittens?" She exhaled a laugh. "You plan to fill

my apartment with felines?"

"I'll fill your apartment with anything you want."

She shifted away from his caress. "Just because I said you are hot, doesn't mean I'm easy. You are hot. You're very, very hot, not that you need me to tell you. It just—it wouldn't be a good idea to—I'm not easy."

"If I thought you were, I'd have taken you upstairs to my bed." His bed. Oh, geez, he had a bed in the building. That thought mired her in the moment. "I'm obsessed."

"Obsessed with what?"

"The sound of your voice." His palm skimmed over her knuckles on the cushion between them. "The second you touched me… Shit, baby, I can't get you out of my head."

No way. It didn't make sense.

"Why would a man like you ever want—"

"No more of that." His fingers slipped between hers on the lush fabric. "I'm attracted to you and I want to explore this. My dad's rich and my mother's kind. You want to get to know me?" Instinct fueled her nod. "Sometimes I don't know when to shut up and I tend to be decisive. I value loyalty, family, and women with their eyes on the prize."

"What's the prize?"

"Devotion. Growing up with parents like ours, we've got a pretty good idea what a healthy relationship looks like."

True. Put that way, their confidence and courtesy made a lot more sense. Talk about pressure on a generation.

"That's a lot to live up to. And your mother wonders why her boys aren't married?"

"Yeah, it's all her fault. Someone should talk to her about that."

Even in an intimate setting with serious words in

the air, he could still relax her with his easy humor.

"Maybe talk to your dad," she played a little. "See if he'll drink some more or start a few extra arguments."

"Oh, he argues... in defense of her, whenever it's needed." Wonder must've painted her expression. "Yeah, sick really, they've been married thirty-five years, and he swears he loves her more every day."

She shrugged. "Sex life can't be too shabby either."

And there she was talking about sex again. At least his mother wasn't around this time. She'd take the victories wherever she could, no matter how small.

His brows rose before his smile broke loose. "Oh, yeah? What makes you say that?"

Seemed dumb to state the obvious. "They have sixteen children."

"Yeah, they do. I get how you could figure that translates to great sex."

She hadn't said great sex, but okay. Maybe she had said it. Who could be sure about anything anymore?

"If it wasn't good, they wouldn't keep doing it, would they?" Something else lit his gaze. "What am I missing?"

"You want some wine or—"

"Darroch," she said, grabbing for his thigh.

His glint of amusement matched his surrender. "Two things Breckenridge men don't share."

"And the second is women, I remember. What's the first?"

"Genes," he said, inspiring her frown. "Most of us, well, some of us, are adopted."

"You're adopted. All of you?"

"Some are biological, some are not. We never ask or talk about it. We're family. It's important to our mom that we're equal."

Huh, gosh, complex, compassionate, and...

How did that feature in a person's psyche? Were the boys curious? Were they allowed to know? Did they care? Any of them? That layered something else into the family, a perspective she hadn't considered.

"Are you adopted?"

His fingers came to hers, stroking between them, reminding her she'd planted a hand on his leg. With his strength above, she couldn't withdraw.

"Would it make a difference?"

"A difference?" she asked. "Maybe if you needed a kidney."

"To you, Cherry. Would it make a difference to you?"

"It's none of my business."

Right, so maybe she shouldn't have asked. The query slipped out all on its own. In a kneejerk response to the statement, she'd just blurted out an insensitive question without considering its repercussions. But, come on, cutting herself a break, could she be surprised by her lack of tact around him?

He didn't seem to share the sentiment. "Sure it is." No offense to be had. "Your guy's business is your business."

"You are not my guy."

"Humor me."

Man, her head was foggy, her senses drowned in this proximity. How could a man so hot live and breathe right there in front of her like that?

Basic functions became more difficult by the second. Focus. *Focus.*

"Okay," she said, doubling down on her effort to concentrate. "What was the question?"

"Would it matter to you if I was adopted?" The thought lingered. The longer she sat there the harder it got to figure out. "Guess no answer is—"

"I'm trying to—why?" she asked, squinting.

"Why what?"

"Why would it make a difference to the woman in your life? If you're together, why would adoption factor into anyone's feelings? Because you're not sure of your genetic history or something? Do people really make decisions about who to love based on their gene pool? What else could it be? Why would a prospective partner care?"

"You want me to answer that?"

"Would I have asked if I didn't?"

Maybe it wasn't wise to be obtuse when they were alone, and it was hot, and… shit, he was hot. There was that lip again, enticement, oh so close, oh so almost within reach.

"Because some, on the outside, might worry the non-blood Breckenridges aren't entitled to an equal portion of the pot."

"The pot?"

Were they talking about brownies again? This guy really scrambled her brain. Know what it was? His cologne. She could practically taste it… in a good way, like how it might be on her tongue if she licked him right—

"Inheritance," he whispered.

And, damn, did that cool the mood fast.

She recoiled, flat out appalled. "You want a woman to love you for your means? Is that your measure of love? Will you only love someone whose fortune matches yours?"

"No," he exclaimed, choosing now to be smacked by offense. "I don't give a shit about money."

Easy to say when he had it.

"There's only one reason finances would become a problem for me in a relationship."

"When's that?"

"If my guy squandered it. Not that every cent

should be accounted for or that he can't spend his own money. But if he was throwing it away on hookers and cocaine, that would upset me."

"If he's squandering it on hookers and cocaine, your relationship has bigger problems."

"I'm serious, Darroch. There are people in this world with real issues and money can make a difference to—"

"I know." He scooped up her hand to kiss the back of her fingers. "Man, you sound like my mom."

"Warning you hookers and cocaine aren't a good long-term investment?" she teased. "Is that what your mother's always telling you?"

"No hookers or cocaine in my life. I'll submit to a physical and pee in a cup if you want."

She laughed. "That's romantic."

He leaned in, intoxicating her with another whiff of those pheromones. "I can do romance, flowers, wine, trips to Florence. Anything you want."

Their mouths got closer. "Anything?"

"Anything."

Inhaling drew their lips together, tasting, in a gentle somehow confident yet hesitant kiss. Kissing Darroch Breckenridge was a bad idea. Beyond bad. She should stand up, walk away. Apologize, move on, and never see him again.

In sync with his hand skimming onto her waist, hers slid up his chest to his strong shoulder. That synchronous signal of acceptance parted their lips, granting the wish of their tongues to meet. Pleasure encircled, prompting her closer and… God, passion hadn't tormented her for so long. She'd forgotten the heat, the rush of endorphins, the tug of desire that swallowed good sense.

The bulge on her hip was—was it? No, her purse, her buzzing purse. Forcing herself back fast, she grabbed for the device inside.

"I—uh—hi," she answered her phone.

"Where are you?" Celeste demanded.

"I was—" quick thinking, come on, work, "in the restroom."

Yes!

"Hurry up," Celeste huffed. "We're leaving."

Leaving, right, that meant—hanging up, she leaped to her feet, tucking her phone away.

"I have to…" As she backed away, he set his hands on the bench behind him. "Everyone is—"

Man, he was hot. Too hot. Pure art for the eyes. Nourishment for long dormant hormones. And this could be her last chance to ever touch such a gorgeous specimen. Leaping forward, she couldn't resist another taste of that incredible mouth.

The moment they parted, he reached for her hips. "Baby—"

"I have to go." Oh, if not for inevitability. "Thank you, I—I have to go."

SEVEN

"I DID IT AGAIN."

"Did what?" Jacob asked.

His voice had come to comfort her. Something about it was wrong, though she didn't have the gumption to ask if she'd conjured that up in her own head.

"Made an idiot of myself."

"I'm sure that's not true. What happened?"

"I had dinner at my boss's house. Our prize for the bake-off."

"You didn't have a good time?"

"The meal was wonderful," she said, lying on her couch, coiling the cord around her hand. "I've never had food like it. In a restaurant, like even the toppest, poshest restaurant I've ever visited. They had staff too. Servers in their actual house." She sighed, her eyes closing as her cord wrapped fist bumped on her forehead. "They can't really live there."

"Why not? What's wrong with it?"

"People like that, in a home like that, it's a palace. Can you just imagine what kind of carnage I could cause?"

"It may look different, but there's no reason to think they'd be less at home there than you are in your apartment."

"Bad example." She squinted, though her eyes stayed closed. "The tougher I find it to sleep, the less I like staring at these walls."

"You could visit a doctor. He could give you something to help you sleep."

"Medication?" She shook her head at no one. "I've seen that path and it's not pretty. No, I'll be fine. I just need to kick myself out of whatever this funk is."

"Seems the root of that is your trauma."

"Why did I call it that? Why did I choose the trauma option?"

"Because being held hostage is a traumatic event. Why do you struggle to acknowledge that?"

"I had a boyfriend when I was fifteen. Not exactly a straight-A student, but I was acting out, I guess. I wasn't the best student."

"And the boyfriend?"

"His thing was tagging any weird place he could find."

"Tagging? Spray paint?"

"Yeah," she said and sighed. "I followed him around like a puppy dog, him and his crazy posse. It's weird, isn't it? How teenagers gravitate toward the kind of people we try to avoid for the rest of our lives? Maybe we don't try, but we should try. Bad boys might equal great sex, they don't equal reliable partners."

"Sometimes it's the labels that provoke the connection."

"Maybe."

"Why are you thinking of him?"

"Oh, uh, we were out one night, way past curfew, in the woods. At the time I thought he was the coolest person to ever breathe. I'd have followed him anywhere. We started in the group. One peeled away, one went home, then another, our numbers dwindled until we were alone. Just him and I. I knew he wanted to get to the witch's house. That's what we called this old abandoned building deep in the trees. We couldn't find it. I thought we'd be there all night searching, maybe we'd never find it, maybe we'd die there, in each other's arms like Romeo and Juliet, forever locked in our love."

"It didn't work out that way?"

"We found it, eventually, it was raining, freezing cold, but I stood in my rapture watching him leave his mark on the wall that once meant something to someone."

"That's true. It may have been abandoned, but someone must've called it home at some time."

"He used to let me put an X under his mark, like my love underlined his genius."

"That's nice."

She snickered. "Nice I was a co-defendant in his crime."

"You got caught?"

"No, if only. On my knees doing this X, he wouldn't let me get back up, not until I… Let's just say, he got his happy ending."

"You didn't want to?"

"I'd never done it before. It's nothing like you think, but… he was so adamant. We were out in the middle of nowhere, if I hadn't opened my mouth for him, we'd probably still be there."

One way or another.

"Did you tell your mother?"

"God, no," she said, that was funny. "She didn't even notice I was gone. Her and her boyfriend were having their own fun when I got back."

"Did you see him again?"

"I went out with him for another three months," she said. "And every time there was an X…"

"There was a happy ending?" he asked. "That's a difficult thing for anyone to go through, especially someone so young."

"But that's the thing. It wasn't a big deal, I got over it."

"Did you?"

Did she? Life was a series of experiences tacked onto each other. Once the train started moving, there was no slowing down, no stopping, no getting off. People had to get on with it, couldn't dawdle over processing and interpreting emotions on every little thing.

"Teenage boys like sex. All men I've met do." The lingering silence got her checking the line was still active. "Hello?"

"It's interesting that you put it that way."

"Put it what way?"

"Men like sex. Implies women don't. You don't."

"I like sex."

"That was a kneejerk response. Instinct. Maybe you tell yourself that or you've said it to others…"

She sighed. "I like the idea of sex. The intimacy, and I love climaxing, who doesn't. It just so happens that…"

"That?"

"The climaxing thing only happens when I'm alone. Most of my sexual experiences are… not like the movies."

"Hollywood movies or the one-handed scroll at three a.m. kind?"

Her expression warmed. "You know, you have an amazing way. You're good at this."

"Thank you."

"I'm sorry I talked about sex."

"You can talk about anything you want to talk about. Didn't I say that already?"

"I want to talk about you." Another silence, only this one wasn't tense, just expectant. "Do you like sex?"

"I do."

"Do you think it can be like the movies?"

"Movies are fake," he said. "Scenes are set up, choreographed. I prefer something more spontaneous, something more tailored to me and my partner's wants."

"So much of life is about sex, isn't it? It's on the TV, in the books we read, on billboards, talked about in the break room, the doctor's office. It's a part of our everyday lives, even when we're not getting any."

"Do you feel that would help? Getting a release with a partner?"

"It's my own fault."

"What?"

"That I can't come with a guy."

"Something Jeremy told you?"

"No, because I've never told anyone about Jimmy, about what happened between us at that house. I don't trust people; I don't talk to people. How can I truly give myself to a relationship or a moment, if I can't trust the man I'm with?"

"That's a good point," he said. "Sex is better with intimacy and that's a lot more than the physical. But I don't think that difficulty translates to any fault on your part."

"You have to say that."

"I don't have to say anything," he said, a laugh in his voice. "I can hang up any time too."

True. "I hadn't considered that."

"I have no intention of doing it."

"You're not paid to be there," she said, curiosity about him growing. "Why do you do it? Why give your time like this? You don't know me, you don't get anything out of this. Are you paying a penance?"

"Guilt? You think the only reason one person would help another is if they get something from the deal?"

"I think I'm one of many people you work with on this line." Her mind drifted deeper. "The stories you must hear… How do you keep it from traumatizing you?"

"I'm here for the long haul. I have clients I've spoken to for years. Hearing someone else's experience is nothing to them going through it." He cleared his throat. "And I have a strong support network. I'd never break a confidence, but if I need a break or someone to keep my mind off it, my family are always there for me."

"I can't even remember the last time I talked to my mother."

"You're not in regular contact?"

"Unless she needs money, not really. We tried to do the holiday thing a couple of times, but it was a joke really. It's hypocrisy in obligation. Just because we share blood doesn't mean we share values or ambition."

"What is the difference between you?"

Licking her lips, she didn't have a good answer for that one. "Just like I said with guys and sex, it's as much my fault as theirs. I've never spent any time digging into my mother's pathology. I've never got to know my sisters, especially as adults. We're blood, but strangers. To love someone, you have to know them. You have to show your love in what you do, not just say the words."

"True."

"I could spend that time."

"Why don't you?"

"Because my inability to trust came from somewhere." Shifting onto her side, she pushed herself against the back of the couch, imagining the support was more than inanimate. "It's harder to say the words and not be heard than it is to just not say them at all. When you open yourself up to someone, you want to think it means something."

"It does."

"Not in my family."

"You're protecting yourself."

"And so the cycle continues," she said. "Sorry, this is… I didn't mean to get heavy."

"Heavy is kind of the point," he said. "You can trust me. It means something to me to hear you talk, to listen to your burden."

"It's not a burden, it's just life." She exhaled. "Thank you for listening, for your time."

"Any time," he said. "And I mean that. I look forward to your calls."

She smiled. "Goodnight, Jacob."

"Night."

Opening her mouth, speaking, it did help. She still wasn't sure exactly what it was that she wanted to say, but being heard meant something. If only there was a way to show the man who'd become her confidante how much she appreciated his patience. Trusting a man she'd never meet in real life, who'd never lay eyes on her, that was easier than witnessing him absorb her words. Someday she'd figure it out. Someday.

EIGHT

WHAT HAD SHE been thinking? Making out with Darroch Breckenridge? Well, with anyone. It was a kiss. What was a kiss? Nothing. No big deal. So why was she still thinking about it?

"Put your name up," Nessa said.

"My name?"

Right, yes, bowling. All day one game would follow another. Every team paid their entry fee and sponsorship, that money went into the charity pot. A percentage of the bowling alley's takings also went to the winning team's charity. Adding up food, drink, the arcade and game room, the prize pot would be heavy by the end of the day.

Sitting at their console, she added her name to the bottom of the list. Bowling wasn't exactly her forte, but it would be fun. There were kids, families, friends, plenty of happy feeling and positivity.

"Hey, team!"

No, that sounded like—

"What a surprise," Celeste exclaimed. "A

welcome surprise."

She couldn't turn around, not if he was there. Why would he be there?

"You're my team."

In the corner of her eye, in the lane by theirs, Caber joined Luxe Leathers. And he wasn't alone, young Astor was with him.

She whipped around kind of hoping to see cute, little Buoy, though wasn't disappointed to find Dougie. His big brother was a much less welcome arrival.

"Come put your name on the computer, Dougie," Yvette said. "I'll show you."

They approached, forcing her up, out of the way.

Drinks.

Maybe she should go get some drinks.

Yes, drinks.

Everyone needed drinks.

Hurrying from their lane to the dimly-lit drinks counter, she needed the time to get her head straight.

The team. That was why he'd showed up. Alice probably sent him there, with Dougie, to keep the boy entertained and support the company efforts. Yep, that was it. Corporate responsibility, civic duty, fraternal bonding. Admirable. And all completely unconnected to her... unconnected to the kissing.

A hand appeared either side of her on the bar just moments before something moved the hair at the side of her neck. Not something. Someone. Darroch Breckenridge's face was buried in her hair, his heavy head on her shoulder.

"You smell incredible."

"What are you doing?" she asked, wriggling to turn and face him. Whoa, bad idea, especially with him stooped so low. "You can't touch me like that."

"Because...?"

"My colleagues are right over there." Her arm

raised beneath his to sort of gesture in that kind of general direction, but fuck, her mouth dried and she swallowed hard. The memory was alive and burning her throat, boy, those lips, that temptation. "People might… they might…"

Unlocking his elbows, his advance was slow, but ended exactly where her mind put them, kissing again.

Except this one was short. Too soon, his elbows locked again.

"You want to keep this a secret?"

"This is not a this, it's a—I don't know what it is, but it's not a this."

"Okay," he said, clearly amused. "I can play it cool in public."

Maybe he could. Her heart beat in the pit of her stomach. The tempted intrigue of her curiosity roused her sleeping hormones. Darroch Breckenridge, in a million years, no one would've predicted this. It couldn't be happening, couldn't be real.

She had to give him a chance to come clean.

"Did you lose a bet?"

"What?" he asked.

"Your mom said you were competitive. Did you lose a bet? Is that what this is? You know like in the movies with the ugly duckling and the hot jock?"

He frowned. "Baby, why would you—"

"It's Jeremy, isn't it?" God, how stupid could she be? "You know him, don't you? You're friends. He put you up to this." Shoving away from the bar, she pushed past his blocking arm. "Get a couple of pitchers of something for the team, please."

The team. The charity.

She valued the work she and her colleagues did for good causes. More than just a way to pass the time, it was part of her identity. One she strived to continue and do better. If the Breckenridges, Darroch specifically, decided to include themselves indefinitely, what would that mean for her? This was her social life and her work life, her reason for getting up in the day. If both were taken from her…

Yvette split from the others grouped around the computer when she returned.

"What's wrong with your face?" she asked.

"Me? What?"

"You look like you want to punch someone."

"Oh, if only."

"If only who?"

"Jeremy," she said.

Yvette relaxed. "So nothing new there." She smiled at her friend's comforting tone. "You've got to get him out of your head. Don't let him rule your life like this. Did he call?"

"Every time I think he's gone for good, he always pops back up."

"You have a responsibility to us married women to make the most of your singlehood. When was the last time you went out on a date?"

"Oh, God, I don't even remember. I don't even care."

"There's your problem. You need to get out there so the next time Jeremy calls, you can tell him where to get off. Better yet, your new guy should tell him where to get off."

"Men are the last thing I want to deal with right now."

Yvette hooked an arm around hers and drew her a few steps to the side. Darroch appeared over her shoulder, walking by with a tray of drinks.

"Got food on the way and set up a regular sugar drop off," he declared to the group, sliding the tray onto the top of the screen. "Got to keep those energy levels high, this is a game of endurance."

Yep, and for the next eight hours or so, she'd stay right there, with the group. No more wandering off, no chance he'd get her alone if she ignored him and stayed glued to Yvette. The joke may be on her, but she'd keep her defenses high. It wouldn't last forever, couldn't. The Breckenridges would get bored eventually. She hoped.

NINE

AVOIDING HIM WAS easier than she thought. She didn't sit next to him and moved whenever he got too close. Dougie was a great buffer and a hilarious little guy. It also helped that with four Breckenridge brothers present, crowds gathered.

Not only did the Breckenridge teams mix and mingle, others, spectators and players, hung out with them. Some asked questions, told stories, jokes, gave pointers, and got them too. Perfect for her. More people diluted any requirement to be anywhere near him.

"Cabe!" Darroch shouted over those around their lane, getting his brother's attention. "Ast!"

With both brothers following his nod, he grabbed Dougie, guiding him through bodies, toward the front of the building.

Being short and at a lower level, she couldn't see whatever he'd noticed. Whispers didn't take long to reveal the secret.

"She actually came," Celeste said, hurrying away.

"Alice Breckenridge again," Yvette said,

choosing her ball. "Guess she's here for the reveal. I never imagined seeing her in a place like this."

Had they ever imagined seeing her anywhere? Alice Breckenridge was not supposed to socialize with the sales staff. That they'd drifted onto her radar was nothing more than pure, dumb luck.

They were only minutes away from the end of the tournament. Breckenridge winners couldn't be decided in a monetary amount because it was impossible to know who'd spent the most. They could've worked on an honor system, though that wasn't likely to succeed with Celeste and Maureen at the helm.

Yvette went to take her shot.

She, herself, had never been a bowling aficionado, but usually did okay. Easier said than done in practice when Darroch Breckenridge's eyes seemed to follow her everywhere. She felt them again, on the back of her neck. It had to be her imagination. No way could—

"Mom, you remember Savanna."

Whipping around, there they were, Darroch with his mom on his arm, right behind her.

"Yes, of course," Alice said. "Have you enjoyed today?"

"Ha, I—yeah, uh, it's been fun." Thank God it was nearly over. Harder to just walk away from the guy when he brought the world's most affable woman with him. "Thank you for coming to support us."

"I had to be here for the announcement of the Breckenridge winner. It's exciting. Have my boys conducted themselves appropriately?"

"Oh, I—" Her eyes rose to Darroch though his were decidedly cooler than usual. "Yes, they're a credit to you, perfect gentlemen. Dougie is especially funny."

The woman beamed. "He does like to please the crowd. I apologize if they've drawn exceptional interest to your station here. Unfortunately, it happens often."

"No need to apologize," she said. "They've dealt with it well and kept their focus. Would you excuse me?"

"Oh, yes, certainly."

Skirting around them, she sped toward the restroom just for somewhere else to be. Yvette would finish her turn and then maybe they could get out of there. The timer showed less than two minutes until the end of play time. There'd be a speech or something from the charity, probably. Their scores would take seconds to print out from—

Someone grabbed her arm and redirected her through a nearby door.

Her back hit a wall and he slammed a hand to the concrete far above to lean in.

"Darroch," she gasped.

"Jeremy's your ex." Was that a statement or a question? "He's your ex, right?"

Question. "Yes. I don't know what—"

"The jerkoff still bothers you?" Though her mouth opened, her jaw tightened soon after and her lips circled, she had no idea what to say. "If he still bothers you, I'll deal with him."

"How?" The word came out before the question fully formed. "Hire some guy to—"

"Hire? No." His low laugh was almost sinister. "I deal with that kind of shit by myself."

"You shouldn't be here." She pushed at his chest. "Your mother is out there. The people crowd too clo—"

"She's with my brothers. Soon as we can stand upright we're taught how to protect her. Think my dad would have it any other way?"

Man, she shouldn't swoon, but that was sweet… and sexy.

"Okay, we should get back out there."

He hooked her chin to raise it up. "No more."

The depth of his calm, of his certainty, lightened the pulse in her chest, allowing it to float to her throat, ascending to the delicate need lingering on her tongue.

"Darroch…" She barely got the word out.

"No more talk of bets or guys like me. I'll do whatever it takes to be with you, Cherry. What I want from you is real, genuine, prompted by nothing except my own desire for you."

"It doesn't make sense."

"Because this Jeremy still lives in your head. Is he in your heart? You still love him?"

She blinked in surprise. "No! God, no!"

"Get him out of your mind too," he said, the pad of his thumb sweeping back and forth on the front of her chin, his other curled fingers still supplying a rest. "Move him out, I need more room in there, baby. That's what I want, to be all you think about."

Not asking much, was he?

"I'm not looking for a relationship."

"No, because one already found you. I'm right here, baby. All you need. At your command."

Descending, the liberty his mouth took with hers could only be intuitive. Whatever they had to say would wait. Despite her objection, the conflict fled in the wake of his mouth's torment. All she wanted was this. Being with him, under his mouth, satisfying his need, it filled her with accomplishment. Her own desire was fulfilled by pleasing his.

A whimper vibrated from her throat to his as she clung to his shoulders, digging her nails in, wishing him closer. Contact, that was what she wanted, full body, full naked body contact.

The seal of their mouths broke, he gathered her hands into his and held them to his chest.

"May I take you to dinner?"

"No," she panted, fixated on his mouth. "No dinner." Freeing her hands, she tried to pull him lower again. "I don't want dinner."

On a rumble of a laugh, he cupped her face in both hands and touched his mouth to hers again for a second, not long enough. "I want the same thing."

"How far's your hotel?"

"We're not doing this that way." He scooped her hands together again, just at the base of his throat. "Dinner."

She yanked her hands free and flattened them on the wall. Looking at him, acknowledging what they were doing, erased her good sense and sucked away her inhibitions. Her eyes closed, her chin rose, and she exhaled.

"What the fuck is wrong with me?"

"The same thing that's wrong with me."

Obviously not, if she was propositioning men in what turned out to be a darkened stairwell.

"This is a bad idea, I can't—I would never…" Though she didn't trust herself to open her eyes, she did steady herself on her feet again, without using the wall for support. "You're my boss and I need my job—"

"I am not your boss and your job is not at risk. My family don't work that way. Can't you tell already? Haven't we conducted ourselves with integrity?"

"Yes," she said, her eyes springing open. "Oh, God, I'm sorry, I didn't mean to imply otherwise."

"But you still think we'd fire you if this relationship didn't work out?"

"No, it's—the people I work with—"

"You want to keep this between us, I heard you. This doesn't have to be public knowledge until we're ready."

"If we go out somewhere for dinner, everyone will see—"

"Private dining, baby. We can eat in private. Or you can come to the house, no one else has to know."

"Except your entire family."

"You've seen how big the house is."

Which meant what?

"I don't know, it's—this is happening too fast, I need to… I need to think." Acting based on heated desire wouldn't put her on a reliable path. "Give me your number, I'll call."

Would she? Maybe. The pondering fled when he stepped back.

"I… don't give out my number."

Another quick cool moment. "Okay," she said with an incredulous brow raise. "Well, that was an easy decision."

Striding past him, she ignored his plea for her to wait and went back to their group just as applause died down.

"Where did you go?" Yvette asked, joining her. "You missed the end."

"It's okay. I'm ready to go home."

"There's talk of the Breckenridge guys taking the two teams out for drinks. The older ones."

Sure, the older ones.

"You have my blessing, but I need to stand in the shower for an hour."

"You and your showers."

"I think better in there."

"Okay, you can go have your shower, after they call the Breckenridge head-to-head."

Shit. Right. The exciting part. Apparently.

Alice stood at the head of the Luxe Leathers lane. Caber was at her back and moved aside to let Darroch stand beside him when he showed up. In a heartbeat, he zeroed in on her.

Shit. She dropped her eyes. Why did he do that?

Yeah, they could have a relationship, sure. In what kind of relationship did a girlfriend not have her boyfriend's number? If he couldn't trust her with that, what else was there? So much for not doing things that way. With that kind of barrier, what more could there be?

Dougie and Astor ran up to their mother, each with a stream of paper.

Alice caught both with a smile and kissed each of them.

"Thank you, sweethearts."

The younger boys went to join the older ones. The four moved aside, two left, two right, giving their mother privacy to read the scores.

"We have a clear winner in our Breckenridge face off," she said and raised an arm. "Congratulations, Luxe Leathers!"

The triumphant brothers rushed to the others to jeer their counterparts.

It wasn't right; she shouldn't be relieved they hadn't won. Yet when Alice announced the winning team would be treated to dinner in an exclusive city restaurant, Breckenridge family included, relief definitely prevailed. Some of the family or all of them? That might be a sight to see.

"Now we have an excuse to get drunk," Yvette said. "We suck at bowling."

"Enjoy yourself." She swept her purse from a nearby seat. "See you Monday."

TEN

"FATE IS LAUGHING at me."

It didn't help that was the first thing Jacob did on that Sunday too. "You think so?"

"Even you're laughing!"

"Sorry," he said, flattening the amusement in his tone. "Tell me what happened."

"No, I don't want to now," she said, tucking the cordless phone between her ear and the pillow. She'd chosen the bedroom for tonight's call. "You'll have to live in wonder."

"I want to know."

"You tell fate to call me, ask that question herself."

"Fate is female?"

"Well, she's not male, that's for sure. You know any guy who can pay such close attention to other people's lives and remain catty at all times? Female. Not a nice one. She doesn't speak for us all, but, yeah, definitely female."

"Okay. And she's laughing at you?"

Because believing that was the easy way out. "I'm blaming her, but it's all me. The signs are there, the red flags, and I'm ignoring them."

"Red flags about what?"

The concern in his voice was so genuine, she forgave his earlier slight.

"Do you believe we're all destined to find one person?" she asked.

"I hope not."

Curious. "No?"

"What if fate deals you or your other a bad hand? How do you know that vehicle accident you passed doesn't hold your other half's corpse? Kids die young, accidents and illness can befall us at any time. You could be out there looking for a guy who died of scarlet fever when he was eight?"

"Do people still die of scarlet fever?"

"I have no idea. The point's the same."

Whatever his point, he'd skewed her perspective enough that optimism could trickle in. "Actually, that explains a lot."

"A lot?"

"Think about how many people are out there in the universe, searching for the perfect partner and they never find them? It's not their fault, just fate's sick sense of humor."

Yeah, okay, so maybe death leading to optimism was a little cynical. Hey, sometimes you've gotta get it where you get it.

"You like to assign blame," Jacob said, "have you noticed that?"

Suspicion narrowed her focus. "Are you shrinking me? Are you some kind of head doctor?"

"Not even close. Another observation? Love is important to you too."

"I don't know about that."

"Love, sex, they come up a lot in our conversations."

"That's not my fa—" okay, maybe she'd give him one. "It's because of guys; the sudden influx of them in my life. Because of Jeremy calling, then you with your voice, and the edible Breckenridge."

Another laugh. "Is that what he is?"

She adjusted the pillow to bring his words closer. "I don't want to talk about him."

"Okay, that leaves Jeremy, my voice, and your hostage experience."

Her eyes sprang open, but only darkness greeted them. Why hadn't she turned on a light?

"When did that come up?"

"You still haven't talked about it," he said. "You talked about Jimmy last time and—"

"That was to make a point."

"Which was?"

Intimacy. That's why she hadn't turned on a light. Talking in the dark emphasized the effect of his voice. And, for some reason, she wanted to lose herself in the seclusion of them alone, absorbed in each other and nothing else.

"I didn't see what happened with Jimmy as a trauma," she said. "Maybe it was, but it didn't stall me like the other thing has."

"Yet you don't call that a trauma either. What is a trauma to you? How do you define it?"

"A trauma's a… it's a… something that damages you."

"And you haven't been damaged? Don't you think about them out there?"

"Them?"

"Your ex and the guy who took you hostage?"

"My ex? Jeremy injects himself into my life way more than I'd like, but he always knows where to find me. Somehow."

"I meant Jimmy."

"Oh…" When was the last time, before story time, she'd thought about him? "Not really."

"He could be out there in the world preying on innocent women. Men like that escalate."

He'd blown it way out of proportion. Had she completely misread this guy? He couldn't be totally naïve surely.

"You're private about your age, okay, but don't tell me you're still a teenager."

"No." Another laugh; its warmth and ease coated her like a blanket. "Not a minor."

"And were you a saint in your teen years? When you were young and horny?"

"I never forced a woman to get me off."

Jimmy would probably say the same. People processed the same event in different ways, lit by the angle of their specific lens. Another's lens may be calibrated to an opposing perspective.

"Sometimes guys just take it too far."

"Sometimes a woman has to speak up," he said with an unexpected stern air. "You should talk to your employer about security and your building manager too."

"Neither of those people are present when I'm getting intimate. And I like to think I'm more assertive now than I was at fifteen."

"Not if you're letting your partner get themselves off in you without demanding a return."

"You can't force someone to care about your needs. They do or they don't."

"If they don't, they shouldn't get a chance with you."

"Now I know why you're not married."

"Why's that?"

Wow, not so judgment free tonight.

"Impossible standards. Are you saying if you were with an incredible woman who checked all but one of the boxes, you'd dump her if you couldn't get off in her?"

"You'd spend your life with a man who didn't care about your pleasure?"

"I haven't found a man to spend my life with. I hope when I find him, I'll talk to him about everything, including that."

Though could she visualize that potential future? No. Not when it was impossible to trust anyone.

"There's nothing wrong with guiding a partner."

"How come sex is always a part of our conversation? You talk about sex with all your clients?"

"If you think I'm being inappropriate—"

"Hey, what is wrong with you tonight? You're on edge."

"I apologize."

"Don't apologize, talk to me. Is it your family? Women problems? If you have something pressing or concerning, go, be where you need to be. I'm okay, we can talk another time."

"This is where I need to be," he said. "This is helping."

"That I don't believe. Tell me."

"I upset someone," he said. "Someone important."

"I'm sorry. Can't you apologize?"

"I will, but I don't know if it'll make a difference." He sighed. "I hoped you'd call tonight."

"You did? Why?"

"Something about your voice."

Her flat feet slid up the bed, raising her knees. "I guess you're not allowed to call me," she said. "If you are and you need to talk… We all need someone. Anonymous isn't bad. People in your life have their own agenda, not necessarily bad, they have skin in the game. I don't. You can tell me anything."

"That's not how this works. I told you the first night, I don't matter. This is about you and what you need."

"I need you to be honest. This has to be honest."

"I'd never lie to you."

"Are you in an office somewhere? At home? In a crowded bullpen?"

She couldn't hear anyone in the background but wanted a better picture of his surroundings. For some reason. The why made no sense. It just mattered to her, he mattered.

"I'm… alone."

In life or just at that exact moment?

"You went through a trauma, you said you had experience."

"Enough to know being held hostage would damage even the sanest of people."

"And I sure couldn't wave that flag to begin with, I hear you. Maybe you're my sanity."

"Then we're both in trouble. Talking about it will help."

So many people seemed eager to tell her that. Okay, so two people, her sanity and her supervisor.

"I thought I was alone. My earbuds kept me company. I was counting, typing, sorting, nothing strenuous. Doing something I'd done a hundred times before."

"When did you become aware of him? Aware you weren't alone?"

"That's one of the things that makes my skin crawl when I think about it."

"You don't know how long he was watching."

That, right there. "I don't know how long he was watching."

"The cops should know, shouldn't they? If they have him on camera."

"They'll know, they didn't tell me."

"You should ask—"

"What difference will it make? The answer doesn't matter, he still had my life in his hands. He could've killed me and I'd never have seen it coming. Maybe that would've been the merciful way."

"If they have him on camera, why can't they ID him?"

"He used the employee access. Less cameras than in the public areas, and basically not patrolled at all. His face was covered the whole time. They have rough height, build, skin color, blue eyes, soft voice, quick to anger."

"They didn't get those last three from a tape."

"He kept his promise. I did what I was told, and he let me live."

"Lighting Darkness has connections in law enforcement. Let me reach out to them and—"

"No. Thank you," she insisted. "No one wins by dredging it up again."

"When did this happen? A year ago? Two? More?"

"Four months ago."

"Shit, baby, no wonder it's still screwing with your head."

He'd never called her "baby" before. Was that a slip of his professional veneer? Could it be that this was becoming a something?

"I have to go."

"I'm sorry, I didn't mean to pressure you."

"No." She sat up, eager to shake off… whatever. "You didn't. I just… have something to do."

"Anna—"

"Goodnight."

Ending the call, she held the phone to her cleavage. They'd never met, never laid eyes on each other, but he knew her. Had heard more of her secrets than any other living creature.

She flopped forward, planting her face in the bed. Damnit. She was making a mess. Whoop-de-do. Just her style.

ELEVEN

MONDAY CAME AND went. Tuesday was good.

On Wednesday, in the systems room, she was busy updating their pricing when Nessa came rushing in.

"Oh my God, you have to get out here."

In the Breckenridge department store, anything could happen. They'd had shoplifters, marriage proposals, even streakers, yes, more than one. And that was in spite of their floor being members only.

Following Nessa out, she caught the door and let it drift from her hand when—she stopped.

Alice Breckenridge stood on the other side of the counter between Celeste and Maureen. Why was Luxe Leathers Maureen on their patch?

"Thank you, ladies," Alice said, leaving them to track her at the counter. "Savanna… is there somewhere we can talk?"

"My lunch is in an hour." Alice didn't move or react, her expectation remained the same. Right, duh. "We can talk in the break room."

This woman and her husband owned the

building. They owned the main store, every sub store. Stores across the globe. With money like theirs, even what they didn't own, they could buy.

Maybe that was why opening the counter for Alice and leading her to the employee only door was just pathetic. They went down a short corridor, bland, beige, not at all glamorous. The break room consisted of an old couch, a dinner table with a few chairs around it, a fridge, and a blessed coffee machine.

"Would you like some coffee?"

"Yes, thank you."

She gestured at a chair and Alice was gracious enough to sit. What was she doing? The woman could take all the damn furniture and kick her out. It wasn't her place to give Alice Breckenridge permission to do anything.

The coffee machine brought her up short. Shit. Coffee? From that crappy machine? She tipped out what was in there and washed the pot. Feeble. What could she do but change the filter and try her best?

Deep breath; she turned. "I don't know what Darroch told you—"

"Darroch?" This wasn't about her son? "He's a good boy for the most part. His mouth runs away with him at times. He's headstrong, all of them are. I can only apologize if he has upset you."

"If this isn't about Darroch… What's it about?"

For the first time, Alice exuded pain. "I didn't know it was you. I'm so sorry, Savanna."

"Know what was me?" The minute the words left her lips, clarity struck. "Oh, that."

"I can't express the depth of our sympathy. I'm so sorry."

"How did you find out?"

"Someone mentioned it to Benedict when talking about the contest. He was appalled, we all were."

All? Did that mean the Breckenridge boys knew? That Darroch knew?

"I didn't want it to be a big deal. I have no intention of suing."

Alice got up to come over. "That is not why I am here." She took her hand. "I came to offer our sincerest apologies. And to provide any help and support I can. You were offered counselling, is that right?"

"Yes."

"Did you embrace it?"

Her insides squirmed. How far should she let this go for courtesy's sake? Honesty was usually the best policy.

"I appreciate you reaching out," she said, "but talking about it makes me uncomfortable."

"Of course, I understand, I'm sorry."

"The only one to blame is the perpetrator."

"It's unacceptable that this man is still out there, a risk to others."

"I agree with you, but I'm not surprised. The world isn't a just place."

"Just because it has been, doesn't mean it always will be," Alice said. "We have to believe we'll make a difference. Why do you spend so much time participating in charity events if you don't believe that?"

"I believe we should do what we can to give back." The depth of her truth remained hidden. "If I didn't believe one person could make a difference, I wouldn't do what I do. That doesn't lead to me believing wholly in justice. What would happen to him? What should happen? It doesn't matter. The deck is stacked against women like me."

"Like you?"

"Women from a lower financial tier, without a relentless support network, survivors of sexual violence. If justice always prevailed, we wouldn't have inequality and horror in the world."

Suddenly, the woman lit, like the sun illuminated clarity. "You're it."

And now she was self-conscious; she didn't want to be it… What did "it" mean exactly?

"It?" she asked.

"I should've seen it sooner."

"Seen what?"

"I'd like you to join me in an endeavor, a pet project. A collaboration I'm excited to be involved with."

"What pet project? I signed up to attend the walkathon already."

"This is something more involved and more discreet. Still in its infancy."

"What is it?"

"A friend of mine is building a foundation. She's tenacious, vivacious, I'm looking forward to working with her. We're building something that will work hand in hand with Lighting Darkness. Are you aware of Lighting Darkness?"

"Yes, it's a Breckenridge-led charity that's grown exponentially over the last fifteen years."

"Yes, it has, much to our delight. My boys handle most of the management. While we want to keep listening, we also want to give people a voice, victims a voice, survivors a voice."

"Oh, you don't want me for that. You know nothing about me."

"You have no criminal record and no negative notations in your Breckenridge file." That Alice even knew that was leery enough. "You have heart, I see it. That's what we have to nurture."

Like maybe she was the side project. "I don't need to be saved, I can look after myself."

"I apologize for implying otherwise. Perhaps I can appeal to your sense of duty. I will invest my time and expertise, as will my closest friend, but this venture is a young woman's game. Those at the head of this project have tenacity and ambition, it will benefit Lighting Darkness to have someone able to keep up."

"Mrs. Breckenridge—"

"Call me Alice."

"Okay." Though it didn't feel right. "I appreciate your sympathy and the offer, I don't have experience running anything. It wouldn't be right to—"

"Have dinner with me tomorrow night."

"Dinner?"

"Yes, I'll have a car sent to your apartment. We'll eat, talk, and get to know each other. No pressure. You'll see this is a genuine request. Your input will be invaluable."

No one says no to Alice Breckenridge.

Guess that made the decision for her.

TWELVE

"I'M SORRY IT'S late," she whispered into the phone. "Did I wake you?"

"No," Jacob said, though there was a rasp in his voice that suggested otherwise. "Are you okay?"

"There's no rule that says you have to answer the phone, is there? I thought if you were off duty it wouldn't connect. Can you turn it off? Your Lighting Darkness phone?"

Or however it worked.

"If I wanted to, I could block any number. I answer because I want to."

"Because you're so sure you can fix me."

"You're not broken, Anna," he said, soothing in his certainty. "No one should go through what you went through. And I know there are things you still haven't told me."

She frowned into the darkness of her bedroom. "How do you know that?"

"We all have secrets. Not everyone has this opportunity to share."

"In anonymity? I admit that does make calling easier. I think about you… a lot."

"Because I can be anyone, anything you want me to be. I understand, even when I don't. I reassure, though I have no power. Supporting you is what I want to do, tell me how I can. Why did you call tonight?"

"I missed your voice." That was honest. "Though there's something weird about it I haven't—"

"The Lighting Darkness lines run through a distorter automatically. It skews our voices, just a little."

"So they can't be recognized," she said. "That protects you, your people. I suppose that means Jacob isn't your real name."

"No, it isn't." A few seconds of silence until ever-patient, he came back. "Is that a problem? Does it hurt you? Upset you?"

"No," she said, briefly closing her eyes. "Maybe a little, in the times I'm thinking of your voice in the dark… How your breath might feel against my skin if…"

"We were closer?"

Maybe not exactly how she'd have put it but thank God he had.

"I'm sorry. That's wildly inappropriate."

He laughed, startling her, though delight soon took its place. "It might be, but you're safe, I promise you."

"I'm safe? What about you?"

"As we've just established, you don't know my real name or even exactly what my voice sounds like. Besides, I take kind words from women as compliments, not threats."

"Guess that's the luxury of being a man."

"You must get your share of compliments." He cleared his throat. "Sorry, that was sleazy."

"It's okay."

"I'll work on the delivery. The question, it's not

judgment… Does the attention of men upset you?"

"It doesn't upset me but… I have hang-ups about it. My ex, Jeremy, he didn't like it when other men noticed me."

"A lot of people experience jealousy. You were never jealous of him?"

"Oh, my jealousy came in how easily he slipped into any conversation. How simple it was for him to connect with people. I'm not one of those people."

"Social people?"

"People who can—God, think about our conversation, I'm always saying something wrong, something stupid. Then out in the world, I trip over my own feet and… For some people, it's effortless. They're not intimidated by a room or aware of every syllable. I guess I can't claim to be either because I'm always…"

"You're hard on yourself. We get along, don't we?"

"I don't have to look you in the eye. I don't have to wonder what your real motive is. This relationship has set parameters." That she'd already violated by talking about his breath on her skin. "I don't mean to do it, say the wrong thing, do the wrong thing."

"We all have hang-ups," he said. "And are our own harshest critics. You need to give yourself credit where it's due. No screw up of yours led to you being held hostage, did it?"

"We fell behind, as a department. My boss was getting divorced, and we'd missed a couple of weeks." Or maybe a couple of months. "We were taking it in turns to work the extra hours to clear the backlog…"

"If it had been another night, it might have been someone else."

Is that what he'd heard? She'd be lying if she said that thought never occurred to her.

"I was the best one," she said, "for it to happen

too. My boss was going through enough, I wouldn't wish any harm on our youngest colleague. And Yvette, she's my friend. She has a husband and a home. He works away a lot, but her life is what many people strive their whole lives for."

"So you think you're expendable?"

"I think I… matter less than my colleagues, in general. I don't have Nessa's rosy optimism, her get it while the going's good attitude. And it's not like I've never posed in my underwear before." Silence. Ten seconds. Twenty. "Jacob?"

He coughed. "Yeah, uh…" More quiet. "Sorry, I…"

"See, I shouldn't talk about this—"

"You should. That's what he wanted? To see you like that?"

"It's the product I work with. I used to do parties for women, like Tupperware parties, just a little more risqué. And it's a premium clientele, you understand, it wasn't like…" Was she explaining or apologizing? "I haven't done it since before… him. I'll do it again, sometime, it'll be different with women, it'll be fine. Truth be told, I need the money. I need to get over this so I can start earning again like I used to before—"

"Your employer will understand. If you explain—"

"No one's pressuring me. No one expects me to… it gives me more time for the charity stuff. Though the longer I go without the overtime, the more *I* become charity."

"You're strapped for cash?"

"Everyone I know is, it's just life, especially these days. Unfortunately, the bills don't care about trauma, they still come due."

"You could speak to your employer, ask them to—"

"I just want to forget it ever happened." Closing her eyes, she rolled onto her back. "I want to go back before the hostage thing, before Jeremy, I want a do-over, that's not too much to ask, is it?"

"Everyone deserves a second chance. And if it was within my power to give it, I would."

"The things you must hear..." And all she did was whine. "The real, true, devastating things people must endure..."

"You were violated, in a space meant to be safe. Someone forced their will onto you. Did you want to model for him?"

"No," she said, her voice small.

"You have to acknowledge it, give yourself permission to feel what he made you feel."

How was that? "I don't know what he made me feel."

He exhaled, almost seeming to calm himself. "When do you think of him? When is it worst?"

"I don't go into the back storeroom anymore." Which the others had accepted without addressing it. The why was obvious. "And at night, when I'm alone." Which was part of the reason she called him. "I feel ridiculous. I'm a grown woman and I've slept with men, been naked in front of them. Why is this guy different?"

"Choice. Did he threaten you?"

"Yes." The ache in her throat almost reminded her of that first moment. When he asked her to... "He didn't have to, I was cornered, the threat was implied but... he had a weapon."

"You deserve justice. You deserve to be heard."

"Thank you," she said, her body heavy.

"For?"

"Picking up. And don't tell me I didn't wake you because I know I did. You didn't have to answer, and you did. You make me feel better. I can't explain it.

Before when I was scared, I'd turn on all the lights and watch infomercials until I fell asleep."

"You know there are streaming services now."

She laughed. "That requires thought and concentration. I just needed the noise, the illusion that I wasn't alone."

"You're not alone," he said. "You have me now. And I will always pick up, sleep or not."

"That a promise you make to all your clients?"

"No." The honesty felt profound. "With you, I… I'm getting something out of the deal."

Saying that was probably against the rules. Were calls recorded? Maybe if his supervisor heard… so she shouldn't ask…

"What do you get out of the deal?"

"You're special, Anna," he said and laughed himself. "And that was another sleaze, sorry."

"Don't apologize. You tell me I have value, that I'm allowed to feel what I feel. So are you. Just… don't show up at my apartment and ask me to model for you." Okay, crappy joke, it fell flat. "Sorry, I should let you get back to sleep and—"

"Don't hang up. You don't want to be alone? You don't have to be. Lay down, leave the line open."

Like she had the first night when she fell asleep by accident.

"Am I that pathetic?"

"No. Anything that makes you feel better, makes you feel more secure, it's important. You're important, Anna. Just close your eyes and exist with me for a bit."

Somehow he knew exactly what she needed to hear, knew what she needed, before she did.

"Thank you, Jacob."

"Shh, baby," he murmured. "Go to sleep. I'm right here."

THIRTEEN

THE NEXT NIGHT, a car took her to a broad glass restaurant flanked by flames. *Blaze*. Not somewhere she'd expect Alice Breckenridge to hang out. Especially given it was situated in the glittering red skyscraper of the Rouge complex, which included the famed, and often scandalous, Crimson nightclub.

Her door was opened and an usher immediately offered his arm. "Ms. Mayden." How did he know her name? "Come this way."

They went inside, and before the maître d podium, he guided her to the right, past a screen and into a private dining room, where Alice Breckenridge already sat. Damn, not a great first impression. Was she late? Should she have arrived earlier? Yes, probably, note to self, always arrive early.

"I'm sorry," she said. "Were you waiting long?"

"No, I've been in the city all afternoon. It was nice to get off my feet. I took the liberty of ordering wine and a selection of appetizers. The boys rave about this place. I thought this might improve my chance of impressing you."

Sitting down, the waiting wine was much needed relief. "Impressing me?"

Hilarious that anyone should think that, let alone someone like Alice Breckenridge. There had to be something else going on.

"My boys have their fingers on the pulse of the city's social hotspots. Tripp does anyway, and he keeps his brothers in the know."

"I don't know how you keep track of them all."

"Oh, they make themselves known. But enough about my family, have you had a good day?"

"Not really."

"No? What happened?"

Honesty would be a good start to the relationship. She'd learned her lesson about lying.

"With this meeting on the horizon, it was difficult to relax. I'm not sure why we're here."

"You seem suspicious, on edge," Alice said. "There's no need to be wary, I promise this isn't an ambush."

"Then what is it? You tell me it's not about Darroch, but some part of me…" The smile that warmed Alice's cheeks only heightened her awareness. "What?"

"I fell in love with Ben the first moment I saw him. I never told him that, not until years later. From money, an only child, he was told all his life that he was destined to be in charge, to get what he wanted when he wanted it. Yet, somehow, he held onto his humility… a sliver of it anyway."

"How old were you?"

"Sixteen," she said. "We'd moved from California, away from the peacocking suitors my mom warned me about. I'd heard of the Breckenridges, everyone had, and our families had dealings with each other, but I'd always been protected, separate from the business. My family had money, not Breckenridge money, but enough to make me a target."

"A target?"

"For unscrupulous men looking to cash in and skip a few decades of hard work." And that seemed… unfathomable. "Don't look so bemused, this was almost forty years ago. My mother taught me the world was a big place, that interests and opportunities weren't always what they first appeared. To say she wasn't a fan of Ben's would be an understatement."

"Because…?"

"Because he was young, attractive, and had the world at his feet. His father was a known philanderer." Okay. Awkward. "I refused Ben's every advance."

"You believed he'd be like his father and cheat on you?"

"That would've been noble and logical. No, my reasons were much more selfish, I was afraid of losing his affection. Mother said men want one thing and once they get it, they move on to another challenge. We were children really, Ben's only a couple of years older than me. So influenced by those around us, wide-eyed and naïve, perhaps. We dated, spent a lot of time together, no matter how much I resisted the physical, he kept making dates, kept showing up. We'd sneak out together in the middle of the night and…"

Alice's wistful sigh sucked her in deep. For some reason, she was invested in the story, even though she knew how it worked out.

"You gave in?"

"No," Alice said on a light laugh. "The opposite. I was deeply in love with the man who'd become my best friend. This was long before the days of social media and the scrutiny that brings. Long before smartphones and email, and constant communication. He was everything to me; some might say I became addicted."

The end being apparent didn't detract from the intrigue of the journey. "What happened?"

"I told him I wouldn't."

"Wouldn't?"

"Be intimate with him."

"Ever?"

"With anyone. Until I was married."

"Wow."

A side door opened and three servers came in with platters of food. They laid them out then departed without a word. Alice selected a plate, put a few samples on it, and placed it between them.

"Do you have any allergies?" Alice asked. "I should've asked before ordering."

"No allergies." Alice took a bite of… something, she couldn't take her eyes away or close her eager mouth. "So…?"

Alice swallowed. "So what?"

"You told him you wouldn't be intimate with him until you were married and…"

"He proposed the next day." Alice dabbed the corner of her mouth with a napkin. "I spend so much time eating with men that I forget some women aren't as forthright. Please, help yourself."

The story was better than the meal.

"He proposed the next day?"

"Very romantic." Again, the woman urged the plate her way. "He pulled out all the stops. Flowers, music, moonlight."

She didn't care about food. "And you said yes?"

While sipping her wine, Alice nodded. "I was so young, my mother warned me not to leap into forever at that age, that I'd come to regret it."

"Have you?"

"Not a single second. Not with Ben or with my boys."

"Did you consciously decide to have so many children?"

"We didn't trip and fall into it by accident," Alice said and laid a hand over hers. "But I'll talk about my boys all night if you let me. I'd love to learn more about you."

"Not much to learn, nothing as exciting as what you live every day. Honestly, it's awe-inspiring. Your family, the way you love each other, support each other…"

"We are blessed." Alice pushed the plate toward her, so she selected a canapé. "Darroch was an advanced child. Less interested in academia, although he was more than capable, he has a knack for reading people."

"Is he your favorite?"

Alice laughed. "Why do you ask that?"

"You talk about him a lot."

"You brought him up first."

Yes, okay, her mistake. "I admit, I'm fascinated. You must have such an affinity with the opposite sex. Men have always confounded me. I tend to overthink and overcomplicate things. I know I do, but… I have never met a man who follows through on promises. Hell, not even promises, just shows some common decency."

"You have now. All of my boys will treat you with the greatest respect, including Ben. And if any of them give you cause for concern or you have questions…" Alice reached into her purse on the table and produced a card. "Call me."

"I can't take that." If Darroch didn't trust her enough to give out his number, what would he say if he found out she had his mother's? Maybe she was some crazy stalker determined to get him no matter what. "It wouldn't be right."

Alice tucked the card into the side pocket of the purse in her lap, all she could do was look at it.

"There, I have given it to you. I'll be offended if you refuse it."

Well, great, hello rock and goodbye hard place. "You mentioned your project."

"There will be time to talk about that." Alice picked up her glass. "Do you have siblings?"

"Sisters. Two."

"And your parents?"

"My mom is… highly strung. My dad isn't around. I met him. At least who my mom says is him." Not a flicker of judgment. "Can anyone be as truly good as you seem to be?"

Alice laughed. "No one is perfect. My mother's words still echo for me, the world is a big place. Everyone has a story and we're not always in control of it. I've seen children neglected and exploited by wealthy parents and less affluent alike. I've witnessed parents who torture their kids simply by being together. And I've seen single parents prevail and excel. Nothing in life is straightforward."

No, and until then, she hadn't put the pieces together. Adopted. Some, maybe all, of the Breckenridge boys were adopted. Were they all adopted at birth or had they lived difficult lives before meeting their saviors?

She wanted to ask.

Wanted to know more.

About Darroch.

Goddamn her.

He'd said he wanted to be all she thought about and he was getting his wish. Maybe the phone number thing was a product of his past. Could he have a phobia? A trauma? Something he may be embarrassed about or wouldn't want to confess so early in their relationship? How could she have been so hasty to dismiss him? God, put in that context, she was an absolute bitch.

"Mr. Breckenridge must be quite a man to

deserve you."

"Ben is thorough and considerate. We have dinner every Friday night, we'd love it if you could meet us for a drink tomorrow."

"And crash your date? No thank you."

"Please," she said, giving her hand a reassuring squeeze. "After thirty-five years of Friday night dinners, I've more than earned one drink with a friend after all those I've had with his business associates. And it's not like our boys never crashed. What Ben cares about is the drink we share on our bedroom terrace at home, when he reminds me of the promises we made and the lifetime we've spent together."

"I don't need to ask where that goes…"

They laughed. "Some things men never grow out of."

"I don't know if that's reassuring or terrifying. Does thorough and considerate continue on from your terrace?"

"Ben knows how to take good care of me," Alice said and reached for a menu. "Join me in a cocktail?"

"Why not?"

She hadn't eaten and this was the boss's wife, maybe that was why not. Something about Alice Breckenridge disarmed her. Stupid maybe, but this was safe, she was safe, and the night was only just beginning.

FOURTEEN

"…SO THEY GET competitive," she said to Alice, topping off their glasses.

Maybe they'd drunk too much, either that or Alice Breckenridge was the easiest woman to talk to in the world.

"Competitiveness has its place," Alice said. "My boys goad each other frequently, but there's never any malice. It's all in good fun."

"I don't think Celeste and Maureen mean to provoke each other. If I'm honest, I think it's helped Celeste through her divorce. We kept her busy, gave her a social outlet. I know how difficult it can be to get out there sometimes. And how distractions hold you up."

"Has it been a help? Since your trauma at Breckenridge?"

"I don't like to call it a trauma, but, yes, I suppose it has. Though this is nothing new for me. My whole life I've done anything and everything for charity that I could."

"Is that rooted in something—"

The door at the back of the room opened. Rather than more servers, it revealed a stunning blonde.

"I heard a whisper…" the woman said, creeping inside.

Alice surged to her feet and the women met in a hug. "Is my boy behaving himself?"

"You know, probably not," the blonde said. "But I'm not the best barometer for that. I like it when he's naughty."

"Oh, my…" With an arm still around her, Alice brought the woman to the table. "Savanna Mayden, meet Roxanna Kyst."

The blonde extended a hand and they shook. "Pleasure to meet you. Call me Roxie."

"Okay, uh, hi."

Alice sat and Roxie slid into the seat beside her.

"Roxanna is spearheading the project I told you about here in the Big Apple. She was gifted a foundation by her fiancé for her last birthday," Alice explained. "And has been working with a friend on the west coast developing something called Huddle Hope. A digital support structure for people who might otherwise be alone or unable to afford talk therapies."

"It's an offshoot from the social media platform Huddle."

"I've heard of it." The platform, not its off-shoot. "I'm sure it's quite the venture."

"Roxanna has a wide network and travels often. Her contacts in New York are wonderful women. Do you know Freya Dere?"

"From Children's Connection? Only by reputation." She'd done some sponsored events for ChilConn, not that Freya Dere needed the money. "She's accomplished so much."

Roxie dipped her fingertip in her drink. "Freya

sends her apologies. She'd be here, but something came up at the hospital."

"Freya prioritizes her work over everything else," Alice explained. "Even her own personal life. Sometimes I think she works too hard, but it means so much to her. She'll do great things in this new partnership."

"Huddle Hope is in its infancy," Roxie said, selecting one of the few canapes left. "As is Lola's Liberty, my foundation, we're basically the money. We will gain a lot of stability and credibility if we work with the existing infrastructure. We're not looking to take over anyone's patch. In fact, we welcome, covet, advice and support from veterans of this field. The stronger the network, the higher the likelihood it will succeed."

Roxie popped the canape in her mouth. The door opened again to more servers with food and wine. Were they going to be there all night?

"Savanna and I are spending some time getting to know each other," Alice said. "Building a more personal bond. She's wary of getting involved."

"Oh, believe me, I know that," Roxie said, stirring the drink in her whiskey glass with a fingertip. There was way too much liquid in there to actually be whiskey… right? When that fingertip touched her lip, Roxie scowled and called out, "Baker!" A server hurried into the room. "Please take this away. I don't know what it is, but it's not Gin and It. It's not even in the right glass."

"Should I make more?"

"No, it's okay, thank you. The Emperor will get me drunk when he's horny later." The server started to leave. "Oh, ah, but, Baker…" The guy stalled. "You know what? Take that drink to him, him and only him. Tell him it's a gift from me. Someone needs an education." The guy nodded and disappeared, then Roxie widened her smile. "Sorry, where were we? Ah, yeah! A personal connection is important to Huddle Hope too, we want people invested in its success."

"I have no money," she said, struck by panic. "I don't—"

"No, no, no," Roxie said, pouring wine into an empty glass. "We definitely don't need money. Working with Lighting Darkness will strengthen our network, there's so much experience there. We need a liaison, someone to act as a go-between for…" Maybe it was the look on her face, but Roxie paused. "Are you seeing anyone?"

"Am I see—I—no," she said, unsure where the question had come from.

"You looking?"

"Not really," she said, unable to look Alice in the eye. What a question, and after what she'd said about Darroch. "Does that matter?"

"No," Roxie said. "It's surprising with Alice having so many options available. Have you met her boys?"

"Not all of them."

"Me either, I don't think it's possible to have them all in the same room at the same time. The universe will implode or something."

Not dissuaded, Alice seemed to enjoy the blonde. "The Cavendishs' Christmas Ball is approaching."

"Even if you got the others there, Tripp would never stay," Roxie said. "I'd bet money on that."

"You and Zairn have been invited for Christmas. We'll all be present then," Alice said. "Will you accept the invitation?"

"That's up to Jane," Roxie said and gestured at the table. "Do you want to take this upstairs? Z's at work, he won't be home for a couple of hours. Even if he shows, he'll make himself scarce, or not, depending on your preference. We could persuade him to strip down to his loin cloth and feed us grapes…" Her chin jutted up at an angle, eyes on the ceiling, fingertips trailing down her throat. "Hmm, how would I persuade him to do that in company?"

Like it was something he did a lot in private? "Z?"

"Zairn," Alice said, "Lomond. Roxie's fiancé."

Ah, okay. "And his work is…?"

The amusement on Alice's face flashed to Roxie for a moment. "Is the nightclub in the building."

"Nightclub? Crimson?"

"Yeah, he's Rouge's Chief and Emperor. Do you like to party? You're welcome any time," Roxie said. "Just tell whoever's on the door that Ballard said it's okay."

"Ballard?"

"Our Head of Security and Logistics. It's safer to use his name. Use mine and Ballard's people will follow you around all night. It's harder to get up to mischief when they're constantly monitoring you."

Alice glanced at each woman. "Tripp could escort her, he spends more time in this building than he does any other. I'm surprised Zairn hasn't evicted him."

"Are you crazy? He might clean out our fridge on a regular basis, but his drinks bill keeps the lights on." Roxie picked up her glass. "Upstairs?"

"I can't… I shouldn't," she said. "I have work tomorrow."

"Right," Roxie said, "regular job. You're with Breckenridge?"

"I work in the flagship store. On the members only floor."

"Ah, members only, I heard, I like that. Shame I don't do lingerie."

"You don't do lingerie?"

"Nope," Roxie said and drank some wine.

"You wouldn't need to," Alice said, laying a hand on Roxie's. "I've seen the way your man looks at you."

"My friends once reminded me of the amount of time he spends at the gym. So rather than repay that effort with lace, I pay in head instead. Nice little rhyme there."

"Roxie!" Alice exclaimed with a laugh in her voice.

"What? He's okay with it."

Alice laughing at—okay, she was mortified, but it put her talking about sex at the bake-off in a different context.

Remaining defiant, Roxie held her posture. "I will not argue against the merits of lingerie, it has its place, and everyone has to earn a living. Maybe I'll swing by some time, Savanna, and you can take a shot at changing my mind."

"Have you had something custom made for the wedding?" Alice said. "If not, we can help with that too."

"Actually, now there's a good point. I have no idea where we are on lingerie." Roxie tapped a finger on the table. "I'll have to get Jane over here."

"Jane?"

"Our wedding planner."

"And one of Roxie's dearest friends," Alice explained.

"She's making all of the wedding decisions."

"Except the honeymoon."

"Except the honeymoon," Roxie agreed and Alice laughed. "She's laughing because Z already took me on a rehearsal honeymoon. And what a commotion that was. I think we'll need another after that palaver."

"Tell Savanna," Alice said, squeezing Roxie's hand. "You can trust her."

"With everything?"

"We want her to put her faith in us, we have to

put our faith in her."

Secrets. She could handle keeping secrets. She was an expert at it actually. Though most of her secrets weren't deliberately held, she just didn't trust many people.

"Where do you want me to start, Momma B?"

"At the beginning."

"We'll be here all night."

And going home, she'd be a changed woman. Already that was obvious. Something about the women's spirit, their dynamism, enlivened her with a curiosity and confidence of her own.

FIFTEEN

IT WAS WRONG that he was on her mind from the minute she got in the cab. Maybe it was before then. Being with Alice, and with Roxie, strong, powerful women, who held it together... Why was she always falling apart?

Kicking her shoes into the bedroom closet, and pulling the clip from her hair, she didn't even bother to change before calling.

It was wrong. To be so reliant on him. Two nights in a row. When would it end? Maybe never.

"Hi."

Oh, the sweet rapture of his attention. "It's late again."

"I told you to call whenever you wanted," Jacob said, the smooth comfort of his voice encircling her. "Did you have a good day?"

"You know how some people inspire you?"

"Yeah."

"You want to be better because they show you it's possible?"

"You met someone?"

Unzipping her dress, it fell to the floor. She didn't bother to pick it up, just hopped onto the bed and lay across the width of the end.

"I'm not a dynamic woman, or the kind of person people notice. How do people do that? Fill the air with positive energy?"

"You're doing it again, selling yourself short."

"I strive to be better, I do. I think we all do, in some way. Fate just doesn't… she doesn't embrace some as much as others. Not that I'm blaming her for anything. The signs that are out there, we can misread them. Even when she's showing us the way, sometimes we miss it."

"You think fate is showing you the way? What did she show you tonight?"

"Good people do exist. There is hope for the future."

"It's nice to hear you're feeling positive."

And if she was in such a good mood, why did she call?

"I think about you too much," she admitted, stroking her abdomen. "Because when I think about you, I'm not thinking about him."

"I'm here for whatever you need," he said. "Are you worried about sleeping tonight?"

"I'm worried I'll never be like them, those kind, dynamic people. That I'll never get over this and be in a place in my life where I can really help others and feel secure in my own life." And maybe it was just slightly more than ridiculous that, at her age, she was crushing on a faceless voice. "Why am I such a mess?"

"Because you don't face it. You hide from it."

Was that true? "When I turned around and he was there, I said nothing. Couldn't think of anything to say. I just stood there."

"Fight, flight, or freeze is a perfectly normal

response.”

Alice Breckenridge wouldn’t freeze. Neither would Roxanna Kyst.

“He asked me my name. I told him. Somehow, just going along with what he asked was easier than putting up a fight. Why didn’t I fight?”

“You said he had a weapon. If you tried to run or rush him, he may have used it.”

“It felt so ridiculous afterwards telling the cops that when he told me I was sexy, I said, thank you.”

“It’s an automatic response.”

“Yes, so I thought too. I went along with it like it was a photo shoot or a lingerie party… Except… instead of changing in private…” She left that to linger. “I can’t let this take over my life.”

“Facing what happened doesn’t mean it’s taking over your life. Process it. Don’t rush yourself. Do you have anyone in your life you’d trust to listen?”

“In my real life?” How sad was she? “No.” Goddamn and it didn’t make sense. “How can I talk to you about it and not talk to anyone at work? Not talk to a professional therapist?” Not that she’d be able to afford it. “I couldn’t talk to Jeremy about it. My ex. The cops called him to come get me that night and he said he had an early day.”

“He didn’t come to you?”

Though his disgust was obvious, she couldn’t feel the same. “It didn’t matter. What could he have done anyway? He said the next day, he hadn’t understood what happened. He hadn’t realized it was a big deal. The cop didn’t tell him—”

“It was a big deal.”

“I don’t know if he thought so, which made it so much worse. When I did think about it… I didn’t want to be intimate with him, be naked in front of him, of anyone. I think he got tired of it, of the drama, he called it."

"Which is why you struggle to talk about it now. You see that, don't you? His response, the way he reacted, diminished what you went through. It minimized your justified feelings. You struggle now to see that your responses are perfectly reasonable."

"How can you see that as a complete stranger, but my own boyfriend couldn't? Did he ever love me?"

Maybe that's really why she obsessed with Jacob. This voice on the line told her she was allowed to feel what she felt, that there was truth and trauma to what she endured.

"He wasn't the right man for you, you'll find someone who does understand, who does let you feel that experience and process every aspect of your life, positive or negative."

"You said you weren't married, but never told me if you have someone to share your life with?"

"Maybe," he said. "She's a complicated woman."

She smiled at the ceiling. "You're safe. That's what you said. That's why I feel connected to you."

"It's a common response."

"Like transference," she said. "Florence Nightingale Syndrome."

"You label everything to marginalize the truth of your relationships. This one is safe."

"I put my faith in this so I don't have to connect with anybody in the real world. If I get my emotional support from you, why do I need to look? Why do I need to be with anyone?"

"You don't," he said. "Some people make that choice for themselves."

"And it's valid?" she asked on a laugh.

That seemed to be one of the buzz words.

His tone acknowledged her joke. "It is."

"I don't want to be alone. I don't want to be in

the wrong relationship. And I obviously suck at it, picking the right man."

"Almost no one gets it right the first time."

Alice Breckenridge had with her husband. Roxie? She didn't know how many serious relationships the woman had before Zairn, but she'd found it too. How had she known? How did anyone know when someone was The One? Had she just never found it or was she not capable of loving like that? Maybe she wasn't designed to be loved like that.

"Do I need to break away? Stop using this crutch?" She closed her eyes. "I shouldn't think about you the way I think about you."

"Like you said, this is safe."

Wouldn't she turn into her own version of a crazy assaulter if she truly fell for him? Ridiculous! It wasn't possible to fall for someone she'd never met, not when he wasn't sharing his life too.

"I'm sorry," she said. "For the things I've said, for the number of times I've called."

"I told you I want you to call."

"Your girlfriend wouldn't appreciate it. I don't know how to get my head straight."

"Maybe you do need to find someone in your life. To rely on. To trust. Is there anyone you're interested in building a deeper relationship with?"

"Not someone who'd want me. For a second I thought maybe but…"

"But…?"

"He's too together. If he had the first clue how screwed up I am, he'd run." On a swallow, she let the truth in. "He could never be happy with someone like me… and I think he knows that."

"Trust him," he said. "Fate put him in your path, didn't she?"

"Fate's proved she doesn't mind being cruel.

What if I like him—if I fall for him and…?"

"It works out? You live happily ever after?"

"You're not that naïve."

He laughed. "Happy doesn't have to mean incident free or constant bliss. Choosing to be with a person is about a partnership, it's agreeing to confront whatever either of you endure together."

Together. She had to admit that sounded good. Imagine having someone to shoulder life's trials with. Alice and Benedict did it. Roxie and Zairn. Yvette and Iain.

"You're right, I'm sorry."

"Sorry?"

"I shouldn't be relying on our conversations to fulfill my emotional needs. You have your own life and your own people, and…" It was embarrassing to learn he had someone in his life. Was she lying next to him when the phone rang? What would she think? "I won't inconvenience you anymore."

"Anna—"

"Goodbye, Jacob."

She hung up and dropped the phone at her side. What was she doing? Where had it all gone wrong?

SIXTEEN

RUSH, RUSH, RUSH.

From work to play again. Her social calendar had never been so full.

What should she wear to drinks with the Breckenridges? She'd stayed at work as long as she could that Friday, putting off having to make a wardrobe decision.

Stepping out of the employee exit into the alley, she hooked her purse strap across her body. "LBD," she said to herself because who could argue with that?

Forget the dress, on the street, still outside work, walk or ride was the more imminent question. Huh, not that she had time to meander.

"Hey, Cherry."

His voice brought her around fast. "Darroch?"

He came sauntering over, smile on his face, like being there was the most normal thing in the world.

"Miss me?" he asked.

"What are you doing here?"

"I missed you."

More likely that he'd been to the store on

business. "No, you didn't," she said and stepped off the sidewalk to hail a cab. "I'm going home."

"I've got a car."

"Good for you."

When the cab stopped, Darroch slid between her and it to open the back door. She got in and gave her address, now she had to decide—

Darroch boosted her across the seat to join her in the cab. What in the actual—

"I want to take you to dinner."

"You told me that already," she said, scrutinizing him.

"Tonight."

"Tonight? Why tonight?"

Had Alice said something to bring Darroch to her?

"I haven't seen you since the bowling."

She smoothed her skirt. "Heard you went for drinks after, was quite a night."

"That you missed."

By choice and with good sense. For once.

"How was the dinner with Luxe Leathers?"

"I didn't come here to talk about that," he said and linked their fingers. "Have dinner with me tonight. I don't care where. We can go for burgers or I'll charter a jet for Italy. Whatever you want."

She caught the cab driver's eye in the rearview. "He's kidding." She shoved him closer to the door and whispered, "I don't want to go to Italy."

"Where do you want to go?" His fingers feathered across her cheek. "Lady's choice."

"I can't."

"Can't or won't?"

"I have a… prior engagement tonight."

She didn't expect him to smile. "Competition? Oh, I can't wait to crush his hopes and dreams."

It wasn't that she didn't want to tell him about dinner with his mother or her appointment with his parents, but she wouldn't play games. Whatever she and Darroch were or weren't was separate from whatever she and Alice were or weren't.

"That shouldn't excite you."

"You heard my mom say we're competitive, right?" he asked. "Tell me about him."

"I'm not going to tell you anything."

"No inside track, I hear you. This guy is good."

"This isn't a challenge," she said. "It's not a big deal."

"It's a big deal to the guy you're going to spend the rest of your life with."

Though she shook her head, his confidence was amusing. "I haven't seen you for a week."

"Won't slow me down."

And his smirk only endeared her more. "I was sulking."

"When?"

"You said I couldn't have your number and I figured that meant you weren't interested beyond the chase."

"Baby, you've got to believe—"

"I jumped to conclusions, just like you said."

"Is this an apology?"

"Let's wipe the slate clean. I have something else on tonight and I'm working tomorrow during the day. But if you want, if you'd like, you could pick me up tomorrow at seven thirty."

"For dinner?"

"For whatever you want."

He sucked in some intrigue. "Risky giving a guy free rein like that."

"There's nothing free about it." Her shoulders pushed back. "Would you like to have dinner with me tomorrow night?"

"You asking me out on a date, Cherry?"

Playing with him wasn't so bad. "Not anymore," she said, sliding away.

He caught her hip to drag her back. "Oh no you don't. The door is open and this horse is bolting. You're on." And she shouldn't get too carried away. "You going to tell your prior engagement about me?"

"No."

Definitely not. She would not mention the Breckenridge son to his parents. They'd said secret and she doubted it would last. Yes, the chase was fun, but what came after the pursuit was the real measure. That was the harsh lesson she'd learned with Jeremy.

"You like to keep things equal. I like that."

Or she could be lying. "You've got the wrong idea."

"What idea do I have?"

"I don't know, but it…" She couldn't see ridicule when he looked at her, yet there was something there she hadn't deciphered. "I'm a crappy trophy and not good in bed."

"I've got no problem with sucking in bed." Such charm, presence, appeal. "Dinner's what you should be worried about."

They pulled to a stop outside her building.

"Why? Do you talk with your mouth full?"

"That a deal breaker?" he asked and produced a card to pay the driver before he'd even told them how much.

"You don't have to—"

He got out of the car before she could finish and offered her a hand to help her onto the sidewalk.

"So this is your place, huh? Nice block."

"Compared to yours?"

He moseyed closer. People moved past them left

and right, going about their lives… or did they? The deep chocolate of his eyes swirled, mesmerizing her.

"I wouldn't mind spending some time here, Cherry."

He had the whole world, yet there he was on her block, enticing, teasing, intoxicating her. When he stooped lower, she froze in anticipation. He scooped her head into his hands and pressed his mouth to hers. In his kiss, she felt like the world, his world. The notion of inviting him inside sprang up and that was when she stepped back.

"People will see us."

"Boyfriend number two live nearby?" Rather than an accusation, he played with her, his fingers drove into her hair as he took more control. "Let him watch. Breckenridge men don't give up."

"You have no competition."

"Great, then call the chump and cancel. I'll take you to Blaze."

Oh, wouldn't that be hilarious.

"I can't cancel tonight," she said, a smile peeking out. "But you can kiss me again."

Because every time their lips met, pieces clicked into place. Her heartbeat settled into a rhythm meant for more.

"Can I come up?" he murmured on her, brushing his kiss across hers. "For a minute. Two if you're lucky and I think about Caber."

She laughed and smacked her hands to his chest to hold him away. "No." He wasn't the only one who could tease. "Someone told me we're not doing this that way."

As she sashayed away, he grabbed for her hip, pinching her like he wanted to pull her back. It couldn't be that the excitement, the intrigue, the potential, could translate into something real, something lasting. Want.

Desire. Need. They didn't last... did they?

SEVENTEEN

"I CAN SEE WHY my wife likes you," Benedict Breckenridge said, topping off her wine glass after his wife's. "You're dedicated."

"It's a hobby. Whenever there's a chance to sign up for something, I do it. Why not? Isn't it better to use our time for good than sit around and do nothing?"

"Darling, you are not to introduce her to Lesley or Ernie."

Alice laughed, then clued her in. "Our friends at the adoption agency."

"One dinner with them and you'll be signed up for three by dessert."

"Ben," Alice chastised, nudging her husband. "You'll scare the girl."

The couple sat by each other, against each other really, Alice's hand and forearm lay twined with her husband's on the table. Yeah, she was kind of the third wheel, but they were the epitome of relationship goals. She couldn't tear her eyes away.

"Are you planning to adopt more? I have to say,

Buoy is just adorable."

"Unfortunately, my wife is attached to him, so he's off the market," Benedict said, flashing a smile at Alice. "Our boys mean more to her than anything."

"They return her affection, I'm sure."

"They do. Vehemently."

"You wouldn't have it any other way," she said, spouting Darroch's words. "Although you're her greatest defender."

"Am I?"

"I like that." Her smile bloomed. "Chivalry is rare, it's nice to discover it still exists somewhere in the world."

"Savanna hasn't had the best experience with men," Alice explained. "I've told her our boys will treat her right."

"Ah, that's what this is," Benedict said and kissed his wife's hair, resting his lips there. "We're interviewing her for a daughter-in-law position? We do have vacancies in that department. Many vacancies."

Terror was cold. "Oh, God."

"You're scaring her again, Ben. We're here because I think she's perfect for our partnership with Huddle and Roxie."

"Roxanna's putting together quite the team."

"We're investing in a solid future," Alice said more to her than her husband. "Something we can be proud of and pass along to our children."

"Which Alice is passionate about."

"Roxanna's friend, Roux, is Head of Huddle Hope Operations in California, the original idea was hers. My best friend, Carolyn Hunt, is taking the lead for Lighting Darkness over there."

"Alice and Carolyn have known each other since they were children," Benedict added. "We trust Carolyn completely."

"Unfortunately, Savanna didn't get the chance to meet Freya last night."

Benedict seemed impressed. "She's an incredible role model."

"Yes, she is," Alice said.

"Another woman my wife would love to have as a daughter-in-law."

"I would never raffle my children off to my friends."

"Not for anything other than charity," Benedict said, smirking.

"I'm happy so long as they are happy."

"Men tend to take longer to settle down," she said. Like how the hell would she know? "They have all the time in the world."

That statement gave Alice the opening to ask, "Do you want children of your own, Savanna?"

"Alice would talk of children all night."

"A mother should be proud of her offspring. And, from what I've seen, she has a lot to be proud of."

"We're both proud," Benedict said. "Communication is our family's greatest achievement. It's not about impossible standards or perfection, we get where we get together."

"Very wise," Alice said, resting her head against him.

On a laugh, he kissed her head again. "She says that because I learned it from her. Every piece of wisdom comes from her. She schools us all."

"I'm honored you listen. And we built this family together. Everything we do is together."

He picked up his wife's hand to kiss her palm. "Always."

That bedroom terrace was in the couples' adoring eyes, which was her cue.

A reflex smile spoke to her wonder. "I'm sorry

I've taken up so much of your time." She pushed back her chair to stand; Benedict immediately followed. "Thank you for your hospitality."

Alice picked up her shawl and rose in one slow move like a delicate ballerina. Her actions were so deliberate, so precise, so graceful.

"We'll take you home."

"Oh, that's not necessary. I can—"

"We would never allow a woman to make her own way home," Benedict said. "It's late and we have a car waiting." Sure they did. "It's no trouble. We insist."

Yeah, because that was what decent people did. They concerned themselves with the safety of others.

When they stopped at her building and she got out, she paused, expecting the car to leave. Instead, Alice gestured for her to go inside.

Going up the stairs, amazement overcame her. Believing the developments in her life were near impossible. Dining in a billionaire's mansion? Having dinner in exclusive restaurants? Meeting for drinks with wealthy moguls and honest-to-God celebrities? Who was she? What happened to set her on this path? Fate was out there, but what did it all mean? She'd never have anticipated these turns and didn't quite know what to make of them.

With good usually came bad, the balance of the universe depended on it. That didn't bode well for what might happen next. Her inner cynic never missed an opportunity to speak up. Could she maybe try to ignore it this time? To think the best might come from recent experiences?

That thought stuck as she unlocked her door but—the moment she flicked on the light, everything came to a crashing halt, including her.

The place was trashed, drawers emptied, furniture upside down. Her kitchen cabinets were open, food was scattered all over, liquid on the floor mixed with dry pasta and laundry detergent. What a mess! Why would someone, anyone…?

"Oh my…"

A spasm of pain clenched her gut. Sinking onto the carpet, she couldn't think. Darkness from beyond the hall parallel to her kitchen, the route to her bedroom, could be sanctuary or her ending. How much bad luck could plague one family? What was fate trying to tell her this time?

****

SOMEHOW, she'd called the cops. The who, what, and where were foggy. Again.

The mess continued into the bedroom. Her closet was tossed, the nightstands. Nothing was missing, nothing valuable, she didn't own anything of monetary value. What had the asshole been looking for?

"It is unusual," Detective Chapman said. "To see this level of mess. None of your jewelry is gone? You sure there are no devices missing?"

"No." She shook her head. "My phone was in my purse. I had it with me."

"You don't have a computer or—"

"I… I left it in my locker at work… I think."

"You think?"

"I haven't used it for—why my apartment? Why this floor and—"

"There will be a complete and thorough investigation."

And he seemed damn adamant about that. Defiantly so. Strange, no, suspicious was a better word. People didn't look out for her, they didn't get worked up and—

"…a nightmare…" the feminine voice stalled her

thoughts.

When she whipped around, it was confirmed, Alice Breckenridge was in her apartment... with her husband.

Their eyes met and Alice immediately rushed over.

"Alice," she said, somewhat in shock as the woman pulled her into an embrace. "What are you doing here?"

"This detective called and I'm glad he did."

"Detective?" she asked, her attention tracking to the thorough guy she'd just been addressing. Ah, see, now his behavior was less suspicious. The word "Breckenridge" probably changed a lot of outlooks. "How did you know to call them?"

"Saw the card sticking out of your purse."

Somewhere on the floor by the door still. Outrage compelled her to say something, but the notion vanished when crime scene techs, white suits and all, barreled in full of purpose.

"What is going on?"

"Detective Chapman will keep track of everything for us."

The world was—she couldn't quite believe this was reality. "What?"

"Call me direct," Benedict said, handing the detective a card. "We want to know who's behind this. Use all your resources."

"Was it random?" Alice asked, arm still tight around her. "Have there been other break-ins?"

"Not in this area. We're not tracking anyone particular around here, but this is a concerning case."

"How so?" Alice asked, genuine in her concern.

That worry was touching and completely foreign. It was almost... maternal.

"The degree of disruption," Benedict said,

scanning a discerning eye across the scene. "The electronics are still here, so it wasn't about money." His attention stopped on her. "Unless you had a significant stash somewhere that may have appeased them?"

Her head shook. "No stash."

"Initial thoughts?"

Benedict and Chapman wandered off, surveying the chaos. Alice drew her to the side of the room to let the techs pass.

"Would you like to pack a bag of your own things? Gather your essentials. Anything personal or sentimental. I'll arrange for everything else you might need brought to the house, new attire, toiletries—"

"The house?"

"Yes," Alice said. "Oh, you can't stay here tonight. Have you called Darroch?"

"No! God, no." So his mom didn't know about any phone phobia or trauma, interesting. "He doesn't need to know about this."

"No, I understand. There's no need to worry him, of course. Tomorrow is a big day for him."

And that lit her intrigue again, but it wasn't exactly appropriate to ask, not in that room at that time, given the circumstances.

"I appreciate your generosity," she said instead of peppering the woman with questions about her son. "There's really no need—"

"Nonsense. If you're uncomfortable at the house, Ben and I will stay with you in the city. We'll take a suite at the Grand Hotel—"

"No, you—"

"This is important to me," Alice said as Benedict joined them again. "Tell Savanna we'd be delighted if she stayed at the house."

"Of course we would. We insist. There's plenty of space."

"You'll be safe there, protected, comfortable." Still at her husband's side, Alice took her hand. "Breakfast with Buoy."

The deal breaker. The woman's smile was so hopeful, so warm. Fighting wouldn't get her anywhere with the tenacious, persistent Breckenridges.

"How can I say no?"

EIGHTEEN

SHE SHOULD'VE SAID NO.

As soon as they arrived at the mansion, Alice shuttled her into a bedroom on the second floor.

"If there's anything you need, anything at all, you can call down the stairs." Like this was some kind of hotel. "Are you hungry?"

"No," she said, shaking her head. The bed was huge, the room was… Her throat narrowed, some kind of apprehension? Fear? Trepidation? Maybe. Why did she feel so…? How did she feel? "Please, you've already done so much. I can't even…"

Fairy lights twinkled in the courtyard below the towering window. A courtyard. How could she be in a home big enough for a courtyard?

"Savanna, dear." Alice came to her side, took her hand and led her to sit on the bed. "We'll keep you safe. Tonight has been such a trauma for you." Not exactly. Though she'd never be safe in that apartment again. Damnit, moving, just what she needed. "We have one rule in this house, it supersedes all other promises and arrangements."

"That's… daunting."

"Support, not judgment. That's the rule here. We communicate and care for each other. You can take as much time as you need, stay here indefinitely." Wow, what an invitation. "You're always welcome." Alice stroked her hair. "Darroch won't be back tonight, unless you want me to request he—"

"No, thank you, I'd appreciate your discretion."

"Of course." Alice touched her cheek and glided to her feet. "You never have to be afraid here. It's a promise Ben and I make to all the young souls who cross our threshold. You're safe now."

Cupping the side of her head, Alice bowed to kiss her forehead and departed without another word.

Talk about being born to do something. Alice Breckenridge was meant to have children, to care for people, to welcome those in need. And damn if it didn't make her feel like a princess and a broken doll all at once.

Accepting the way family made her feel would take more than a minute, maybe more than a year. It didn't help that she was tired, exhausted. The comfort of the bed beneath her hadn't escaped her notice.

That was what she needed. Slipping off her shoes, she dug her heels into the mattress and pushed back into the cloud of a duvet that held her just right. Safety. Just like Alice promised.

***

SHE'D OPENED HER eyes refreshed… and kinda wriggly.

A possible explanation for the weird buzz that carried through her dreams came in the morning.

The bathroom was bigger than the bedroom in her apartment. The cologne by the sink shifted her mind's gear. This was—it wasn't a guest room, the bedroom belonged to someone.

And one whiff of the scent answered the question of whose. The occupier of the bedroom.

Who is Darroch Breckenridge?

Damnit.

What if he'd come home? What if he…? He could be on his way there now. Right that second.

She stripped, showered, and dressed so fast that her skin was still damp as she swiped on her makeup.

Hospitality was not something she ever liked to stretch. How would she explain to Darroch that she was in his room? The closet was a step too far. She didn't dare venture in there, from the threshold she saw the line of jacket sleeves and had to turn away.

She stuffed her things back into her gym bag and got out of there fast. Take a right to the end of the hall, another right to the staircase Alice and her boys greeted the Intimates team from the first time they arrived for dinner.

The grand front door was tempting. She could run out, run away. Would she make it out? Probably. Would she make it all the way down the driveway? The thing was a mile long. Ducking in and out of trees, hiding from passing vehicles would be more than a little ridiculous.

Oh, but that meant seeking people out. It would only be polite. Sneaking out the morning after was less than classy.

Decision made, she tried to remember the way to the dining room.

Taking her time didn't stop the inevitable. She crept through the house and opened the dining room door slowly. The memory of the long table brought trepidation. How many people would be—

One.

The little guy, sitting with his back to her concentrating on something. Breakfast with Buoy turned out to be a private affair. When she closed the door, he twisted his little body around to see who'd joined him.

Odd that she'd be intimidated by a five-year-old.

"Sav-Na." Aww, what a cutie pie. "Want to color with me?"

She went closer. He wasn't sitting, he was propped on the chair on his knees, a thick cushion beneath him.

"Careful you don't fall, honey." His weight was on his arms against the table as he scribbled furiously. She pushed in his chair a little more; it didn't slow him down. "What are you coloring?" She sat next to him, and he leaned back to turn his paper her way. "Wow, is that a dragon?"

He pushed it aside to spread the blank ones out. "You want a lion or an oc-too-puss."

That was just how he said it, so cute. "You pick one."

He pushed the octopus picture to her and his tin of pencils over to between them.

"Which color?"

Buoy picked out a red one for her. "Red's my best color."

"Mine too," she said, coloring the picture. "Have you had breakfast? Do you want food?"

The spread had clearly been picked over, maybe by a pack of hungry gannets, but there were still pastries and pitchers of juice. No coffee though, hmm. She was late to the party. Had that made her the topic of conversation?

"What's your favorite animal?" Buoy asked, distracting her from the lack of caffeine.

"Tiger."

"Yeah?" he asked and stopped coloring to

narrow his eyes at her. "Do you like pussy cats?"

"I do."

He went back to coloring. "Mommy said we can't get a pussy cat."

"Well, it might get lost, this is a big house."

His pencil paused on the paper and then kept going. "We could get a doggy. A big doggy won't get lost. Boa never gets lost."

Boa? A friend's dog, maybe? "Are you home all day to pick up after it? Big dog means big poop."

The pencil stopped again. This time, rather than just keep going, he craned his little head around to blink at her. Was that a bad word? Had she said something wrong? Great, corrupt a kid, her new special talent.

"Are you marrying my brother, Sav-Na?"

Shit. Well. She wasn't the only one spouting the bad words.

Luckily, she got a pass when Alice entered. "Oh, Savanna, sweetheart, good morning. How did you sleep?"

"Amazing." Too amazing. "You have wonderful beds."

"And an abundance of them." She kissed the top of Buoy's head and surprised her by bowing to kiss her cheek too. "Buoy and I are going to a tea party at the stables today."

"Lovely."

Had she ever used that word in that context? It felt right in that moment, though a little awkward on her tongue.

"Would you care to join us?"

"That's very generous of you."

"Of—"

"But I have to get back to the city. I'm working today."

"You're working—oh, yes, you're working."

Alice laughed. "Ben assigned Ferguson to your detail. He's been apprised."

What the…? "Detail?"

"He'll take you wherever you want to go. He'll drive you and ensure your safety."

"There's no need—"

"Haven't you learned there's no point resisting. We'll always—"

"Insist, I know," she said and sighed.

The generosity did make her uncomfortable, because how would she ever repay it? How could she show her own gratitude for their kindness?

"Would you like some coffee?" Alice asked just as a side door opened and a server came in with a tray. "It's fresh."

What a contrast to the coffee she'd offered Alice at the store.

"Thank you."

"If there's anything specific you want to eat or you have special dietary requirements—"

"Coffee's fine," she said as it was poured for her.

"Color," Buoy said, pushing her paper closer.

Alice sat at the other side of her youngest. "Be polite, sweetheart," she said and kissed his head. "Have you had enough to eat? We'll pack snacks for the car. Do you want to take cookies or cakes to our party?"

The woman was always looking after other people. So attentive. So kind. The family was truly blessed.

NINETEEN

OF COURSE A man like Darroch Breckenridge would be on time. Her heart pumped hard as anxiety shook her fingertips. That last customer took forever to ring up, and then the woman just had to throw in some extras… which she "absolutely had" to try on first. Why did these things happen at the worst possible time?

A shiny black car outside her house was conspicuous enough. Two was a neon beacon. The one already there had to be Darroch. She, as in the shiny black car carrying her, pulled up right behind the first. Shit. If Darroch was waiting, she was more than late. Damnit.

"Thank you," she called to Ferguson and bolted out of the car. Darroch appeared from the rear of the other vehicle at the same time. "I know, I'm late…" Walking backward while addressing him, she searched her purse for her keys. "I will be ready—I will—"

"Babe," he said, looking pointedly at the car she'd just emerged from, then back at her.

Ferguson got out right around the same moment

driver one exited his car too. The former set her in his sights, somehow immobilizing her.

"You need both of us?" Driver One called, she guessed to Darroch. "Tripp's looking for a ride."

"Tripp's always looking for a ride," Darroch said and raised his arms. "Go. Might as well. I have no idea what's going on."

Okay, so Mrs. Alice Breckenridge took discretion seriously.

"Miss Mayden," Ferguson said, opening his palm. "Keys."

"Right. Keys."

She handed them over and quickly spun to hurry after him when he entered the building and went upstairs.

At work, his presence hadn't been too conspicuous. When anyone asked a question or looked for too long, he said he worked for Benedict Breckenridge and that shut them up. Helped that he was nice enough not to stand too close to her. Yes, he was always in her field of vision, but he got the meaning of discretion too. And, as far as she knew, no one had seen her get in or out of his car. Until Darroch anyway.

"Wait here," Ferguson said, unlocking her door.

Darroch came upon them. "What the hell is going on?"

Ferguson opened the front door and Darroch moved like he intended to follow.

The suited driver stopped him with a hand on his shoulder. "Stay."

Darroch's head dropped a couple of inches to the side. "Gus—"

"No. Stay."

The guy went inside, swinging the door almost closed behind him.

"Wow, I didn't think he'd talk to you like that,"

she said.

"We don't treat our people as the help," Darroch said, his eyes widening as his head shook. "You want to fill me in on why you have your own Breckenridge bodyguard? Did something happen at work today?"

"No."

"Ferguson is heavy duty. The best we've got when it comes to kicking ass, which means he's reserved for imminent danger. Cherry—"

"Take it up with your mother."

"My mo—I will."

He fished a phone from his inner pocket and woke it. Before he could do more than that, she laid her hand on it. Shit, she hadn't actually meant for him to…

"Don't call her. I didn't mean for you to—I told her not to call you. This is my fault."

"Your fault?"

"I couldn't argue in front of Buoy, could I? Not that I'd argue with your mother. Your parents are a freight train when it comes to looking after people."

His brow descended. "Looking after people? Looking after you. That means you were in trouble, something bad happened. You better tell me what the hell that is before I take a trip to BHQ."

"No, you shouldn't… You know what? You should go home. My apartment's a disaster, I don't want you seeing it like that. I'll be mortified. Your house is just, it's like a palace, a perfect, pristine palace. We should reschedule or just forget it; maybe fate is telling us this is a bad idea. If you want to—"

The door swung open again.

"All clear," Ferguson said, handing the keys back. "All lights are on and the phone line's active. Any issues, there's a panic button by the bed. Carry it at all times."

"There's really no need for—"

"Unfortunately   for   you,   it's   Benedict

Breckenridge's name on my paychecks, not yours. Want me to back off? Take it up with the gaffer. Until then, I'll be right here."

Ferguson nodded at Darroch and sidestepped, spine to the hallway wall by the door.

"You can't stand out here, that's crazy. Come inside."

"She'll get used to it," Darroch said, taking her shoulder to direct her inside.

No way he could—argument fled at the sight of her apartment. "Oh my God."

Darroch closed the door behind them. "What?"

The place was spotless. A complete contrast to the insanity she'd come home to the previous night.

Just when she thought things couldn't get any more incredible, the Breckenridges surprised her again.

"Moisture warmed her eyes. "Shit," she whispered.

"Is this about boyfriend number two? Jeremy the Germ? If some asshole is hassling you…"

Spinning around, she dropped her purse and keys. "The Breckenridges are the most incredible and generous people."

Grabbing his face, she pulled him down to join their mouths. His surprise didn't discourage her kiss. It couldn't. Enveloped by the kindness of his family, right then, there was no other way to express her appreciation.

Though she pulled away, the heat of that union turned her lips into her mouth to relish every last remnant of him.

"That was pretty generous that right there, Cherry." His hands slid from her waist to splay on her lower back as he stooped closer. "Dinner's not supposed to be optional."

"If you let me go, I'll get dressed."

"So if I keep holding on, you'll get naked?"

She laughed. "Darroch!"

"Okay, okay," he said like he was loathed to free her from his embrace. "If you want to get changed, I'll call my mom and get the skinny."

"Don't call her. Please. It's no big deal." She hurried down the hallway to her bedroom beyond, calling to him. "Just a little drama last night." She tied her hair high on her head and turned on the shower. "You don't mind waiting a few minutes, do you? Do we have a reservation?"

"Take all the time you want, they won't turn us away." No, not a Breckenridge. "What wasn't a big deal?"

"I'll tell you in a minute!"

She showered almost as fast as she had that morning. As much as she didn't want to keep him waiting, she wanted to be fresh more. Wrapped in a towel, she did her makeup while waiting for her hair styler to heat up.

"Time's run out, Cherry," his shout came from closer than before. "I'm calling my mom."

Was he in her bedroom? Wait, what did he say?

Dashing to the doorway, she caught him right there by her bed, phone in hand. "Don't!"

"Don't? Call my mother?"

"I didn't tell her we're seeing each other tonight."

Why hadn't she told Alice? It wasn't a secret, it just didn't come up. She could've brought it up… no, she'd never have done that.

His hand dropped to his side. "You've got to help me out here, baby. You and my mom are best buds now?"

She swallowed and went closer, tucking her towel in tighter. "I swear I'm not a crazy stalker person. I didn't track your family down to hound them or get closer to you. You probably don't believe that. I know. I wouldn't in your place."

"Baby—"

"You should go. Take Ferguson too. Your parents shouldn't pay for—"

"Your safety? That's what they're worried about if you have Ferguson. We're standing here alone in your bedroom with you in nothing but a towel and I am asking questions instead of working my magic." He tossed his phone to the bed. "Talk to me, baby, my chivalry only runs so deep."

"I told you, it's not a big deal." Her fingers sought his wrists, though their eyes stayed locked. Snared in his gaze, she couldn't liberate herself. "Someone broke in here last night." His muscles bunched like he clenched his fists. "They trashed the place but didn't take anything."

"Were you here? Alone when—"

"No. No, baby, I wasn't here. The place was fine when I came up after we…"

"After I kissed you in the street."

And that memory might've colored her cheeks a little. "I went out for my prior engagement and came back. Alone." For some reason, that was important to state. "I couldn't believe it, I came in and the apartment was trashed. Everywhere was a mess." Not that anyone would be able to tell given its current state. Good chance she'd get her security deposit back. "Your mom is an incredible woman."

It could only be the Breckenridges. She hadn't even considered cleaning up while they'd taken care of the whole hurricane zone.

"Doesn't give the rest of us a fighting chance, does she?" It calmed her that he was being so good natured about it. "Were you looking for me? When you called?"

"I didn't call, the cops did. Your mom's card was

in my purse, a detective fished it out and called her."

"Let me guess," he said, his smile lighting his eyes. "After that, you were just a passenger?"

Inhaling, she got a whisper of his cologne and her stomach flipped. How crazy was it that just a quick hit set her senses soaring on high?

"I left my wand on in the bathroom."

The distance in her words wasn't matched by their magnetism, there was nothing subtle about the gravity drawing them together.

"Cool." His fingers curled around her waist, strengthening, tightening, pulling her closer. "Your wand for casting spells? You don't need it, I'm bewitched."

Her breathing shallowed. Shit, she was panting, fighting to hide it made it worse. She couldn't catch her breath or tear herself away.

"I mean if you don't excuse yourself like a gentleman, this whole place will go up in flames."

"I feel the heat too, baby. I know how to ride it, don't be afraid."

Except it wasn't fear. Pure hot, wet anticipation mottled her skin.

"We're not doing this like that," she whispered.

"Fuck me for ever saying that."

But he had and it was the wake up call she needed.

Easing his hands away, she backed toward the bathroom. "Chivalry's my hero."

It didn't take long to finish up and settle on a boatneck in midnight blue. Nothing fancy. Nothing compared to what he'd be used to, but she couldn't do anything to change herself. Not in such a short window anyway.

"Are you sure you want to do this?" she asked, walking into her living room.

He stood from the couch and turned, mouth

open, but he stalled, and his mouth closed again.

She smoothed her dress. "What's wrong?"

"Guys are going to be staring at you all night." History had a way of repeating itself. Would she ever learn? "Tell me if the competition moves in while my back's turned."

It got cold. "Are you mocking me?" Her dress stopped just above the knee, that wasn't too much flesh, was it? "Angry?"

"No," he said, unfazed, sauntering around the couch. "I said you didn't know it, didn't I?" He stopped within a few inches, forcing her neck to crane. The pad of his thumb traced her jaw. "You're beautiful."

Dipping her chin, she caught his thumb's caress with her kiss. Desire enveloped them, squeezing her, holding her right there beneath his gaze.

"Help me out, baby," he murmured. "How do I lock this down?"

Could this guy be for real? She couldn't believe it. If one of them didn't remind them of the itinerary, they'd never leave that spot. Though, in truth, that didn't sound so bad.

"Where are we eating tonight?"

"It's a surprise," he said, taking her hand. "Are you ready to go?"

"Ready as I'll ever be," she said, then felt like an idiot.

Credit to him, he didn't laugh or sneer, just led her outside to follow Ferguson down to the street where he put them in the back of the car. All the while, Darroch kept hold of her hand.

"Would you like something to drink?"

He reached over to open a concealed fridge.

"Not if you want me to keep my hands to myself." It was the quick shot of shock he flashed over his shoulder that forced her words to sink in. "Sorry, I shouldn't—I don't know why I—" she squeezed her eyes closed. "I'm doing it again." Getting all tongue-tied around him. "I slept too well… which isn't my fault. Your bed's too comfortable—"

"Whoa." He dropped back into the seat. "My bed? You slept in my bed?"

"I… I think it was yours."

"By special request?"

That really would make her a crazy stalker. "No! No, no. I didn't figure it out until this morning. It might not have been yours, maybe I made it up in my head—"

"Second floor. Right at the top of the staircase then a left? The east wing, second door down?" She nodded and he surprised her with a quick kiss. "Man, I wish I knew that last night."

"I didn't mean to—I didn't ask to sleep at the house. In fact, I was more than a little mortified when it came up, but your dad was just so… Your mom said you wouldn't be home…" Now it was clear why Alice pointed that out. "She said you had something important on today."

"Not more important than you in my bed or you in need of support and affection."

"What was it?" she asked. "What were you doing today?"

"Had my first student."

"You're a teacher?"

"Flight instructor."

Damn, that was impressive. "Wow, you're a pilot?"

He shrugged. "It's a hobby." He brought her hand to his lips to kiss the back. "Leif bet me I wouldn't do it."

Those competitive brothers again. "Leif? Another brother? How do you keep track?"

"A lot of practice. Mom has flash cards."

"Where are you in the lineup?"

"Third… or fifth, depending who you talk to." Okay, she didn't quite get it. "We battle over age and maturity."

What a family. They might be alone in the back of that car, but she could feel he carried the others with him.

"Teaching people to fly takes maturity, I'd think."

"A friend of ours owns an airline company." Naturally. "Bastian Hunt."

Oh, a name she knew. "Carolyn's son?"

Could be husband or cousin or—

Surprise startled him. "You really have been chatting it up with mom."

And for some reason, his intrigue and her triumph was a potent mix. Resting a hand on his thigh, she was tempted to beg another kiss.

"You're lucky to have them."

"I know it," he said, curling his fingers around hers.

"And they're lucky to have you."

That triggered his smile. "I'd be lucky to have you." She tried to take her hand back, but he held it tighter. "Don't be afraid, baby. Why do you pull away from me?"

"Because I relied on a man once and he left me broken." All in one rush of unchecked breath, she'd revealed such a vulnerable part of herself. She wanted to pull it back, but couldn't, she couldn't tear her eyes from his. "I wasn't enough for him. There's no way I can be enough for you."

"Let me be the judge of that."

Descending, he cupped her face as he joined their mouths. The kissing was supposed to come after the date. They hadn't even been on an official date and how many times had they kissed now? God, she was losing her mind, losing her senses, losing her…

TWENTY

HER SIDES ACHED. They'd had a private dinner, maybe a few drinks, and were in the back of the car again.

Darroch was an apt storyteller. The Breckenridge boys' antics could be made into a movie, a series of them. Money and madness led to a bunch of craziness. They had means and often put them to good use. Every story was some other secret that he and his brothers kept from their mother.

"I can't believe you did that!"

"It wasn't my fault, I was just a guy there. Tripp, he's the one, it was all on him."

She tugged a Kleenex from the box above the fridge. "You blame a lot on him," she said, catching moisture at the corner of her eye. "He's always in the thick of these things."

"Just the way it is, baby." Locking his fingers between hers, he pulled them to his lips. "You have an amazing laugh. I could listen to that sweet sound all night."

His lips were still there, lingering on her skin, as

he assessed her.

The Kleenex sank to her lap. "I've never laughed so much in my life."

"It's a barrel of fun being a Breckenridge," he said, tracing his lips back and forth. "You'll see."

Had she thought resisting her attraction to him would ever be possible?

Parting her lips, she filled her lungs, searching him for what she found in herself.

"You're an incredible man."

"Who's interested in you. Don't think I'm just an ass who talks about my family all day long."

"You're proud of your family." Just like his mom. "They're amazing people."

"I want you to be comfortable. For as long as you want, I'll fill the silences and keep your mood up. When you're ready to talk to me, really talk to me, about you, I want every word. But I have no intention of rushing you. We have all the time we need."

She didn't expect such calm understanding and patience. The least she could do was give him honesty, voice her misgivings.

"My life isn't like yours, my upbringing was different..." except she didn't know that, did she? "I know you said this wasn't going to be... I don't know how to be with men like you. This life is a fairytale, and I come from a completely different world. I'm just not... made for it."

The car stopped, her building loomed large beyond the side window behind him.

"You wear them on your face," he said, stroking her jaw with his thumb. "Your emotions." Did she? "You're nervous about going upstairs. Do you want me to come up with you?"

Her focus shifted from the distance to his eyes.

"You want to spend the night?"

"If that's an invitation…" he said, once again provoking her laugh. Somehow he managed to make her feel better. "I can have Ferguson check it out."

"He'll spend the night?"

"Ha, not a fucking chance I'll send another man to your bed."

She leaned in. "Who said anything about bed?"

"Sorry, the thought's always in there when you're around."

Another laugh. "Thank you. For tonight. I've had fun. It's been a while since I—"

"You don't have to go upstairs. You should never be afraid." Intent, his sincerity was subdued but adamant. "Come back to the house with me."

"No! Whoa, no. You want your mom to think I'm some harlot? I like your mom."

"I like her too." He squinted. "Help me out, how does one relate to the other? She's married, if you were considering making a move. And, if you're looking for some side action, I'd put good money on Mom chewing me out for not bringing you home."

"Do you bring a lot of dates home?" To his parents' house? That seemed kind of crass and disrespectful of the class his mother exuded. "Into your parents' house? Do they get breakfast with Buoy?"

"You stayed at the house last night. Was I there?"

"No."

"And I don't have to be there tonight. Breckenridge House is a safe place for anyone who needs it," he said. "I'm betting my mom told you that."

"She told me I never had to be afraid there. Support not judgment."

"And there's the answer," he muttered then called to Ferguson, "back to the house."

They were driving again. Before her mouth could close, they were turning off the block.

"I shouldn't, Darroch. She already thinks…"

"Thinks what?"

He curved an arm around her, pulling her tight to his side.

"I don't know, but she brings you up like she… suspects something."

"She doesn't suspect, she knows."

"Knows what?"

"I'm attracted to you. I want you. We can't hide that shit from my mom, gave up trying to do that before puberty, she reads every one of us. And she knows we're dogged. Giving up? A Breckenridge? Not a chance."

"So it's inevitable?" she teased.

"Yep, you should just give it up now."

He caught her face to try guiding it around, but she resisted.

"Is that the cost of safety at Breckenridge House?"

"Shit, you want my mom to disown me? We don't extort anyone, and we sure don't exchange sex for safety." He kissed the top of her head. "Sometimes it scares me."

"What scares you?"

"The way you talk, the things you say… You don't owe anyone anything. Ever. Not me or my mom or anyone. If someone makes you feel differently, send them my way."

She slid a hand across his stomach, settling against him.

"Who I am, what I came from, doesn't match what you and your family have. I've never met such…"

"Generosity?" he asked with a smile in his tone.

She peeked up. "Have I used that word?"

"Once or twice. My mom is generous with her time. My father is generous with his money… to a point."

"Unless your mother is involved. Then it's all her."

"You got that right. Me, I'm generous with something else."

"Yeah? What's that?"

"One day you might be lucky and I'll show you."

"Oh, is that your game?" she asked, restraining a laugh. "You tease women with maybes?"

"I'll maybe you right here, baby, if that's what you want."

"Tell me more about your family," she said, coiling his arm around her. "I like the sound of your voice." She closed her eyes, resting her head against him, basking in his scent. "I don't care what you say, just talk."

Looking at him got her in a muddle and speaking to him didn't always go well. But absorbing those words and the rumble of his chest beneath her ear, she could spend a lifetime right there.

TWENTY-ONE

WHEN THE CAR stopped, she jolted awake. Sleep? Had she been sleeping? Oh, God. How long had she been out?

Pushing away from the man holding her, she couldn't shake her senses straight.

"Cherry." The bass of his voice struck her, she gasped and grabbed for the closest stable force: his thigh. Oh, embarrassment knew no limits. "Baby, you okay?" His fingers locked between hers. "You want to sleep out here?"

His tease woke her enough to smile. "In the car?"

"Right here in the driveway."

"Promising more maybes?"

He slid along the seat and got out, still holding her hand. "Think you've got the wrong idea about me."

"The wrong idea?"

Those twinkle lights, like the ones in the courtyard, lit up the stairs and trees flanking the grand front doors of Breckenridge House.

"I can follow through, baby. Follow all the way

through.”

He took her inside and without pausing, up the stairs. The first time she arrived there, the intimidation of the place made her feel so small. When he walked in those halls, they gave him strength, power, a gravity that tugged at her need.

Like they'd done it a million times, he led her into his room and the lights came on automatically, just dim enough to be intimate.

“What time is it?” she asked.

“Late.” He removed his jacket as he went into the closet. “You have this much stuff last night?”

Stuff? Following his path, she peeked around the doorframe.

“I didn't venture into your closet.”

“Feel free. There's nothing bad in here,” he said, taking out his cufflinks. “Nothing that should scare you off. And this…” Spinning around, he opened the second drawer in a rack to reveal underwear, women's underwear. “Wasn't here when I left yesterday, so I'm guessing it's for you.”

“Your mom did offer to have new things brought here. I had no idea she…”

“She expects you here indefinitely.”

“She…? How do you know that?”

“Support not judgment,” he said, unfastening his shirt buttons. “If you'd told me that sooner, we'd never have stopped at your old place.”

Old place?

He'd undone three buttons; a long slice of tan skin came into view on his way to the fourth.

She spun on the spot. “Don't get undressed in front of me. Do you have no mercy?”

“I'll change and get out of your hair.”

“Out of my hair?”

“Yes. I told you this wasn't extortion. My mom

put you here, this is your room. Your safe space."

A belt clinked, a zipper zipped. Unzipped? Hell, did he just drop his pants?

"Why would she put me in a room already occupied?"

"Because you're flanked by Caber and Acre," he said. "Rankin is opposite. You're basically surrounded by men taught to care for and protect others. Surrounded by people who know the value of a safe haven. Nothing will happen to you here."

Just like Alice said. "And where will you be?"

A strong arm came around her, pulling her back against his hard body. "You want me close, I'll bunk with Caber." He kissed the top of her head. "Or there's an empty room by Rankin's."

"You shouldn't have to bunk with anyone in your own house. This is ridiculous." She pushed his arm away and crossed to stand at the end of the bed. "This is your room."

"And I'm happy for you to be here." His voice betrayed he was on her heels. "I'd rather you be here than anywhere else."

Because of her apartment break in.

With him in a tee-shirt and gray sweats, there wasn't much keeping her skin from his. Yet when he raised her chin on a curled finger, she laid her hands on his body and accepted his kiss.

She didn't hear the door open.

"Savanna, I was so—oh."

He broke the kiss, and her chin dropped. Shit, had Alice seen…?

"Mom."

"Darroch Breckenridge, are you taking advantage of this poor girl?"

Was she poor? God, she really was a corrupting harlot.

"Getting her settled in," he said. "I'll switch to the first guest."

"I was pleased to hear Ferguson brought you home, Savanna," Alice said, gliding across to them. "How have you been feeling today?"

"Okay."

"Ben has a meeting with Detective Chapman on his calendar this week. He'll expect progress."

"I'll get in on that." Darroch got his phone from his pocket. "You should've called me last night, Mom."

"We managed without you, sweetheart," Alice said, resting a hand on her son's cheek. "We were very proud of you today."

"Yeah. Yeah." Though it sounded like he was sick of hearing it, his smile told a different story. "I'll be back in the office next week."

"I need to usurp some of your time this week."

"Whatever you need, Momma Bear."

"What time did you get in tonight?" mother asked son. "We thought you were with Tripp."

"No, we sent Schmidt to him and stuck with Gus."

"We?" Alice asked, drawing her eyes from Savvy to her son.

"We had dinner."

"You did?"

"Look at her brimming with happiness," Darroch said and bowed to kiss his mom's head. "I'm easing Sav into it."

"Everyone's been so kind."

"And generous," Darroch said. "She uses that word a lot."

"We were so scared for you, Savanna. Thank you for staying with us, we appreciate it. I wouldn't sleep if you weren't under this roof. Darroch, sweetheart." Alice took her son's hand. "Her safety is paramount."

"I'm not putting the moves on her, Mom, I swear."

"He's being a gentleman."

"Good," Alice said. "Because his father is upstairs waiting for me, and scolding his son is not on our agenda."

"Is his father on the terrace?"

Alice laughed and rested a hand on her arm to kiss her cheek. "A woman can dream. Goodnight, dears."

She sailed out of the room, closing the door almost soundlessly.

"The terrace?" Darroch asked.

She just shook her head. "Girl talk."

"You girl talk with my mom now?" He caught her wrist when she started to turn and pulled her back. "I better watch out."

Relaxing against him, her head fell back as he coiled both arms around her. "Maybe you should."

"Might not sleep well tonight with you under this roof, just out of reach."

"I can go home," she pouted, distracted by his mouth. "If you'd prefer me far away."

He yanked her even closer, holding her so tight her lungs could barely get air. "I prefer you as close as possible. I'll have to dream of you."

"Or you could stay right here." His flash of surprise was funny. "Can you be a gentleman in bed?"

He narrowed his eyes. "Is this a test?"

"No," she said. "An honest request. I don't sleep well alone." Though that might give him the wrong idea. "Not that I go around asking men to sleep with me. You shouldn't think that I—I'm not like—"

"I'd be honored, Cherry."

It helped that he was so supportive. A Breckenridge trait she may otherwise have assumed was in their genes.

She wriggled from his arms. "Can I borrow a shirt?"

"Take whatever you want."

That was a loaded statement. "Wait here."

He'd given her permission to enter the closet, but she still got a zip in her belly when she crossed the threshold. Shedding her dress and bra, she slipped into one of his shirts and fastened all the buttons save the top two.

This could be a crazy idea. Maybe they'd had too many drinks. Or maybe she was finally admitting to herself that she felt safe with this guy. And she needed that. Needed to feel safe and protected. Hadn't she been searching for it her whole life? If her gut was right, this was the closest she'd ever been to finding it. Why couldn't she let herself give into it all the way?

The pulse of adrenaline tingled all over when she went back to the bedroom. But climbing into that bed to kneel in the middle was the most natural thing in the world.

"Never seen a more inviting sight."

"You're the one dragging your heels," she replied. "Turn off the light and get over here, Gentleman."

He clapped twice and they were plunged into darkness.

Holy shit, such a classy house and...

Laughter burst out of her. "You have a clapper?"

"No, just a guy in a secret closet with his finger on a switch."

In the darkness, his arms came around her and they dropped down to the mattress together.

"This doesn't count as a relationship concession," she said, rolling her head in his pillow to avoid his mouth. "It's not intimacy, it's safety in numbers."

"Safety in numbers, right." He kissed her carotid. "Your skin's silk."

"And you promised to be a gentleman," she whispered. "I want to be safe with you."

"Always." He eased her one way and went the other, then pulled her back against him, spooning her body against his. "How's this?"

The vibration of his words, his breath in her hair, closed her eyes. Safety captured them. Locked in that embrace, nothing could harm her.

TWENTY-TWO

WARM LIPS TOUCHED her ear, the cushion of her hair pressed against her as the kiss went lower.

With a whimper, she arched into the caress, the weight of a dream cascaded around her as her body softened to accept the rigidity of his.

"Darroch," she whispered, moving with the hands that stroked her belly, her arm, that cupped her face to tip it higher. "Baby…"

"Sweet Cherry…"

Her eyes opened. It wasn't a dream, she really was in his secure embrace.

"Darroch." Laying her hands on his, she parted them to wriggle out of his arms. "This feels like the moves."

You know, the ones he'd promised his mother he wasn't making.

"Saying good morning."

He kissed the back of her head and her lips quirked. Guy could be such a goof, endearing, and sometimes infuriating, but exactly what she needed.

"You have an amazing bed."

"I like to think the company makes all the difference."

Relaxing to her back, she slid a hand up his arm. "It does." She accepted a short kiss. "Can I take a shower?"

"Can I join you?"

"I do not want to be wet and slippery the first time you see me naked. No."

"I like that," he said as she shimmied to the edge of the bed. "That was a when statement, not an if."

Rising, she peeked back at the guy with his hands locked behind his smug head.

"You keep on dreaming, Gentleman," she said, slinking into the bathroom.

***

WHEN SHE FINISHED her shower and came out, he was nowhere around. Having snuck down for breakfast before, she expected to replay the experience after creeping down the stairs. That was until she reached the table's adjoining room. Talking, laughing, a general hubbub of noise betrayed people awaited. Shit.

Should she sneak back the way she'd come? Curiosity awakened. If there were many people in the dining room, odds were that she'd know at least one of them… right?

She couldn't stand there all day, so ventured in, head held high.

A guest, that maybe the ranks weren't aware of, did draw attention. With Benedict at the head of the table, Alice and Buoy in their usual places, she had allies in the room.

"Savanna! Good morning." Of course she could trust Alice to give her a warm welcome. "Come and sit down, there's fresh coffee."

Dougie, Astor, they were familiar. No sign of Darroch or Caber. Aiming for discreet, she checked out the three additional men there.

Alice was pouring coffee at the place by Buoy where she'd sat before. "Savanna, meet Brant, Troy, and Ward."

"It's nice to meet you," she said, taking her seat, unsure which Breckenridge was which. "No elusive Tripp?"

"Why is he always the one people want to meet?" one of the trio asked.

"He's a popular boy, Brant," Alice said, seating herself again. "Darroch would have a better idea where he is."

Except Darroch wasn't around to ask. Not that it mattered much.

"I've heard his name a few times, that's all."

"You'll meet him at the Cavendishs' Ball. All our boys will be there."

"Except the four we have in college," Benedict said, swiping something on the tablet by his plate.

"Wow, four," she said. "Must be expensive to…"

Huh, except, yeah, this was fairytale land.

"Like we care about the money," Brant scoffed. "It's nothing."

"Brant, sweetheart," Alice said. "You know I don't like that kind of talk."

"Sav-nah," little Buoy said, pushing his plate away to get at the papers beneath. "I brought you one special."

He scraped through the various pictures until he found the right one, which he held up in triumph.

Accepting it from him, she gasped. "Oh my goodness, I love it!"

His proud smile glowed. "It's a tiger, for you."

"It's amazing!"

"You can keep it forever."

"Thank you, beautiful boy."

Leaning in, she kissed his hair.

"Hey, those are for me."

Darroch's voice drew her attention to the door he'd snuck them out the night of the prize dinner. Caber sauntered at his side until Darroch peeled away to join her. He put a hand on the back of her chair and bowed to kiss the top of her head.

"Uh, discretion."

Darroch descended into the seat by hers. "This is discretion," he said then cleared his throat to address the table. "Sav and I are keeping us under wraps for a while."

"Because she's screwing the boss?"

"Brant!" Alice chastised. "What is wrong with you this morning?"

"Watch your mouth," Benedict said, his voice deep. "Apologize to our guest."

Brant exhaled. "Sorry, Savanna."

Darroch's hand slid down her thigh beneath the table.

"It's okay," she said. "Thank you."

Benedict wasn't done with his son. "And your mother."

"I'm sorry, Mom," Brant said. "I don't get why they'd lie about being together."

"Would you admit to dating Roch?" Caber asked, grabbing a croissant. "I wouldn't."

"Hey, she's never kissed me at the breakfast table."

She held up her picture. "You never colored me a beautiful picture," she said, proud and touched Buoy thought of her. "Even the littlest Breckenridge is generous."

"I'm not worried about the competition," Darroch said with an exaggerated throat clear. "I can reach the top shelf. Boo Boo can't beat that."

A dope, but a sweet one. His hand remained there on her leg, warm and heavy.

Didn't beat the picture that still held her in rapture. "Can we put it on the wall upstairs?"

"Anything you want, baby." Darroch squeezed her leg. "Want me to get it framed?"

She blinked around at him. "Would you honestly or are you making fun of me?"

"No, baby, I'll do it."

"Then maybe you'll earn yourself a kiss at the breakfast table too."

"Oh, yeah?" he said, leaning in to press a brief kiss to her lips as he took the picture. "You were right, Dad." Darroch swept her hair from her face to admire her. "Keep the wife happy."

"Told you, son," Benedict said absently, swiping again.

Tearing her eyes from Darroch, the others at the table didn't want to see them mooning. "How was your tea party, Buoy?"

"I had a cookie and two cakes with chocolate candy."

"Wow!"

"You know…" Caber noted, finishing his croissant. "Buoy usually doesn't speak to strangers."

"Sav-Na is my friend."

"Yes, she is," Alice said. "I'd like to add, Buoy wasn't just eating cakes all day. He drank his fresh squeezed juice and rode his favorite pony too."

His favorite? She'd never ridden a horse in her life much less had a favorite.

"This his favorite at the Boldwind Stable?" Caber

asked. "Why don't you move him here?"

"He has pony friends," Buoy said, trying to make a bigger space for his pictures. She moved the crockery and cutlery from his reach, providing more room. "Which you want to color, Sav-Na?"

"Uh…" She took her time checking out each one. "Which one are you going to color?"

"Bring his pony friends here," Caber said.

"There's nothing wrong with where he is," Alice said. "Buoy enjoys going to the stable."

"One of the few places he does enjoy going," one of the new brothers said.

She leaned back against Darroch, craning her neck around to murmur. "Which one's Troy and which is Ward?"

He kissed her hair as he dipped his lips to her ear. "Troy then Ward," he answered and switched angle. "Troy, tell Sav where you got your eyebrow scar."

"No, we do not want those stories at the breakfast table," Alice said, though she was smiling as she delicately covered Buoy's ears. "How many times must I remind you boys that you're role models."

"Shit, that's a terrifying thought," Brant said.

"Language."

"Someone thinks he's back in his frat house," Caber said, spreading something on a bagel.

"You have four brothers in college?" she asked Darroch.

"Yep. That's where they're supposed to be at any rate. Not sure they're learning anything," he said. "There's a lot of talk of beer pong and co-eds."

"And you, I suppose, were a saint at college. Does your mom know about your brownie days?"

Caber laughed. "More stories she won't appreciate from the role models at the breakfast table."

"Have you eaten, Cherry?" Darroch asked.

"Everything you see's on offer. Bet there's some steak in the kitchen, quail eggs? Caviar?"

"I'm not hungry." Raising her cup, she sipped the coffee. "This is all I need."

"She was asking about Tripp," Troy said.

"Be careful asking for the Breckenridge boys together," Caber said. "You'll meet everyone at Christmas."

"Yes, all my boys will be home for Christmas," Alice said, brimming with excitement.

"Thought we were going away this year," Troy said. "The Deveraux place."

"It's not big enough for all of us."

"We may host them," Alice said. "The Cavendishs have invited us to their Christmas Ball."

"We're always invited to that," Ward said. "Everyone's invited to that."

Not her. Not regular, mortal folks.

Troy laughed. "Yeah, hence why Tripp goes in disguise every year."

"He barely got over the threshold last year before he split. I think he was there a max. of three minutes. The guy who can get into any party, the most exclusive on the block, runs for his life on the corporate ticket of the year."

"Last year was Mischa related," Caber said, standing to put the segmented bagel in front of Buoy, who paused in his coloring. "She won't be around this year. Isn't she engaged now?"

"I think she was engaged then too."

Buoy picked up a bite-size piece of the bagel and stuffed it in his mouth before returning his pencil to the paper.

Now that was sweet. Without direction, Caber had spread jelly on the bagel and cut it into little pieces for the youngster.

A hand slid down her forehead to briefly cover her eyes. "Don't go gooey eyed over Caber."

"I've never met a family like this."

His hand continued down until his elbow was on the back of her chair and his forearm hung in front of her. Somehow, maybe on purpose, she'd angled herself toward Buoy, so her back was semi to Darroch. When his forearm got closer, without touching, it eased her back against him. Being in his invisible cocoon only drew her deeper into the family. With him there, she didn't seem like an outsider, it was almost as if she was a part of the family.

"We have an engagement with Chester Foundation today."

"Ma, come on, that's what this thing is?" Ward asked. "It's a cattle market."

Benedict's attention left the tablet. "Do we need the boys?"

"Yes, we need the boys. I told Audrey we'd have them with us. Savanna, you should join us."

"Yes, please, join us," Darroch said, jumping on the suggestion. "You can protect me."

"How come Tripp gets out of this? And where's Acre?"

"At the office," Benedict said.

"Ours or his?"

"Can I go to the office too? Any office?" Ward asked, smirking. "I suddenly feel productive."

"No, buddy, I tried that already," Caber said, tossing something in the air to catch it in his mouth. "If it won't work for me, I won't let it work for you either."

"I've got a pass, surely," Darroch said. "What about Sav?"

"It's for charity," Alice said, her smile almost amused. "She won't mind for charity. You don't mind for charity, do you, Savanna, dear?"

"Uh… no." Not that she had any idea what they were talking about. "And I can't join you, sorry. I have to get back to the city today."

"Working again?"

"Not today," she said. "I have to deal with my apartment."

"Of course. We'll pick you up and have dinner in the city before we return here."

"Thank you, but I… I have a thing tonight."

"A thing?" Caber asked. One set of expectant eyes bred another until she was under blanket scrutiny. It wasn't accusing just… innocently expectant. "See the thing is in a family like this one…" He gestured a circle. "There's no such thing as a secret."

"We tell each other everything," Troy said. "Someone always knows something."

"No secrets," Ward agreed. "No judgment."

Maybe it wasn't such a great idea for her to be part of the Breckenridge family.

Darroch's thumb extended to stroke up and down her arm. A comfort? Or was he agreeing with his brothers?

"A thing?" Caber prompted again.

"It's something for a friend. I promised I'd make an appearance at his event to support him."

"Him?" Ward said and grinned at his brother. "Competition, man."

"Don't I know it," Darroch said. "She's made no secret of that. I'm just happy to be in the running."

Did she really come across as the type of woman who'd string several men along at once? If anyone asked Jeremy, he'd say yes.

"It's not like that, we met at a fundraising event years ago. He's passionate about the community effort. It's for a children's center."

"Oh, wonderful. It's in the city?" Alice's

shoulders went slightly back. "Why is that not on our calendar?"

"Don't ask me," Caber said, though she may not have been actually asking him. "We're finding out there's a lot not on our calendar."

"No," she said on an exhaled laugh. "This is small scale, tiny, they're hoping to raise thousands, not millions."

"Luxe Leathers going to be there?"

"No, this is not through work, it—" She cleared her throat with an eyeroll. "We went out one time."

"Ah, so it is like that."

"Competition," Darroch said, closing his arm around her.

"No, not at—he's an amazing man, but he has serious issues. Well, his family has serious issues. He's a… His work means everything to him. I said I would make an appearance to support him. It means a lot to the kids he works with."

"He works with children and prioritizes charitable efforts?" Alice asked, her eyes slinking around to join hers. "Darroch may not be the only man at the table with competition."

Wow, a joke she didn't expect, but she appreciated it with her friend. Friend?

"You hearing this, Dad?" Troy asked.

"I hear everything," Benedict said, typing into the tablet. "And what's our first rule with women, boys?"

"Do it better," the men chorused, startling her.

Benedict surprised her by giving her his focus. "Learn everything you can about the man, then do it bigger, better."

"Okay, to do it better, I have to see it," Darroch said and kissed her hair. "Dinner first? What time does the event start?"

"Eight thirty. But it's invitation only, they don't

have a lot of space for——"

"Will a million get us through the door, or should we make it five?" Benedict said. "What's the guy's name? I'll give him a call."

"Oh, I… I'm sure it will be fine."

"Good," Benedict said. "We'll pick you up at the apartment at six."

"Remember Tripp's thing's tonight," Caber said, seemingly addressing only Darroch. "You sure you want to miss it to double date with Mom and Dad?"

"I'll miss it to be with Sav," Darroch said, tracing his fingertips up her shoulder. "Take Troy."

"Yeah——"

"Ah, no," Caber said. "Tripp up, that was the stipulation."

"I dread to imagine," Alice murmured.

"Breck going to be there?" Troy asked. "The whole Tripp up thing is BS."

"This again? He's the transition. From the upper Breckenridge men to the lower Breckenridge boys."

"I'm closer to his age than I am to Brant's," Troy said. "I'm the eighth, that makes me the midpoint."

"Boo Boo was unexpected," Caber said. "We're the role models, you guys are the screw ups."

"And you think Tripp falls into your group?" Brant snorted as he laughed. "Shit, he's up for anything. Any time, any place. Didn't he just have some orgy in Hawaii with Roman?"

"He was with Struan and it wasn't an orgy."

"Twenty women," Brant said, cynical. "That's an orgy."

"I don't think he slept with all of them. I don't know if he slept with any of them."

"Roman did."

"How do you know that?" Caber asked. "You think you can trust anything out of that guy's mouth?

See, that's why you're in the screw up group."

"You see Sway in the news?" Troy asked. "Roman too."

"We're used to seeing them, but Struan, wow, that came as a shock, right? Anyone know where this Bambi came from?"

"That's one mess I'm happy to have no part of," Caber said. "The woman must be something."

"Tripp's met her."

Whoever these people were, they obviously meant something to the Breckenridges. The boys anyway. She was… clueless.

"The tone of conversation this morning leaves a lot to be desired," Benedict said. "We have a guest."

"I'm sorry, Savanna," Alice said. "We haven't raised brutes, I promise you."

But she smiled. "That you're sitting around a table at all is far more civilized than my family ever got. I was raised around all kinds of language."

"It's not really you," Troy said. "Dad's reminding us this is the dress rehearsal."

"Yeah," Ward agreed. "Because Grandma's coming to visit."

"Oh, God, that's right," Darroch groaned.

"When is that again?" Caber asked. "I need to take a vacation that week, or, you know, pay for some horrifically gruesome fate to befall me, so I can be in hospital under sedation."

The brothers laughed; the parents weren't so amused.

"Your grandmother is looking forward to seeing you all," Alice said. "I've threatened to chain Tripp to this very table to ensure he eats meals with us during her stay. And don't think I won't do it. Savanna, she'd be delighted to meet you."

"Uh, maybe not a good idea," Darroch said. "We

might stay at Savanna's that week."

"All of us," Caber said to another laugh.

"You think it's a joke until one of you says something hurtful in front of her," Alice said. "Please, remember she loves you."

They had a lot of love, around them, in them, for them. What a way to grow up, and an incredible way to live. Support just oozed from all of them. It wasn't the money, it was the rapport. Had she known a family could actually enjoy each other's company? Not using hers as an example, no. Maybe there was another way.

TWENTY-THREE

"SHE'S NOT THAT BAD."

Darroch sauntered into his bedroom as she tucked her phone into her purse.

"Who? Your mom? I love your mom."

"My grandmother. She's from California, you know what people from the Golden State are like."

"No, actually," she said, flashing him a quick smile. "I've never been to California."

"Oh, they're all drama queens."

"Isn't your mom from California?"

He came to plant his ass on the bed by her purse. "More girl talk?" She shrugged. Snagging both her hands, he guided her into the vee of his thighs. "You know more about my mom than you've told me about you."

"You said that was okay. That you would wait until I was ready."

"And I will," he said, kissing her knuckles. "You belong here, Cherry."

"In your bedroom?"

Except he wasn't playing. "You don't feel it?

How right this is?"

"Says the guy sitting on the bed we slept in together last night."

"What are you implying, Sweet Cherry?"

"I don't know," she said, sliding one knee onto the bed and then the other to straddle him. "That maybe you're a man with one thing on his mind."

He grabbed her ass and flipped her to her back. "Always with you around, Cherry."

The point was to go back to the city, to… did he have to be so good? The heat of his mouth pressed hard. Her tongue begged his and it didn't disappoint. Bold, broad, he sheltered and seduced her with the deep need of—

"Darroch!"

Shit, that wasn't an adult voice.

Darroch sighed. "Astor."

"Are you having sex?" the eager thirteen-year-old asked.

"No, and if we were, you should be backing up fast."

"Are you touching her boobs?"

Another exhale from Darroch, but she laughed and patted his shoulders, signaling him to let her up.

"Nothing untoward," she said, turning on the spot. "We're fully clothed."

"And in our bedroom, which means we can do what we like."

"It's daytime," Astor said like that meant something.

"People have sex during the day," she said to no one.

Darroch, at least, heard her. "Not when Astor's around," he said. "Whatever you want, Ast, it better be good."

The boy came over, waving paper in the air.

"Need you to sign this."

"Shit, who can tell Breck spent the night out?" he said and snatched it. "Did Caber say no?"

"He's on the phone."

"Oh, he's on the phone." Darroch went to a drawer to get a pen and sign before coming back to her side as she sat on the edge of the bed. "I was on Sav." She socked his thigh. "You're more important than a call, baby, was my point. He wanted to just happen upon me undressing you, that's the truth."

A teenager wandering in…? Could be completely innocent… or not.

"What are you signing?" she asked.

"Good point. Why am I signing a gym pass on a Sunday?"

"Mom will know if I do it in the morning."

"And Breck's not here. You're freaking he won't be here in the morning."

"Is he with Sequoia again?"

"I don't know, buddy," Darroch said, handing the paper back. "Ask Mom."

"He's never here."

"That's nothing new." Darroch dropped onto the bed by her. "Call him."

"Dad has my phone."

"Sending dick pics to the seniors again?"

"Darroch!" she chastised.

Color rose in the teen's cheeks.

"High school seniors," Darroch said. "Not senior citizens… If you shock someone to death, is that murder?"

Poor Astor just stood there making fish faces.

"I don't listen to him, honey. It's okay."

"Yeah, don't worry, she'll be around long enough to tell your future wife about this."

"I would never—why would you—"

Silenced by Darroch scooping the side of her head under her hair to pull their mouths together, oh, she'd take it. Mm, his tongue slid along hers and her hand rose, hanging there in midair, unsure where to land with a teenage spectator.

Darroch broke the kiss but stayed so close his lips caressed hers as he spoke. "Scram, kid, you're not getting schooled by my girl."

After some muttering, the bedroom door closed.

"Your little brother—"

"Isn't as innocent as you think."

"I thought your family didn't keep secrets."

"We don't. We only pretend mom doesn't know about the notes. And it's not that everyone knows everything, there wouldn't be enough space in any one head. But someone else, or some people, always know. None of us can keep anything to ourselves. Except women…"

He kissed her again, a long, slow pressure that eased then returned. Guiding his hand down the side of her neck, her shoulder, she kept going until it closed over her breast. His rumble of satisfaction echoed again when she let go to grip his thigh. Without relenting his prize, his fondling grew bold.

Swaying back, she licked her lips and his. "Wouldn't want to disappoint him."

"He won't hear it from me," he said, coiling his other arm around her. "Let's stay right here today."

With a tug on her waist, he got her on her back again, though this time he stayed at her side.

Admiring him as his fingers combed through her hair, she sank into the mattress. A dream was all the moment could be compared to. The flecks of hazel appeared almost gold in the rich cocoa of his eyes, framed by long lashes. The man got the details right, not just the broad strokes.

"You're a good brother. And a good son."

"You're a great girlfriend." His hand descended to her hip to yank her against his hard form. "My girl."

"Darroch—"

"I know, the competition, I haven't forgotten. I never forget." His loose fingers drifted across her cheek, to her temple, forehead, around her eyes. "I'm fucking jealous of a guy I've never met. I'm jealous of this guy we're meeting tonight."

"There's nothing to be jealous—"

"We don't have to let this guy tonight know you're keeping your options open, do we?"

And as she opened her mouth to correct him, Jacob came to mind. What a stupid time to think about him. He wasn't her other man… was he? They hadn't talked for a while. Maybe that was why she'd had so many moments of insanity. She always had moments of insanity, but with him, somehow, he accepted her and made everything okay.

"I don't crave male attention, I never have."

"We can't help it, baby. You're a walking wet dream."

Stilled by a chill, she left the bed. "I have to go."

"Baby—"

"Will you thank your mom? Please." She grabbed her purse. "I'll stay at my place tonight. I'll pay for whatever she can't return in the closet."

"Whoa, something changed there fast." He swooped in to body-block her route around the bed. "What is it, huh? I hurt you." His thumb met her jaw. "Tell me how. Tell me so I never do it again." Except she wasn't sure the words would come out. "What you feel is real. It's valid. How will I learn you if you don't trust me? If you don't help me, I'll just keep fucking up until you convince yourself this relationship isn't real, that it's broken." It was like he could see right through her. "You can trust me, baby. Come on. Please."

Trust? Maybe. But could she humiliate herself?

"Jeremy used to say I was desperate for men to notice me." She couldn't meet his eye and fixated straight ahead on his tee-shirt. "That if I talked to a man, I was flaunting myself; I wanted them to take me home. He said I was an embarrassment, to myself and to him." The thump of her heart inside her chest was familiar territory. And there she was, so embarrassed that it shook her eardrums too. "I didn't mean to upset or embarrass him—"

"Baby..." He took her head in both hands to align their gazes. "You are beautiful. Men can notice all they want, that's not on you. You're kind and gracious and always conduct yourself with class. I told you to erase that shithead from your thoughts, didn't I?" He kissed her forehead. "I know it's easier said than done. When he comes to mind, remind yourself he's feeble and pathetic, beneath you. Kicking his ass to the curb was a mercy because he'd never be worthy of you."

"And how am I in any way worthy of you?"

"I'm the panting dog over here." He smiled and bent his knees to stoop lower. "You're an incredible woman. And I intend to spend the rest of my life treating you like a queen, because you deserve no less."

Talk of forever. Of spending their lives together. The peculiar thing was...? He meant it. Conviction bled from him. Determination glowed. He wasn't feeding her lines, his sincerity was absolute.

"Kiss me," she whispered.

When he did, there was nothing but them. He kissed her until Jeremy was gone from her thoughts and Darroch was all that existed. She'd found the medicine to cure her fear and insecurities. Nothing would ever be simple again.

TWENTY-FOUR

DESPITE THE DISTRACTIONS of that morning, she got a lot done in the city. Though not everything. Back at her apartment, under the pressure of time, her desperation was beginning to show.

"I get that," she said to the infuriating guy on the phone.

"Now, if you want, we can put something in the books for next week."

Her hand landed on the kitchen counter. "No," she said into the handset. "I don't have—"

"What's your destination address?"

"I don't have—" The tap on her front door brought her around. It opened and she glimpsed Darroch coming inside so turned her back again. "I don't have it for sure yet."

"Listen, sweetheart, you want me to come help you out?"

This guy was rubbing her all the wrong ways. "You don't have to patronize me."

"You got a guy looking out for you, sweetheart?"

The snicker in his voice was the last straw.

"You know what?" she asked. "Forget it!"

Hanging up the phone, she screamed at it once and whirled around.

Damn! Her anger evaporated into lust in less than a second.

That wasn't just Darroch. That was Darroch in a black shirt, black jacket, perfect hair; the headliner of female fantasies.

Shit. The glint of his cufflink matched the glimmer in his eye and—the phone fell from her hand. She dropped to scramble it up, only the thing flipped free again. She tried to rise and boom, fuck, the damn kitchen counter was closer to her skull than she'd thought. Fuck.

"Babe—"

"I'm okay," she called out, stumbling forward, fumbling with the skittering phone and another dull thwack shot pain through her abruptly halted toe.

Damnit!

She couldn't even get upright, couldn't move without tripping over her own hormones.

"Baby," he said, right there at her level as she froze in her crouch.

"Do you have to be so delicious?" she asked as he parted her hair, searching for a bump. "You just walk around injuring unsuspecting women, how are we supposed to go about our lives with you oozing your hotness everywhere?"

"You've got the cure, baby."

Giving up, she sank to the floor on her butt. "I do?"

"The only person on the planet who does," he said, pinching her chin to tip her mouth up to meet his.

Mmm, the biggest aphrodisiac. The only person on the planet who...

Pushing him down, she climbed on, slipping her

hands under that jacket to squeeze the impressive globes of his shoulders.

"Darroch," she breathed, her chin rising as he kissed her throat.

Oh, maybe she should've thought about her silk robe or how easily he could loosen the belt and skim his hands across her tingling flesh. When his fingers bit deep into her ass, forcing their bodies together, she growled and pushed down, claiming his mouth with hers again.

The tingle became a buzz and a ringing in—she pulled back to meet his eye.

Grumbling, he sank a hand into his inside pocket and raised a phone to his ear.

"Yeah!"

Okay, he didn't have to shout. Sitting up, she closed her robe and knotted the belt. He immediately grabbed it, shaking his head, but the interruption was the sanity she needed.

"Yeah, two minutes," he said into the phone as she got to her feet. "Yeah... Baby?"

"I have to get dressed."

She rounded into the hall and hurried to her bedroom. Hair and makeup were done. Or, huh, maybe she needed to freshen up the smudges of lipstick and smooth a little more serum over those flyaways.

As she dug lip gloss from her makeup bag, his reflection appeared in the mirror above hers. Wrapping her in his arms, he stooped, the warmth of his kiss on the side of her neck never got old.

"We started something in there..."

"What happened to eating with your parents?"

"They'll wait."

She laughed and bent closer to the mirror to apply her gloss.

"Mmm," his groan of satisfaction moved her hips.

Was it fair to undulate against his impressive arousal? Maybe not, but, shit, she didn't have a choice. Biology drove her hormones and worked her muscles of their own accord. Wasn't her fault biology was horny.

He caught her hips, pulling them close, then sinking back, trailing his kiss to the groove between her shoulder blades. With a feather's touch, the caress of the tip of his tongue quaked through to her bones. Adoration and need fought to conquer better sense.

"Darroch," she whispered, somehow rolling against the vanity to face him. "Your family?

His mouth stopped seeking hers to release a groan. "Cherry—"

"I have an early appointment tomorrow."

"What? Why'd—"

"Stay tonight. Here. With me."

That was her train of thought. For a few seconds, his gaze was sharp, then just as quickly fogged with desire again.

"Cherry—"

"Think about it."

"Oh, I will, believe me."

How was he just so perfect?

"We have to go downstairs," she said. "Can I put on my dress?"

"Can I watch?"

Shoving him out of the bedroom, she laughed. "No! Go in the living room, be a gentleman."

"Only 'cause my mom's watching."

He cast another look over his shoulder on his way out and closed the door.

They hadn't been anywhere yet and she was already excited about how the night would end. Her original dress choice was ignored in lieu of a dark gray cowl-neck. It would go much better with Darroch's outfit. For some reason, matching him, complementing their outfits, turned her on. She wanted to be his and to show the world he belonged to her.

Geez, talk about getting ahead of herself.

She snagged her purse and hurried to the living room. Darroch stood by the front door, smiling as soon as she came into view.

"What are you smiling at?"

"I'm a lucky man."

"Yes, you are," she said, stopping in front of him. "Dating me is a dangerous pursuit. I'm surprised you've made it this far without permanent injury."

"You're worth the risk." He fished something from his pocket. "Got something for you."

"For me? What did you—"

He popped open a velvet box and there inside was a necklace of two red gems and a green. "It's a cherry," she whispered.

"Figured before I ask you to give me yours, I should give one up for you. May I?"

And how could she possibly say no? Turning, she hooked her hair out of the way and held her breath as he fastened it.

It settled in the center groove of her collarbone.

She spun around to show him. "How does it look?"

He held out his splayed hand. "Just like the rest of you: perfect."

Laying her hand on his, their fingers linked and they went downstairs. Ferguson opened the limo's back door. Alice and Benedict sat opposite with their back to the driver.

"Sorry, we didn't mean to rush you," Alice said when the door closed behind Darroch. "Did we interrupt?"

"The baby making? Yeah, almost."

"Darroch," she scolded then turned contrition

on Alice. "We weren't. I promise you we would never—
"

"Relax, Cherry. Did you forget she loves babies?"

"Maybe next time, I'll ask Alice to bring her baby along. Buoy is so much more polite."

To her surprise, Alice laughed. "Oh, I do love seeing you together. Darroch, son—"

"I know, Mom. One step at a time."

Good thing he knew because she was completely in the dark.

"Did you achieve what you wanted to achieve today?" Benedict asked. "Savanna?"

"Me?" she asked, surprised to be the center of attention, because why would any of them care? "Oh, uh… Not exactly. I saw three apartments, one I like, but it's complicated. My current landlord said I could leave at the end of the month without penalty. She painted recently and has a waiting list, she'll fill the unit fast."

Given what happened, maybe because of it, her landlord had been incredibly understanding.

Alice was all concern. "You're moving?"

"I can't stay there now. Once, in the past, when I was young, my family was burglarized, and it taints a place. I wouldn't be able to sleep there again."

"You're welcome to stay with us."

"Yes," Darroch said, pressing his lips to the back of her hand. "For as long as you want. Permanently."

Her smile was contrite. "I appreciate the offer, I do, but it wouldn't be right to accept."

"Why not? We have plenty of room. We wouldn't at all dream of forcing you and Darroch together, if that's what you're worried about."

"No, it's not that, it's… For one thing, I don't drive. It's a forty-five-minute journey by car, I have no idea what that would translate to on public transport."

It would probably take her an hour just to walk down the driveway.

"You have transport," Darroch said. "You're sitting in it. Technically, we're in your ride tonight."

Generosity didn't do their invitation justice.

"I can't live off you for the rest of my life."

"If she wants to stay in the city, she's entitled to do just that," Benedict said. She appreciated the support but was surprised it came from him. Even when the man seemed busy or distracted, he was always switched on, always interested, when he didn't have to be. "What's the problem with the apartment you like? The end of the month is Thursday, isn't the new place ready? Darroch, I shouldn't have to tell you—"

"I'll make a call. Consider it done."

These men were problem solvers. They didn't see challenges, only opportunities.

"Thank you, but it won't help. The new place will be ready on Tuesday, but the guy has someone willing to move in on Saturday. He gave me 'til noon tomorrow to decide or it goes to the other person. I have a couple more places to see tomorrow, and I'll have to find time to pack."

"Pack tomorrow," Darroch said. "Move into the new place Tuesday."

Her lips stayed closed as she sighed. "I haven't had any luck with that."

"Luck with what?" Alice asked.

"Finding a mover I can afford who has availability. Everyone I've tried has a premium for emergencies, which since we're talking about moving in less than forty-eight hours, this counts as apparently." She couldn't really argue with that. "But I have work on Tuesday and I don't want to call Celeste…" She took a breath. "Sorry, it's been a busy day." And she sounded like a crazy person ranting about it. "How was the

Chester Foundation?"

"We can help," Alice said, ignoring her question. "If you need time off or funds to—"

"Thank you, but I would never ask you to intervene or cover expenses, it's just not who I am."

"Darroch," his mother beseeched. "Have you nothing to say?"

"Nothing," he said. "Zip. Not a word." That surprised both parents, one appeared disappointed while the other was more judgmental. "I'm waiting for Sav to remember I have fifteen brothers."

TWENTY-FIVE

IN THE BACK of the car, she shifted to face him. "What has that got to do with anything?"

He shrugged off one side of his jacket to plant her hand on his shoulder. "You feel that? It's not nothing."

"No," Alice said, optimistic again, almost joyous in her pride. "It is not, you're right. The boys will do it."

"What boys?"

Darroch leaned in. "There are sixteen of us."

"You don't mean… No, I couldn't—you couldn't…" After a glance at the Breckenridge parents, she edged closer to Darroch. Her chin dipped as her volume lowered. "You're billionaires, you don't… you know…"

"What?" he asked, straight-faced and without discretion. "Work for a living? Look out for the people we care about? Get our hands dirty?"

"My boys have built homes in Africa and South America, and assisted with disaster relief in many conditions."

For charity, sure. Is that what she was? Charity?

"What if one of you got hurt?" she asked.

"Oh." Alice waved away that concern. "We've donated millions of dollars to most of the hospitals in this city."

Benedict concurred. "We can afford excellent medical care. And take your pick of the Breckenridge trucks too."

Astounded, she blinked, dazed by Darroch's gaze. "You would really…"

"Never had a boyfriend offer to do you a favor? If we didn't have money in the bank, would you expect me to help?"

"No! Never! I would never expect anyone to—"

"Your previous partner wouldn't have helped?" Alice asked, perplexed.

"Jeremy?" That was a laugh. "God, no. He would never offer to pay for anything or give it away for free. He said it's how the rich get rich, being frugal."

Maybe that was too—she shouldn't have said that. Wrong audience.

Darroch raised her eyes to his. "Don't know if you've noticed, but the Breckenridges are doing okay for dimes, and frugal doesn't figure in our house. We can be pretty generous, if you give us the chance."

His smile warmed hers. Physical help would make the world of difference, but that wasn't the reason sentimentality bloomed in her chest.

"You actually care," she whispered.

Had anyone ever…? So openly…? She couldn't get used to this, if she started to believe being part of their family was an option… Imagine being accepted, supported…

"Yep, me and my fifteen brothers."

She hadn't met them all, but they cared about each other. That was enough for Darroch, for any

Breckenridge. They took their support of each other for granted, because, she'd bet, it hadn't failed them yet.

"At least three of your brothers are minors and four are in college."

"Okay, so I have eight brothers," Darroch said. "And BKS is nothing but muscle."

That last part was for his nodding mother. "Acre will help."

"He never turns down a chance to sweat," Darroch said.

"Is all the furniture yours? In your apartment?"

"Not all of—"

"Would you trust Darroch with a key? Give him the authority to take care of the logistics?"

While she went to work and let the move happen in the background? She would leave for work from one place and go home to another, not a jot of effort required on her part.

"Of course I trust him, but it would be unfair to—"

"This is what real boyfriends do," he said, kissing her hand again. "Authentic, regular boyfriends, not weirdos like Jeremy the Germ." She pursed her lips to contain her laugh. "You want me to come with you while you sign the new lease tomorrow? Make sure this guy isn't giving you a bum deal?"

Alice sighed. "All I teach them and they still think men are better negotiators. They forget how many hours I spent negotiating them into socks and snowsuits, never mind how many deals were struck over the consumption of green beans."

Adorable. She could imagine little Darroch and Caber resisting the constriction of socks each morning before school. And how many times had they tried to persuade their mother they could brave the cold without outerwear in their haste to get the best spot for snowball fights?

All those kids and all that land, growing up in such potential must've fired their imaginations. No wonder they were confident and bold, the Breckenridge men had been given room to bloom their whole lives.

"Cherry?"

"Don't you have work?" she asked. "I could never ask you to—"

"You're not asking me, I want to," he said. "Dad's getting the hang of running the place without me. We need to take the training wheels off sometime."

None of them could ignore that quip, especially when Benedict's deadpan eyes rose from his phone screen.

Alice laughed and leaned against her husband. "What do you think, my love, can you cope without Darroch at work tomorrow and Tuesday?"

"I can cope without him all week. For the rest of his life, in fact, if he wants to find himself alternative employment."

Darroch kissed her head. "Don't worry, baby, we'll be okay. I've got a trust fund."

"Underwritten by Brecken," Benedict said.

"You give that guy too much responsibility."

"You think I wanted to be the one wrangling the lot of you?" Benedict asked. "Your brother deserves a raise."

"Well, I know who to talk to about that."

"Brecken?" Alice asked and laughed.

Funny, sure, but she had to ask. "Do you really have a brother called Brecken Breckenridge?"

"Oh, no, dear," Alice said.

"Rankin is the oldest," Darroch explained. "Rankin is mom's maiden name. And everyone called her dad, my maternal grandfather, Rankin. Got confusing."

"So he became Brecken?"

"Colloquially," Benedict said, and put his phone away as they stopped at the curb. "Ready?"

"Blaze?" Darroch asked. "Who booked this? Tripp?"

"I did," Benedict said. "At your mother's request."

"Why would—"

"The salmon," she said on a gasp.

"Yes!" Alice exclaimed. "They've created an entree for us."

"Wow, really? I think maybe not so many cocktails tonight."

"Live a little, my dear. You deserve a break."

Benedict helped his wife out of the car. She expected to go after them, but Darroch pulled her back.

"Salmon? Cocktails?"

"Yes," she said, happy to be bold. "You haven't figured it out yet?"

"Figured it out yet?"

She kissed him quick. "Your parents are your competition."

"My...?"

"My prior engagement was drinks with your folks."

"Here?"

"No, me and your mom ate here alone before that, on the recommendation of her sons."

"Darroch," Benedict said from the sidewalk. "We're going inside."

Hand in hers, Darroch moved a few inches closer. "You know what this means?"

"What does it mean, Gentleman?"

His lips curled slowly. "We're exclusive."

She flattened her affect. "No."

That switched off his smugness quick. "No?"

"No. I plan to keep seeing your mom."

He laughed. "She can't reach the top shelf either."

"What's on the top shelf that's got you so obsessed?"

"All the best things come from the top shelf, Cherry. You should know, it's where I found you."

"On the shelf?" she asked and laughed when his faced dropped. "My hero."

"That's not what I meant."

"With the porno mags?"

He squinted. "Do they still print porn magazines?" Like she would know. "I'll ask Astor. That kid's probably got his own operation running."

"You trying to deflect?"

"No, baby!"

"I suppose I should be grateful you scooped me up," she teased, fighting her smile. "Off the shelf."

"I'm grateful. Remember I'm the panting dog."

Letting go of his hand, she slid hers up his body and leaned against him. "You've got the cure," she whispered.

"The only person on the planet who does?"

Without waiting for a response, their mouths met, and the question was forgotten. So was their location and the fact the door was still open to the street.

"Get a room. You can afford it, brother, have some class."

Their mouths parted in deference to the invading voice.

A guy. Hot guy. Hands in his pockets, bowed over, checking them out. His finger combed hair was probably a million-dollar style, but it hit roguish, rakish playboy on the nose.

"Hey, what you doing here?" Darroch asked, slapping his hand to the guy's in a familiar shake.

"Demand he treats you better, Savvy. Don't fall

for the good guy act, he's a player."

"Says the world champion of charming women out of their underwear."

"How do you know my name?" she asked.

"Roch talks about you. A lot."

"Cherry, this is—"

"Tripp, right? The guy always on the go."

"Smart and pretty. You did good, bro."

Tripp offered his hand to help her out of the car. He was gracious, gentle, didn't stop Darroch taking her hand back the moment they were on the sidewalk.

"Come in and eat with us," Darroch said to his brother.

"No, thanks, Fernando's not talking to me."

"What did you do? His daughter or the dirty on his debt?"

"Nothing that fun," Tripp said, still smiling at her, curiosity pinching his lower eyelids. "You really are beautiful."

She glanced between the men. "Are you screwing with your brother?"

Because he couldn't be coming on to her for real.

"No, just surprised."

"Don't hit on her," Darroch said, relaxed. With his humor on, a tease flavored his voice. "Have some class, brother."

Tripp laughed. "Man, you are possessive of this one. Cabe was right."

"Yeah, what you doing down here when your thing's tonight?"

"Not for hours," Tripp said. "You bringing your girl?"

"Yeah, 'cause I'm fucking insane. Where were you at tonight? If it was dinner, where's your date?" He bumped her arm with his. "Tripp can only eat food if there's a beautiful woman at the table with him."

"A lot of things I can only do with a beautiful woman present," Tripp said, full of confidence. "And not to disappoint, but no dinner date. Not yet anyway, I might pick one up on the way upstairs. This is me getting home from last night."

"Why do I even fucking ask," Darroch said, smirking and shaking his head. "Is Roxie home?"

"You want her to be? Bring your girl up, we'll find out."

"No, raincheck, we have something on tonight."

"Oh, yeah? Standing me up?" Tripp snickered. "I'd do the same if Savvy was my alternative." From nowhere, he snapped his fingers. "Sizzle Girl."

She gasped. "Oh my God! You don't—you know about that?" Laughter released her tension and anxiety. "Really? How do you know about that?"

"I know things, and I never forget a face or a body," Tripp said, his gaze traveling down her form. "Where you working now? No way I heard right that you're still at Breckenridge, you can do so much better."

"Thanks, but I…" She shook her head. "I don't do that anymore."

"'Cause of this lug? You can do better than him too."

"No, no, Darroch's amazing."

"You must've got him on a good day." They laughed again. "But, seriously, think about it. I can get you representation. Great representation. Whatever you need. I've seen it, you can write your own ticket. There's a shoot in St. Barth's next week—"

"No, thank you. That chapter of my life is closed. Completely."

"Shame," Tripp said. "You ever change your mind…"

"I know where to find you."

"You'll never get away with sneaking out on

Mom," Darroch said, getting them moving.

"A double date," Tripp said, joining them. "Breck better step up his game."

"Tripp!" the maître d called the moment they crossed the threshold.

"Julian," Tripp reciprocated and did the double cheek kiss thing. "You know Darroch and his beautiful beau—"

"Savanna, our chef has created a dish just for you."

"You've made an impression already," Tripp said, strolling along like they had all the time in the world.

Whether it was deliberate or not, the Breckenridges, and their associates, were the most welcoming people. Fundamentally good, so pure of deed, it was difficult to believe people like them existed.

TWENTY-SIX

"IF YOU'D RATHER NOT—"

"We are honored to join you," Alice said. In the back of the car again, they'd just stopped outside the community center. "Our eyes are willing to be opened to every cause."

Darroch's hand slid down her thigh as he leaned in to kiss her ear and murmur, "You want me to get them out of here?"

She tipped her head to push her hair against his mouth. That physical support held up her inner self too.

The lights at the community center may not be as delicate as those outside the Breckenridge home, but they were just as welcoming.

Though when the four of them hit the sidewalk, butterflies danced in her belly. What was she scared of? That her guests would be unwelcome or that her cause would embarrass her guests?

Darroch locked his fingers tight between hers.

He squeezed and kissed her head. "Get your checkbooks ready."

"After you," Benedict said, sweeping an arm toward the door.

It most likely wasn't normal for the Breckenridge patriarch to defer, yet he didn't hesitate. He was a man confident in himself and his masculinity, and he'd taught his boys well.

A sign indicated they should proceed to the main hall at the other end of the corridor.

Thankfully, the hall, much like a high school auditorium, buzzed. Maybe not full to the rafters, but the kids running around and music brought the place to life. Wooden tables lined the room with games and knickknacks. Some of the art against the walls was interesting. Everything had a price tag.

"Savanna Mayden, you've gone down in the world."

The familiar voice brought her around, smile wide on her face matched by his.

"Quade," she said and accepted his kiss on her cheek before they hugged. "I brought along some friends."

"I see that," he said, and continued without introductions. "Darroch Breckenridge."

"Quade." The two shook hands. "Been a while."

"You know each other?"

"Wonderful Quade," Alice said, taking his hand and accepting a kiss. "It's been too long. Why don't you come and visit anymore?"

"I'm not in the neighborhood much anymore, Mrs. B."

"We had no idea you were a part of this. What a wonderful venture!"

"It's not something my mother likes to advertise."

Absorbing the scene, Alice glittered. "It's magnificent."

Quade and Benedict shook hands too. "Your brother was in my boardroom last week."

"You have my sympathies."

"Oh, Quade," Alice semi-chastised. "Your family love you. Your mother must miss you terribly."

"She knows where I am."

"Your sister dotes on you."

"And I her," Quade said, stepping back to her side. "Della's the bright spot in all of our lives."

"If it wasn't for her, I dread to think how awful things might be. It's such a tragedy how this has worked out. A tragedy."

"Unfortunately, this is the only way it can be."

"How do you know each other?" she asked, behind the curve.

"I went to school with the Breckenridge boys," Quade said. "Alice and my mother are friends. Though they're so different, I have no idea what they talk about."

"She was at the high tea last week. She smiled, but this must tear her up. From a mother's perspective, I can't imagine any of mine being so distant. It will be breaking her heart every minute."

"If that were true, she'd accept my choice, like you'd accept any of your sons'," Quade said and smiled. "Enough about family. Would you like to see what we've built here?"

"We would love to! You should know we'll fund whatever you need," Alice said. "Are you too proud to ask for help? You spent most of your younger years at our house. Once you were just another of my boys." Darroch got his mother's attention. "You should keep in closer touch."

"Yeah, especially if he's thinking of moving in on my girl."

"He had his chance."

Quade laughed. "And I blew it, so I'd say you're

safe. Though, Savvy, I've got to say you could do so much better than Darroch Breckenridge."

"You know you're not the first man to tell me that tonight."

"Better step up my game." Darroch tucked her against him. "I've got to start screening who you're talking to."

The tease was taken in humor.

"The other man who said it was your brother."

"So I can kick his ass without a police report? Excellent."

"Darroch." Alice tsked yet smiled. "Your brothers respect your choice and Savanna's."

Quade's smile grew. "I don't know, he's doing something right, there's a lot of choice at Breckenridge House. Tripp still single?" And that got a laugh from everyone. "The Breckenridge everyone wants and no one can have."

"Someday the right woman will steal his heart," Alice said.

"I just hope it's before we hit retirement," Benedict added and nodded. "Show us around."

TWENTY-SEVEN

"I DON'T KNOW which to ask first."

After a stop to drop them off at her apartment, the Breckenridge parents continued their journey home.

In her bedroom, she freed her hair from its bounds. "You want to know how I met Quade?"

"And how you know my brother—or how he knows you?"

"Don't worry," she said, the zipper of her dress gliding loose until the fabric dropped from her body. "You've seen more than he has."

"Is there a story?"

"Not really," she said, putting her dress in a dry-cleaning bag. "It was a swimsuit thing I did a couple of years ago."

"They called you Sizzle Girl?"

"It was written on the page. I told you I did modeling?"

"Yeah."

"I was at a party and there was this photographer… anyway, I ended up in the Breckenridge catalog and later on, there was a calendar. It was just a stupid thing, but people used to request me for parties. You know our floor is members only?" He nodded. "Apparently, there was a boost in membership numbers and people would come in, men and women, to request me specifically."

"Sizzle Girl."

She shrugged it off with a smile. "I don't know how Tripp knew about it."

"Tripp knows things," he said, casting off his jacket. "Especially when it comes to current fads and beautiful women. You didn't want to pursue the opportunity elsewhere beyond Breckenridge?"

"Oh no," she said as he undressed. "Jeremy hated it."

"The Germ again?"

"At first, I thought he was being protective. Things went downhill from there. I don't know why, how he thought it changed things between us. As far as I was concerned, it didn't. Maybe it did change me, maybe I did crave the attention."

"Hey," he said, coming to gather her against him. "We're not letting the asshole in, remember?"

"Do I flaunt myself? Is it something unconscious that I do? Am I a lush?"

"You are beautiful, Savanna. That doesn't require any flaunting. But, no, you don't seek attention, male or otherwise."

"I'd never make a fool of you." Sliding her hands higher, she linked her fingers at the back of his neck. "Tell me you know that."

"I know that." One arm stayed around her while he tucked her bangs from her forehead. "And you should know I'm not worried."

"About me?"

"About other men."

Her lips curved. "Because you're a Breckenridge?"

"We always do it better," he said and winked. "And I see the way you look at me."

"Okay, Hot Stuff."

Never had a man accepted her with such ease. It wasn't until right then that she caught up with the truth of Darroch Breckenridge, of all the Breckenridge men. They were well adjusted. Honest. Honorable. And, by far, more secure in themselves than any other men she'd been in relationships with.

Spinning her around fast, he stole her breath. "You got it, baby."

"Did you lock the door?" she asked when he backed her up against the bed.

"I locked the door."

"Are you sure? Because—"

"Baby…" His embrace clamped tight. "No one will get near you while I'm here."

Odd way to put it, maybe, but the break-in had freaked her out. So much so that she hadn't slept there since it happened.

When he picked her up and laid her down, all worries and fears faded away. This man, the one above her, kissing her mouth and caressing her body, he was something unique. Cut and smoothed to fit exactly against her, in body, in soul, in every way a man and woman could be made for each other.

Thinking like that was dangerous. She'd kept an abstract hand firm against him, elbow locked, to save both her heart and her dignity. This was a Breckenridge, a man bold and strong, a man cradling control of her life in the palm of his hand. If she lost her job, if she couldn't get a reference—

He would never do that to her. Never. The faith she had in him matched that she had in his mother. Alice raised her boys well, she gave them morals, decency—but, God, it was difficult to remember that when his hips moved against hers, when the thick length of him pressed hard against her, teasing her, daring her to beg for more.

And she wanted more than his lips on hers, on her body, tormenting her skin. They'd waited long enough, hadn't they? They could give into the heat and arousal of endorphins electrifying every pore and hair.

Could Darroch be her forever man? Like the story Alice told, about her certainty over Benedict, had it felt like this? Despite that certainty, Alice held true, stayed strong, followed through to ensure the future was secure.

Grabbing his shoulders, instinct urged him away. "Darroch."

"What?" he panted. "What's wrong?"

"I just realized something."

"What?" With that huffing need in his voice, he couldn't really be listening or thinking straight. "Baby?"

Pushing him further away, she clambered out from under him to get to her feet. "I have to call your mom."

"My mom? What are you—my mom?"

"Yes."

"It's late." The couple would still be in the car on their way home. "She'll panic and turn them around. Why do you need to call my mom?"

"She told me the story of her and your dad. That she loved your dad from the moment they met."

"Yeah."

As she paced the length of the bed and back, he sat, knees up to support his loose forearms.

"But she told him she wouldn't have sex with him until they got married. Her mom warned her about men, about how they lose interest after the chase, after women give it up to them."

"My grandma's full of pearls of wisdom like that, why—" his frown relaxed from its confusion and quickly morphed to dread. "No."

"Don't you see?" She stopped. "She told me that story so I'd know; so I'd know to do the same. She told me so I wouldn't be a cheap and easy date."

He flew off the bed. "That is not why she told you that story."

"Why else would she tell me that story?"

"To bond, I don't know, girl talk."

"Women like your mom, kind, positive women, they advise, pass on their experience, so younger women don't make the same mistakes. Your grandmother passed that wisdom to her and she gave it to me."

"That is not why Mom told you that story." Though from the look on his face, he was coming to terms with the fact it wouldn't happen for him. "Let's call her."

"You said it was too late."

"When I thought I was getting lucky, this is an emergency situation."

Valid point, though not the one he was making. "If you call her, you'll scare her. She'll think something is wrong."

"Something *is* wrong."

"You're proving your grandmother's point," she said, fists rising to her hips.

He scooped them off to loosen her fingers in his. "Things were going so well…" he directed her arms around him to mosey up close. "We were relaxed…" she held the embrace when he let her go and raised her jaw with two loose fists. "Having fun…" he kissed her. "Being together."

"I have to talk to your mom," she said after his next kiss.

"If I don't need my mom's permission to have sex, you sure don't."

"Were your other girlfriends close to her?"

"No woman has ever asked my mom's permission to have sex with me."

"I'm not asking her permission, it's more like… guidance." When he tried to retreat, she pulled herself against him again. "This is a compliment."

"Struggling to see it that way, babe."

"I want you to stick around." She kissed his torso. "I don't want to lose you. Isn't that a good thing?"

"Would be if you weren't also implying I'm a shallow jerk only interested in getting lucky."

"I don't think that." She laughed. He didn't. She cleared her throat. "Your mom has taught me so much about valuing myself and how purpose can matter. Maybe I want to tell our future son's future girlfriend how we got our start."

"Hard to have a son if you won't have sex with me," he grumbled then threw both arms around her. "Whatever you want, Cherry."

"Am I not worth the wait?"

"Whatever you want." He kissed her again. "Happy wife…"

She smiled. "Thank you, Gentleman. You'll still protect me?"

"Even more. I haven't caught your pussy yet."

When she shoved him, he pulled her onto the bed with him. Gentleman was right. Other guys may not be so understanding. The Breckenridge men really weren't like any others.

TWENTY-EIGHT

"YOU'VE BEEN AMAZING TODAY."

"I'm amazing every day," Darroch said, stacking the latest box on top of another.

"You spoke to both landlords, helped me pack, listened to more than one of my meltdowns."

"It's my job, Cherry, as the designated guy in your life."

And he hadn't lost his shit or sulked once. Maybe coming from such a large family taught him the art of diplomacy… and patience.

"It's almost midnight," she said, glancing down at her phone screen. "You got any juice left?"

"Juice for what?" he asked with an intrigued double brow bob as he swooped down to the floor beside her. "You talk to my mom today?" Wasn't that just the question. And a hilarious one. How often had that been on his mind? "I heard you on the phone before dinner."

"When you were taking a shower? Were you eavesdropping?"

"Maybe a little bit. What did she say?"

"You're eager as a schoolboy," she said, draping her arms around his neck when he pulled her into his lap. "Yes, okay, I spoke to your mother. I said we were getting frisky last night and I put a stop to it because I was worried about losing your affection."

"And she told you her boys weren't like that, she'd been wrong about my father, and reminded you I'm crazy about you."

"No," she said, rocking against him. "Actually, she said I did exactly the right thing." He frowned. "She used the words 'never prouder,' I think she's considering adopting me too."

"Ah-ha," he said in a false laugh, his arms closing tight around her. "You had me 'til then. She knows how desperate I am to knock you up, she'd never pass up a chance of having babies around."

"Knock me up, huh?"

"You wanted a son…" Slowly, deliberately, he laid her down. "I can make that happen."

"My hero."

"I will be."

"How do we always end up here?" Her fingers combed through his hair. Wrapped in each other, admiring, basking, dreaming. "Our duties aren't done yet, we still have to take the bed apart."

"I know an excellent way to do that."

"Mr. Breckenridge…"

"Less of the formalities with the father of your future children."

Their mouths found each other, tilting to taste deeper. Both wanted to explore this, whatever it was between them. Was it smart? No. After spending the day with him, dealing with one apartment and another, they were a team. He didn't take over, his consideration bolstered rather than stifled.

Turning her head, she broke the kiss. "We have furniture to dismantle."

"I'll do it in the morning."

"You can't do it alone."

"Brothers, baby." He kissed her cheekbone, the corner of her mouth. "Let me worry about the heavy lifting."

"So I should just lay back and let it happen?"

"Couldn't have said it better."

As her muscles relaxed, her eyes closed. He really had the technique down, a gentle kiss, a caress, the brush of his tongue.

"Mmm, Darroch." Her hips rose and his body pushed back, accepting the challenge. A fingertip tucked into her neckline, drawing it down, exposing sensitive flesh that he teased with his tongue. "Mm, you're good at that."

And that encouragement took the indulgent weight of his body from hers just long enough for him to rid her of the top completely. Her own fingers wandered beneath his tee-shirt as he cupped her jaw to join their mouths again.

Now it wasn't enough. "Darroch," she whispered again as his lips descended to her throat.

Gathering his tee-shirt at the back of his neck, she wanted rid of the fabric keeping their skin apart. They'd waited long enough. Hadn't they? Couldn't they—shit, she didn't have Alice's strength, any strength.

"Cherry…"

"Yes," she said, yanking at his tee-shirt to get it over his head. "Did we pack the condoms?"

He kissed her quick. "Do we need one?"

Her phone rang, startling the moment. Clearing her throat, there was a good chance her voice might fail her.

"Don't—"

"Hello?"

She didn't know who she expected. Not reading the screen was probably a mistake, definitely a mistake, when his voice broke through.

"Sav?"

Coughing again, the hoarse quake in her throat scratched with lingering desire.

"Jeremy?" she asked, pushing Darroch aside to stand up. "What's wrong?"

"Nothing. I miss you."

"No, you don't," she said, closing her eyes and covering them with a hand, blocking out the interruption, and his voice, at least she tried to. "Why are you calling?"

"Heard you were in Blaze the other night."

"Heard from who? Who are you talking to about me?"

"Just came up. You win a prize at work or something?"

"Yeah, that's it," she said, not owing him any explanation. "What do you care?"

"I could come over."

"You could," she said, unimpressed. "You wouldn't get in but knock yourself out."

Another good reason to move. She might just omit Jeremy from her list when sending out change of address messages.

"Don't be like that, sweetie."

"Don't," she said. "Are you drunk?"

"No!" Offense joined the word, she doubted it was completely honest. "I want to come over and see you."

"You want to come over and have sex with me."

"That too," he said on a chuckle that shook her head. "You know how good—"

The phone was plucked from her hand.

"Listen, asshole, you've got a problem, a serious problem. You call this number again and that problem will visit your doorstep, you understand?" He turned away when she eventually caught up to what was happening. Darroch, on her phone, talking to Jeremy. Shit. "That's right. New guy, only guy. And believe me, man, I have the power to make your life hell." Her jaw loosened. "You'll lose your job, your apartment, and never get laid again. You so much as think about Savanna and your problem will become my life's cause. Lose this number." He hung up and threw the phone onto the couch. "I can't believe that jerk called you."

"Happens sometimes," she said to his back as he ran a hand through his hair.

"Better never happen again." He spun around, his brow low. "Block his number."

"I don't think I need to." Over the surprise, she licked her lips. "I can't believe you spoke to him like that."

"I'll speak like that to any guy who propositions you. He's got some fucking nerve, the way he treated you makes me fucking sick, but the fuck still thinks—"

"It's okay." Resting her hands on him, she boosted onto her tiptoes. "I've never heard you swear so much."

"I'm mad."

"Okay," she said, heat rising within her. "Let's do something with that energy."

Except as she slid her hands up to his neck, he resisted her pulling him down. "No."

"No? You don't want to…?"

"No!" he exclaimed, easing her away. "Definitely not. Hard no."

Oh, right, yeah, Jeremy still had that effect on her love life. "Oh…" Now it just felt weird and awkward. A few minutes ago they'd been getting hot and heavy, ready to give in to what they'd resisted since they met. "It's getting late."

"Yeah."

"You should go."

She couldn't even look at him. It made sense. Why wouldn't he be mad? Finding out her ex still showed up for booty calls? He had to think the worst.

"No, I don't want to go."

She tucked her hand behind her when he tried to touch it. "I'd like you to go."

"Cherry—"

"I appreciate all your help today. It's late and I have work tomorrow so..."

"What happened to not sleeping well alone?"

"I'll get by," she said, catching a quick glance up at his frown. "I got by before you."

And she'd be fine without him, didn't it always work out that way in the end?

"Baby—"

"Please," she said, crouching to pick up his shirt to hand it over. "Go home, Darroch."

Without giving him a chance to say anything else, she went to open the front door. What was the point of dragging it out? Just the idea of putting his hands on her was repellant to him. All it took to find that out was the right call at the right moment.

Maybe she should thank Jeremy for revealing that truth.

Though he muttered something else, he strode past her and into the hall. Goodnight, Darroch. Was it goodbye too?

TWENTY-NINE

AND, BOY, WAS she in a pickle. It plagued her all day. Tuesday. Moving day… or it was supposed to be.

Yesterday, with Darroch, she'd accepted the new apartment and the keys. She'd also informed her current landlord she'd be leaving. What the hell was she going to do now on her own? This was why she should know better than to rely on people.

Moving the furniture was out. Even if she could get a truck, she couldn't lift such large, heavy pieces by herself.

"You're a million miles away," Yvette said, joining her at the counter.

"It's been a busy day," she said on a sigh. "Sorry."

"You don't have to worry about moving, I'll help you. We'll go tonight, rent a truck from… somewhere."

"I can't afford it." Turning her back to the store, she leaned against the counter. "It seemed like a good idea at the time. Now I'm locked in."

"Is anything urgent? Maybe the landlord will store whatever we can't move."

"That'll cost money I don't have." She sighed. "I'll probably be charged for abandoning it there too."

If the landlord had to pay someone to come dispose of her junk, that cost would be passed onto her, no doubt.

"Or she rents the place fully furnished." Good thing they hadn't gotten around to dismantling the furniture. "Iain's away for another sixteen days."

"Don't worry about it, I'll figure it out," she said, squeezing her friend's arm. "Thank you though, your support means a lot."

The apartment was one worry that she could at least attempt to tackle. The other things on her mind, the other thing, Darroch, was less tangible.

No matter how many times she told herself it was for the best, that they would be better apart, she couldn't get him off her mind.

"Hmm, maybe that will cheer you up?"

"That?" Her friend's gaze was aimed at the door. "What?"

Pushing off, she twisted around and couldn't believe there were Breckenridge boys out there on the concourse between their store and the leathers department opposite. Darroch, Caber, Ward, and Troy split off in pairs. When Darroch headed toward them with Ward, she turned her back again.

"Think our teammate heard about the latest sign up?"

"Ladies…" Darroch's voice vibrated the counter from the other side, that's what it felt like anyway. "Busy day?"

She bit her lip.

"Celeste call you?" Yvette asked whoever was on the other side of the counter.

Wouldn't that be the icing on the cake? If her boss had Darroch's number and she didn't.

She didn't care. Didn't matter to her. Just relax. Exist without taking up any space… was that possible? If she could invisible herself, that would be the time to do it.

"About the car wash? No, but our mom did. Yvette, this is Ward."

"Another brother?" Yvette asked. "Nice to meet you. Are you joining the team too?"

"Get one, you get them all," Ward said.

"Same here." Yvette took her shoulder to turn her around. "This is my colleague Savanna."

"Savanna, huh?" Ward smirked. Okay, so they'd met at the breakfast table, but he played along. "Who's on for the walkathon?"

"That why you're here?" Yvette asked.

"Nessa around?" Darroch asked. "You should introduce her to Ward. They'd make a dynamic recruitment team."

"Oh, yeah, sure," Yvette said and gestured Ward to follow on the other side of the counter.

Half a dozen steps later, when they were out of earshot, Darroch laid both hands on the counter. "Want me to fall to my knees?" She didn't want to lift her head. "I stayed at the Grand last night; it was as close to you as I could get. I couldn't sleep without you." That startled her enough that instinct raised her eyes to his. "There's my girl."

"Darroch—"

"Look, I'm sorry. I could've handled last night better. Hearing you talk to him, and knowing—my blood was hot, I admit it. That guy, you were with him, and he calls you up to… I'm sorry."

"You don't have to apologize."

"I charged in, I was rude—"

"Really, Darroch." She forced a smile. "You did nothing wrong. Your response was completely natural."

"Yeah?" he asked, squinting. "Doesn't feel like my Cherry's with me."

"Savanna's here." She sighed. "It's good that this happened, that it happened now. We got carried away."

"No, see, this is exactly what I didn't want. You've convinced yourself our relationship is broken."

"Darroch, you made it clear you didn't want to be with me—"

"I want to be with you. I am with you. That Germ though? I don't want him in your head, I don't want him anywhere near us when we're making love."

"That won't be a problem." Because it wouldn't be happening. "Darroch—"

"Have dinner with me."

"Darroch—"

"If I have to start at zero all over again, hell, if I have to start at zero twenty times, I'll do it. Breckenridge men don't—"

"Give up?"

"No, we don't."

"I'm not a challenge to overcome. I'm a person."

"I get that."

"And I think you're incredible, but if you haven't noticed, my life is a mess right now. I can't even think about dating until I straighten things out."

In her entire life? Yeah, that was an unachievable goal, maybe she'd never have sex again.

"What's the problem?" he asked. "Whatever it is, we'll figure it out together."

Yeah, 'cause that worked out so well the last time. "This is my problem. It's my problem I have two apartments. It's my problem that I don't know if I can afford either. If I can't pay the moving stipend, it'll be storage, or my old landlord will—"

"What are you talking about?"

Why was he confused? This wasn't difficult.

"What do you mean what am I talking about?" she asked. "You forgot we spent yesterday filling boxes? Now I have to get everything from A to B and—"

"It's done."

Just nothing. The look on his face was completely neutral, yet she was absolutely lost.

"What's done?"

"The move," he said and frowned. "That was the plan. We did the paperwork and the packing yesterday; me and the guys did the heavy lifting today while you were at work. Cleaners went in to do their thing too. Gave my keys back to the landlord. It's done."

Even her mind stuttered. "But… we—last night we—"

"Last night didn't change anything. Together means together, argument or not." How could he be so…? Oh, where were her defenses? "Baby…" His hand rose, but she pushed her shoulders back, leaning away while scanning the store. No customers and Yvette was busy with Nessa and Ward at the other counter. The cameras would be watching though. "Have dinner with me. Please, Cherry, you have to let me touch you."

"Not here," she murmured under her breath. "You know we can't."

"Have dinner with me." His voice got a little stronger. "Tonight, tomorrow, this weekend, whenever you want." What was right? God, that determination in his eyes, tinged with pleading… "I'm your guy."

And whatever went on last night, he'd proved himself that day. He'd proved himself a million times over. He wasn't petty or petulant, Darroch Breckenridge was a real stand-up guy, solid, dependable. Oh, God, she could be in serious trouble.

Celeste appeared behind the others and gasped in elation. "What a surprise! Wonderful."

"Tomorrow," she whispered with Celeste

barreling toward them. "At eight. I'll meet you at Blaze."

"Darroch," Celeste said before he could acknowledge her murmur. "What brings you to us today?"

"Missed you." He walked Celeste's way. "Come and meet Ward."

As Celeste turned he glanced back and winked. Yeah, he got it. Tomorrow gave her something to look forward to.

THIRTY

SHE DID LOOK forward to it, until she got there. Fernando seated her in a private dining room that gave them cover to conduct their romance in secret. Excellent! Only… there was no "they" yet. Being the only one in there made her isolation all the starker. Nothing to see here. Just a woman by herself, she shouldn't be humiliated yet, should she? What was the clock on being stood up?

Okay, so she'd shown up early, eager to thank him for what he'd accomplished the previous day. The Breckenridges didn't just move her things, the old apartment was spotless, and her things had been unpacked at the new place. Not her clothes in the suitcases though. Good. Gave her something to do and a little dignity. Everything else was in cabinets, in drawers, even the TV had been wall-mounted upstairs in the bedroom loft. Not where she'd have put it, but, okay.

They'd built her furniture, made her bed—it was so much more than she'd anticipated. And if she'd had Darroch's number, she might have called to tell him that.

Just as well she didn't or something inappropriate may have crossed her lips. A man like him was a blessing. Genuine, honest, kind, he didn't know how to disrespect her.

Except… clearly he did.

Why couldn't they get it together? If it was supposed to happen, it would happen. They had to decide to jump in or clear out. By that logic, if they weren't supposed to happen, these obstacles would continue to shoot up in their way. At some point, eventually, she'd have to take fate's hint.

Was that why he hadn't showed? He'd changed his mind? Decided she was too much trouble? Found someone far more glamorous and—no, not that last one, he wouldn't ditch out like that. What kind of guy wouldn't ditch out on an apartment move but would on dinner?

Nine, he'd be there by—okay, so nine thirty… How long was she going to sit there drinking wine she couldn't afford?

Damnit.

Finishing the bottle, because why the hell not, she gulped down the liquid.

Fernando came in. "Miss Mayden—"

"I know, he's not coming." She stood up, holding her phone. "Can I have the check, please?"

"We just heard… something."

"Something?" she asked. Why was he pale, so reticent? "Fernando, what?"

"An ambulance was called to…"

"What?" she asked, her heart leaping to her throat.

"We don't know exactly, but Tripp left his suite upstairs in a hurry about two hours ago. Took Roxanna's car to Laird's."

"Laird's—Laird's Hospital?" With a gulp, he

nodded. "Oh, God."

"Go," Fernando said. "There's a car outside." She got around the table and took half a step back. "Don't worry about the bill."

"Thank you," she whispered and bounded over to kiss his cheek before rushing away. "Thank you."

What was she doing? Whatever it was, whatever had happened, it was none of her business. Still, in the back of the car, speeding through the city streets, all kinds of scenarios rushed through her mind.

Damnit. Whatever happened, it must've happened fast. Wouldn't Darroch have called the restaurant? God, the Breckenridges were close, all of them. What if it was one of the kids? Buoy? Darroch wouldn't be thinking straight, none of them would be. What heartache, what worry, their kindness didn't deserve to be repaid by tragedy.

She leaped out of the car and ran into the hospital. Only as she reached the desk in the mobbed emergency department did it occur to her that finding the Breckenridges may not be easy.

Taking up space, she stood dumb for at least a minute.

"Can I help you with something?" asked a man on the other side of the desk. "Are you sick?"

"No, I'm looking for someone."

Not very descriptive.

"You family?"

"No, I'm—"

"We don't give out patient information to anyone except family."

Good rule that made a lot of sense. Though it left her stuck and—a feminine laugh cut through the rest of the noise. The why was unimportant, but the woman beyond the admissions desk ignited her hope again.

"Freya Dere," she called out, louder than she'd

meant to because more than one person turned. Luckily, one of them was the woman she needed. "You're Freya Dere of Children's Connection."

"Yes," the woman said, coming around the desk. "I've got this, Rufio." The admin guy wandered away. "Do you have a child in need of medical care?"

"No." She shook her head. "No, this isn't about ChilConn." She didn't think. Though Buoy's little smile chased her. "You don't know me. I'm Savanna Mayden—"

"Oh, God." Spiked with shocked concern, Freya came rushing around the desk to take her hand. "Why aren't you upstairs with Darroch?"

Alice must've mentioned her... and her connection to Darroch. So much for flying under the radar.

What was the point of denying it when concern had to be written all over her face?

"I just—where will I find him?"

"Third floor west, room three nineteen. Do you need me to—"

"No, I'll find him. Thank you."

All she needed was to be pointed in the right direction. The elevator took too long, so she vaulted up the stairs instead.

Third floor, left or right? Choosing right, it was disconcerting not to see anyone in the corridor.

Light signaled the space opening out to a nurses' station. Two women sat there, not so pleased to see her, but she kept going and they didn't stop her. Fourteen, fifteen, left, right, eighteen, she stopped.

The next door was slightly ajar. The susurration of voices, male, came from in there. The blinds were down on the nearest window. This was family.

Why hadn't that occurred to her?

No one called her. This wasn't her business. She

sat in the middle seat in a row of chairs against the corridor wall. Intruding would be wrong, barging in on the private scene would be the epitome of insensitive. Someone would come out eventually and she'd offer support. Not condolences. No. Whatever happened, they couldn't be saying goodbye. It didn't bear thinking about.

The floor was quiet, the lights low. Maybe it was a floor reserved for VIPs. Further down the corridor, light glowed from some of the windows by doors. Were they private rooms? A door, a long window, was that a whole room? Quite big. Weren't hospitals supposed to be bustling? Desperate for space?

The Breckenridges admitted donating to the hospitals in the city. And if the situation was serious enough, it might even make the news.

A couple came out of a different room and disappeared around the corner.

A half hour went by. Was she crazy to be sitting out there? The Breckenridges had been kind to her, supported her. Being on hand was the least she could do.

As she inhaled and her head turned, she saw it. Saw him. Entertaining himself, little Buoy spun into view in the crack of the door. She almost screamed with joy. The littlest one was okay, suiting himself, hopping, jumping, spinning. Joy filled her cheeks.

He stopped and froze, then tilted until his little eyes blinked to hers. She raised just her fingers from her knee in a semi-wave. Without a word, he flipped a one-eighty and re-appeared with a tiny superhero backpack.

The door didn't move as he squeezed his little body through the gap.

"Hey, sweetie," she whispered, suddenly aware of the echoing peace of the medical halls. "How are you doing?"

"Color with me." He pulled a couple of books

from his backpack and dragged out a bunch of bright markers. "Can we share the frogs? I saved it..."

Flipping through the pages, seeking the picture, he showed a flurry of others already completed.

"You're an amazing artist," she said, sinking down to sit on the floor by him.

He found the frogs page. There were two of them on adjoining lily pads.

"You do this one." He handed her a blue pen and pointed at the closest frog. "I'll do the big one."

"Okay."

Only a few seconds went by before a stern male voice intruded.

"What do you think you're doing?"

Wow, tall, severe, whichever Breckenridge this was, he didn't kid around.

"Sav-nah is my friend."

"Sav-nah?" he quizzed.

"Savanna!"

Alice's exclamation brought her immediately to her feet. Thank goodness she was okay.

"Oh, Alice, I'm so sorry."

"My girl." Alice swept her hair from her face to hold it in both hands. "We couldn't find you."

"Couldn't find me?" She scanned left, right. Men, a lot of them, with one glaring omission. "Oh, God..." The words slipped out under her breath as clarity iced her veins. "Where's Darroch?"

"Savanna—"

"She doesn't know," someone said.

Except she did, not right until that moment, but she did now.

Feet moved and she pushed through bodies until she was in the room. Yes, it was big, one bed with a curtain partially pulled around it, cold, sterile, everywhere but there. Him. Darroch. In bed, head elevated, a tube in his arm. Eyes closed. Was he breathing?

"He's okay," Alice said, putting an arm around her while rubbing the other. "He's going to be okay."

"He doesn't look it." Rushing to his side, she stroked his hair from his forehead leaving her hand there. "He's warm. What happened?"

"We don't know exactly." Benedict, she didn't have to tear her eyes away to identify him. "He was found in the alley by BHQ, unconscious, blunt force trauma to the head."

"Your smart mouth," she murmured, pushing to her tiptoes to rest her lips on his. "Anything to get out of paying for dinner."

"There are drugs in his system, keeping him out."

"They say he'll wake up soon." Not soon enough. "All we can do is wait."

She kissed him once, and again, stroking his forehead and cheek. "Gentleman."

"She better be the girlfriend, or we're all just standing here while she assaults him."

The speaker thought that was bad? Only straining every ounce of restraint prevented her from crawling into bed with him.

"Darroch belongs to her," Alice said, rubbing her back and easing her down into a chair by hers.

Her hand drifted to Darroch's. Still fixated on his face, her other one sought Alice's and brought it to the bed to join hers and his, locking the three of them together. Whatever happened, they'd need to wait until he woke to get answers.

THIRTY-ONE

VOICES BY THE door had been mumbling to each other for a while. She heard the occasional word as tempers frayed.

"Stop with the squabbling."

"Mast should be on a plane," someone said.

Brant.

She'd barely looked at him before another voice rose.

"No."

A single word from the man half in shadow in the corner.

That authority could only belong to one man. "Breck?" For the first time she looked at them all in turn. "Caber," she knew. The two beside each other with the thick biceps had to be, "Acre. Axon." A nod. "Ward, Tripp, Troy. Brant," were familiar as well. The next boy got a smile. "Astor. Dougie," and not to be left out, "my favorite Breckenridge, Buoy."

"Still can't reach the top shelf."

The croak from the bed brought everyone's

attention round fast; her and Alice shot to their feet.

"Darroch, my sweet boy."

By rote, he answered, "I'm fine, Mom." Though when he ventured to crack an eye, his inspection turned to a frown. "Am I fine?"

"Brant, get the doctor," Benedict said.

"Baby…?"

"You stood me up, Gentleman." Her heart leaped. Darroch's eyes closed, but his heavy arm tried to rise. Helping him out, she immediately pressed his hand to her cheek. "You scared me."

"Cherry—"

"What happened?" That stern male voice again. "Darroch?"

"I don't know."

"There are drugs in your system," Tripp said. "Serious drugs. GHB. How did that happen?"

"I don't remember."

"They found you passed out with a skull fracture. When you wouldn't wake up in the ER, they drew your blood."

"Sweetheart," Alice said, laying a hand on his shoulder. "What is the last thing you remember?"

"I was at the office. On my way to meet Sav." He forced his eyes open a sliver. "I never made it?" She shook her head. "I'm sorry, baby, I—"

"Shush," she said, a tear skittering from her lashes to meet his hand. "You can spend the rest of your life making it up to me."

"Everyone heard that, it's a promise."

"Please don't joke," she said, reaching to kiss him again.

When she tried to stand, he caught the back of her head to pull her back. She didn't resist when his tongue touched hers. The whole family might be there, but she'd give Darroch whatever he needed. Anything.

"Geez, man, have some class."

Tripp again, just like before.

Darroch's grasp relaxed and she slipped free, though he was quick to snatch her hand. The interruption was funny. Or so she thought. Darroch's face said something different.

When he tried to sit straighter, the whole posse advanced in one loud, "whoa."

"He's staying put," Benedict said when a pair of doctors came in with Brant. "Do you need to assess him?"

"Yes."

"No one's assessing squat," Darroch said, eyes closed again. "I'm fine."

"You don't know that," Alice said. "Let these people do their jobs."

The brothers filtered out as the doctors got closer. She tried to let go of his hand, but he tightened his grip and yanked her down.

"I'm sorry about dinner, baby."

"Forget dinner and cooperate with the doctors."

"What do I get?"

"You just stuck your tongue down my throat in front of your mother."

Yet somehow, the elation at seeing his eyes again erased all inhibitions.

"You saying I get to do that again?" His arm snaked around her, his hand trailed up the back of her thigh, in between them and—

"Hey!" she objected, catching those wandering digits to free herself. "At least pull the curtain."

"Go for it."

She laughed. "This is frisky, even for you."

"The drugs lower sexual inhibition," the younger of the doctors said.

"Think it's you being in the room that does it,

doc," Tripp said, swaggering a few steps closer, putting a blush in the doctor's cheeks. "I'm coming down with a case myself."

"Oh, Tripp," Alice said, taking her son's arm, "let the woman alone."

Darroch squeezed her hand. "If you don't walk back through that door with the rest of the family, I'll come find you. Skull or no skull."

Okay, he'd find it pretty hard to do anything without a skull, but she got what he meant.

"I'll come back," she said and kissed him again.

A good few seconds passed before he let go of her hand. His parents were by the door and ushered her out before closing it.

The mass of Breckenridges clogged the hall.

"Take the boys home to bed," Alice said to the big biceped Breckenridges. "We'll wait to see what the doctors say."

"Carver will take them. We have to talk to Darroch, find out if he was targeted."

That possibility startled her as much as Alice. "Do you think...? No, it has to be random."

"Maybe. But that won't be the only avenue investigated." This Breckenridge brother was no nonsense, which was good, the night didn't call for it. She followed his eyeline up to a couple of unknown guys loitering further up the hall. Plainclothes cops? Maybe they'd heard Darroch was awake too. "We have to look at this from every angle."

"If someone is hurting Breckenridges," Savanna said, "neither of you should be anywhere near it."

Unfortunately, the potential cop nearest her made eye contact. That was enough to bring both of them through the other Breckenridges to her side.

"Mr. and Mrs. Breckenridge," the blond cop said. "Ax." So they knew the bicep Breckenridges. "And you are…?”

Wow, not so subtle.

“This is Savanna,” Alice said, twining their arms. “Darroch's girlfriend.”

And weren't partners always the first suspects?

“Girlfriend, huh? Where were you tonight?”

“Sitting in a restaurant, waiting for Darroch to show up.”

“So you had plans? You knew where he'd be?”

“Actually no, I didn't know where he was coming from. We were meeting there.”

“Is that typical for you?”

“Savanna is not a suspect,” Alice said. “She would never hurt Darroch.”

“Alice,” Benedict said, putting an arm around her waist. “This is their job.”

“I don't mind answering questions, I have nothing to hide. No, Darroch usually picks me up.”

“Why was today different?”

“I don't know. I just told him to meet me there.”

“Because…?”

With his whole family watching, she didn't want to go into minute detail. “There was a thing, we had a thing.”

“What does that mean?”

“Mom,” Ax said and side nodded.

Benedict got it and eased his wife away.

Great, just great, the Breckenridges moved away in a flock. Their intention would be to give them privacy. They wouldn't suspect her of anything… would they?

“A thing?” the cop prompted.

“Darroch was at my place a couple of nights ago. My ex called and we fell out about it.”

“This ex still a feature?”

“No.”

“He and Darroch know each other?”

"No."

"Could this ex be pissed you're with another guy?" Honestly pissed? Like because he still cared about her? No, not Jeremy. She was beginning to wonder if he'd ever cared about her at all. "Is he the jealous type?"

"I don't know. Maybe. But he wouldn't do this. He wouldn't hurt anyone. He knows I'm seeing someone else, he doesn't know who that someone is. There would be no way for him to know it's Darroch."

"A Breckenridge isn't hard to identify."

"Yes, but Darroch and I, we're—" God, it seemed so stupid now. "Our relationship is—"

"Open?"

Was it open? Maybe. No. They had kind of called exclusivity.

"No."

"It's strained?"

"No. We were meeting for dinner. I didn't know where he'd spent his day. I still don't. No one in my life would know we're together. I haven't told my colleagues, my friends."

"Why not? Because of this ex?"

"No, because I work for Breckenridge."

And that shame pulled her limbs in tight. Did he have to look so disapproving?

"At BHQ?"

"No. In the intimates department."

"In the store?" She nodded. "That how you met?"

"No," she said, cupping her elbows, holding them close. "Do we have to get into all that? I know you want to find whoever's responsible, but—"

"That'll happen faster if we have the full picture."

Why would someone hurt Darroch? He couldn't have enemies, the Breckenridges were too good to have anyone pulling against them.

THIRTY-TWO

"MRS. BRECKENRIDGE."

The doctor's voice brought her around; the junior professional ducked back into Darroch's room. From the hallway, the Breckenridges stampeded after the young doctor. When she attempted to follow, the second cop blocked her way.

"Breckenridges have enemies."

"I'm not one of them, sir." Honestly, who could have beef with the kindest family in the world? "They've been nothing but generous."

"People like that, with money like that, some see them as a soft touch."

"So I'm a gold digger? If I was, what would I gain from hurting him?"

"Savanna?"

Caber, on the threshold of Darroch's room.

The cop wasn't ready to relinquish her. "Just a minute—"

"No, Niddrie, now, or we'll have a problem." Caber tipped his head toward the room. "Sav. He needs you."

Maybe, or the family were losing the battle to keep him still.

Inside, Darroch's frown was the first thing she saw.

"What's the problem?" he asked, his arm rising toward her. "Cherry?"

"No problem," she said, hurrying her pace to thread her fingers through his. "What did the doctors say?"

"Tripp's got your ex-wife's number, Niddrie," Darroch said like it was some kind of threat.

Tripp slipped his hands into his pockets. "Got his current girlfriend's number too."

"Just looking out for you, Roch," Niddrie said. "Someone's behind this."

"Not Savvy."

"He's right," she said. "Someone did this to you." She gently combed her fingers through his hair. "Where does it hurt?"

"Will you kiss it better?"

"He'll have to stay here for observation," the young doctor said. "For a day, maybe two."

"We have to talk to you, Roch," Niddrie said. "The more you can tell us, the faster we'll find this guy."

"Did you see him?" Ax asked.

"There's no cameras around there," Acre said. "Think he knew that?"

"You got beef with Ms. Mayden's ex? Where'll we find him?"

"At this time of night—"

"Guy's an asshole," Darroch said. "The way he treated Sav, if the guy showed his face, I wouldn't hesitate to—"

She touched his lips before he could make a real threat. "You told him off. He knows I'm yours."

"Which could be the guy's problem."

"Jeremy's a social climber," she said. "He'd be more likely to make friends with Darroch than fight him. Breaking through with the Breckenridges would be a Lotto win for him."

"You should talk to the police," Benedict said to Darroch.

A short knuckle tap on the door preceded a tall guy sticking his head around it. Broad, yummy, another Breckenridge? Couldn't be. He looked older than college age and she'd met all the others.

"Who needs a ride?" Buoy went running over and leaped up to be caught by the newcomer. "Astor, Dougie. Brant, you coming with us? Tripp, you going back to Crimson Palace?"

"I don't know, are we staying here tonight, Mom?"

The doctor didn't allow Alice to answer. "I'm sorry, we can't—visiting time is over, the patient has to rest," this from the older, more authoritative doctor. "We have to ask all of you to leave."

"Leave?" Alice said, dismayed, seeking her husband.

"We'll stay in the city," Benedict said. "The boys will go home."

"All of you can go home," Darroch said. "Sav will call you if there's anything to report."

"Sweetheart—"

"You have to get the kids to school in the morning, Mom. We'll be okay."

"Okay," Alice said, touching her face. "If you're sure. Do you want us to stay, Savanna?"

The doctor was insistent. "Everyone will have to leave."

"We need answers," Niddrie said.

"Talk to the police," she said, keeping hold of

Darroch's hand and coiling his arm around her hips. "Whoever hurt you has to be punished."

"They shouldn't be out on the streets," Acre said. "Want us to call Stone?"

Niddrie opened his arms. "We're standing right here."

"You'd rather we question your ability behind your back? 'Cause I do that too."

"Boys, don't fight," Alice said. "It does no good. We're on the same side."

"We think."

She didn't have to look to know Niddrie was focused on her.

In case anyone else was unsure, Darroch highlighted it for the room. "Keep looking at her like that and your problem will be right here."

She leaned in, desperate to soothe. "The partner is always the first suspect. It's an honor they're picking on me… unless you have a squad of other girlfriends for them to question."

When his scowl flew to her, she smiled.

"Only you, baby."

"I know," she whispered and rested her forehead on his for a second.

"Please, everyone," the doctor said. "Darroch has to rest until the drugs are fully out of his system. Let's give him a few minutes with the police. Then all of you can come back tomorrow."

"Okay," Alice said, kissing her boy. "We love you, sweetheart."

Benedict laid a hand on his son's forehead, then shifted it to his cheek. "Call if you need anything."

She kissed him, intending to leave, but sprang back when his embrace strengthened. His brothers were calling out their goodbyes, squeezing toes and patting legs, heading out.

Darroch didn't seem to notice; his mesmerizing eyes entranced her.

"You better be back."

"First thing."

"Within the hour."

"Baby, she said no visitors."

"You think that would stop me?"

No, it wouldn't. If she were the one laid up, he'd never let her out of his sight.

"Okay," she whispered and kissed him again. "Be good."

"Only until you get back."

"Are you sure it's a good idea for—"

"I don't sleep well alone."

Those were their magic words and all she needed to hear. She nodded before pressing another kiss to his lips and drifting away. This time, he did let her go, though his eyes stayed on her the whole way out. Every time she cast a glance back, their intensity grew. The cops were left inside and closed the door.

Alice hugged her in the hallway. "Do you want to come back to the house?"

"No, I want to be closer than that," she said, which put a smile on Alice's face that she switched to her husband. "He's strong, he'll be okay."

"Yes," Benedict said and kissed her cheek. "Call us if you need anything."

Just like he'd said to Darroch. Alice hugged her again and kissed her, squeezing her hand just before their fingers parted.

Caber, with Axon next to him, surprised her from behind. "How many guys you seeing?"

"I—"

"He talked about competition."

"It was a joke," she said, glancing at one then the other. "Darroch's the only man I'm seeing."

She could act offended, get upset, rush back in and tell Darroch they'd questioned her. But she wouldn't. These men loved their brother. That was something to be celebrated not resented.

"And the ex?"

"I'll give you his information, but he's a wimp. Trust me, this is not his style."

"Roch have any trouble with either of your landlords?"

"No."

"Any arguments when you were out together?"

"I honestly can't believe anyone would want to hurt him."

"Someone did."

Yes, they did. "And I want him found too. Darroch gets along with everyone, you know that." Except Jeremy. "You could talk to Quade, but I didn't see any trouble at the community center event."

"The one you went to on Sunday with Mom and Dad?" She nodded and the men looked at each other. "It's worth asking."

"Other than that, we were at Blaze. Always in private dining. Tripp said Fernando was mad at him, at Tripp, not Darroch. Maybe ask him what that was about." Though she really couldn't see Fernando hurting anyone either. "The girls at work don't know about our relationship. The Breckenridges are the only ones who know about us. You and Fernando..." She caught Caber's forearm. "Check with your team too, the leathers girls. Again, I don't see them doing something like this but..." And another thought. "Ask your dad about Detective Chapman. He's the cop investigating the break-in at my old place. I know your dad and Darroch were keeping in touch with him. Neither of them has said anything to me about there being a problem but—"

"It's worth checking out," Caber said, surprising

her by stepping in to kiss the top of her head. "Come on, we'll take you home."

"It's okay, I can—"

"Someone out there is targeting Breckenridges," Axon said. "We're taking you home."

Should she tell them that she didn't intend to stay home? No. Some things stayed between a woman and her man.

THIRTY-THREE

THE HOSPITAL'S REAR stairwell got her to the third floor without seeing anyone. Knowing where the room was, she snuck through the hallways, while trying not to look like she was sneaking, just in case.

Darroch's door was closed. Good. Without making a sound, she opened it and slipped inside, closing it just as quietly. The curtain was pulled around the bed too, another bonus. The more barriers, the more protection they had from prying eyes.

Finding the split, she slipped between the fabric edges. His eyes were closed, though as she slipped off her shoes and laid her bag on the chair, his head rolled her way. She couldn't even tell if his eyes had opened at all, but the curve of his lips betrayed she'd been made.

"Scoot," she whispered, picking up the sheet to slip in next to him. He shifted a little across the bed and put an arm around her to hold her against him. She tucked the covers around them and relaxed. "God, you feel good."

"What took you so long?"

It hadn't been much more than an hour since she'd last been in the room. "Your brothers took me home. I had to get changed."

"I liked the dress."

"I put it on for you."

"For me to take off?" His mouth moved in her hair. "Come up here."

Laying a hand on his chest, she rose to meet his eye. "If I kiss you…"

"What?"

Just admiring those lips was enough to draw her breathing deeper. "You know what."

One inch would lead to a mile. Man, the stirring of need and gasp of want, her inner muscles clenched. Being in bed with this man was risky.

"We're allowed, I'm your guy."

"I'm sorry."

"For…?" he asked, his hand sliding up to clasp the back of her head. "The apology should come from me, I stood you up."

Dinner? Old news. "I don't want us to be broken."

He guided her mouth to his. "We're not broken."

His lips were sure, so familiar and every promise her heart craved.

She eased away. "I held back from us, for so many reasons, which I can't even remember now."

With his grip still on her head, he angled her a little for the next kiss. "What matters is where we are now."

"You have to rest."

"You've got something on your mind, beautiful," he murmured and kissed her again. "What do you want to say to me?"

Because tonight had proved they may not always have time to waste.

"You make me feel like—I've never felt like this, the way I feel when I'm with you."

"I told you, it feels right."

"It does and I—that scared me, I think. I didn't want to be the stupid airhead tripping over myself for the GQ model, but I—I am tripping over myself for you, Darroch Breckenridge. I want to be with you."

"You're my girl."

"I want us to do this. Together. Us. I want to be your partner, to face whatever the future has for us, together."

His next kiss was a smile. "Baby, I've been yours since before you offered me your cherry."

"Even if the sex sucks, we'll work through it."

His quiet laugh vibrated through her. "The sex won't suck."

"But we'll work through it, won't we? I don't want us to lose each other, to give up, because something isn't perfect or there's a flaw that—"

"Partners," he said, his fingers digging into her skull. "It's what we both want. You know what I come with, my ridiculous family—"

"I come with no family. None I'd be proud to share with you."

"Perfect doesn't matter. Real matters," he said. "Family, work, whatever we do in our spare time, our friends, future family, partners are united. All we have to do is listen to each other."

"Respect each other."

"Exactly."

"Like your mom and dad?"

Her smile bred another laugh from his lips. "Yeah, just like them."

"You know, thirty-five years isn't a bad innings."

"No, it's not."

She squinted. "Not sure about the sixteen kids

though."

"It starts with one, we'll go from there."

"That's about ten steps ahead of where we are," she said and breathed out, closing her eyes as she rested her head against his face. "I thought we were all screwed up after Jeremy called."

"You thought we were done? That why you thought I'd ditched out on the move?"

"I thought we were in a fight."

"Even if we were, it doesn't change the foundation of us. We're still together. Our commitment remains solid. We just make up and have lots of sex after we've calmed down."

"Oh, do we?"

"Yep. New policy. We keep our word and follow through. We always follow through."

His hand went from her hair to her hip and before she could object, he'd boosted her on top of him.

"Darroch—"

"Shh," he said, squeezing her hips to pull her higher. "Forget about the hospital—"

"And the head injury?"

"And that."

"And the drugs in your system?"

"They've got to be gone by now."

"Want to tell your cock that?" she asked, wriggling against him in case the eager erection had escaped his notice. "You're under the influence of a date rape drug. This isn't the right time."

"This is the perfect time," he said, pelvis rising. "Know how easy it would be to—"

"I am not telling our future children..." She gripped his waist to slide back to her previous position next to him. "That you were high the first time we had sex."

"You going to tell our kids about our first time?"

"Maybe. Anyway, remember your mom's rule we're not allowed to do it until after—"

"There's something I've been meaning to ask you," he said, pinching her chin to bring it up. "Marry me."

"Ha, ha, very funny," she said, slithering higher to kiss him slow. "I will not accept a marriage proposal while you're high either."

"Not ideal, I know, but I'm a little behind. When my mom made that rule, my dad proposed the next day."

"That's true, you slacked off, you waited days. A sign you're not all the way sure?"

"I wanted to find the perfect ring first."

The warm, comforting heat of him joined her aura, blending them together. With an arm across his middle, she pulled herself tighter into him. "Thank you for inviting me to come back."

"I need a protector."

And that chilled her mood. "Did talking to the cops bring anything back?"

"Only that Niddrie's an asshole." The next time their eyes met, hers were unimpressed and he sighed. "I don't remember, baby. I want to remember. I was at work, I took a shower, changed. There was a call right before I walked out the door. I was pissed because I didn't want to be late."

"And then?"

"Nothing," he said. "It's fuzzy, I don't even remember much about the call, just that it happened. Next thing was us kissing and Tripp telling us to have class."

So he didn't even remember waking up. "It's normal. Axon said in the car that head injuries can lead to memory loss."

"Docs said it might come back."

Might was no guarantee.

"Acre thinks it's possible you could've been targeted. Do you think you were? Have you been fighting with anyone?"

"Only crossed words were with the Germ."

"I gave Axon Jeremy's information. Told him everything I could about anyone we've interacted with."

"Good girl." He smoothed her hair and used the move to pressure her head to his shoulder. "As long as you're safe, I'll be fine."

"How do you think that works for me?" she asked, stroking the cotton on his torso. "Anything could've happened… I don't think Jeremy's got the balls to target someone like you, and he never cared enough about me to really be jealous, but… If this was anything to do with me, with your connection to me… I'll never forgive myself."

"It was random."

Except BHQ wasn't in a rough area, the service alley not some place people might stumble across to hang out in. There may not be cameras behind the structure, but security guards patrolled the building. How could someone be there, meaning harm, at the exact moment Darroch was there too? Especially if he was late leaving. Could it just be one of those things? Maybe. That didn't make her feel better or any more secure about his safety.

"You should take Ferguson," she said.

"Where?"

"Anywhere. Everywhere. All the time."

"My head is harder than yours. If anyone is going to take the blows, it's me. You're more important."

"Than you? I am not."

When she tried to lift her head, his strength held it down.

"Let's not fight about it."

There, in the hospital, they had to keep the volume down. And they should both be safe with security and so many other people in the structure. For someone to come to the room to finish the job, that would be more than random and even more than targeted, that would be someone with a serious vendetta.

"Darroch?" she murmured, closing her eyes.

"Yeah, baby?"

"Partners?"

He kissed her head again. "Partners."

She shouldn't be there and would have to sneak out before morning. Being with him justified the bending of hospital rules. She wasn't there to hurt him or to push him. More than anything, she wanted him to be better, back at full health. If he needed her with him to speed that process, she'd stay at his side for as long as it took.

THIRTY-FOUR

"OH MY GOD!"

The exclamation jarred her from sleep.

"What the—"

"Darroch!"

Alice's voice cut off the one from beneath her. Damn. Her vision still blurred, but there were vague figures standing around. His parents. His doctors… his brothers. Oh… no… Darroch, the hospital… it was coming back, and it wasn't good.

"This is unacceptable," a doctor said.

"Hospital sex, nice."

"If there was intercourse, it will have to be reported."

Were they different doctors? Why were there three of them now? What did that last one say?

"Interco—no! We didn't have—there was no intercourse," she said, burying her face against Darroch.

"Not for lack of trying on my part."

"We'll have to test if you're still under the influence of drugs."

And if he was, she'd probably need to talk to the cops… again.

"I'm sorry," she said, breathing him in once more before sitting up to slither off the bed. "I meant to leave before you all got here."

"We did nothing wrong."

"Rest is vital to your recovery."

"Yeah, we know that."

"I guarantee he slept better with his girl next to him than he would've alone," Caber said. "Savvy settles him."

"That's true," Alice said. "I'm sure they meant no harm. Young love finds a way, Doctor."

"We have to take him upstairs," the doctor said, unimpressed. "He needs a full evaluation."

"Because he slept with his girlfriend?" Caber asked. "Whatever disease she's got, she gave it to him before this."

"Hey!" Darroch chastised as his brothers laughed.

"Please don't tease him," Alice said, going to her son, stroking the hair from his forehead. "How do you feel this morning, sweetheart?"

"I was better when Savvy was with me."

She crouched to seek her shoes beneath the bed. "I'll come back later."

"Come back?" he asked. "Where are you going?"

"*You* are going upstairs, Mr. Breckenridge," the doctor said as two men in hospital uniforms came in to free Darroch's bed from its brakes. "No family allowed. This shouldn't take more than an hour or two."

"Savvy's coming with me," Darroch said, sitting up straight only to then grasp his head.

"Darroch?" Alice asked.

Concern hung around every brother.

Without thinking, she was there next to him,

holding his head in both hands. "Gentleman?"

"Head rush," he said and smiled. "Worked for me." He slung an arm around her. "Come with me."

"I have work today," she murmured, stroking his face.

"Shit."

Pulling his mouth to hers, she kissed him. "I don't start until noon."

"You'll be here when I come back?"

She nodded, her nose bumping his. "I'll be waiting."

He kissed her as the bed started moving again. They wheeled him out, doctors in tow, until only the family remained.

"Were you here all night?" Benedict asked.

Though she squirmed, she didn't want to lie. "Yes."

"Good," Benedict said, setting a hand on his wife's hip. "We have to make arrangements for him at home."

"Yes," Alice agreed.

"Depends what their scans and tests show," Caber said. "Do you think they'll let him out today?"

Alice was calm. "Let's wait to see what the doctors say."

"I should…" She rushed to return to her shoes and slip them on. "Get going."

"You just said you'd be here when he got back."

Didn't take long for Caber's mood to switch.

"If I leave now, I will be back in time. I have to get ready for work."

"Back to your apartment and—"

"I brought things," she said, grabbing her bag from the floor. "I just need to find somewhere to shower."

"They have facilities in the women's locker

room," Tripp said, attracting all eyes. He shrugged and snickered. "What?"

"And you know that because…?"

Swagger bled from him. "I never forget a body… or a liaison."

"Do you have to work?" Brant asked before his brother had any further chance to explain.

Did she have to work? What good would she be at the hospital? Being with him, near him, made her feel better, but he'd have his family around him.

"I can stay with him today," Alice said, giving her the out. "Get yourself something to eat." The woman embraced her like a mother. "Tripp, eat with Savanna once she's ready. Look after her. Ben will call and have something brought to the family lounge."

"Thank you," she said and accepted her kiss.

"Make sure there's enough food for the nurses Tripp will pick up on the way," Ward said, laughing with Brant and Troy.

"Doctors, admins, patients…" Tripp said, coming over to slide an arm around her. "All are welcome to apply."

"Yeah, yeah," Troy drawled.

"Jealousy's an ugly color on you, brother."

"Tripp," Alice said in that tone. "Ward. Troy."

The tone that told them to behave.

The Breckenridges once again came to her rescue. Now she had to beat Darroch back to the room, so he'd never know she was gone.

THIRTY-FIVE

AN OVERDUE EXCHANGE of numbers at the hospital meant she'd been in touch with one Breckenridge or another all day. All except the one she craved.

Without going home, or really stopping to breathe, she got Yvette to cover close with Nessa and left work early to race to the hospital. Damn, even with all the assurances in the world, she couldn't relax.

Not until she laid eyes on him again.

Rushing into his hospital room brought every face around, her awareness stuck on him.

"Am I interrupting?" she asked.

"Yeah," Darroch said. "Eight hours too late." He gestured. "Get over here."

Crossing through the bodies, she dumped her bag, kicked off her shoes and climbed onto the bed on her knees, facing him.

Maybe she should've had more decorum, but instinct drove her to cup his head to match their mouths.

"How do you feel?" she murmured and kissed

him again. "I was worried." Another kiss. "Did they take you for the other scan?" One more. "What are they saying?" Oh, she couldn't stop with the kissing. "Are you in pain?"

"Only when you're not here."

"She going to settle the debate or are we doomed to watch this show all night?"

"When was the last time you got some, Brant?" one of the brothers asked.

"Yeah, you're damn bitter these days, man."

"Stop teasing him," Alice said. "We have to make a decision."

"What's the debate?" she asked, rocking into Darroch's grasp when he tempted her mouth back to his for a longer tender kiss.

Thank God he broke the union, she would've stayed there forever otherwise.

"The doctors want me to stay another night."

No debate. "Then you stay."

"I don't want to stay."

Her fingers sank into his hair. "I don't care, you take your medicine."

"You don't want me home?"

To be alone in bed with him, watching him rest? Safe and healthy? More than anything in the world. What she wanted didn't matter. He'd do what was best for him, what would keep him with her for the longest time.

And she wasn't ashamed of that truth. "I'd rather you spend one night out than a lifetime in the ground."

"That's kind of dramatic, baby."

She kissed him. "You like that?"

"Kissing you?" This time he was the one drawing their mouths together. "Every damn time, baby."

Her face stayed in the cradle of his hands, but she swayed away when he tried again to kiss her. "Harder to kiss me if you're dead."

"She's got you there, bud."

"If you're staying another night, we'll have someone posted in your room," the white coat guy said, coming closer.

"I'm going home," Darroch said.

"Against your lady's wishes?" Troy asked.

"They're posting a guy on the door, security, to keep us apart."

Any barrier between them made her uneasy. A person responsible for standing between them…? Yeah, it upset her, but these doctors were professionals. If they believed he needed to be observed, could she advise against that?

She told the truth. "I want whatever is best for you."

From him, she looked to Alice. If anyone else could appreciate her dilemma, his mother was the one.

"Ben is making arrangements," Alice reassured her.

"Arrangements?"

"It would be best for Mr. Breckenridge to remain here," a doctor type said.

"For observation," Darroch added. "You've been observing, I'm fine." He squeezed her knee. "And the drugs are out of my system."

"Okay…" Benedict's voice brought her attention around to him entering the room. "We have a neurologist on his way to the house and two home nurses will be there within the hour."

"Mr. Breckenridge," the doctor said. "If something goes wrong, it could happen fast. Having a specialist on site does not matter if they don't have the facilities and equipment—"

"We'll have a chopper parked on the grass," Benedict said. "It's arranged, the pilot will be ready to go at a second's notice. We'll have two pilots, and a dedicated flight doctor, just in case."

What a family. As incredulous as she was, and impressed, her smile didn't do her thoughts justice.

"What?" Darroch asked, catching her lowering chin with a finger. "Why the smile?"

"Our children will know nothing but love, will they?"

He smiled and eased her close. This time, he resisted the kiss. "They'll have the best of everything in the world."

And he wasn't talking about material possessions. The next joining of their mouths was slower, deeper, much better suited to a bedroom than a hospital room… filled with his family.

"Does that mean we've decided?" Brant asked.

When they parted, all eyes were on her, including the patient's.

"Promise you'll take your medicine?"

"I promise."

"And you'll listen to the professionals?"

"I'll listen."

"Will you be honest, Gentleman? Don't hide symptoms from us."

"I won't, baby."

She sighed.

One of the brothers spoke up. "I'd add to that it's probably best she goes on top for a while and…"

Outrage loosened her jaw.

As the brothers jeered, Darroch smirked. "He's got a point there, Cherry."

"The safest course would be abstinence."

Whichever brother said that got a cheer. As dismay hit Darroch, triumph visited her. Yeah, sometimes life wasn't fair. As long as he had it, everything would be okay.

THIRTY-SIX

SO HE WON THE battle to be allowed back to Breckenridge House. Despite his objections, he didn't win the next one regarding a wheelchair. No amount of brothers would shake her and Alice from their insistence. If he wanted to be home, he had to prove his ability to compromise.

That was how she learned Breckenridge House had an elevator. Behind a regular door, it wasn't a typical metal box, nor was it very big.

"I'll meet you upstairs."

She darted away before anyone could object and ran up the stairs.

Two women at Darroch's bedroom door stalled her.

"Let me—it's locked."

"It's not locked, it's—"

"Can I help you?" she called, bringing them around. One wore a knee-length trench and what might be hospital scrubs. The other… were those fishnets?

"We're looking for Darroch's bedroom," said the

fishnets woman.

Yeah, and if she was a more suspicious person…

"For what reason?"

"Bright!" Tripp called from behind her. "Hey, baby."

"These are your nurses?" Brant asked. "Shit, wait 'til Mom sees this."

Tripp swerved past her to curve an arm around the fishnet woman's waist. Had he called her Bright? Her actual name or a nickname?

"Your brother? That's why you called me?"

"Yeah, don't worry about that, Bright, baby. His girlfriend's standing right there."

"What's going on?"

Darroch rolled up with a couple of brothers.

"Mom and Dad are downstairs with the neurologist and a nurse, Tripp—"

"Jodi, there," he said, gesturing to the woman in scrubs. "The best nurse you'll ever meet. We…" He backed off keeping the other woman pressed to his side. "Will see you all at breakfast."

Tripp was happy to saunter off, down the hallway.

"Brant, take Jodi downstairs to Mom."

The woman went when Brant raised an arm the other way.

Caber opened the bedroom door and entered before Ward wheeled Darroch in.

The first thing she did was double clap, then pulled back the covers.

"Help me get him into bed."

"Baby, you don't need no help with that," Darroch said, planting his feet on the floor as he bounced forward in the chair.

His brothers grabbed his shoulders to hold him back. "Dad was clear on this, fresh meat. Mom and Sav's word is law."

"She wants me in bed, you heard her say that."

"I heard her ask us to help you in bed."

"Okay," Darroch said as Troy came around to fold back the feet rests. "You know we're not playing that game. Help? With Savvy in bed? Not a chance, Sunshine."

Caber took one arm, Ward the other, they pulled him up and did more of a toss than a help.

He took it with a laugh and flipped himself over, she was less amused.

"Okay, maybe I'll just help him get ready for bed alone," she said, trying and failing to contain her offense. "Go and check when he next needs his meds, please." She pushed the chair toward them. "Go on."

His kind of taken aback brothers shuffled out with the wheelchair.

"Cherry—"

"We don't want you to get too hot." She kneeled at his feet to take off his sneakers and socks. "Your sweats should be okay for—"

"Cherry," he said, sliding a finger under her chin to elevate it. Nothing but tenderness bled from him when he witnessed her gathering tears. "What's wrong, baby?"

Rising, she touched her mouth to his. "Sit back," she whispered, climbing on as he shuffled back to lean on the headboard. Straddling him, she held his face in both hands. "I've never been so happy to see a man in his own bed."

"I'm over the fucking moon every time you're here."

His wit remained healthy.

"Is there anything you need?"

"Yeah, what you didn't give me last night."

Though his mischievous eyes betrayed he didn't

expect her to yield, he underestimated how pleased she was to have this opportunity.

"You have a crack in your skull," she said, unzipping his hoodie, helping him liberate his arms. A longer kiss. "The doctors said no strenuous exercise."

"What they don't know…"

Mm, their tongues smudged together. Sliding her hands up under his tee-shirt, it was so difficult to be careful when his body felt so vigorous.

She released, then kissed him gently. "You need to relax."

"Best way to do that is with my girl."

His tee-shirt went the way of the hoodie and their mouths joined again. How could she do anything less than forever with the man who'd awoken her carnal soul? In that bed, they'd grown closer, slept wrapped in each other, shared heat and intimacy. Shared safety.

"This feels like…" she broke their kiss just long enough to get her top off, "a violation of your mother's trust. I'm…" Shit, it didn't feel right to do anything with her mouth other than consume his. "I'm supposed to be looking after you."

"Cherry…" his hands surged up her back into her hair. "With you, I've never felt healthier."

No, he hadn't. Mm and they'd never had circumstances come together so… Undulating her hips, for once, she was actually allowed to enjoy how he felt. How would he feel inside her? Power, that's what he gave her, what she felt like being intimate with him. That response, his cock, hard and ready, massaging her pussy as she tilted closer to rouse her clit, that was hers. He was hers. Awaking the heated pressure, the demand of the other was ready to be satisfied, ready to be released.

Before she'd shed her bra from her arms, her breasts filled his hands.

"Darroch," she whispered his name when his

head urged hers aside. "Gentleman—"

"Not tonight," he growled against her. "I've got you, baby, and there's no fucking way I'm letting go."

Yes, those were the words she ached for. Squeezing his arms, her fingertips wandered down and across to his abs and lower to—

The door burst open, she barely got a chance to—

"Savvy's naked!"

She grabbed for her chest, pressing herself to Darroch. From that angle, all the youngster would see was her back, but that didn't account for the shock of his presence.

"Get the fuck out of here, Astor. You little—"

"Mom's orders," came an older voice from outside.

Ward appeared carrying the end of a couch.

She caught Darroch's hoodie as he wrapped it around her. With her arms in the sleeves, she climbed from his lap, zipping it up.

Ward and Troy carried in the couch. Axon and Acre were right behind them with another.

"What are you assholes—"

"Shh," she whispered, touching his lips. "They care about you." The guys set up couches, brought in Barca's and a huge projector screen. "You told me your mom didn't let you take your wealth for granted, don't take their love for granted."

"And how long you think my girl will stick around if I don't show her love?"

She grazed the stubble on his chin. "Would you leave me for not giving it up?"

His arm around her clenched, pinning her to him. Dipping, he kissed her, just for a brief moment; even in that whisper she tasted his possession.

"Soon as you give up your heart to me, I'll never

surrender or abandon it."

"If you two are done with the gooey gazes, pick a movie."

"A movie?"

Breckenridges as far as the eye could see. The young ones were on the couches, now there were three in the room and a couple more on the recliners.

"Thought I was supposed to rest," Darroch said as his brothers passed around popcorn and snacks.

"Do that," Caber said, dropping onto another chair, smirking. "Pretend we're not even here."

Though he stayed quiet, Darroch's irritation showed in his face.

She laughed and kissed him. "They wouldn't be your brothers if they didn't wind you up. I think it's cute."

"There may be another Breckenridge injury tonight. Next one won't be mine."

"We can cuddle," she said, raising his arm over her head to wrap it around her.

"Cuddling," he said with no intonation. "Every guy's wet dream… when he's thirteen."

"Oh, am I in the wrong place?" She raised her interest. "Should I be cuddling with Astor? He won't mind I'm not wearing a bra, will he?"

His arm clenched tight around her. "Not a fucking chance."

"Good." Wriggling, she relished his heat and solidity. A real, tangible man, her man. "I don't take this for granted."

He kissed the top of her head and that was enough. Surrounded by his family, the lights were dimmed, and the movie started. Being in the Breckenridge bubble was a blessing. She hardly recognized her life. Fate had a great way of making her point.

THIRTY-SEVEN

MMM, THE SMOOTH texture of his heated skin demanded the salve of her kiss. Without opening her eyes, she angled her chin, rolling her cheek against him to taste his pec, his sternum, his—

"Cherry."

The rasp of his rough morning voice inspired her leg to slide over his and her kiss to ascend. His throat, his chin—

"Baby, I love your thinking, encourage it—"

"Shh," she whispered, resting her fingertips on his lips, rubbing her cheek against his stubble. "You feel so good."

"Uh huh, again, appreciated," he said and coiled his strong fingers around her delicate wrist to liberate his lips. "Any other day—"

She kissed him, freeing her hand to slide it down his stomach.

"I'll feel good, baby."

"Oh, that I know for sure." As her nails met the waistband of his sweats, he grabbed her hand hard. The sudden startling act opened her eyes to blink down at him. "You might want to check the end of the bed before putting the stick in drive."

The bed? Twisting to do as he—his brothers. Astor was peeking over the back of a couch, more than a few smirks occupied other faces around the room, even those with closed eyes. But it was Buoy, sweet, little Buoy lying on his stomach on the end of their bed, coloring as always, that made everything okay.

God, she'd almost...

Her guy snatched her wrist, pulling her hand from its place of support, collapsing her body onto his.

He kissed her palm. "Any other day, Sweet Cherry. Though... I could use a shower."

And everything fell into perspective. "No, you cannot. Caber and Tripp will help you."

"Help what?" Caber muttered from somewhere.

"Help your brother shower."

He snorted. "Yeah, not doing that."

"I'm not strong enough to support him on my own."

"I can stand on my own two feet," Darroch said.

They ignored him. For good reason, one head rush or a bout of dizziness and he could crack his skull all over again.

"Isn't that what the nurse is for?" Caber asked.

The nurse? As in the woman she'd met last night?

"She wouldn't be much stronger than me." And she didn't want to take risks with his safety. Neither would his mom. "I'll ask Alice, they might be able to find male nurses—"

"I don't need help in the shower. I'll be fine."

But she wasn't as optimistic. "Your mom will agree with me."

"She's got you there," Caber said, waking to sit up, stretching his back, fingers interlinked over his head as he forced his palms toward the ceiling. "We'll figure it out, Sav."

"You promise?"

Caber snickered. "Yes, I promise."

Slapping a hand to Darroch's cheek, she brought his gaze to hers. "I have to go to work."

"You don't have to—"

"It's my job."

Yes, maybe he did own the business, and she'd concede the day would be hers if he made a call. Not just a call, all he'd have to do was nod at one of their people and it would be done, like a magical nose twitch, but that wasn't the point.

"I'm laid up, baby."

"I see that."

Her heart jumped when he thrust a fist into the mattress to sit up against the headboard. Her open hands hung there, close, not touching him. Such a virile man shouldn't feel fragile, and it wasn't that she feared breaking him… or did she?

He caught each of her hands to press them against his torso. "You can't leave me alone with these assholes."

"Watch your language," she murmured, glancing back to Buoy. "He's so beautiful."

"Okay, I'm over here." The amusement in Darroch's voice matched his smile. "When he gets older, you know we'll tell him you were nuts about him."

"I'll always be nuts about him." Would she be around to experience that jeering? "Don't get up today, okay? The hospital didn't want you to leave last night. The compromise is this, that you do what you're told. Stay here. Safe. Please." Amusement no longer lit his gaze. She leaned closer to brush her lips across his and whisper, "Would you do that for me, Gentleman?"

"I would do anything for you, Cherry, but—"

She kissed him. "No but. No risks. Please don't ask me to see you in the hospital again." If she got that call at work, she'd have a heart attack on the spot. "Stay in bed. Bathroom's the only exception, and you have to use the one here. Only this one."

Searching him, she bit her lower lip. He scooped a hand around the back of her head and forced their mouths together. Not like in the hospital, this kiss was so much more amorous, and with their audience—

Laying a hand to his chest, she pushed back, lowering her eyes.

"I'll stay in bed," he said, his kiss almost, nearly catching hers. It closed her eyes again, tempting her mouth higher. "For everything except the bathroom, our bathroom only."

Blinking, need glistened in her gaze. "You will?"

"I promise."

That dropped her shoulders slightly. "Thank you, Gentleman."

Another kiss, then she scooted off the bed. Before going into the bathroom, she looked back to him watching her. Whether it was one day or a million, she'd never get over it. Him, such an honorable, passionate man was hers. How did that happen?

THIRTY-EIGHT

"HEY! COME ON."

Closing her locker at work, she turned to Yvette hanging in the break room door. "Come where?"

Only place she wanted to go was to her guy.

"We have an idea," Yvette said, smiling as she side-nodded.

Out of curiosity, and because she had to go that way anyway, she followed her friend out of the room and to the staff exit that would take them to the stairwell. Celeste and Nessa were there waiting.

"What's happening?" she asked.

Nessa held up a bottle of Scotch while Celeste opened a card.

"We're going to take them to him. Gifts. A card."

"Take them…?"

"Sign the card," Celeste said, thrusting a pen and the card her way. "Write something nice."

Closing it over, the big, "Get Well Soon" words covered the front, top to bottom. Something nice…

Hmm, what was she supposed to write to her

secret boyfriend?

"Hurry up!" Nessa urged her on.

"How can we take them to him?" she asked, writing a generic get well message and signing her name. "In the hospital?"

"He went home," Nessa said. "That's what Cinda said, she said he was back at Breckenridge House."

Word really did travel fast and far. "Just today?"

Was it dishonest to plead innocence?

"How would she know that?" Yvette said. "Where did she hear it?"

"It doesn't matter," Celeste said. "Going to the house would be an overstep, and it's forever away." Yeah, what would be the point traipsing over there just to immediately come back. A cab would cost a fortune. "We're only going to BHQ."

Oh, so much better. A shiver quaked in her spine as Nessa opened the stairwell door to venture on. All followed her, so what choice did she have? Traipsing out after them, she had to ignore the alley where she usually got into the Breckenridge car and follow her coworkers to the street to get in a cab.

"I've never been to BHQ," Nessa said after a block or two. "Think our employee credentials will get us in?"

"Do you think Caber will be there? He should be able to pass on our best to his brother."

And if he wasn't? Unlikely Astor or Dougie would be there, they were school age, not corporate overlord age. They'd met Ward, maybe he'd be around. Would he play it cool? He had in the store, though that was no guarantee. The more time she spent with the family, the more difficult it became to remember her and Darroch weren't common knowledge.

Nessa opened the bag looped around her wrist to put the sealed card inside. "You take this."

The young woman thrust the gift bag into her hands. Peeking inside to the chocolates and grapes, there were a couple of other boxes in there too.

Nessa's shift finished earlier, she must've gone out shopping before returning with her wares.

"This might be an overstep."

What the hell would she do if someone recognized her and said something? How far did discretion go? Damn, what if Benedict was there? Would he feel obliged to receive them because she was part of the gang? The man was too busy to field visitors.

"Nonsense," Celeste said. "He's our teammate. It would be rude not to send him our best."

"Can't we mail a card?"

If she volunteered to do it, she could save herself the cost of a stamp and give it to him in person. She hadn't spoken to him all day, she missed him. It was crazy, but her worry eclipsed every other emotion. Customers suffered for her distraction. Maybe she should take him up on that time off. Nursemaid would be a role she'd happily adopt, if he agreed to be compliant. Though she was one to talk, from their kissing the previous night before his brothers showed up, they may not be the most trustworthy together.

The cab stopped. Wait. They were there?

The driver must've been paid because there they were piling out onto the sidewalk in front of the building her guy had been attacked behind. Oh, it made her sick. Someone hurt him. Took advantage and—why would anyone do that?

Yvette snatched her hand. "Come on."

Celeste and Nessa were already inside, by the time they caught up, the other two were holding open the elevator.

Shit.

Okay.

The top button lit and they ascended way faster than they should've. Okay, maybe not than they should've but she wasn't ready. Ready. Could she get ready for—

The doors opened to a bustling bullpen. Not exactly what she expected. Maybe they didn't get all the way to the top, or—glass rooms around the far perimeter were definitely offices. Shit, there was Ward, and Troy. What were they doing there? Why wouldn't they be? God, this was a disaster already—

"Miss Mayden?"

Her head turned before her eyes followed. And there was Schmidt standing with security at the access turnstiles. Were they turnstiles? Glass access doors, there but… not there.

"We came to give Mr. Breckenridge our best," Celeste said.

Nessa raised the liquor bottle again.

"Okay," Schmidt said.

The other three security guys looked to him for direction. And, of course, he was staring at her. Oh, this wasn't going well.

"If you could pass these things along," she said, raising the bag, trying her best to tell him not to recognize her.

He had. Obviously, he had.

Damn, what was she supposed to—

The elevator behind them opened again, this time Ferguson joined them.

Oh, fuck. He'd know better but—

"Yes, we will…" Schmidt's voice diverted her attention back to the—

In the corner of her eye, a side door opened. Those glass walls were opaque and the rabble of men who emerged—no. Mouth open, she couldn't breathe because there was no way. Laughing, his head came around. The moment their eyes locked, his amusement died.

Oh, anger had never been so—

"Darroch!" Nessa exclaimed. "Wow, you look so good. We didn't think—"

"Get fucking well," she said throwing the gift bag over security toward him and spinning on the spot.

Thank God the elevator was still there. She marched in and hit the button. Repeatedly. Yes, she heard him calling her name, but she didn't give a shit.

Swiping angry tears from beneath her eyes, the numbers lit as she descended. Fucking idiot. Her, not him. Why would he—it didn't even matter. No.

Thundering outside, she got in the first cab waiting by the door and gave her address. She couldn't breathe through whatever churned inside her. Anger, upset, grief, anger, yep that one again.

When they got to her apartment, she paid the driver and rushed up the stairs. What would she do with this—she had to do something with this—damn, this was why people shouldn't be trusted.

THIRTY-NINE

PROMISE. Did that mean nothing?

Going through her front door and up the stairs, she tossed her purse toward the couch and went into the kitchen. She couldn't stay still. What was she supposed to do? Good luck to him. If he wanted to take risks with his life like some kind of thrill seeker—was one bout of unconsciousness not enough for him? How could his mother have let him out? She wouldn't. No way. That meant he'd snuck out, like some kind of creep—

"Cherry!"

"Don't you—" Storming to the balustrade above the stairs, she shouted as he ascended. "I am not your Cherry! I am not your anything."

"Yes, you are," he said, reaching her level. When he tried to touch her, she raised her arm out of his reach. "Partners, remember?"

"No," she said, backing up as he advanced. "Partners don't lie to each other. Partners don't make promises they have no intention of keeping."

"Baby, it wasn't like—"

"When I left this morning, what did I say?"

His nod acknowledged surrender. "You told me to stay in bed."

"No!" She pointed up at him when they stopped. "No, I *asked* you to stay in bed. I said I was worried, and I didn't want you taking any risks. Didn't I?"

"Yes."

"I asked you to stay in bed, only get out for the bathroom, that's it. You could read, watch TV, do whatever you wanted, but I asked you to stay in bed. And what did you say?"

"I said I would."

"You *promised* you would. Completely of your own volition, you promised! I asked if you would do that for me and you said, you said…" Still panting, her gusto winded her. "You said you would do anything for me. I asked you to stay in bed and you promised you would."

"I'm sorry, baby," he said, maneuvering in a few slow moves to put her back to the kitchen counter.

"You don't promise a woman something, anyone something, if you have no intention of following through."

His humoring smirk wasn't appreciated. "I had every intention of following through. I underestimated how boring it was to be in that bed without you."

"Don't flirt with me, don't charm and—you hurt me, Darroch."

His smile immediately dropped. "Bab—"

"You lied to me." Much as she tried to convey it, she wasn't sure he got it. "I can't be with a liar."

Suddenly, he got way more serious. "You are not ending this because I got out of bed."

"Lies, Darroch. I need a man who doesn't lie to me. Who takes partnership seriously." She exhaled and ran a hand through her hair. "What was I thinking? This isn't a partnership, I don't even have your phone number."

"I scared you; I shouldn't have been so insensitive to your concern."

"You shouldn't exploit someone else's feelings like that. It's like you don't even care."

"Of course I care," he said, landing his fists on the counter, looming over her. "You know how I feel about you, baby. This is forever and I'm going to make it happen, whatever it takes."

"How can I believe that when you just flagrantly disregard my—your mother has my phone number, by the way. Partners consult each other. If something happened or something changed, Alice could've got in touch with me. Did that even occur to you? Probably not, 'cause I'd bet you're hiding from her too. She would never let you—do you know how scared she was? We sat there together, holding your hand—"

"I know, baby."

"Your family—your brothers might think this is some joke, that it's okay to josh around like you're some badass out there picking fights with—"

"I get it," he murmured, bending his knees to come lower. "Okay? I get it. I'm sorry."

"I trusted you. How can I ever do that again?"

"Because whatever you want right now, it'll happen. You're the boss, okay? Strike one, I get it, I won't fuck up again."

She shook her head as it dipped. "You already have a mother, an incredible one."

"You're not my mother; you're my partner."

"We're not equals."

Curling his finger under her chin, he brought it up. "No, but I'll try my damndest to reach your league. Give a guy a chance."

Except she had given him a chance… hadn't she?

"You're mocking me."

"God, baby, don't ask me to lose you when I barely got a taste."

Scared. That's what he'd said. What was wrong with that? Nothing, except, that's what it was: fear.

"What if you hadn't woken up?" she asked. "If that guy hit you just a little harder… And if I'd come to your bed tonight and you were gone…"

"You're right. You're right, I didn't think about it like that. Truly, I'm sorry."

This time it was his gaze that drifted. The guy had been through so much and, if anything, the fear only made it more palpable. He had her heart. Her love. She'd fought it, but having known the world with him, she couldn't bear to think of it without him.

Good sense didn't care about heartstrings and Hollywood endings.

Taking his hand from the counter, she linked their fingers to lead him up the stairs to the loft bedroom. Putting his back to the bed, she let go.

"Baby—"

She touched his lips to quiet him. "This is your do over. Your one do over."

Gathering up his pullover hoodie, she needed his help to remove it because he was so much taller, same with his tee-shirt. Laying her hand over the center of his chest, she felt his heartbeat against it before leaning in and kissing his sternum.

"Belongs to you."

"What belongs to me?" she asked, caressing his torso with her cheek.

"Me. All of me. Everything."

"If that's true…" She reversed a few inches and pushed his hips downward until he sat on the end of the bed. She crouched in front of him. The wonder in his eyes might be hopeful, but she wasn't that over their spat yet. Instead, she slipped off his sneakers. "You'll stay in this bed with me until I release you."

"I can handle that." He planted his hands on the bed behind him. "It's the 'with you' part that's the clincher."

"You will do as you're told?"

"I will do as told."

"Socks on or off?" she asked, squeezing his ankles.

"Your call, Mistress."

"If they stay on, you'll only get so close to me."

"Off it is," he said, toeing off one then the other like a professional.

"Okay," she said, finding her laugh. "Bet you're happy your boys put that TV up for you now." She nodded at the nightstand. "The remote's on your side, pick whatever you want."

"Where are you going?" He caught her hips before she could retreat. "What happened to 'with you'?"

"I'm going to get my purse and something for us to drink." And to lock the front door. "Are you hungry?"

"Haven't had much time to go grocery shopping."

"I have pasta, some sauce, or I can go out foraging?"

"Not out, stay in, we can order something. Are you in the mood for something specific?"

She screwed up her face. "I don't want anything greasy."

"Okay, pick, any restaurant in the city."

Her fingers combed through his hair. Damn, he was like a work of art yet approachable; soft, with just the right amount of hard.

"That's not the way restaurants work," she said. "Typically people go to them."

"Either we take the bed with us, or we make it worth their while."

"Bribe them to deliver?"

"Whatever your heart desires, baby, I'll have it brought here with bells on."

"Okay," she said and pushed away with another laugh. "Go lie down, I'll get my phone and we can check out our options."

She grabbed what they needed. By the time she got back upstairs, Darroch had the TV on pause and the pillows stacked to keep them close.

"I went with action. We'll watch the panty melter next."

"You have a head injury, stop thinking about sex. Good thing I knew you before this or I might think it was a symptom." She tossed her phone to the bed beside him. "Will you call your mom and let her know you're alive? Please."

"Then she won't bother us later," he said and winked. "Good plan, Batman."

She pulled her blouse from her skirt and drew the zipper half down before taking the pins from her hair.

"Check she's okay with you staying here."

"Been a long time since I asked my mom's permission to have a sleepover."

"You have better facilities at the house." She paused. "Maybe you would be better at home. Though we are closer to the major hospitals here."

"Stop worrying, baby, and lose the clothes."

Her head turned toward the mirror and there was his reflection in the center at the top of the bed, eagerly awaiting… Why would a man like him—no, he didn't like her thinking that way.

"You've seen me in less plenty."

"Never gets old," he said, tapping her phone to fill the air with ringing.

"Do not tell her I'm getting undressed," she said and stalled to catch her skirt. "She'll think I brought you here for—"

"Sex? I'd be okay with that."

"Savanna?" Alice's voice stopped the ringing. "Oh, my dear, those boys—"

"It's me, Mom."

"Darroch?"

"I'm sorry. I didn't think about how my actions could upset everyone. There's no excuse. I was insensitive."

Alice sighed. "That girl is good for you, my sweet boy."

He smiled at her. "I know it."

"Did you make it up to her?"

"I plan to," he said. "We're staying at hers tonight."

"Unless you want him home," she interjected.

"Savanna, sweetheart," Alice said, "his home is wherever you are, and his home belongs to you. I trust you to look after each other." A second passed. "Darroch."

"Yes, Mom," he droned.

"I love you," Alice said.

The line disconnected.

She went to retrieve the phone and plugged it into the nightstand charger. "She does that with all of you, when she says your name like that…"

"It's her way of telling us to behave. She's had too many teenage boys in her life to ever forget what we're capable of."

"Why are you all boys?" she asked, sliding off her skirt and shirt to put both in the laundry hamper.

"We identify that way and all have dicks, honey," he said. "You know mine but will have to take my word for the other fifteen."

He picked up the covers for her as she crawled into the bed next to him. "Why did your parents choose boys?"

"Boys are harder to adopt." He tucked her in close and kissed her head. "Girls are more popular."

"Would you ever do it?"

"Do what? Adopt?"

"You make a lot of jokes about family and what you want…" Twisting her head, she looked up at him. "Is a family what you want?"

"We have a family. We are family."

"Your mom wants you to be happy. All of you. Sometimes I think…"

"What?" he prompted.

Her eyes met his again. "Sometimes it can feel like no matter what you do, it's not enough."

"You think she isn't doing enough?"

"I'm in absolute awe of her, I think she's the most incredible, inspiring person I've ever met."

"So you think you aren't doing enough? Cherry—"

"I get it. I don't know her reasons or their source, but motivation, the drive to give back… It's not about chasing a high, it's never being enough. I can never repay all that was given to me."

"You don't owe anyone anything," he said, combing his fingers through her hair.

"I feel like I do," she admitted, vulnerability quaking in her belly, quieting her voice. "Growing up, my mother would take whatever she could get, whether we needed it or not. Charities picked us up. The goodwill of others gave us a lifeline we wouldn't have survived without. There were times we needed it, after we were burglarized, and we had a fire… more than one fire." And she wasn't so sure they were all accidental. "But it didn't matter. If my mom saw an in, she'd take from those who might need it to have more for herself. Makes me sick to think about it now."

"That was your mom and you were a kid. You're a good person, an amazing person. But I have no problem with giving back or taking on other responsibilities. Whatever life we build together, Cherry, I will always be on your side. I'll always support you."

She couldn't probe and ask more about what he wanted from life when her own vision was still hazy. Alice Breckenridge showed what was possible. How did that inspiration shape her own future? Their future. Together. Together?

FORTY

MOVIE ONE FINISHED. Somewhere in the second movie, she lost the battle against sleep. Something roused her, a touch, a tingle, a special kind of zip between her thighs.

"Mmm," she murmured, moving with the caress of the mouth on her breasts, the hand sliding across her hip to— "Darroch." Instantly awake, she tossed back the covers to find him there, all innocence and arousal. "Darroch! What are you doing?"

"Give me a minute and it will all make sense."

"Get up here," she said, grabbing for him. "You are not doing that."

"You're awake now." Kissing her once, and twice, brushing his lips across hers, to her jaw, her throat. "Now I can really astound you."

"Stop," she said. All he did was peek up from her cleavage, darkness drew them closer. "You're not allowed to do that."

"I'm your guy."

"My head injury guy." Pushing him away, she got

him onto his back. "You're supposed to be resting, not… not resting."

"New rule…"

"Rule?"

"We spend every night together. Here, at my mom's, at a hotel, I don't care, but we sleep next to each other every night." He must've read the question in her expression. "Then we don't have to worry about each other or lose track. We'll always know where each other is. Give me your phone."

She rolled away to grab it. "It's probably too late to call your mom."

"Not calling Mom," he said, typing into her phone. After a second, another ring razed the air, but it died quickly. "Now you have my number."

"You called your phone from mine?" she asked, and he nodded while handing it back. "I didn't mean to pressure you into—"

"No, you're right. It's ridiculous that I don't have a way to contact you. We never would've fought earlier if I'd just called to tell you what was going on."

That was true.

When she settled, he was quick to pull her into his arms to start the kissing again. "You're still in recovery."

"I'm fine. The docs are overprotective."

Smart that he put it on the doctors and not her and Alice. "We're supposed to be watching a movie."

Though the room was dark, TV off.

"You fell asleep and I don't care about the movie."

"No?" she asked, hitching her playful chin. "What do you care about?"

"This woman in my bed," he said, rolling them over to put himself on top again. "It's never felt like this, Cherry. Tell me I'm crazy."

"Folie à deux."

"Damn, I hope so."

When he tried for a kiss, she laughed and ducked away. "Kissing isn't part of your rehab."

"Feels so good, it'll cure me."

"Your momma told you to behave."

"Yeah, and my woman ordered me to bed. I've got to keep her happy. No brothers here to interrupt."

"Okay," she said, laughing as he went left and right countering her avoidance of his kiss. "Lie down."

"Huh?"

"Lie on your back," she said, planting her hands on his shoulders and moving with him as he complied.

"I'm liking this," he said, running his hands up her back as she straddled him. "What comes next?" She unhooked her bra and tossed it away. "I'm the luckiest guy alive."

Her fingertips met his lips before she sank forward to replace them with her own. "Your luck is directly linked to your ability to control your smart mouth."

"You're not the first woman to tell me that," he said. Her switch of head angle provoked a different smile. "But you will be the last. My last. Ever."

Damn right, because she wasn't getting into this for the short-term. He'd been hurt. Alone. And she knew what that felt like. Despite their differences, something in them called to the other. What other explanation could there be for how they were drawn to each other. Fate, it could only be destiny.

Running her hands across his body, up, down, her fingers danced in each muscular valley. Why was it she got to feast on such an incredible guy?

Her exploration descended and descended. She wanted to be able to say her lips had touched every part of him, every pore and freckle. Learning him, earning him, would become her new hobby.

It helped that as she kissed and licked, her body rubbed on his, on a specific part of him pleased by her attention.

Her lips grazed his navel, traced the line of hair descending to his groin and—

A phone rang.

Startled, she rose, not much, enough to make him gasp.

"Ignore it, it'll stop."

"It might be important."

"It's too late for Mom."

"What if Tripp needs a ride?"

"He can afford a cab," he said, his hand landing on her head with a reluctant pressure that eased and returned like he wasn't quite sure what to do.

The ringing stopped and she relaxed against him. His cotton covered cock found sanctuary between her breasts.

When it seemed he'd stalled, uncertain what to do next, she rested her mouth on his torso.

"You don't disappoint, Mr. Breckenridge. Am I disappointing you?"

"Baby, you keep doing what you're doing and I'll blow my pride right here. You want to see it?"

"No," she whispered, surging up to kiss his lips. "I want to taste it."

His arms came around her fast, but she sat straight, thwarting his effort to take the lead.

"Baby—"

"If I'm not pleasing you, I'll stop," she teased, arching her back to grind against him. "You want me to stop?"

"I want you to marry me."

She kissed him again. "One thing at a time."

Their next kiss was longer, slower, more

learning? Sure. But it helped they were skin to skin and neither of their hands missed the opportunity to explore.

Sometime, whenever, eventually, his phone rang again.

Again, she broke their kiss. Their eyes questioned, begged, worried.

He exhaled, stroking her hair, tempting her mouth back to his. "Leave it."

"It could be important."

If they didn't understand the value of being present and available, they hadn't learned anything in recent days. He groaned as she wriggled from his arms and down the bed.

"More likely it's Caber or Ward messing with me."

"Messing with you how?"

"They've met my girlfriend," he said as she leaned off the end of the bed to snag his hoodie. "And they know we're doing this."

"How do they know we're doing this?"

"I boast." Her flat expression prompted his laugh. "I'm kidding, Cherry. I'm kidding. They know you're hot and we're spending the night together. If we weren't doing this, I'd have to hand back my Man Card."

The phone stopped ringing as she dug it from his pocket and turned to walk on her knees up the bed on her own side.

"Angie," she said, stopping halfway up. "Two missed calls from her and—" She frowned. "I thought you phoned your phone from mine. There's only one other missed call and it's from Anna."

"Babe, forget the phone," he said and tried to grab it, but she held it out of reach. "Come here."

"Just a second." Dialing her number, it was weird that the glitch erased her number and no one else's. Except when she pressed call, the phone on her nightstand lit up. And there it was on his screen again: Anna. He had her number saved in his phone under Anna for… the answer came in the two smaller pale gray letters beneath the name. LD. Lighting Darkness. Anna. Lighting Darkness and…

"Baby—"

"Oh my God," she whispered and threw the phone to her pillow as both hands flew to her mouth. "Oh my—"

"Let me explain."

"You're nineteen oh eight. You're… you're Jacob."

"Baby—"

"No, no, no—" Scrambling off the bed, her hands still stifled her words. "No, it can't—I can't—"

"Listen to me." Throwing back the covers, he was on his feet in an instant. "Baby, it wasn't a—"

Maybe he was still talking, saying words or… One man, two men, no, one man, listening to her secrets, asking her to bare her soul, telling her she was safe, and all the time—

She swept his clothes from the floor and dumped them on the bed. "Get out."

"No!" His adamance might mean something to him, but it changed nothing. "I'm sorry, Cherry—"

"Stop it!" Squeezing her eyes closed, she scrunched her hair in her fists at her temples. "No more. No more! God, I was an—the things I've said—the things I—" Words blocked her throat. There he was, at the side of her bed, standing there in his underwear like… "I don't know who you are."

"Yes, you do. You do."

When he tried to approach, she leaped back. "Please don't make me call the cops."

"Call them, I don't give a shit, I'm not going anywhere."

And they wouldn't make him. Who would law enforcement send? Someone who owed the Breckenridges? Someone close to the family with their own agenda? Safety didn't even exist in those paid to protect.

"Was it some kind of sick game? Another bet? Another deal?" This time as her eyes closed, her head went right. "Why did I ignore my instincts? God, I'm such a fucking fool. I deserve everything I get."

"You're not a fool and it was not a bet. Everything between us was real, *is* real—"

"Don't insult me," she growled, her jaw so tight her lips hardly moved. "You got your kicks, now get dressed, and get out of here."

"Cherry—"

"Get out! Get out! I don't want you here! I don't want you near me!" Tears burned hot like acid fueled by fury. Swiping up his hoodie, she threw it at him. "Take your shit!" Next was the tee-shirt, everything there, of his, his clothes, was thrown at him one after another. "Get out of my apartment! Out of my life! Take your money and your flirting and your goddamn—get out of my house, Breckenridge! Now!"

"Ba—"

"Everything! I want it gone! You gone! Take your cars and your drivers! Take your brothers! Your family! Your private dining! Get the fuck out of my life! I never want to see you again! Never want to see—"

"Savvy—"

"Do not call me that like you have any idea who I am," she spat.

Except he did. He knew more of her than most people alive. He'd been twice the presence, the real, the oral, the physical, he'd had two sides to her. Reluctant to corner herself, she had no choice because she had to get her phone from the bed. Then it was three digits, she typed and turned the phone to show him.

"Get out," she said again, showing certainty with her composure. "Or I will call the cops. I'll call the media. I'll call the goddamn—"

But no, she wouldn't wait for him to acquiesce. His access, his money, it gave him rights and privileges not afforded to people like her. Opening her nightstand, she grabbed sweats to pull them on.

"What are you doing?"

"You don't have to go anywhere, I get it, your power gives you—" She snatched a tee-shirt from a drawer. After putting it on, she picked up her purse from the floor. "I'll never have access or freedom in the way a Breckenridge—"

"This is your place." Was it really? It didn't feel that way. When she stood, he opened his hands. "Okay, wait, I'll go." And that would be it. Over. "I get you need time to process this." Was he really going to talk to her like that? Snagging a hair tie from the lamp, she put her hair up. "No…" He started to dress. "I'm getting changed, I'm leaving. Baby, I need you to understand, to know what I—"

"I don't have to do anything," she said, numb as she went to the stairs. "Get dressed and get out. Take the car, Ferguson, everything, I don't want anything Breckenridge anywhere near me."

And, God, she already owed them so much. Descending the stairs, she went through the door to the left, the bathroom, and locked the door. She couldn't lose it, wouldn't lose it, not until he was gone, until it was over. Over. They'd been promising each other forever not so long ago. Now it was… over. Resting against the vanity, she listened to his movement above, down the stairs.

Eyes closed again, breath held, she waited.

"I love you, Savanna Mayden," his solemn voice

came from the other side of the door. "Believe it or don't, but I never meant to hurt you. I wanted you and I couldn't give you up. I love you, Cherry." Silence. Still, she didn't breathe. "You know how to find me."

Not that she would need to. His footsteps faded and the front door closed. Her knees buckled and she went to the floor with a wail. Over. Forever. Oh, God, what was left of her this time?

FORTY-ONE

NOTHING BRECKENRIDGE MEANT no job. God, she wouldn't make rent if she didn't find something, anything, soon.

Online, she scrolled through listings, sending her resume to anything even remotely suitable. Something had to work eventually. Fate hadn't been her friend, what was karma going to say? Something in her favor, hopefully, maybe. Life didn't work that way. Twenty-five years to learn that lesson. That was just fucking embarrassing.

Any time her phone rang, she grabbed it with hope some employer was getting back to her. Nothing yet.

Celeste, Yvette, Nessa, all of them called, but she hadn't answered. Her resignation email was her final word, should be her final word. There was no way to explain it to them. She'd never get through the tale anyway, her shame was beyond stupidity.

Darroch Breckenridge? Any Breckenridge? What

a complete idiot. That wasn't her life. She'd known that and been seduced by… Well, he'd played it great, or she'd heard what she wanted to, felt what she wanted… Another lesson it took twenty-five years to learn. If something was too good to be true…

And she couldn't even unload on anyone. Get out all the tension and stupidity and emotion. Yvette had enough on her plate, and what would she say anyway? How could she explain her reasons without admitting her shame? Her association with Darroch had been private. What would be the point of admitting it now it was over?

No, she wouldn't dwell on it. Over meant over. New chapter time. Time for something completely different.

Someone knocked on the front door. Who'd be visiting? Doubt a job just sauntered up to say hello and offer itself to her. If only.

She went down the stairs and checked the peephole. Darroch wouldn't—

She stepped back.

Was that really?

No.

Sliding back one lock while turning the other, belief didn't kick in even with her eyes on the guest.

"Roxanna Kyst?"

The woman held two bottles aloft. "I brought wine."

Stepping aside when the woman strode on in, the guy on the threshold, the tall, built, gorgeous man on her threshold, took it upon himself to lean in and close the door.

"How bad is it?" Roxie called from upstairs. "Do we need glasses or are we chugging straight from the bottle? I have Astrid on standby if we need anything stronger."

Getting with it, she hurried up the stairs. Roxie

had already kicked off her shoes and taken her hair down.

The corkscrew on the couch next to her looked like hers. Had Roxie…?

"So here's the thing about Tripp Breckenridge…" Roxie twisted the corkscrew in. "He's the catch-all brother. The one everyone else goes to with their oopsies." She paused to show her a palm. "And that is not to minimize what happened. God, no. No way." Straining, she held the bottle between her thighs and pulled at the impaled corkscrew. Except the cork stayed stuck. "Ballard!"

The scream was so loud, she ducked like it had physical mass. The downstairs door opened and the scowling door-closer came stomping up. Roxie, without seeing her rise, scampered across the room to meet him at the top.

"I swear to fucking God, Little Rox," he murmured not so under his breath.

In a single pull, he freed the cork. Roxie grabbed his neck in one hand and the wine in the other, she pulled him down for a cheek kiss, then waved him away.

"I keep him on the reservation," Roxie sang to Ballard as he glared to stamp on out and slam the door. "Makes his job easier, Ballard's job. See once upon a time…" In a twirl, Roxie snagged her arm in hers to link them and continue to the couch. "Once upon a time, my guy could be all kinds of grumpy and erratic. He'd get stressed and need to disappear or be reckless with his safety."

Arms still looped together, Roxie dropped to the couch, forcing her to sit too.

Her guy? "Zairn?"

Roxie tilted the bottle toward her. "Mm hmm."

"I'll get glasses."

As much as to buy time than anything else. Leaping up, she hurried to the kitchen for a breather.

If Roxie knew, did everyone know? If they did, it would be from Darroch's tongue, not hers. Who would share something so shameful? Someone proud of their achievement, that's who.

So much for not a dare or a bet. Damn, talk about misjudging someone, or in this case, a whole family.

"Do you need some help?" Roxie called, reminding her she wasn't alone.

"No, I'm good."

Just lost in her own kitchen.

"So when I got with my guy…" Roxie's raised voice carried like they were next to each other. "He told the whole wide world, on international television, he was in love with me, and we were going to be together forever."

Joining her guest, she sat down. Roxie poured into the glasses she held.

"That was romantic."

Roxie stopped pouring. "Before me. He told international television before he told me. Before we ever talked about being together, publicly, for real."

Okay, so, wow.

"Were you mad?"

"Oh, I lost the plot. And I lost him."

She sighed. "But you figured it out, got each other back."

"All relationships go through turmoil."

"You heard something about Darroch and me?"

"Yes."

That was it? No elaboration.

"We didn't have a squabble or disagree on whose turn it was to do a random chore. What he did…? It's unforgivable."

"Nothing is unforgiveable, forgiveness is a choice. The big kicker is malice. See I got so lost in rage that I didn't see Z's admission for what it was. He didn't do it to hurt me, he did it because he couldn't keep it in. He did it because he believed it. He did it because he needed me in his life. There was no malice, he was just… that in love with me."

"Is that why you're here?" she asked, prickling a little. "To tell me to forgive? What does it matter anyway? I'm not going to the press and I already quit my job. The Breckenridges won't ever hear from me again."

"Is that what you want?" Roxie put the wine bottle on the coffee table and curled her legs up beside her as she leaned against the couch arm. "To never hear from them again?"

"I appreciate you coming and…" Setting the glass on the table, she slid to the front of the couch. "I'm not in the mood to talk about it."

"Okay, so we'll talk about something else." Smiling, Roxie sipped her wine and propped an elbow on the back of the couch, clearly not planning to go anywhere. "Want to hear how Zairn and I reconnected after the tour?

"I don't—"

"It's a sex story…" Not tempting. "Want to hear how Jane and I went on a secret mission in CollCom? Disguises and everything, real comedy caper."

That was… "No, thank you. I'd prefer to be alone."

"I could tell you how Lilya and her husband met." Roxie still smiled. "He was naked at the time. At work." Okay, that was… naked? "Want to hear how Zairn set up my secret birthday party?"

She exhaled. "Roxie, I appreciate what you—"

"Maybe you don't want to hear the good stuff. I could tell you how I got arrested, the first and the second time."

"You were arrested twice?"

Roxie's fingers moved in a midair wave. "Both were in LA, I should be safe on this coast."

"What were you arrested for?"

"Inciting a riot, I think," Roxie said. "The first time. The next time was breaking and entering… or maybe stalking. I don't know, Zairn took care of the details."

"He bailed you out?"

"Yep, and I wasn't even sleeping with him the first time. We weren't so much bailed as released, I suppose. His people made the charges go away, for all of us. Which is something in LA because Ackley, the DA, hates him."

"Hates Zairn? Why does he hate him?"

Now Roxie wasn't so gleeful. "Because Ackley thinks my guy is a murderer." Okay and now… her mouth stayed a little open and she just breathed. What the…? A murderer. "He's not, by the way, and it upsets me when people think, or imply, otherwise."

Yeah, 'cause would Roxie be with him if he was capable of… Eyes still on Roxie, her hand found the glass and she raised it to her lips as she folded her own legs onto the couch at her side.

"Is that why you can't be in LA?" she asked.

"I can be in LA. I'm in LA all the time."

"Alice said you had someone working for Huddle Hope in California. Isn't that because you can't be there?"

"Roux's in California. She's the juggernaut behind Huddle Hope, it's completely her baby, she deals with operations and executive decisions. I work more in recruitment and motivation."

"It's an amazing concept."

"We have people all over. I'll try to get everyone together somewhere soon. I know there's video calls, but it's not the same. That from someone who spends long stretches of time celibate because her guy thinks it's okay to run his business in other countries." The irritation was fake, Roxie's smile soon betrayed that. "We're becoming kind of a crowd. We have no assholes, not on the female side of the equation, I can't vouch for all the men. You'll get along with everyone."

"Oh, I—I can't be a part of… anything."

"Why not?"

The question seemed sincere.

"Ah, well, because I… I don't know what you know, I guess you know something… But I'm no longer affiliated with the Breckenridges."

Didn't that sound sterile.

"Uh huh." Roxie was completely understanding yet blank in genuine confusion. "What does that have to do with anything? You think we were hiring you because you were boning the Breckenridge boy?"

"Oh, I wa—"

"Alice trusts you, so I trust you. And you haven't done anything to change my opinion on that. I've heard about the work you do, from various sources. You have passion and determination; qualities that can't be taught. We need someone who wants to help people. Someone with compassion, understanding—"

"Roxie, I haven't talked to Alice…"

"Since you and Darroch broke up?"

"We didn't—we were never—"

"Yes, you were," Roxie said, finding her smile again. "Maybe I should finish what I was saying when I came in."

"Finish?"

"Tripp Breckenridge is the catch-all brother. If anyone messes up, embarrasses themselves, does anything horrendous, they go to him. Tripp has never judged anyone in his life. Anyone can say anything to him, he's never been repulsed or ashamed of anyone.

He's their priest, you know? He's everyone's priest, not just his brothers'."

"Darroch talked to him?"

"I don't know, I guess so."

"Guess?"

"Tripp wasn't explicit, he just hinted it might not be a bad idea to check in with you. That there may be waves in need of calming." Wasn't like he could do it himself. His brother would have his loyalty, as he should. "So this is me… calming." Her lips quirked higher. "Not something I'm famed for."

"I didn't spend much time with Tripp."

"You don't have to spend a lot of time with him for him to care about you. Actually, I'm not sure he has to spend time with anyone to care about them. He and I met in the Ruby Room, Crimson, right here in New York. He's our playboy-in-residence, 'cept the funny thing about him is…" Roxie touched the surface of her drink with a fingertip. "In his frivolity, there's ferocity. Tripp doesn't go home with the hottest girl in the room to show off to his buddies. He always has his reasons. Just like he had his reasons for sending me here." She paused, giving that a second to filter in. "You and Darroch were together?"

She couldn't talk to any of her friends. Roxie might not be a neutral party, but she was there… with wine.

She gulped the rest of the glass, then let the glass sag to her thigh. "We flirted, messed around, we were… something. I thought we were something."

"And now you're through?" Roxie asked. She nodded in response, unable to look the woman in the eye. "Do you want to be through?"

"With the man I thought he was? No. Shame that's not who he is."

"How do you know? He fucked up? What did he

do? Screw around?"

"No! God, Darroch would never—" What the hell did she know? Not the truth of him. "I thought he was someone else."

"Guys get weird when they're falling in love. Believe me, I've seen it in many crazy forms. Sometimes we act crazy too and—"

"No, I don't mean…" Blowing out her shame, she had to do it or give up. "How are you at keeping secrets?"

"I'm the goddamn Vatican. Tripp might be a priest, I'm his Holy Father. Wooo, the things I know about that man."

Roxie wouldn't want to hurt the Breckenridges if Tripp was one of her best friends. And it wasn't like the woman could hurt her, she'd quit her job, which entailed cutting off friendships. Maybe Roxie could be her one last thread of sanity. And, it turned out, a job had just sauntered up to say hello and offer itself to her.

FORTY-TWO

ROXIE WAS A lifeline. She hadn't completely agreed to join Huddle Hope, but hadn't discarded it as an option either. Who was she kidding? If it wasn't for Roxie's Breckenridge connection, she'd have signed on already.

Over the last three days, her newest friend had called six times. Other callers, she ignored. Roxie? She picked up. If the stories were even half true, Roxanna Kyst knew no limits. The woman was not about hollow threats. There was something about her, an openness, a welcomeness. She'd challenge anyone to dislike or discourage Roxie Kyst.

At least she was getting out now. Groceries, pharmacist, boring errands, but it was better than moping around the apartment. Walking down the sidewalk, she found herself checking the faces that passed by. No Breckenridges. Post-contact with that family, their tentacles slunk into every area of her life, her consciousness.

With a bag on her hip, another around her wrist, she fumbled in her purse to retrieve her ringing phone.

Good, she needed a distraction.

"Hello?"

"Want to come to the club tonight?"

"Roxie," she said and smiled. "You ask me that every day."

"Eventually, you'll say yes. Everyone does in the end. Take a break from job surfing and type my guy's name into Huddle Hunt. That's Z-A-I-R-N."

She laughed. "And why am I putting your guy's name into a search engine?"

"He's hot. Really, smokin' hot."

Life got lighter with this woman's support. "And you're charging for viewings?"

"Oh, I would if I could, believe me, I would. Unfortunately, he believes in flashing it all over the place, wrecking my chances of exploiting his beauty. Lucky for you, it's more of a sucker punch in the flesh. You've got to see him up close."

And she might consider it, except… "Tripp lives in the building."

"Unofficially. And he's usually all for mending a woman's broken heart with his spunk. Unfortunately, that doesn't extend to his brother's girls… I think. I've never seen verifiable evidence either way. If there was an exception to that rule, it would be Brant… if he could ever get a girl."

"I don't want to crash his party. I've cut ties with everything Breckenridge."

"Until you come home to Huddle. Come on, honey!" Roxie whined. "Get back on the horse."

"Horse?"

"Yeah, I'll find you one, don't worry, Toria's vetted a lot of eligible men since she moved here. We'll start you off gentle, find you a real nice steed to ride."

The last thing she could think about was men or relationships.

"I'm swearing off dating." Indefinitely. "I don't have the energy."

"So we'll have a girls' night. Freya would love to get to know you better. At the very least, you should come to dinner."

"Dinner?"

"It's Thanksgiving, honey. You promised you'd come over on Thanksgiving."

She paused, scrutinizing the middle distance. "I did? Wait, it's Thanksgiving?"

"Yeah, you didn't notice the hullabaloo? Try going a few blocks over, there's a big clue there."

"I didn't even…" She hadn't even known what day it was. "Wow."

"Yeah, men can do that to us," Roxie said. "I've already sent a car. If you don't get in it and come here, I'm bringing everyone to your place. There's like fifty people here, do you cater? Should we bring chairs?"

Oh, God. "No, okay, I'll come over, except—"

"Tripp's at Breckenridge House. Think Alice would let her boys out of eating with the family?"

No, and it was actually reassuring to know that. "Okay, let me get changed."

"Yay! Okay, Fernando says you have no allergies, right?"

"No allergies, but… aren't you at—"

"Crimson Palace? Yes, but please, honey, you think I stuffed the turkey? With these nails? That would be a helluva place to lose my ruby. Come have some fun, honey. Anything goes here. I was drunk before noon, I'm not even sure which of the guys roaming around here I woke up with this morning… or which one I'll go to bed with."

She laughed. "Rox—"

"Dinner's in an hour."

The line went dead and her heart sped up. Less

than a block from her place, she hurried to get inside. Her keys didn't want to liberate themselves from—with another yank, she freed them from her purse just a few feet from her front door. The bag at her wrist cut into her, she hooked it over the handle to—the door opened.

She hadn't even put her key in the lock and it gave under the weight of the bag. Weird, but—no, she sighed. Just classic her since she'd broken up with Darroch. God, she had to be more careful. What had he done to her brain that she'd forget to lock a door? Her! Oh, her life was a mess.

Thank goodness everyone was more interested in giving thanks than raiding her apartment. Putting her groceries away, it was nice to see something in her empty fridge again. Okay, so it was salad and wine, but something was better than nothing. Damn, had that really been her Thanksgiving dinner?

She tossed her things in the hamper and jumped into the shower, taking Roxie's threat seriously. The car could arrive any minute and she didn't have time to prepare as well as usual. Thank goodness there were no men in the equation.

Doing her hair and makeup downstairs, she only had to go up to the loft bedroom—why were there panties on the floor? Had she been so harebrained when waking up that morning? Two pairs on the floor and another hanging out of the drawer.

Damn, she needed to get with it. Thank goodness for Roxie, maybe a friend would help her right the ship.

The phone rang just as she was checking her lipstick.

"Yeah?" she answered, rushing to grab her shoes. "Hello?" No one said anything; the line had to be bad. "I'll be downstairs in a minute."

Shoes, purse, and one last look. What was she

thinking? Going to dinner with billionaires? This wasn't her life, had she forgotten that lesson already?

The phone rang again. "Hello?"

"Hello, I'm your driver. I'm downstairs."

"Yeah, I just—" maybe he hadn't heard her the first time. "Okay, one second." Dinner. Locking eyes with herself in the closet mirror, she inhaled. "You can do this."

Forget Darroch and the past. Forget her job woes and her family troubles. This was a day to give thanks… even when she didn't have much to be thankful for.

FORTY-THREE

ROXIE DEFINITELY FELL into the category of "friend." That definition was nowhere near enough. She'd been nervous showing up to these fifty people Roxie referenced. As soon as she walked in, she was hit by the noise of people, music, and the scents of food and liquor.

This wasn't fifty people. It was way, way more than fifty people. Just as she was about to spin on her heels and leave, Ballard appeared from nowhere to take her arm and lead her to Roxie.

Yep, Roxie had given him special instructions to single her out. Not only did her friend welcome her like a long-lost sister, but she kept her close all night. Not just checking in every once in a while, Roxie was glued to her side. She spent more time with her than the woman did with her fiancé.

Her deliciously delectable fiancé who bled charisma over every person in a ten-foot radius. She'd been seated with Roxie and her friends, yep, they had their own table. Zairn wasn't at that table, no, the affianced sat separately. In fairness, with the number of people there, there were a bunch of tables. Seating her friends at one was a saving grace because Roxie spent a lot of the evening flitting from one table to another, while Zairn sat at the head of his table admiring her from afar. Honestly, every time she looked his way, he was transfixed by the woman wearing his ring.

The meal itself was over, but no one was in any hurry to depart. They seemed to have the entire floor for festivities. One corner had been used for dinner. While plenty of people still sat at their tables having wine and scotch refilled, others filtered through to the bar area.

"We have to get changed," Freya said from behind her. "Are you ready, Savanna?"

Twisting in the chair, she found Freya wasn't the only one waiting for her response. "Change into what? I don't have anything to—"

"We have Roxie's closet," Toria, another of Roxie's friends, said and grabbed her arm to pull her up.

"Where's your grandfather?" she asked Freya. "Won't he miss you?"

"Oh, Truman has a million friends through there. He knows I'm safe at Crimson. You've seen how he dotes on Roxie. He's probably already disinherited me in favor of her."

On a wave of women, she was carried to the elevator and up to a penthouse. Huge. Gorgeous. Full of light, from outside, from within, even the floor sparkled like it was diamond encrusted.

"Wow," she exhaled, awed by the view of the city spread out beneath them.

"Yeah," Toria said, snagging her arm. "Wait 'til you see the rest of it."

Their troupe rushed down a corridor and into a bedroom. Oh, hubba, the man in the center of the space fastening his watch under his open shirt was a better view than any stupid city. Hair damp, Zairn crooked a brow at Toria.

"What?" the woman asked on an innocent shrug. "I knew you were done."

"I'd apologize, Casanova, but give the woman a break." Whirling toward the voice, Roxie sat up slowly in a huge bed, clutching the sheet to her chest. Didn't take a genius to figure out what they'd interrupted. "Toria's been desperate to catch you in bed since before I even knew you existed."

Expecting they'd excuse themselves, she edged backwards. Toria caught her arm to hold her in place.

"Behave yourselves," Zairn said, going to his fiancée in, what had to be, their bed. Planting a fist on the mattress, he loomed over Roxie who draped one arm around his neck. "No shenanigans tonight, Empress."

"Reminding me of my responsibility to our brand? You know I'd never make that promise. I will do whatever the night calls for, in this, our beautiful home." Her smile brightened. "All part of the adventure of loving me, Scroogey."

"And this is the woman I chose to bear my children," he muttered, seemingly more to himself than anyone else.

"And I suck your cock. You always forget that one."

"Mm hmm."

He leaned in closer to kiss her and retreated, only to go back in for another kiss.

"Maybe we should just…" Freya caught her and Toria's hands to lead them at her flanks into the closet. "Oh, Roxanna."

Excitement got the better of Toria. "Time to suit up!"

"Why are we in here?" she asked. "Why are we changing clothes?"

"All part of the process," Toria said, pulling various dress bags from the end of the closet to hang them on a rail facing them. "Roxie's idea."

"What's Roxie's idea?" When Toria produced a bag with her name on, she was startled. "Why is there one for me?"

"Because you're Roxie's girl," Freya said, putting an arm around her to give her a hug. "She adopts us."

"One by one, we're doomed."

Toria unzipped each of the bags one at a time, inside each contained the same dress, short, beaded Bardot neckline. Gorgeous. And, yes, of course, every one was red, rather, crimson.

"Astrid, Merci, Rainie," Toria said, handing out dresses to the women.

"Oh my God," the younger one whispered.

Yep, her sentiment too.

"Everyone happy?" Roxie came in behind them, wearing an unbuttoned man's shirt that she held closed. "We have strapless bras, tit tape, chicken fillets, anything anyone needs. Panties are optional, wear them or don't, but it's at your own risk. Management takes no responsibility for damages, accidents, losses, or thefts of pussies or their contents."

"How does someone steal a pussy?" Astrid asked.

"I'll explain later, honey," Roxie said, winking at her friend. "Any questions? No. Good. Hair and makeup are setting up in the salon. Touch-ups or cleansing only, each one of you is beautiful, and extremely fuckable, in your own right. Anyone says otherwise, bring them to me."

As the others got into it, she backed up to Roxie. "I don't know if I should—"

"Of course you should," Roxie said, stroking her arm. "It's for charity. I've heard you can't say no to charity."

"Charity? How is it—"

"The car wash is tomorrow, honey. We'll be chatting it up all night with the big dogs hoarding bundles of cash, and many, many cars. Imagine how much we'll raise and all it takes is a little cleavage!"

"But I can't be on the—I'm not on the Breckenridge team, I quit and—"

"No, you're on the Crimson team," Roxie said, reaching past her for the dress Toria presented. "You're one of us, beautiful." Roxie kissed her cheek. "Let's get changed."

FORTY-FOUR

IT WASN'T ONLY the woman's affable nature that got her in the mood, the wine helped. As did the Gin and It drink freely handed out to the women. God, it felt like a million years ago.

"Savvy!"

That call was way too bright and cheery for a morning after the night before. Was that Roxie? How did the woman stay so fresh and bright all the time? Roxie was a professional partier. Yeah, that had been repeated to her several times the previous night.

She couldn't even remember getting to bed. But she had. Because she was in one. Sitting up, eyes barely open, the city view was very bright. Too bright. Oh, the city. That vista? This was Roxie's penthouse.

"Whose idea was a car wash event in November?" she mumbled to herself.

"Up, shower, I'll have your uniform brought in."

At a guess, the "uniform" would be crimson. Roxie sure was big on branding.

Shower. Right. Slithering out of bed, her head

dropped into a hand, why was it so heavy. It didn't help that even when she got to the shower she couldn't work the thing. There were spouts and sprays and rainfall and—who needed so many options in a shower? Even Darroch's wasn't so—no. No Breckenridges allowed in her brain.

Shit, last night, she said something about—oh, God, it was to Zairn Lomond. What were she and Zairn talking about on the couch? How had she even got on the couch? No one got on the couch. That startled her into a little more sense. Zairn… Zairn Lomond, damn, she'd poured her heart out to the world's number one playboy. Why the fuck would he care about…? Here was hoping the guy could keep a secret… or had amnesia.

Her bed was made by the time she got out of the shower with a towel wrapped around her. Who made her bed? When was—they must have staff for everything. Her head rotated on her neck, scanning for any hint someone may be watching. How did they know she was up?

And what was…? Red sneakers on the floor by the end of the bed drew her eye. Oh, God, the uniform… Was that a shirt dress? Small mercies and all that. At least it wasn't a… opening the shirt dress laid on her bed, the required bikini was beneath. Okay. She sighed. She shouldn't be surprised, the Breckenridge team had discussed the same thing. Breckenridge. She swallowed. Darroch could be there. Not on her team, so he wouldn't get too close, but it was the first time she'd be seeing him since…

"You better not be obsessing in there," Roxie called. "Are you decent?" The hostess didn't wait for her answer before swanning in. "Forget about him." She came over to hug her. "Start charging rent if he's taken up residence in your head."

"How did you know I was—"

"Because we all do it, honey," Roxie said, stroking her hair. "I obsess about Z all the time too."

"You don't obsess he'll blindside you, or humiliate you, or that you might accidentally meet his eye and melt."

"We won't let you melt. You're Team Crimson. Darroch won't be allowed near you. No fraternizing with the competition."

It was charity, not industry, but she appreciated Roxie's solidarity. The Breckenridge teams would be head-to-head, as always. Having that competition go on while not being a part of it would be a first. She'd never thought it mattered to her, now she wasn't so sure.

"How would we stop him? It's a warehouse site. I don't think we can bring security, people will need to drive in and out."

"Oh, we'll have security for sure. Ballard's been out half the night casing the joint. Our equipment arrived early, that takes a while to set up."

"Our… equipment?"

What equipment did they need for a car wash? Everything needed to wash cars was provided, soap, water, sponges…

"Mm hmm," Roxie said with a glint in her eye. "You'll see when we get there." She got a squeeze. "Get changed quickly, you have to meet the rest of our team."

"The rest of our—we're only supposed to have six."

"A maximum of six doing the washing at any one time. We're allowed to have as many people on our team as we want. We'll swap out."

"And everyone else will just—"

"Keep the party going and round up more cars."

"You don't like half measures, do you, Rox?"

"Never met one that could handle me," she said and kissed her cheek. "Now, come on, you need to have breakfast, this is going to be the hardest some of us have worked in a while." She leaned in. "Sex doesn't count as exercise, my personal trainer tells me. I think he only says it because if sex did count, what would Z and I need him for?"

On another laugh, Roxie faded out of the room. Uniform. Team. Okay. In the name of charity.

Getting changed didn't take long. And when she departed her bedroom, she didn't have to wonder where the party was at. The sound of laughter and conversation drew her to the gang.

And she wasn't the only one wearing the uniform, thank God. All the faces from last night welcomed her. She approached the food spread on the kitchen island and those perched on stools around it. No Zairn, but… She stopped. There was a man there, one, and it wasn't their host.

"Okay, no food fights," Roxie said, rushing over to take her wrist. "Tripp is under strict instructions not to talk to you." And the guy stood there, cup in hand, exuding more contrition than anger. His shirt was red, just like the women, only he had nothing on underneath. Well, shorts, he had red shorts. Guy could be a Baywatch extra… or superstar. "He's here for the female element. Plenty of women with cars too. And, you know, he bleeds Crimson."

Another reason she shouldn't be there. "I shouldn't—" A woman stepped from behind Tripp. Not that she'd been hiding, she put her cup on the counter and just stood there. "That's Sway Sheridan."

"Yes," Roxie said, raising her loose arm. "Yes, see! Oo! Sway Sheridan, right there." She leaned in. "You like Sway Sheridan? She selling it to you?"

"I didn't see her yesterday."

"Yeah, by design," Roxie said, guiding her over to the island. "She was in the building, just chose to keep it low-key." The hostess sighed. "You're a fucking Queen, Sway. Since before I even knew what a Crimson Queen was. You have more right to be here than most of the freeloaders we catered to yesterday, me included. More right than him, he's not a Queen."

As the only man there, Tripp raised his cup in thanks. "Not for lack of trying, Rox Out."

"I don't know where the Rox Out thing comes from," Freya said, licking her fingertips after selecting a croissant. "Should I know?"

"It came from London," Tripp said. "When she—"

"Ah!" Roxie held up a hand. "What happens in London, stays in London."

"Then you caught a break, Rox Out."

"Does Zairn know?"

"He has a way of knowing these things," Roxie said, grumpy like a petulant child. "I swear he drugs me and fucks it out of me."

"You know, there's a chance that's true."

"We're getting close to—"

"Yes," Roxie said to young Astrid. "Once a timekeeper, always a timekeeper. Thank God for you, Ast, where would we be without you? Late! That's where we'd be. Buses are waiting, has everyone eaten? Grab food, fill up those insulated java lifelines, it's time to go!"

Waving both hands, Roxie got everyone moving until catching something in the corner of her eye. The hostess immediately switched to go around to Sway.

So this was charity, Crimson style? She turned to follow the others, but someone snagged her wrist. Tripp.

"What do you want?" So much for not allowed to talk to her. "I didn't know you'd be here. If you think this is some scheme to force your brother—"

"I know better than to ask where your head's at," Tripp said.

Nice of him not to insult her intelligence by playing dumb. "Good, so what do you want?"

"A truce. A peace treaty," he said, setting his damn smile to smolder. "I'm friends with plenty of women, my exes, my brother's exes, I'm Switzerland in these things. Anyone can talk to me about anything—"

"Roxie told me." She relented a little. "You're a priest."

"*The* Priest, but whatever…"

Relaxing, his exhaled laugh loosened her muscles. "I won't pour my heart out to you."

"I'm here, if you need to," he said. "I don't repeat what's said or read between the lines." He shook his head, oddly stern. "I don't interpret, or game play, or meddle… like Roxie."

"Like Roxie what?" the woman called, coming over, Sway's hand in hers. "Hey! You're not supposed to talk to—"

"It's fine," she said on a sigh. What was she going to do? Run and hide from the guy all day? "We're fine."

"You really are good, Priest," Roxie said and made brief eye contact before leading Sway out, leaving her and Tripp alone.

"I listen, that's it. Confess your sins, I'll absolve you."

"Did you absolve Darroch?" With a smile, he touched a knuckle to the front of her chin and walked past. "Tripp?" Turning around, her eyes followed him to the threshold of the room. "You don't pass messages, okay, but…"

"Might make the exception when it comes to family."

"Thank you…" She crossed to join him. "Could you tell Buoy I'm sorry I haven't come over to color with him… please?"

"Buoy," he asked, his face lighting to a grin.

"Wow, kudos, that boy works fast."

"I don't want him to think I abandoned him. I miss him."

"But not Roch?" he asked. When she recoiled a fraction, he took her hand. "Sorry, I get it. I wouldn't date him either." She slid her hand from his. "Buoy…" He got in her way when she tried to pass. "He's never taken to anyone the way he did with you. Hasn't let some of his brothers that close."

"He's a good boy, I miss him."

"You don't have to, Mom would have you over anytime."

She winced. "It's too…"

"I get it. If you want me to bring the little guy over to your place…"

And she believed him. That was a huge concession from someone unrelated to her who owed her nothing.

"Make sure he knows he did nothing wrong."

"Sure thing."

Their hands joined again as they walked out together. Strange he should be such a comfort. Roxie was right. No animosity. No anger or judgment, he just listened, accepted, and went on with his day. Priest.

FORTY-FIVE

A BUS WAS RIGHT. There were so many bodies, talk about entourage. Roxie came with a bunch of others, some not in uniform. What a sight. The bold hostess stood at the front of their ride, taking control of the music and lighting—yes, there was music and lighting—pepping them up, answering questions, encouraging everyone to sing along. Geez, the woman must have some helluva pharmacy in her bathroom. How was she always on?

They drove into the concrete lot. The gates weren't open to the public yet, so they'd have a little time to set up. Others had the same idea. People milled around, some with purpose, some with little. Some wore uniforms, some had a more conservative or functional look.

The bus dropped them off behind the warehouse. Inside, each team's station was designated by temporary walls on three sides. The external wall of the warehouse ran behind them, leaving a small channel between for access and storage, backstage. From the front, cars were driven onto ramps and—

A broad black curtain at the head of the room fluttered. What were they hiding back there?

The lights died only to rise again with flashing colors and strobes scattering across the ceiling of the massive space. Shit, they couldn't be a permanent feature. Why would a cold warehouse need—maybe they had rave parties there or something.

"Whoa, someone called the professionals," Tripp said, slinging an arm around Roxie and crossing one ankle over the other. "You go full power, baby."

Tripp kissed her head and wandered off to join a woman from another team who'd been gesturing at him. Actually, there were more than a few. Even those not gesturing seemed mesmerized by him. Guy sure could work it. And he thought Buoy worked fast? Could there be a cat fight? Roxie scampered over to a group near the vast entrance and...

Darroch.

She hadn't seen him, not at first, but he was there, three stations down with the Breckenridge Intimates team. In a cruel twist, he spotted her just a second later. She wasn't ready, didn't know what to say. Should she say something? Go over there—she couldn't. Closing her eyes to erase the view, all she could do was pretend he wasn't there. No one in this building was an ex. No one in the building made her laugh and shared her bed and—damnit.

This was never going to work.

Leaving their bay, she went backstage to the water cooler. That was all she needed, a drink, a moment, she'd pull it together. It didn't matter that he was there, she'd ignore him, forget him.

Full of gusto, she whirled around and—someone body-blocked her.

"Jesus," she gasped as water sloshed out of the

cup onto both of them.

"Sorry!"

"Darroch!"

"I didn't mean to scare you."

"You can't just sneak up on—" She frowned. "What's that smell?"

"Smell?"

She groaned when she figured it out. "Oh, man, it's you, isn't it? Why do you have to do that? You always do that."

Unable to look at his face, she heard the smile in his words. "What do I do?"

"You can't ambush a woman just going about her life. It's not right. You know it's not right. I've told you before and—walking around, cornering us, attacking us with that masculine, over-powering—you have to stop. Just stop being…"

What? Hot? Not like he could do much about that and the scent. It was like wild, irresistible pheromones, did the guy release them on purpose? Either way, he didn't have to top it off with the deodorant and cologne and… himness.

"You're the only person on the planet with the cure."

And that swagger was enough to wake her up. "No." Sickness narrowed her throat. "I'm doing it again, how do I always…? What an idiot—"

"We need to talk. I need to talk. You need to listen, baby, I've—"

"No," she said, tossing the cup into the trash then backing off. "I don't want to talk, I'm over this—"

"I'm not over it." He caught her arm, and in her pulling it away, her back hit the wall. "I'll never be over it. I'll never be over saying I'm sorry, never be over making it up to you. Whatever it takes, I'm going to prove to you just how sorry I am."

"You can't because I won't believe it."

Except when his fingertips touched her waist, she could feel him getting closer and was struck immobile. It wasn't fear, she didn't fear him. The worst part was she missed him, missed this, being near to him, adored by him. What she'd thought was real, wasn't. What else didn't she know? If he could lie to her about something so huge, what else could he be lying about?

"I miss you, Cherry. I can't sleep, I can't eat, you're all I think about."

"What difference does it make if you're tired or hungry? We won't be together either way." Closing her eyes, she checked herself. "Not that we were ever together."

"Strike two, Cherry, I—"

"Strike two?" Anger landed her gaze on his. "Try three, four, and five too. No. Some things are unforgiveable." Forgiveness is a choice. Shit. Did Roxie have to be in her brain right then? "I don't forgive. I won't forget. No."

"I didn't mean to hurt you, it got away from me. On the phone you… I don't know what it was, I was connected to you, felt connected to you—"

"Ah!" She raised a hand. "I don't want excuses." And that was exactly what he was dealing. "I don't want your words."

"Actions," he said. "You want me to act?"

Closing her eyes didn't help her anxiety. "No!"

"What do you need me to do? Name it and it's done."

"I don't want anything from you, nothing from you. I want you to leave me alone, that's what I want."

"Roch."

His brother's voice turned him. "We're fine, Tripp."

"You guys want to see this."

Just as he retreated, a blast of sound captured them.

"Everyone ready to make some cash?" a woman hollered, a woman with a microphone.

They rounded to the Crimson station just as the huge black curtain fell and music blasted loud.

"Oh my God," she said, glancing around at the exuberant faces fixated on— "That's Kari-K."

"No one we can't reach," Tripp said, extending an arm to offer her a hand. "You're on the Crimson team. Quit harassing our team, Roch, go back to your own."

He didn't interpret, game play, or meddle… but Tripp was still his mother's son. Though Darroch's jaw didn't appreciate his brother refereeing, she did.

Taking Tripp's hand, she rounded Darroch to let herself be led to the others admiring Kari-K blasting out one of her classic tracks.

"How did we get—how do we know Kari-K?"

Tripp looped an arm around her to prop himself against her. "There's no one we can't get."

"Isn't this costing a fortune?"

"Everything you see is from Crimson, or it's been donated, including time." He kissed the top of her head. The first stream of cars appeared. "Time to get to work."

FORTY-SIX

FOR A MINUTE there, she couldn't break free. Powerful as Roxie was, it wasn't coercion. No, somewhere mid-evening at the car wash, she'd admitted the truth to herself. Being part of Crimson, Roxie's entourage, surrounded by safety, she didn't have to think about real life, about her real troubles. The escape might be available, but taking it, keeping it too long, she'd risk losing her confidence. More of her confidence.

Roxie invited her back to Crimson Palace, but she declined. The woman said she wasn't done with the persuading, which was her cue to sneak away. Darroch was somewhere in the building and things were winding down…

Although it felt like an age since she'd been in her own place, getting there was welcome. She stripped off, got in the shower, and made plans.

A job, that's what she needed. To stop relying on others to bail her out. She couldn't lean on Roxie, couldn't lean on the Breckenridges. The city was expensive. Too expensive for her limited savings. If she didn't get a job soon—Huddle Hope was an option. Tripp proved he wouldn't pressure her, in fact, he'd saved her from his brother, a couple of times.

Was that leaning? How long would it take her to get over Darroch? No, she was over him, how long would it take him to get over her? Except that was stupid. He couldn't be into her, not really, so why was he still trying to talk to her?

Wine. Yes. She turned off the shower, stepped out to wrap a towel around her and went into the kitchen for—the fridge was open. Wide open.

Pausing, she glanced around. Had she been so out of it that she hadn't noticed that on coming in? Damnit. Just when she couldn't afford extra utilities, she went and blasted the shit out of the electricity. Maybe she could offer her services as a screw up. Surely someone would get a laugh out of her wrecking everything good in her life.

Snatching the wine, the cold glass slipped a little in her hand, but she caught it. No damn way she'd lose the only friend she needed that night. Grabbing the corkscrew, she didn't bother with a glass. No, this was a straight from the bottle night.

The wine got her attention before the blow-dryer, during the blow-dry, and after. Shit, if she kept going this way, she'd pass out. Food. That would be smart. Something to soak up the alcohol.

Okay, so the only sustenance in the apartment was the salad she bought yesterday. Takeout was too much effort. Maybe there was some dressing left… somewhere. Though if the fridge had been open the whole time she'd been out, would the salad still be good? The wine was cold, icy cold, if it stayed that cold in the open door—

She swung it open and—salad wasn't the only thing in there. A small box on the middle shelf was open to display a single chocolate. Okay, that wasn't something she'd ever...

Peeking around the door, she checked out the room. No one. Slamming the fridge again, she went to the front door and... locked. If she'd locked the door and—did she miss the gift on getting the wine? Maybe, it was in the door, and she—only Darroch had a key.

Stomping upstairs again, she went back to her wine in the bedroom. Now she wasn't hungry, no, she was angry. What the hell gave him the right to sneak into her home? Maybe it hadn't been him. No. He could've sent anyone, paid anyone to—that was beyond crossing the line. So far beyond that there weren't words to describe it.

Her phone rang.

Good.

Snatching it up, she anticipated who it would be. "What?" she snapped. "You better not think that—I can't believe you—what do you have to say for yourself?"

Nothing. No apology. No explanation. Just breathing. Slow, steady but deep, inhales followed by exhales prickled every hair on her body.

Checking the screen, expecting his name, all she read was "unknown."

"Who is this?" she asked to no reply. "Answer me!"

Something on the line clicked, a few seconds passed, and then the drone of disconnection.

Was she losing her mind?

Startled when the phone rang again, the sight of "unknown" prompted her to switch the thing off.

Whatever this was, whoever it was, the walls were closing in. She had to get out of there.

FORTY-SEVEN

THE MOTEL MIGHT be cheap, it might be far from home, but what was home anyway? Running out of her apartment the way she had the previous day was maybe an overreaction. Maybe. Except she still hadn't turned her phone back on.

One thing the trip showed her was life beyond her usual stomping ground. Maybe it was time to move. Where would she go? Where did she want to go?

That was the predominant thought on her walk around the block. Clearing out her head, thinking of the future, and… hmm, she was hungry. She hadn't eaten since Roxie's.

Heading to the motel front desk, she glanced around as she approached the counter.

A woman, late-teens-ish, sat in a chair with her feet up on the unit holding the TV. It was on, but she was lost in the cellphone she held.

"Anywhere around here do takeout?"

The woman leaned back to pick up a menu and held it up without taking her eyes from the screen.

"Thank you."

"You seven?"

"Am I...? Yes, room seven."

"Got a message."

"A message?" Her hands went to the counter again. "For me? *I* have a message?" No one knew she was there; she hadn't spoken to a soul since fleeing. "From who?"

"Some guy." The receptionist tore a sheet from a nearby pad. "Here."

The menu was discarded in lieu of the new slip.

Know where you are. Still watching. We'll be together soon.

She read it once and twice and still it didn't make sense. It did but she couldn't understand what it meant.

"That's it? Who was he? Did he leave a name or a number? What did he sound like? Did he have an accent?"

The clerk just slouched in her chair and returned to scrolling through her phone. "Nope. He sounded like a guy, just a guy."

Heart racing, her mouth opened to allow in short pants. Her throat got smaller, tighter. This couldn't be, how could this be happening? The only vestige of hope that remained seemed unlikely. It couldn't possibly be... God, she had to hold onto something.

Rushing away from the office, her hands shook as she turned the room key and closed the door behind her. She flung the paper to the bed and scrambled over to the nightstand to pull her purse from the bottom drawer.

She yanked out her phone and turned it on. God, it seemed to take an age to show its shining, too bright, symbol of life. Panic reigned when it asked for her passcode, she fumbled the first attempt and took a deep breath before the second. The last thing she needed was to lock herself out.

Patience. Easy. Breathe. The home screen flashed for less than a second, she'd already stabbed the call button and scrolled to his number. Clutching the device in both hands, she held it tight to the side of her face, pressing herself against the side of the mattress. She hadn't even got up off the floor.

It rang once. Twice.

Then he answered, "Cherry?"

"Say it was you," she said so quickly the words were almost one syllable. "Please tell me it was you. Breckenridge men don't give up. Just say it was you, Gentleman, please, tell me it was you, and it will be okay again. I'll be okay again."

"Slow down," he said with a depth of concern. "Where are you? What happened?"

"At the apartment, the fridge, that was you," she said, "and upstairs. The drawer, the underwear. The chocolate. The call." Suddenly, everything was suspicious. The oxygen thinned as the air got thicker. Why couldn't she draw in breath? Why couldn't she fill her lungs? "That was all you, right? Tell me it was you. I'll believe you. You have a key. You're the only one with a key. Please. Please, Darroch. Tell me it was you."

Yet her heart betrayed the opposite.

"Something happened at the apartment?" he murmured her words without recognition. "Baby, where are you?"

His alarm freed the tears from her lashes. "A motel in White Plains."

"Share your location to this phone. We have a chopper on permanent standby. I'm coming to you."

"What? But I—"

"I'm on my way. Wherever you are, just stay

there. Lock the door, the windows, close the curtains. Don't open the door to anyone but me. No one, baby."

"I—" she stuttered. "Okay." At least with a plan, she had a focus. "I don't know how I—"

"I'll help you. It's okay. Can you share your location?"

"I don't know how to—"

"We'll do it together."

He talked her through the steps to give him her location. When it was done, he said he'd be there soon, then silence.

"Darroch?"

He was gone.

She was alone.

God, she better be alone.

Phone still clutched to the side of her head, the nook between the nightstand and the bed seems safer than anywhere else.

He hadn't said it was him. He hadn't said it wasn't.

Why would he do those things? Hadn't she considered and discounted his involvement with each individual event? Why had she called him? What a stupid, stupid—ridiculous, pathetic. Why hadn't she called the cops? Why hadn't she packed her stuff and gone somewhere else?

Because fleeing hadn't worked when her apartment was burglarized. She'd moved apartment and the cops hadn't found a perpetrator. She hadn't called them with the fridge and the underwear because it seemed ridiculous.

What would she do now? Tell them some random person left a message at the front desk for her? Oh, scary. Wasn't it just as possible that the young, not-exactly-engaged, clerk made a mistake and gave the message to the wrong room?

The creepy message.

"We'll be together soon."

He must have said it in a positive way. If being happy or cheery was possible with words like that. No one would hear something like that, engaged or not, and not immediately think creepy. Then again, the world took all kinds of people, and these days, sometimes, everyone was creepy.

What was she doing? Obsessing. Obsessing wasn't healthy… or helpful.

Loosening her hands, the phone fell to the floor. She covered her eyes and pulled her knees up closer to her chest as she twisted to rest her back against the bed. Why was this happening? She didn't understand. What made sense?

It would be better.

Would it be better?

Scrambling across the floor, Darroch could be anywhere, she hadn't even asked. It could take hours for him to get there.

God, please don't take hours.

She yanked open the mini bar and grabbed a handful of shooters. Darroch. The liquid would pass the time until he got there. If nothing else, alcohol should numb the pain, the fear, the terror.

Courage had to come from somewhere. Where were her wits? Her senses? He'd be there soon. He wouldn't let her down. She whispered reassurances to herself, unscrewing the cap and sealing her mouth around the top while tipping her head all the way back, soon couldn't come quick enough.

When the screech of brakes startled her around, she was still on the floor. A few shooters in. Maybe a few too many. How long had it been? A minute? An hour? Two? Could that be him? Oh, God, please—

Hammering on the door quickly answered that

question.

"Cherry?" he called.

She pounced to a crouch, scrambling a few feet on her hands and knees before rising in the phases of evolution barely coming upright before her hand found the key.

In the next second, she was trapped against him, his strong arms shielded her from every danger.

"Darroch—"

"I've got you, baby." Seizing one fistful of hair at her crown, he gritted her teeth against her head. Kissing her hard once and twice in the same spot, he locked his other arm around her shoulder blades steadying her. "You're okay, baby, I got you." Hand still tangled in her hair, he kept her close. "I'm here, I got you."

Eyes closed, when he crushed her temple against his body, she didn't care where or what was happening.

"Thank you for coming," she said on a series of sobs.

"I'm here. I've got you. I've always got you."

Whispering his reassurances into her, he let her cry and curl her fingers into the fabric of his shirt so tight she probably damaged it.

She'd never needed anything more than him right there, right then.

"Oh, my dear," Alice's voice was the first thing to open her eyes.

Not that she moved an inch.

"She's okay, Mom," Darroch said, still holding her tight, maybe tighter. "I've got her."

"Do we have a description?" That was a male voice, Breckenridge male. "We need to know what the hell went on."

"Give her a minute, would you? What's the damn hurry?"

That was another woman's voice. One that

forced her to twist, though her fingers stayed coiled tight: Rox.

The cohort of others came into view. Roxie and Alice weren't their only audience. Caber, Axon, Acre, the corkscrew guy Roxie brought to her apartment.

"You—all of you—"

"Forget about them." Darroch planted a hand on either side of her head and brought her eyes to his. "Tell me what happened. Why are you here? The fridge? The underwear? Talk to me."

"It was stupid. I thought it was stupid. It wasn't anything. I was just freaked out at being in the apartment by myself. I told myself I made it up… In the hallway, when the front door was open—

"You went into the apartment when the door was open?"

"Unlocked. I didn't know it was—"

"Why put yourself in danger like that?"

"What choice did I have?" she asked. "It wasn't danger. I didn't think it could be danger. Why would it be danger for someone like me?"

"You should've called me."

"It was pathetic."

"Not if it brought you out here. You were scared enough to leave the city."

"I just needed a few days. I thought I would calm down. My head's been such a mess. I don't know what I thought—"

"Someone's tracking her," a Breckenridge said.

"That's helpful, Acre. Yeah, thanks, freak her out even more."

"Tracking her?" Darroch said, searching her.

"Something scared her today," Acre continued. "That's why she called. These things happened at her apartment, and she came out here. Something else happened here that scared her, something bigger. That's why she called you."

Her fear was real, but in this room of such strong, resilient people it was feeble to let something like this triumph over her. She should've handled it alone.

"It's nothing." She tried to pull his hands from her face. "I overreacted."

"Don't tell me it's nothing. I'm not going anywhere," Darroch said, the crease of his brow proving his resolve. "What happened?"

"It's on the bed," she said. "A message. Someone called the motel and left a message for me."

He spun around and went straight for the loose piece of paper teetering near the end.

"Still watching you? We'll be together soon." His horror struck her before it became anger and landed on someone behind her. "What the fuck is this?"

How could he be angry at people who hadn't known anything about—

"Mr. Breckenridge…" that was a new voice. She spun around to find Detective Chapman, the same cop who'd come to her apartment the night it was burglarized. "We can only investigate crimes we're aware of. Did you contact the police department, Miss Mayden?"

"Don't put it on her," Roxie was quick to jump in. "If you were doing your job right, you would know who'd gone through her things. Maybe stolen from her. Did you follow up? Did you keep an eye on her? It's your job to keep her safe."

"Protective custody?" Axon said.

Acre shook his head. "Don't trust it."

"You can stay at the house," Alice said immediately extending her hospitality.

"No," she was quick to answer. "I'm not putting any of you at risk. If there is some lunatic out there…"

She wouldn't let it touch these gracious and good

people. These people she'd summoned to her, possibly into the path of this crazy.

"Crimson Palace it is then," Roxie declared.

"Good shout," Tripp agreed. "No one gets to the higher floors without clearance."

"They're strictly ours and have their own elevator," Roxie said. "It won't move without clearance. Trust me, I know from experience."

"I can't put anyone else at risk."

"Good luck to them scaling seventy-something glass floors," Tripp said. "There's only safety there."

"We can have officers in the building," Chapman said.

Roxie laughed. "Oh, I don't think so, sir. You can wait outside."

"We're officers of the law—"

"Who couldn't do your job in the first place," Roxie said. "This person, whoever they are, they're fixated on someone we love. How would you feel if your loved one was burglarized? If their home was invaded? This maniac has been watching her, everything she does. He knows where she lives, knows what she's doing and who she's doing it with. Don't you get how terrifying this is? This crazy person knows everything about her life, and the people she cares about."

The people she cared about… If the same person broke into her old place, her new one, went through her panties, left the chocolate in the fridge… She met Darroch's eye, resisting his effort to capture her too tight in his arms.

"If he followed the move, and followed you here, Savanna," Acre said. "He could be watching right now."

All the things that happened to her, the perpetrator watched. That meant he saw her and Darroch kissing in the street. Saw Darroch take the lead moving her out of her previous apartment and setting her up in the new one.

"He hurt you," she whispered.

Roxie was right, coincidence was unlikely.

"What's important is he doesn't hurt you," Darroch said. "Set it up."

"You can't go back to the house," she said. "If this person is watching—" Just being in his arms was a bad idea, yet when she tried to free herself, he yanked her body to his. "Darroch. He could see us."

"I don't give a shit if he's watching. Let him watch. This fucker thinks I abandoned you. We should never have been apart."

"Stop," she said, wriggling out of his forceful embrace. "You have to be safe."

"We'll keep him in the tower too," Tripp said.

Roxie nodded and opened a hand to her Breckenridge bestie. "Phone."

Tripp slapped his onto Roxie's palm; the beauty reversed through the others to dial.

"We'll increase security at B House too," Acre said.

She couldn't take her eyes from—this person, this criminal, might have scared her, but he could've killed Darroch. How could he stand there like it was nothing? He could've lost his life, and for what? Just for being with her?

FORTY-EIGHT

"ANYTHING YOU WANT, you'll get," Astrid, one of Roxie's young assistants said as they traversed the sleek, carpeted hallway high in the Crimson building. "Roxie's made that clear. To everyone. Your comfort and safety are our highest priority."

"Thank you."

"There's a directory in the phone that will link you to anyone you need. We're twenty-four hour equipped, none of our services close. And only a trusted few are allowed on this floor. If you want spa services, Roxie's people will come to you, day or night." Astrid stopped by a door. "Tripp is the door we just passed." The young woman indicated that way. "My number is in the directory too, don't hesitate to call if you need anything. You want an outside line, dial nine, though Rouge logs every call in and out of the building, just to make you aware. If you want to make a private call, you'll need to come upstairs."

"Which is…?"

Astrid smiled. "Only Roxie and Zairn's is above

us."

"I would never—"

"Your cellphone isn't monitored." The woman's smile was meek. "Sorry, I'm used to Roxie's not being an option."

Astrid slipped something from her pocket.

The box was familiar. "What's this?" It couldn't be… She popped it open to see, yes, it was her cherry necklace. "Where did you get this?"

"Your apartment. Well, I didn't. Ballard did. They got a few things for you."

"They?"

"Anything that's been missed can be replaced or retrieved. Please wear the cherry, it's your security pass," Astrid said and opened the door an inch. "Everything's taken care of here. Crimson Palace is a place of pleasure, as Roxie likes to remind me all the time. If you're ever anything other than happy here, just pick up the phone and we'll change that." She boosted open the door while staying in the hallway and gestured inside. "Enjoy."

The assistant left with a smile before she ventured to go in. Right there in the middle of the sunken living room stood two men. Two Breckenridges. Tripp and, of course, Darroch.

"I've checked it all out for you," Tripp said, his usual affable self. "Your room's on this side." He pointed one way, then the opposite way. "Roch's at the other."

They'd be sharing?

"Just for safety," Darroch said, reading her mind.

"My place is just…" Tripp gestured higher in the direction of her room.

"Astrid told me."

"Cool." Tripp slipped his hands in his pockets. "Yeah, you need anything, or get scared in the night, just bang on the wall and I'll come rescue you."

The way his smile turned to a smirk was enough

to curve her own lips a little.

"How much are you actually here?"

"On this floor?" He raised a shoulder. "Be here more if you need me here." His hands were next to go up. "As a sister. You're one of Roxie's girls. There's rules about that. Serious rules to be taken seriously."

Said like a man who'd heard that more than once. Tactful, diplomatic, Tripp was smarter than people gave him credit for. Smooth though? Everyone knew that about him. He'd put her at ease without raising her connection to his brother but still conveying the point he had no intention of crossing any lines.

"I'll leave you cats to get settled in. I'll bring food and people later. Leave the party to me." Tripp laid a brief hand on his brother's upper arm, then did his mosey thing that could be quick or slow, everything with him was effortless. Coming in close, he kissed her cheek, and raised his lips to murmur in her ear. "We've got you."

His serious eyes met hers for just a flicker, then he walked out and closed the door.

On her and Darroch.

Yep, that was them now, completely alone in their new home.

Living room in the middle, long dining table to the left, sort of semi office area to the right, all open plan. Double doors in each of the far corners, to the bedrooms by Tripp's indication.

"If you want your own space—"

"It's fine," she said. "This isn't—Roxie and Zairn are being incredibly generous. I don't think it's time to start making demands."

His own lips quirked. "Good, because I was going to tell you tough. There's no chance of me going anywhere."

Maybe the humor was supposed to lighten the mood or lessen her burden. The danger superseded whatever was going on between them personally, she got that. In her weakness, her stupidity, of reaching out to him might've sent the wrong message.

Except it was worse than that. Whatever they'd been, that they were no more, had possibly put his life in jeopardy. This man may still be in physical danger over a relationship they no longer had.

"I'm sorry," she said, which quickly wiped the amusement from his face.

"You're apologizing to me? What the hell have you got to apologize for? If you and the Germ—"

"For this," she said. "You're here in this mess because of me."

"I'm here in this mess because of a maniac stalker. I completely understand how he could be obsessed with you; I'm obsessed with you. But if I ever scared you—"

"Don't compare yourself to him."

Though in some ways they were alike, not necessarily the scaring thing, Darroch had occupied two roles in her life. Been two people to her one. No, she couldn't think that way. She couldn't obsess about what was because it never would be. The hurt didn't matter anymore. As soon as this mess was over, she'd apologize again and let the Breckenridges go on their way.

"None of this is your fault," he said, venturing closer while she stayed near the door. "Che—"

"Please, just let me say this, your family are kind and generous and do what they can to make this a better, brighter world. You should be proud of them. You are proud of them. I know you are. And what happened with us, yes, I… I did get caught up in it and let things go further than they should have. It was flattering to have the attention of a guy like you, someone I'd never normally cross paths with. And I don't just mean the money, it's who you are and the way you carry yourself in the world, you're a catch." He was smart enough that his eyes narrowed with suspicion. "For someone else. For someone who isn't me."

"I apologize," he said, "and I'll keep apologizing."

"No, that's why I'm saying this now. This is it, the period at the end, at the end of the whole episode. I don't know how long this will take to get cleared up—and I'm glad that we're sharing space, I want to know that you're safe, and it is easier for Roxie's people and your brothers… It's easier for everyone protecting us to have one site rather than two." Divide and conquer was how these people succeeded in the wild. Could she really compare this to that? "You have your room and I have mine, and we can be polite. There's no need for things to be awkward, and there's no need for us to rehash everything over and over again. Let's just let this be what it is. And when it's over, we say goodbye."

"I don't accept that." Though his good humor was gone, he didn't push. "But the point of this isn't to figure us out. You're right about that, so I'll play things your way. I'll do whatever you need me to do to make this easier, because there's no way I want you uncomfortable or thinking about leaving this safety. You're the boss. If you want to keep your distance, I won't make it difficult for you, but I'm here. I'll be here every minute for whatever you need."

And after?

She didn't ask the question out loud because they'd only end up going in circles. Being over was easier when they were apart. No, it had never been easy.

There, at least, she knew he was okay and didn't have to wonder what he was doing, if he was thinking of her… spending time with other women.

Which was his right. She closed her eyes. He could date whoever he wanted, kiss whoever he wanted… make love with whoever he wanted.

"Okay?" she asked, sidestepping to skirt between the living room and the office. "I'm going to get settled in."

FORTY-NINE

GETTING SETTLED IN was an excuse. She thought organizing her space would give her a chance to get her head straight, not just about Darroch, but about the whole mess. Except when she got into her room, the closet was full. There were things from her apartment, things she didn't recognize, things from Darroch's closet at Breckenridge House.

Her toiletries were on the vanity or in the shower. There was even a charging dock on her night table and a landline phone next to it, the link Astrid referenced that connected her with everything she could possibly want. A palace of pleasure.

Rather than walk out of the closet and return to Darroch to admit she actually had nothing to do, she curled up in the chair next to the bathroom and downloaded some fiction to get her through the day.

The windows were tempting and the view beyond beautiful, but she didn't think it was smart for someone possibly being watched by a nefarious stalker to showcase herself and pinpoint to him exactly where she was. Maybe she should highlight that to Darroch too… except she didn't want to go out there again.

At some point after the sky was dark in Empire City, voices carried from the other room. No big deal. Darroch was allowed visitors and had plenty of contacts, it was no surprise he'd be sociable.

Another voice joined. A feminine laugh raised her head. Would he…?

A second later, the door burst open. Roxie swung herself inside, still holding the handle, anchoring herself with a grasp on the static door.

"It's dinnertime!"

"It's—"

Roxie had already disappeared. She put her phone aside; she hadn't thought about eating and couldn't claim to be particularly hungry.

"They can come upstairs for Christmas," Roxie's voice floated above the others.

She crept toward the door.

The room was alive with people up, moving, being joyous. Uniformed people set the table and laid out food from lines and lines of carts. Roxie was there with her fiancé and Tripp, Darroch, both Breckenridge parents, other Breckenridge boys.

"What do you think?" Roxie asked, popping something into Zairn's mouth. "Savvy?"

"Think about what?" she asked.

She hadn't so much as brushed her hair and everyone else looked so glamorous.

"Christmas! If this is still going on at Christmastime, we're having Christmas upstairs. Just us, family only, no hangers-on, guests or outsiders."

"You've never met an outsider in your life," Tripp said. "As soon as you meet them, you make friends with them."

"Yeah, like you're the Grinch," Roxie retorted.

"You know what I mean, people we trust. People we know aren't crazy, psychotic stalkers. I'll make a list."

"Check it twice," Tripp said, laughing at his own joke.

Some of his brothers joined in.

"What a terrible job," Roxie said, "being the one who writes the lists."

"You'd give presents to the naughty ones and corrupt the nice," Zairn said, pulling out a chair that, with a brow twitch, he got Roxie to sit in.

"Nice is overrated. No," Roxie said, reaching for the wine glass Zairn was still filling. "Jane is nice. She's been on the nice list her whole life. She's nice with merit, with honors, top of her class. I wonder what people have to do to be on the naughty list. No one's good all the time."

"Except Jane," Tripp said.

Roxie nodded, gesturing with her wine glass as it approached her lips. "Except Jane."

Tripp frowned. "Where's Toria? She going to jump out on us?"

"She and Sway are doing some spa immersion thing that takes like six hours or something, I don't know."

"Toria's your co-defendant when it comes to corrupting the innocent," Zairn said, sitting next to his woman.

"Uh, liar, we lived with Jane for a million years and she's still good."

"She also, at your request, broke into her boyfriend's place of work."

"For Lilya."

"And used sex to distract him so you and Lilya could go sleuthing."

"You men don't care if we use sex. You get sex out the deal, what's the problem?"

"I should warn Knox to keep you away from their kids."

Roxie swooped her glass up to rest on her lower lip. "Something you can't do for yourself, Skippy."

"No, unfortunately, you know all my secrets and our genetic material has already been fused."

"Oh," Roxie said, lowering the glass an inch. "That's a hot word."

Zairn leaned right up close to her ear. "Fused?"

Roxie shivered and laughed. "Turn me on all you want, Casanova, I live in this building."

"You two are all sex, all the time," Brant whined, sinking into his own seat.

Her blonde friend checked herself out. "Uh, I am not having sex this second."

Zairn licked his fingertips, which then quickly disappeared under the table. "Give me a second to change that."

On another laugh, Roxie swatted at his hand. "You want me to drag you through to Tripp's place and force you to finish it like a man?"

"My place? What about right here? There are two beds in this suite."

"Yeah, but they're being chased by an evil madman, honey," Roxie said, leaning over the table to pout at the man currently taking Savvy's hand to lead her to a seat. "Your bed's probably already soiled."

"Live in the building but you don't have clean sheets?" Zairn dished food onto Roxie's plate. It was sweet, watching him care for her despite them antagonizing each other. "I'd talk to management."

"I would, but he'd want sex out the deal and for that, I'd want more than sheets."

When the spoon was back in the bowl, Zairn took Roxie's hand, pushing up her ring finger as he raised it for them both to admire.

"How about a rock the size of Gibraltar?"

"Hmm…" Roxie sighed and put down her glass. "Okay then."

On her way to the chair, the couple's mouths met and she, like everyone else, averted her eyes… Did hers have to land on Darroch's staring right back?

The banter, the flirting, it spoke to her romantic side. Few wouldn't swoon over how the couple interacted. They exuded love. With a loose arm on the back of his fiancée's chair, Zairn owned the woman next to him while giving her complete freedom to fly.

Once upon a time, she'd wanted love like that, wondered if it existed. In the past, if she'd witnessed a similar show, she'd daydream about love like that, certain there was a chance it existed up ahead.

Except it didn't for her. Not anymore. That love, her great love, was in her rearview even as he stared right back across the room. Forever, gone in a flash. Nothing lasted forever.

FIFTY

THE BRECKENRIDGE PARENTS left not long after the meal was over. It wasn't that they didn't have life in them, she got the feeling they wanted the younger ones to let loose.

Ha, like they were teenagers with the house to themselves for the first time, the alcohol did flow a little freer after their elders departed. Festivities had progressed to a point their hosts invited everyone downstairs to the heart of the always beating building.

"Come down to the club," Roxie beseeched, shaking Savvy's hand. "We'll kick everyone out. And you'll be safe, the Ruby Room Dyce glass is bulletproof."

Just what everyone wanted to consider on a night out.

Darroch was by the still open door, speaking to Tripp, the only other person left with them.

"Empress!" Tripp called. "Get moving!"

Roxie did glance back but took one more opportunity to turn on her doe eyes.

"Not tonight," she said because the last thing she

wanted was anyone else in danger. "It's been a long day."

A ridiculously long day.

"Okay." Roxie hugged her and kissed her cheek. "If you change your mind, call; Ballard will send up a phalanx of guards to bring you down. Not bring you down, bring you down… escort you, is what I mean."

"Okay," she said on a laugh.

Tripp materialized to commandeer Roxie's hand and lead her across the room. "Yeah, she gets it, Rox Out."

Once Darroch closed the door behind the pair, she breathed out.

"Tired?" Darroch asked, sauntering toward her in the middle of the living room.

"Not really."

"I'm sorry about everyone descending on—"

"They care about you. Didn't you once say you don't take that for granted?"

"Once said a lot of things." He stopped in front of her. Closer than maybe he should've. "We both did." Instead of backing away, her chin rose until their eyes met. "You know I'd never let anything hurt you, don't you?"

Maybe. Yes. But she'd trusted him before and that turned out to be a mistake. Would he let anything hurt her? What a question. He'd let himself hurt her, broken her heart. Mocked her, lied to her, gotten God knows what kick out of pretending to be someone he wasn't, two someones he wasn't.

Argh! She couldn't let herself get bogged down in the whys of the past. Maybe this time together was a gift. Fate gave her a last chance to taste what had been cruelly stolen from her so suddenly.

"This isn't about us," she murmured, drugged by his gaze. "Are you attracted to me?"

A crazy lush, the betrayal didn't change her

fundamental attraction to him. How could it still be so potent? His body, once apparently hers, had never shared itself with her. Why did she need that now?

Of their own accord, her hands skimmed up onto his body, so solid, and so close.

"Every fucking second, Cherry, baby—"

"We're just two people." Simple biology. "Here, alone." And that was an advantage she hadn't expected. Pressing her nails just a little deeper, she licked her lips. "Kiss me."

Scooping both hands beneath her ears to cradle her skull, he dipped to capture her mouth with his. They were good at this. The pressure of need in that kiss promised more security than any building could provide. And, no, she didn't mean forever, but in that moment, this man was—

"Baby…" he gasped, parting their mouths a whisper. "I've missed you so goddamn—"

"Not about us."

Planting her hands on his chest, she pushed him back and went for the zipper on her dress. His flash of surprise heightened the mischief searing desire into her veins. God, she wanted to feel him, to lie under him and give in to the oblivion of just being a woman enjoying a guy hotter than sin.

Dropping her dress, she didn't feel exposed or vulnerable. Under the shroud of his desire, her skin tingled, every hair quivered.

"Sav, you're my whole world, there's nothing I wouldn't—"

"Then do this," she said, guiding his hand to her waist. "Give me what I need."

"I don't understand what—"

"Didn't you say this was my terms? That I'm the boss?"

"Yeah, but—"

"If you reject me—"

"Not possible."

She opened her arms at her sides and strolled backward toward his bedroom. "Then come get me."

Offering herself to him was selfish. Insanity. So risky. Yet slipping out of her underwear and crawling on to his bed was the most natural thing in the world. Just like the first night they'd slept together at—no.

Lying on her back, on a kind of diagonal, her heavy eyes scrutinized his slow advance. Good idea or bad idea, the man came up close, absorbing her every atom, scrutinizing the figure he'd seen before. That didn't matter, not according to the heated message sent by his gaze.

And though he opened his mouth on a quiet inhale, he thought better of whatever words almost passed his lips and unbuttoned his shirt instead. Ripping it from his shoulders, he had his pants off a breath later and then he was on her.

A kiss. A touch. The blanket of him protecting her, she writhed, raising her hips as he guided her leg high around him, holding it close and pushing his tongue deeper, forcing her head into the mattress.

Yes.

Yes!

Oh, she wanted to scream, wanted the world to exist in the long, hot shaft pressing against her, moving slow, massaging her, ripening her body for an advance.

And it was that advance she needed.

Rising from the kiss, he searched her eyes through the dim light supplied by the city beyond the windows.

"Are you sure this is—"

"What I need right here in this moment?" she asked and laid a hand on his face. "Yes."

With a switch of his hips, the blunt head of his

cock pushed against her. Still reluctant, he didn't take his eyes from hers like he expected her to run out of there. She wouldn't. He could take all night if she didn't move things along.

Pressuring his chest, she rolled with him as he landed on his back. On the next inhale, she impaled herself deep, whining out the ecstasy of the plunge. What a world to live in. How could one simple act feel so good?

"Mmm," she moaned, eyes closed, head back, she rolled her hips, pushing into the cradle of his hands fondling her breasts. "Darroch." The taste of his name had never been so intimate. The head of his cock rocked against her G-spot and she sped up, teasing and caressing the space within that had never been so easily reached. "Oh, baby…"

"Cherry…"

She should tell him not to use that name. That moment wasn't about them. It wasn't intimacy, it was safety in numbers.

Pushing up, she dropped, squeezing and massaging him, taking all she wanted, enlivening herself on the gift buried deep within her.

And then she was on her back. In one swoop with his arms around her, he changed the game and took his turn hammering her deep, faster, harder, more than she'd been, yet the juxtaposition of styles fired her hormones to work overtime.

Oh, she couldn't stop touching him. Every part of him was there for her, running its energy on pleasuring her and itself. Was it? Was her body pleasuring his?

"Are you… are you…" Each gasp was too much and the pressure within her burst out in a scream. Her body bucked, arching hard, squeezing tight, clinging to every vestige of the pure lust in physical form that electrified her body.

"Baby…"

He was quick to follow, plunging deep, releasing a long, powerful groan as he poured his seed into her. Without moving from above, he swept the hair from her brow.

Forcing him up, she was quick off the bed. "Thank you."

"Babe!"

Despite his calls, she kept on going, leaving his room to cross to the living room and ensconce herself in her private space.

Or what was supposed to be her private space.

Darroch quickly invaded it. "Baby—"

"No, not baby," she said, snatching her robe from the adjoining bathroom to put it on.

"Savanna. What was that? We're—what was that?"

"What I needed," she said. "Thank you."

"Don't thank me like you—baby, I lo—"

"Don't say that. Don't say anything. It is what it was."

"And what was that?"

"What I needed." She forced a smile, pushing her hair back with both hands. "Physical, Darroch. I needed the physical."

"So you used me for sex? As a punishment?"

Didn't that just change the hue of the conversation.

Her smile transitioned to a frown. "Used you? If you didn't want to sleep with me—"

"I do want to sleep with you, that's why I'm here. Sex? You want it, you got it, but you don't have to run away the second we're done."

"We're not a couple," she said without intending to be cruel. Her words might hurt—ha, that was a laugh. He hadn't spared a thought for how his actions hurt her.

"I'm sorry, I thought you understood."

"That it was physical."

"Whatever I need, that's what you said."

Some of the bluster left his aura. "Whatever you need." He exhaled. "You know how to find me."

As he walked on out, she stayed put. They were attracted to each other, two people in an intense situation who needed comfort. What was wrong with that?

FIFTY-ONE

BREAKFAST WAS LAID out on carts near the windows when she emerged the following morning. Darroch was at the dining table, a laptop and other office type things laid out around him.

"Why are you over there?" she asked, going to pour coffee. "There's a desk here."

That the actual desk was closer to her room didn't make it hers.

"See the stack of stuff on it."

Yes, she did. Files, a laptop, some thick stacks of documents bound together.

"What about it?" she asked, inhaling the scent of the coffee before drinking it.

"That's your work for today."

"My work?" Was that some kind of joke? She didn't even have a job. Going over to check what he could possibly... "Huddle Hope."

Everything was related to the scheme Roxie wanted her to be a part of.

"Time to familiarize yourself."

"Hmm." She sat down to take a closer look. Wouldn't hurt, right? She hadn't signed anything, there was no commitment. "At least I'll have something to do to pass the time."

Somehow she couldn't see herself vegging out in front of the TV and forgetting about the drama in her life. Work would give her a focus.

"How are you feeling this morning?"

She sipped her coffee and started to spread everything out. "Good. Considering. Any news?"

"I haven't seen anyone this morning. But no calls, no emails. I've got a call with the task force at noon, if you want in on it."

"The task force?" she asked, feeling sort of swanky while simultaneously holding in a laugh. "There's a task force?"

"This person is pursuing you."

"Yeah," she said without hiding her smile. "But a person like me doesn't get a task force. We wouldn't even get a call back." She edged her cup aside. "Guess that's what money gets you."

"Want me to disband it?"

Twisting around, she caught the back of her chair to look across the room at him. "Disband—no."

"No problem for me, baby. I'll live here forever with you, sounds ideal."

Some might expect that to be snide. It wasn't. Darroch Breckenridge couldn't slight her if he tried. Her shoulders dropped. Except he could. Why did she have to keep reminding herself that the man she thought he was didn't exist?

"No, you're right. The quicker this is over, the better."

"You sure about that? 'Cause I could relive last night for the next fifty-something years, if you're with me."

Last night being locked in there together, dinner? Family…? Sex?

"Look, I'm sorry if I confused things. Maybe I had too much wine, I don't know, it just felt okay, like it was okay to…"

"It was okay. Is okay. I'm here for whatever you need. Just like you said."

He said it first. She wouldn't ask if their recklessness sent mixed signals or messed with his head. Even addressing it would start a conversation they didn't need to have.

"The coffee's good," she said, returning to it and her work. "It'll take me all day to get through this."

"Maybe all week."

He might be willing to stick around, but she hadn't considered it. Just how long would they be there? What if it took a month to find the guy? A year? Would they be trapped there together indefinitely? That they didn't know was the very definition of the word. Damnit.

Okay, so she couldn't claim hardship. They were in a luxury building, one of the most expensive stretches of real estate in the country, maybe the world. Everything was brought to her, every need catered. And, on top of that, she was able to take physical advantage of her hot roommate any time she liked. In theory. As to whether that was smart…

Being with him, crossing that final line, had been such an amazing high that she almost feared going there again. Could she get addicted? Honestly? She might be already. Once felt like nothing. It definitely wasn't enough. They could be there for months, or they could be snatched from each other again in a second, ending their association for good. That would mean never again. She couldn't handle never again, not yet.

Rising, without thinking too much, because that was when she got into trouble, she was drawn across the room to him.

He glanced over the top of his laptop as she rounded the head of the dining table.

"Need something?"

"Maybe," she said, sliding her butt along the edge of the table toward him.

Without hesitation, he swept his computer and papers aside to stand, snatching her hips to yank her in front of him.

"Whatever you need."

That growl ignited the moment, their mouths clashed and clothes were shoved aside. The seal was broken. With that release came permission for pleasure like she'd never known.

"Darroch," she whispered, her head falling back as the lust became unquenched satisfaction. "Fuck me, Darroch."

Already seated on the table, she dug her knees into him until his hand between them took control and filled her with the gratification she craved.

"Yes," she whispered on a rush of breath grabbing him for stability and pushing into every thrust. "Oh, God, yes…"

"Feel good, baby?"

"Mmm…" she moaned, her teeth finding her lip, dragging it free. "Incredible."

"Any time you want it, it's all yours."

The words reminding him this wasn't about them may have flitted across her mind. May have. That link of their bodies, the friction building, the buzz of a rise that she knew would end in an explosion of pleasure just like the previous night, was way more important.

The flood ascended through her gut, it squeezed her heart, speckled in her eyes. Sex had never been like this. Never even close to the high of him. Snatching his shirt in her fist, she yanked him closer though his hips kept on working. With a strong forearm locked behind her waist, he supported her as she leaned back, raising the gradient of her hips to perfectly feel his—

"Yes, yes. Yes!" Her calls didn't stop there, didn't quiet. She released all her need, pushing, pulling, begging, pleading. "Darroch. Darroch."

Her pant matched the moment her body again caved into orgasm with his landing right on time.

The heave of their bodies continued. Catching her breath wasn't possible, her chest hurt. The sharp snap of pain wouldn't subside. How did she…?

He pushed back just enough to meet her eye. And there it was. The cure for the ache that—no, she shouldn't—except when she tried to push him away, he caught her jaw, tipping her head back to consume her mouth.

Their hello was as potent as what had to be goodbye. And there was that pain again. Grabbing for his shoulders, she sucked air in through her nose and gave back. Not just gave, she forced him to feel her pain, her anger, her fear. What this man had always been was—

"No." The word burst from her mouth onto his. When she shoved again, he still stayed put. "Move, Darroch, or I'll—"

"What? Scream?"

"Don't mock me." He hadn't minded her volume a second ago. "Let me go."

"That's one thing I'll never do, Cherry."

After another few jabs at his shoulder with the heel of her hand, he acquiesced and backed away enough for her to slither off the table onto her feet.

"Cherry—"

"Please don't call me that," she said, shimmying down her skirt and righting her shirt as he put himself back together too.

Kinda.

No amount of smoothing clothes would hide the creases of what they'd done.

When she tried to walk away, he grabbed her arm to pull her back. Rather than say anything, his eyes stayed matched to hers as he touched the gem in the nook of her throat.

"Astrid told me to wear it."

"It's your security pass, I know. I didn't just give it to you because it was pretty." Wait, what did that…? "Your safety, and your ability to access safety have always been my primary concern."

"I don't want to talk about this."

So why couldn't she look away? He might have her arm, but that didn't explain why she couldn't tear her eyes from his.

"I know what safety means to you. You've never had security or someone to look after you, to put you first. And what you went through that night at the store—"

"Stop it," she said, yanking on her arm without freeing it. "Darroch!"

"I am that person, Savanna Mayden. And I will always be that person whether you want me to be or not."

"I don't want to talk about this."

"There is nothing I wouldn't give you." His fingers bit deeper and he stooped lower. "Nothing I wouldn't do to keep you safe."

And suddenly the walls felt less than luxury. No one could get in without clearance. Did that count for out too?

A knock on the door didn't break their stare. Neither did it opening.

"What's going on?"

"Nothing," she said, recognizing Caber's voice

though it was behind her. On the next jerk, her arm was liberated. "We're finished."

"Yeah, looks that way."

It wasn't her job to address the brother's concern, so she went back to work.

"Coming next door for the—"

"Yeah," Darroch said, cutting Caber off. "Sav, if you—"

"Go, play with your brothers." She didn't even look up. "Why would I care?"

He muttered something and a few seconds later, the door closed.

On an exhale, her head fell into her hands. What the hell was she doing?

FIFTY-TWO

DINNER WAS A different affair that night. On purpose or not, the call came to say room service was on its way up. At the sound of the main suite door opening, she went out to find only Darroch waiting with the guy unloading his cart.

As soon as that guy was gone, she snagged her plate from the table and ignored her roommate calling her back, choosing to eat in her room.

The next morning, she lingered in the shower. Usually she found peace there. With water cascading through her hair, somehow her thoughts would order, she'd emerge refreshed.

Not that time.

Breakfast had probably been and gone; she couldn't hide in her room forever. Darroch spent most of the previous day with his brothers, or out of the suite anyway, she hadn't asked. They hadn't spent that much time together. Any time together.

Maybe he'd been right. She'd used him and no one deserved that.

Opening her bedroom door quietly, she peeked around. Resting her forehead against it, only one half of her face would be visible to the room beyond. Either he had supersonic hearing or he could sense her, because he zeroed in immediately from his place behind the laptop at the dining table.

Darroch Breckenridge.

She didn't fear him. So why was she avoiding him? Because she didn't want to have the fight? Why not?

No pressure. No rush. No rage. They just scrutinized each other from opposite corners.

"I didn't mean to use you for sex."

Her voice was small, matching how she felt.

"Never had a problem with the sex," he said, the smooth cadence of his voice so calm that she envied him. "I'm here for whatever you need."

"I can't forgive myself for causing this."

"You aren't causing this."

"I told you if you getting hurt was anything to do with your connection to me I'd never forgive myself."

"That's not why you're pushing me away."

"Are you Darroch right now or Jacob?"

In the time he took to shift position, his tongue met the center of his top lip. "I can be whatever you need me to be."

"Is that what you think of me?" Given her behavior in the last couple of days, he could be forgiven for it. "I'm not a callous user only interested in taking what I can get." Her confidence waned fast. "Am I?"

"No," he said and actually smiled. "Far from it. You're a woman with her eye on the prize." Devotion. Which was what he said he wanted. "I can give it to you, Savanna. I can give you everything."

"That's not what I wanted. I never wanted that."

"What do you want, baby?"

And he just didn't get it. "What do *you* want?" she asked. "What did you think you'd achieve? Lying to me every day, every minute. You'd have to know how I'd react. I told Jacob upfront that I—" Closing her eyes, she appealed quietly to the powers above. "We can't have this conversation."

"Why not?" he asked and rose to dart around the dining table, maybe enlivened by the apparent in.

She immediately pulled the door closer. "Don't come over here. Stay there."

"Because you don't trust yourself to be near me?" he asked, though did stop. "That's exactly how I felt. Every time we were together, I wanted to tell you, then I got scared."

"Men like you don't get scared."

"Want to bet?" he asked. "I might've said the same until I met you, Savanna Mayden. I feared seeing the light in your eye fade. The way you looked at me then, the way you look at me now. Cherry, I—"

"Don't call me that. How many times do I have to—"

"Why not? You never had a problem with it before."

"I thought we had a chance then. That we were partners."

"Nothing has changed."

"Everything has changed!"

The door burst open and Roxie came running in. "Come! Come with me!" Grabbing Savanna, the woman attempted to reverse course.

She resisted. "What are you—"

"They got him! You've got to come! Come! Come!"

Got him? Oh, God, they—Roxie's urgency fueled hers.

They got him? The guy? Her… Oh, God!

Running down the corridor, the elevator opened automatically to swallow them both. Roxie stabbed at the button then tossed the hair from her face.

"How did the elevator know we—"

"It knows when I'm coming."

Wow. "How—"

"I don't ask questions, I just get the perks," Roxie said, smoothing both of them as they descended. "Are you okay? How's your heart rate?"

Yeah, wow, her chest was rising and falling fast. Because of this news or her conversation with Darroch?

"Where are we going? How did they get him?"

"Trying to get in here!" Roxie scoffed in affront. "Can you believe it? Asshole. Not a chance in hell."

She shivered. "He was here?"

"Is here! It's happening right now!"

"Happening right—"

The moment the elevator doors opened, Roxie grabbed her again, dashing out to weave them around a half dozen obstructing people into a long, windowless corridor. Suddenly, they stopped. Roxie turned right into the wall. Except it wasn't the wall, a secret door gave way and they were in a room. A small room with what had to be one-way glass.

"Do you see him?"

"Do I...?"

As the whiplash subsided, she peeked through the people beyond and out to the street. A dozen police vehicles crowded around the chaotic scene. A guy, dragged down the sidewalk, fighting, objecting.

"It's amazing," Roxie said, clearly buzzed. "Want to know who he is? He's—"

"I know who he is," she said, chilled.

Roxie's adrenaline faded fast, and then she was stroking her arm. "You know him?"

"Yeah, he's the guy from Breckenridge. The guy

who came in and—"

When her voice broke, Roxie gathered her into a hug. "Oh, honey."

For a minute, it was nice to relax into the comfort.

Quickly, she cast it off. "Sorry, I—"

"No, don't be sorry. This is a huge thing. You need all the support you can get right now."

And somehow that took her back to Roxie's comment about forgiveness being a choice.

"I'm sorry you've had to put up with this."

"Put up with what?" Roxie smiled. "You're my friend."

Except she wasn't. Not when this started. This had been foisted on her. How could Roxie be so patient? With all the money and charisma in the world, Roxie Kyst could write her own ticket.

She had to ask, "Why do you care?"

"Excuse me?"

"Why do you care about me?"

"I care about you because I am you, we're all you. People come into our lives for a reason. You're a good person. I like surrounding myself with good people."

A commotion attracted their attention back to the street. When she saw Darroch out there, storming right past the cordon, pushing cops out the way—cops!

"What is he doing?" she asked and tried to head for the door.

With an arm around her, Roxie pulled her back. "Oh no, you're not going out there."

Darroch came up against a line of cops, forcing him back when the perp was his clear target.

"I can't leave him out there with—"

Breaking from the others, Tripp and Ballard got hold of Darroch to drag him back.

"There you go, see," Roxie said with a happy

smile. "All's well."

They tossed the asshole into the back of a police van and the door was slammed. The press crowded in from the other side, and she lost sight of Darroch and the others in the crowd nearest the door.

For a beat, she just breathed. "Is it over?" she asked, appealing to Roxie after the words escaped. "It's finished?"

"You'll have to talk to the cops. They'll want background."

They'd find it in their own files, but she'd talk to them. "Then I can go home?"

"You can stay here as long as you want. Don't rush right out—"

"I need to go home," she said. "I need to just…"

"Get back to being you," Roxie said, intuiting it. "I get it."

Linking her fingers with Roxie's, she cherished the woman's understanding. "Will you stay with me? They're going to ask all kinds of personal questions about—"

"No, they won't," Roxie said, tucking her hair behind her ear. "Not while I'm there, and I won't leave you for a second. This here is my house, baby."

***

FOR HOURS, law enforcement questioned her. Roxie did as promised, sticking by her side the whole time. And her friend brought in a lawyer too, just in case. Imagine that. Having the ability to conjure a lawyer from thin air at a second's notice.

Darroch probably had questions of his own to answer. What was he thinking of storming out there like that? How could anything good come from a confrontation with a crazy person? She'd object to the asshole seeing Darroch's face, though she was sure he was responsible for the attack on Darroch too. Meant he'd seen Darroch's face already. He'd seen all their faces.

With her essentials, she'd got in the car provided by Roxie and promised to call the following day. Roxie wanted her to call that night, but she just wasn't sure she had it in her. So they'd settled on a text.

As promised, after crossing her threshold and ascending the stairs, she texted Roxie to say she was back home safe. The driver, who'd walked her all the way to her front door and checked out the apartment before she went inside, would tell Roxie that too. But a promise was a promise.

The place was so... foreign. Yes, it was hers, but had she stayed there long enough to really feel safe? Her head was such a mess.

She just stood there, taking it all in. When her phone rang in her hand, she jumped. Would it be Darroch or Roxie or—no. Yvette.

Her friend hadn't stopped calling since she quit.

For the first time, she answered. "Hey."

"Oh my God! Savvy, what the hell! Where have you been? What happened? I've been calling and calling—"

"I know. I know, I'm sorry." She closed her eyes. "Life's been a clusterfuck and I... I don't even know what to say."

"What happened? Why did you quit work? Why did you stop taking calls? Why did you—"

"Can I come over?" she asked. "I have a lot to tell you."

FIFTY-THREE

THERE WAS SOMETHING to be said for familiarity. Going to Yvette's had been kind of renewing. Iain's trip was extended, so she ended up staying a night, then another, until a week had passed since she'd last been in her apartment. With Iain coming home that night, it was only right she gave the couple their privacy.

And, yes, she really needed to start her life over again. Sitting around forever wasn't an option. Not for someone like her.

She got a cab back to her place and went inside reminding herself of the lessons she'd learned. If something was too good to be true it—

Darroch.

Why was Darroch Breckenridge sitting at her kitchen island with paperwork spread in front of him?

"You hungry?" he asked without lifting his head. "I haven't eaten yet."

How did he know she—wait. "What are you doing here?"

"Waiting for you."

"Waiting for—I haven't been here for a week."

"I have. I've looked after the place. Nothing to report." He tossed down his pen and went to the fridge. "Want a glass of wine?"

Like this was just any normal day. She dumped her bag and went another two steps.

"Darroch. What are you doing here?"

He closed the fridge and put the wine bottle on the counter before meeting her eye. "Waiting for you."

"You said that. Waiting for me for… what?"

God, he was hot. And it wasn't just the square jaw and perfect skin. No. She'd seen inside this man and believed for a minute that—what happened to those lessons learned? She hadn't seen anything and karma didn't owe her squat.

"To finish our conversation."

It wasn't like him to be serious. Where was his smile? Where was his…?

"Our conversation," she said and immediately shook her head. "What—from the suite? No. I told you we're not having that conversation. That conversation is finished."

He opened the cabinet to retrieve glasses. "Cameras are being installed in every hallway, stairwell, and alley of Breckenridge property."

"Good. If they'd been there before maybe you wouldn't have got hurt."

"I'm more interested in your safety."

"I don't work for Breckenridge." Though she had ventured into work with Yvette and been offered her job back by Celeste. Several times. "But I'm happy its people will be safe. Thank you for letting me know." He put the wine back in the fridge. "You can leave now. And in future, a text will suffice."

"I texted you this week."

More than once. "And I told you I was fine. I am

fine. Everything is fine. He was denied bail."

"I know. I was there to make sure of it."

She wasn't. "Okay. Whatever. Will you leave now?"

With his advance, she tensed, she wouldn't retreat, couldn't but… please be strong enough to hold it together.

"Nothing has changed," he said, putting the wine in her hand.

"Everything has changed," she whispered.

"We're partners. We face whatever the future has for us, together."

"The problem wasn't the future," she said. "It was the past I never knew we had." Peering closer, she wanted to be in his head, to know. "How could you do that to me? How could you think behavior like that was okay?"

"I'm in love with you, Savvy."

"Don't," she said, rounding him to put the glass on the kitchen island. "This isn't like that. This isn't one of those billionaire things where you get to demand what you want and it's laid on a platter for you. I'm a human being. Sometimes I struggle to…"

Except he knew. Jacob knew.

"You struggle to acknowledge and trust your own worth. You don't trust yourself or believe you deserve anything good."

Whirling around, his proximity impacted her without taking her gusto. "How was it good that the man I wanted to make a life with lied to me? Not once or twice, but the whole time we knew each other." Her fingertips met her hairline. "I honestly believed we—and all those times. Those times you said you'd be patient and wait for me to open up? Talk about bullshit."

"It wasn't bullshit," he argued. "There's so much more to you than those calls. Yes, I should've told you, but I didn't know how. I didn't expect to walk into that tent and—Sav, what's between us is real, it's undeniable. I've known it from the second I laid eyes on you."

"Known what?"

"That you're the woman I'm going to spend the rest of my life with. Dad said when you know, you know, and with you, there's no mistaking it. You're going to be my wife. We're going to build a life together."

"Don't talk to me like that," she said, narrowing her eyes. "Don't talk to me like you get to make all the decisions and I should bow down and capitulate. I'm not your employee anymore, you don't get to decide if I can pay my bills or not."

"I never decided that."

"But you can decide I'll marry you?"

"I love you."

"Life isn't that simple. And how am I supposed to believe it? Why can't you understand? On the phone, how many times did you tell me my feelings were valid? What about Jeremy, huh? You said his reactions diminished what I went through. That he minimized my justified feelings. What the hell do you think you're doing right now?"

"Your feelings are justified. I fucked up and I apologize. I didn't do what I did for kicks, I did it because I love you and I couldn't bear the thought of losing you. What would you have said? If I'd told you?"

"I don't know," she admitted. "I honestly don't, I... I let myself be vulnerable on those calls. Opening myself in a way I never would've with you in person."

"And I want that side of you. I want you to give me every part of you, and never worry how I'll respond. I'll always be with you, Sav. It doesn't matter what you tell me, I'll support you in everything."

"Then support my decision to end our relationship."

"No," he said with a single head shake. "I won't give up on this. I won't stop pursuing you or apologizing. I will stay in your life if I have to live on the damn sidewalk outside this building."

"You can't do that."

"I can do whatever I damn well want. We're partners. I belong to you and you're mine. I'll do whatever it takes to prove that to you."

"Then how are you any better than him?" she asked. "Any better than the guy sitting in jail for hurting you and hunting me?"

"I would never hurt you."

"And you have the cash to appease the cops that's a big difference. Bet your family donates a bunch to the department."

"Is that what you think of me?" he asked, mirroring what she'd asked him. "That I'd buy my way into abusing you?"

Pain flared in her chest. The cold hurt in his eyes might be masked by a serious brow, but she could see it. That was the man she'd thought he was, the man who'd called himself lucky on their way out for the night.

"I'm embarrassed," she confessed in a small voice. "The things I said to Jacob on the phone…"

"You said them to me. The man who loves you and cherishes every second with you." He captured her hand at her side. "That connection you felt, the breath you wanted on your neck—"

"Oh God." Extracting her hand, she turned her back. And the wine was right there. Thank God for it, she gulped half and set it back down. "I was ridiculous. I am ridiculous."

"No."

"I can't believe I—who falls for someone they've never met?"

"I fell for you the first night. We were never

supposed to be at that bake-off, but I knew if I mentioned it to Mom at the breakfast table…"

Peering over her shoulder, her surprise had to be obvious. "You came to see me?"

"Yes."

The truth. She turned back to him. "On purpose? Did your mom and Caber—"

"No. You know what my mom is like, it was foolish of me, cowardly, all I had to do was mention it and I became a passenger. She did all the work to get us there, get me to you."

He'd felt that connection on the phone too? Even that early?

"How am I supposed to move forward knowing that?"

While she'd been making an idiot of herself with cookies and cupcakes, he'd known her secrets. And, goddamn her, but hadn't she called Jacob back that night?

"Accept my apology and give me a list of what I have to do to fix this."

"Every second of what we were, you were mocking me."

"No," he said, his hand sliding onto the island until, somehow, she was hard against it. "Every second of what we were was my reason for being. Don't you understand, Savanna Mayden? I am your servant. Completely at your mercy. From this day until my last, I will serve your will. Whatever it takes to make you happy, I'll do it."

"Then go home, Darroch. I always thought I was crazy to think I could ever be a part of your world." She licked her lips. "But it's the other way around. Men like you don't belong here, in my world. In this world, we grind, we live what's real because it's all we have. We don't have time for games or double lives; you played a game with me, I lost. Go find someone else to play with now."

"We're not different. We live in the same world. And if you need me to reject the trust fund and shun my family to prove that to you—"

"I would never ask you to do that. Your family are incredible, none of this is on them."

"Yet you're punishing me for being a part of them."

Was that what she was doing? "Women like me are supposed to be shit on by assholes like Jeremy."

"You, Savanna Mayden…" he said, grazing the knuckle of his index finger down her cheek. "Were made to live your life with me. Fuck how much money anyone has or where we come from, we've both known from the beginning that this was different to anything we'd had before." She should've switched on a light, suddenly, as he got closer, it got darker. "You've known it, baby, tell me you didn't."

How could she blame him for lying and then do it herself?

She swallowed. "I… I can't."

There was the smile. "You've been scared to admit it."

"Different doesn't have to mean forever."

"That's exactly what it means. You think any guy will ever measure up to me? Any relationship will match this?"

Could she live the rest of her life knowing she'd walked away from her only chance at happiness?

"I didn't say thank you… When I called… when I was scared…" It didn't feel real. Her impulse to call him at the motel was unthinking. Terrified, she'd picked up that phone and… "You came. You came to be with me."

"Always will, Cherry. That's the truth of who I

am, that guy. The guy who would give up the world for you. No thanks necessary, it's a given, I'll always be by your side, I'll always protect you."

"You're confusing me."

Except when she tried to push past, he pressured her body with his, keeping her still. "I lied to you. Every time your voice came onto that phone, I wanted to tell you the truth, but I lost myself in it, in you. I'm addicted, baby, and I won't live another day without you."

"I can't be with a liar."

"What we felt, in person, and on that phone, was real, it was true. There was no lie in that. There's no lie in our love. That's all we need: love. And my pledge I will never lie to you again, about anything. Won't be so much as a surprise party in your future unless they keep it from both of us, I swear."

Oh, did he have to be goofy like that?

"I'm scared to love you." Her heart beat hard in her quaking throat. "Ending this protects me because I can't ever be hurt like that again. I knew I was in love with you and on that screen, on your phone, I saw those letters and… I was ready to give you everything I could, and the humiliation—"

The memory closed her eyes though he caught her chin to raise it back up. When the brush of his lips met hers, she wanted to give in. Instead, she planted a hand on his chest to push him back.

"Love me, Cherry, and I will always be your Gentleman."

A warm tear escaped the corner of her eye. "It's better to lose you now than let us destroy me later."

"No," he murmured. "Better to start forever now, than to regret losing another second of us. I love you, Sav." He peered closer, beseeching her. "Trust that. Trust what you feel. You will never lose us. There's nothing to fear. Nothing has the power to destroy either of us so long as we're together."

"Together?"

"Partners." A word she'd got from Jacob. One he probably got from his parents. "Trust, Cherry, please."

It was never her intention to have him beg. It was never her intention to lose him. Both men, Darroch, Jacob, what they'd felt for her was real, and what she felt in return was the same. Had fear driven him? One thing was clear, it was driving her decision to push at him.

Trust? Could she do it? Be with a man like Darroch Breckenridge? Didn't take much consideration. Didn't everyone make mistakes? She had to trust his heart, as he trusted hers.

"Thirty-five years isn't a bad innings," she whispered.

Another smile. "No, it's not."

"Not sure about the sixteen kids though."

He brushed the hair from her brow. "It starts with one, we'll go from there." Oh, this was a big deal. "Trust me."

"Trust you."

"I've got you, baby."

Forgiveness was a choice. Could she deny being in love with him? No. And maybe it wasn't just about trusting him. She had to trust herself, her instinct. Every part of her burned to belong to him. They belonged to each other and forever started now.

Read more from the Roxiverse in
Nothing to Deny...

Thank you for reading this tale!
If you can, please take the time to review.

~

Ask your local library for more Scarlett Finn
novels!

~

For all things Scarlett Finn
check out:

www.scarlettfinn.com

Next in the Roxiverse: